The Family Hightower

The
Family
Hightower

a novel

Brian Francis Slattery

Seven Stories Press

New York / Oakland

Seven Stories Press
140 Watts Street
New York, NY 10013
www.sevenstories.com

College professors and high school and middle school teachers may order free examination copies of Seven Stories Press titles. To order, visit www.sevenstories.com/textbook or send a fax on school letterhead to (212) 226-1411.

Library of Congress Cataloging-in-Publication Data
Slattery, Brian Francis.
  The family hightower : a novel / Brian Francis Slattery.
      pages cm
  ISBN 978-1-60980-563-0
  I. Title.
  PS3619.L375F36 2014
  813'.6--dc23

                            2014005055

Book Design by Jon Gilbert

Printed in the United States

9 8 7 6 5 4 3 2 1

Prologue

So listen: You have to accept the coincidence, because nothing is stranger than the truth. It's March 10, 1968, or 10 Dhul Hijja 1388, in the late morning of the first day of Eid al-Kabir. A Russian woman is in labor in a village near Midelt, Morocco, in a house the color of burnt clay. Her husband, Rufus James Hightower, an American, helps her squat by the bed, says he'll go get the midwife. *How bad is the pain? How long has it been going on?* Rufus says. *Not bad, not long,* she says. She's lying. She's been in labor for hours already, since just after midnight, but she doesn't tell him that. He's high, and since she hasn't seen him since yesterday afternoon, she assumes he hasn't slept, either. He's just been smoking. But she still wants him here and knows how little it takes to scare him off, even when he's straight. So she's grateful that he doesn't know her well enough to read the tension on her face. He thinks she's telling the truth. They met each other less than a year ago, got married only after she knew she was pregnant. In the doorway, Rufus turns, holds up a hand—*are you sure you're okay?*— and gets a glare.

Outside, the narrow streets are filled with blood. The knife sharpeners have all gone home and there are bonfires on every corner. Two men, obvious friends, are walking down the middle of the street; there's blood on their machetes, blood on their hands. Three girls play with a sheep's head before giving it to their parents to roast; they ask it questions like it's an oracle. *When will I be married? Will I ever go to Paris?* two of the girls ask. The third girl pretends to be the voice of the sheep, speaking in a bleating monotone. *You will marry when you are seventy-six years old. You will go to Paris tomorrow.* Then they put the head in the fire, laughing, while the people around them pray.

Rufus finds the midwife behind her house, where she and her family are sacrificing a goat. Her husband has just slit the animal's throat, and it lies on the stones of the small courtyard. There's blood pouring out of it, and the midwife is sweeping it into a drain. Soon the butchery will start.

"My wife is in labor now," Rufus says, in Arabic.

The midwife looks at him. He can tell she doesn't have any patience for him today. It's supposed to be her day off.

"It's her first?"

"I'm pretty sure."

The midwife shakes her head, turns to her husband. There's some bickering between them in Berber, which Rufus can't understand. Then she turns back to him. "Give me twenty minutes."

Rufus helps her carry her things back to his house, a stack of towels, a bowl for fresh water, a long, sturdy pair of sharp scissors. But they're too late. At the doorway, he hears a choking wail that doesn't mingle with the children's voices or the cries of the livestock dying outside.

"What's that?" he says.

His wife's voice from inside, in Russian-tainted Moroccan Arabic. "Your son."

Within the year, she'll leave him, after one fight too many. *This is not the life I want,* she'll say, then speak in a way she knows is too blunt, but her Arabic, her English, won't let her do better. *I don't want you. I don't even want the baby.* And Rufus will look down at the child in his arms. *I do,* he'll think. *More than anything else in the world.*

Now it's 2:47 in the morning on July 2, still 1968, in Cleveland, Ohio. Muriel Hightower, Rufus's sister, is at the end of a long labor on the kitchen floor of an apartment near University Circle. She's a stone hippie, and she's still reeling a little from her father's death two years before, and what it did to the family. She's been living in what people will later call a commune, and the family doesn't hide their condescension now, but they don't know what it's like: the Tiny Alice shows, the hang, the talk about how to make things better around here. When the Hessler Street Fair starts up, her lifestyle will get a little more respect, though that's a year off, and the midwifery movement—Ina May Gaskin, and the Caravan, and the Farm—is still two years away. But the idea's been catching on for a while. So the end of Muriel's labor happens on an old school bus. The midwife has gotten some training from an obstetrician in town who figures she's going to try to birth babies whether he helps her or not, so he might as well help. The labor's hard but it's not complicated. The midwife catches the baby, cuts and ties the umbilical, and puts the baby to Muriel's chest. Then she delivers the placenta. The baby cries and pees all over his mother. Muriel doesn't care; she's so happy to see the boy.

"What are you going to call him?" the midwife says.

She takes a breath. *I'm giving him my last name, not his,* she thinks. The second male in that thought is the kid's father, her ex-boyfriend, who split for the West Coast as soon as he learned she was pregnant. She turns her head to the nurse.

"Peter Henry Hightower," she says. "After his grandfather."

The family doesn't find out about the coincidence you have to accept— that Muriel's brother Rufus gave his son the very same name, for the very same reason—until 1974, when Rufus makes his first visit to the United States since the death of the original Peter Henry Hightower: the Ukrainian kid from Tremont, the self-made man, the patriarch, the charmer; the son of a bitch, the criminal, the sellout, and for the last thirty years of his life, one of the most powerful men in Cleveland.

Rufus comes back to Cleveland in 1974 for the wedding of his and Muriel's older sister, Sylvie, at the house in Bratenahl where they all grew up, and where Sylvie still lives. They're on the back lawn that drops down to the lake, a long stretch of grass full of wildflowers, from the shoreline to the top of the rise, where the mansion runs from one wall of the estate to the other. All the windows are lit, and in the last light of the day—the sun went down a half an hour ago—the house looks like a distant city. Sylvie's set up wide white tents, floors on low risers, gaslights on metal stands. A big band plays 1940s swing and the Motown of a few years ago, brings out the middle generation and their parents, the swarm of kids always. The oldest ones there, old enough to be grandparents—the ones who know all the stories now, or at least think they do, and can't be shocked by anything anyway—sit at the back tables with colorful cocktails. Sylvie's dress is a light gray to match her husband's hair. The husband, Michael Rizzi, is sixty-two years old, twenty-six years older than she is, and was a close associate, business and otherwise, of her father's until the day he died. None of the siblings was aware that Michael and Sylvie even knew each other until they announced their engagement, and now all of Rufus's brothers and sisters are bonded in polite confusion: Muriel, of course, with her husband—Terry, whom she met and married not long after Peter was born—and her three children, the youngest just a baby; Henry, the eldest son, and his wife with their only daughter, Alex; and Jackie, twitching, on the arm of uncle Stefan, their father's brother. Rufus notices the siblings are all seated at different tables and smiles. That's Sylvie all over. Understanding why they all might not want to talk to each other for long, even eight years after their father's funeral; giving them the chance to avoid having to pretend that they get along.

Rufus still has the thick mustache he had the last time they saw him, wears loose linen clothes, slicks his hair back with oil, but puts his son—a black-haired boy with bright hazel eyes like a German shepherd—in a shirt and shorts he bought in Higbee's in downtown Cleveland the day before. Though nothing can hide that his boy isn't from Ohio. His skin is far too tan for the sun Ohio gets, his haircut is all wrong. He's an alien in this place.

"Jesus Christ, Rufus, you look like Lawrence of Arabia," Henry says. "Who's the kid? Is he yours?"

"Of course he's mine," Rufus says.

Henry laughs. "Don't act like you're insulted. What's his name?"

"Peter. I named him after Dad."

Henry looks across the reception toward Muriel and her oldest boy, a dirty blond, clean and sharp in a powder-blue suit the same cut as his stepfather's.

"Same middle name, too?" he says.

"Yep," Rufus says.

"You're kidding."

"No," Rufus says.

"Unbelievable."

"What?"

"You really need to stay in touch more."

By the end of the reception, there have been at least a dozen conversations about how the two boys are almost opposites. Muriel's boy moves from table to table asking everyone how their wedding is going. He dances with Sylvie, with his mother, with Jackie. A great-uncle gives him a bite of his cake, and the boy returns the favor. *Here, have a bite,* the kid says. *I can't eat all of this.* Rufus's boy, meanwhile, climbs on the tables, then hides under them. He runs off to the shore of the lake and someone has to drag him back. They find spoons in his pockets before he leaves, walking with his head down, clinging to his father's leg. *It's no surprise,* Muriel says, her baby on her hip, *the way Rufus is raising him, dragging the boy halfway across Africa and back, no mother, no home to speak of.* She's a long way from her hippie days by then, but she's not trying to be mean to her brother; she's concerned about the boy and can't help herself. *Bet he's slept outside more often than he's slept in a bed. Yes,* she says, *one of these boys is going to be real trouble.* She's right about that, dear reader; she's just pegged the wrong boy. And Rufus never comes back to America again.

Okay so far? Because whenever trouble's visited this family, it's been big, and the kind that comes along in 1995—that snares first one boy, then the other, and then the rest of them, in some way or another— leaves a chain of corpses from Cleveland to Moldova. But it's also conjuring some of the old Peter Henry Hightower's dark magic, calling up his ghost to build empires again, hold together and destroy everyone around him. Looking back, it's easy to see how it all fits together, to feel that stale air of inevitability, to forget that at the time it was all open promise—always was, still is now. Those two ideas, of infinite possibility and singular doom, held in direct tension: If America doesn't have a lock on it, at least we've done it best in all the world so far, and it's a small part of what makes us great and terrible, from the first days of religious and political radicals making profits and slaughtering the natives to our final days, whenever they may be, but which are always coming sooner than we think.

Still with me? Good. Let's go.

Part 1

1995

Chapter 1

Every story's a kind of violence perpetrated on the facts. You cut off their arms and legs, stretch them out, break their ribs until they fit where you think they're supposed to. All of it in search of meaning. Some stories, the job is so clean, everything's arranged along an arc so bright that you can't see the carnage that went into making it.

But this story isn't like that. There is blood everywhere, pieces all around us. There are so many people involved: the Hightower family and all the people they touched, all the people they hurt. People and politics and history, of the family and four countries. This means we have to move around a lot. If you're looking for the kind of story where you follow one person from beginning to end, and the clock ticks forward, sentence after sentence—well, it's not going to go like that around here. You won't be confused at the end, you'll know everything then, I promise. But where do we start?

We could go to that strip of land that, in 1995, three countries claim but nobody's governing, the triangle at the intersection of Ukraine, Romania, and Moldova. We could bend a hundred years of history into a perfect circle and call it whole. Would it satisfy you? Almost without a doubt. But it wouldn't be true. We could start in Cleveland in 1966, give you the pinion of the drama. We could start with a single dollar bill, because this is all about money in the end. The things people do when they don't have enough, or think they don't. The impossibility of knowing when we have enough, because not one of us knows ourselves that well, and the man who says he does? Don't trust him. All these things matter, all of them could force the story to mean something, to mean a lot of things. But that's not what we're here to see. We are here, you understand, to see the bodies and the blood. The muscles and the tendons. So maybe we should start with cords: a telephone line running unbroken from Cleveland across the Atlantic to Granada, Spain.

It's August 1995, and Curly Potapenko, in Cleveland, is doing the calling. He's been trying to reach the younger Peter Henry Hightower—Muriel's boy, whom everyone calls Petey—all day. He's trying to warn him, but nobody'll pick up the phone. Curly Potapenko is scared to death that this is because Petey's dead already. It's not a stupid thing to think: The only reason Curly has a phone number is because he paid a guy off to give it to him—a double cross—because he knows the people he's been working for in Kiev have been tracking Petey down in the hopes of killing him. They have a couple guys out, one heading to the Romanian border, one heading east into Russia. Another one heading west, into the rest of Europe. They're even talking about sending a guy somewhere in Africa. They're following all the leads they have.

Curly doesn't know that nobody's picking up the phone in Spain because the young man who lives in the apartment is out. That's all. The bigger problem, though, is that Curly—and that means the people in Kiev, too—in this case, have the wrong Peter Henry Hightower. They've found Rufus's son, not Muriel's, the one who's on the outs right now with his dad for what he thinks is for good, though it doesn't stop him from feeling bad. Our man Peter, who's about to get involved in a plot he doesn't want any part of.

It's 9:06 p.m. in Granada, and Peter is leaving the Art Deco movie theater on the corner of the Plaza de Gracia. He's been to that theater a lot, because he knows almost nobody in this town. He lives by himself in a studio apartment, makes a living from tutoring Spaniards in English: students, businesspeople, a pampered spouse who thinks of language acquisition as a quirky hobby. He sells freelance articles about Granada to magazines, too. The angles come to him without much work, a relic of his days as a more serious journalist: the travel angle, the culinary angle. He's a good investigative reporter, too, when the story grabs him. But often, the story doesn't grab him. These days, no story seems to. Sometimes that Spain feels like a dream to him. For the first five seconds of every day, he has to remember where he is; he keeps expecting to wake up somewhere else. There's the maze of the Moorish quarter. The Generalife, so complicated and peaceful at the same time. And then there's the haze of the place during siesta. He has never adjusted to sleeping during it, or even resting, so he stays in his apartment, sweating in the heat, or goes for long walks. The city's eeriest to him then; it's as though everyone got a piece of news he missed and abandoned the place, and he's the only one left behind. All of Spain seems strange to him that way, and it was like that the day he arrived, by plane into Madrid, and took the train south, riding in the beige smoking car, like living inside a cigarette, staring out at the blank landscape outside the city. It has all been believable as a hallucination.

Peter's thinking of that now, at 11:27, after a slow meal of North African tapas at a bar two blocks to the north of the theater, because, as the clock moves from noon to midnight, the Plaza de Gracia travels back in time. The tiny, buzzing cars, delivery trucks, and scooters of the afternoon give way to bicycles. The modern buildings near the theater, the bright magazine kiosk, get pale in the light of the lamps in the square. The cobblestones, the palm trees, the old buildings of wood and white plaster, come to life. Two Romanis play a tarnished violin and an accordion missing four keys. Their cases are out and already lined with pesetas. Beyond them, an acting troupe has set up a small stage, two floodlights, five rows of ten chairs each, which are one-third occupied. Three actors onstage, two women and a man, in peasant costumes, all scream at each other in Spanish, too fast and slangy for Peter to understand, though it's holding the small audience. They gasp when one of the men attacks the woman, breathe hard when the second man stabs the first and red silk pours from the first man's embroidered shirt. They're quiet for the last minutes, then stand up, clapping, shouting bravos. Whether they're just family and friends is irrelevant to the actors when they're onstage, or maybe all the more meaningful. A man with a black jacket and white hair approaches the stage and waves down the victim of the murder, who's up and bowing. They hug like an uncle and a nephew do, the older man patting the younger one on the back.

A heavy realization—*I've had way too much to drink*—settles into Peter's head. All of a sudden, he can't remember his bed ever feeling so far away. He puts his hands in his pockets to steady himself, keeps his head down. Passes back through the Plaza de Gracia, weaves through the alleyways around the Cathedral, where three Romani women are laughing in a corner, all red scarves, flowing skirts, dangling bangles. He can almost hear it, the past roaring up around him, and he's ashamed, ashamed and sorry for himself at the same time, as only drunk people can be.

It's a year ago, in 1994. Peter is in Cairo with Rufus, his father. His dad, as usual, has moved there for what he says is work, though also as usual, Peter can't figure out what he does. He leaves the house at odd times, makes calls from Egypt's industrial-strength pay phones. Comes home sometimes not with money, but things: a long piece of meat and a basket of vegetables, three pairs of new shoes, a bicycle. It seems good enough. But Peter can see in his father's walk that he's getting bored, nervous. *We could go back to Nairobi,* he keeps saying; he hasn't been there since 1983, and even Peter knows—with all that Rufus has tried to protect him from—even Peter knows how unhappy he was there by the time he left. But he's still talking like that: *We could go to Bissau.* At last, Peter comes home to find the bags packed in the hallway, his father spinning a key ring on his finger that Peter doesn't recognize.

"What are those for?"

"A car. A Peugeot 405, to be exact. Egyptian model. They're making them here now, you know."

"You bought a car?"

"What do you think, I stole it? Don't answer that."

"Where are we going?" Peter says.

"Casablanca."

Peter just looks at him.

"I know what you're thinking, Peter," Rufus says.

"You always say that, Dad, and you never do," Peter says. "You never know what I'm thinking."

"All right. What are you thinking?"

"That you're in trouble again. That your latest scheme, whatever it is, has fallen through, and now we have to skip town."

"That's not true."

"Then why are we leaving?"

"Okay, okay. Part of what you say is true. Or what you're saying is part of the truth."

"Dad, are you high?"

"No. No. I'm saying you don't know the whole story."

"Then tell me. Tell me already."

Rufus opens his arms. "Look at me. I'm most of the way to sixty. I don't want to live like this anymore. I can't afford Europe, but I can't stay here, either."

"What do you mean by *this,* Dad? How is it we've been living?"

"Please, Peter. This is the last trip. I promise you, when we get to Casablanca, I'll stay there for good. You'll have to go there to bury me."

They've been through this before, five times in the past nine years. The first time—in 1986—Peter's only seventeen, but knows he could pass for what white people understand as twenty-two, maybe twenty-five. He's already tall, with cold eyes; the circumstances of his life, the things he's seen, make him carry himself like few kids in rich countries do. They're living in Cape Town then, after having moved from Harare, from Lagos. He only sees his father leave the house, come back, always at different hours, wearing different clothes, holding bundles of cash. Their apartments, though, are almost always the same. Plaster walls, a cracked tile floor. The sun driving through thin windows. Never any curtains. Bare furnishings: A table, two chairs, a hot plate, sometimes a gas stove lying on a counter, the line coiling to a propane tank on the floor. By 1986, Peter's been to thirteen schools, managed to learn to read, write, do math. He's learned how to fit in, how to move around; he can do it with an ease that almost compensates for having no sense of who he is, or where he's from. But one day in May, with the summer turning to fall, he decides he's tired of it. At the time, he doesn't quite understand what he wants—a home—so he just waits for his father to come back, and then tells him he wants to see his aunts and uncles, his cousins. It's night. His father glances out the dark window and squints.

"You really want to see them?" Rufus says.

"Yeah, I do."

They don't have anything you want, Rufus almost says, but stops himself. Realizes it'll only make him seem small-minded, uncharitable, things he tries hard not to be, even though he wonders if it isn't better sometimes, or at least useful, to be petty. His devotion to his son only makes it worse. Rufus wants to teach his son to open himself up to the world, to do what he can't do himself, and he doesn't know how to reconcile that with his conviction that he would destroy entire villages to protect his boy. He doesn't say anything. He goes to the foot of his bed, bends down, and pulls out a metal box with a padlock on it. He unlocks it, pulls out a wrinkled brown folder, and hands it to Peter. Inside, there's a spiral-bound stenographer's notebook filled with addresses and phone numbers, and an envelope with several thousand U.S. dollars in it.

"This is for you. You should start with my brother Henry." He searches for the words. "He'll understand you the best, I think."

Peter's counting the money, his mouth open a little. It occurs to Rufus that his son has never seen that much cash in one place before. That's one thing he's kept him from.

"This . . . this is a lot." Peter says.

"Not as much as you might think," Rufus says.

"If you had all this money, why have we been living like this?"

"It's not my money, Peter. It's yours."

Peter doesn't know what to say, and Rufus feels bad for him, wonders in that second if it was a mistake to raise him like he did. But it's too late now.

"Do you want to go or not?" Rufus says.

Peter spends the summer of 1986 in shock. His uncle Henry's place in New Canaan, Connecticut, is smaller than the palaces around it, more secluded, but finer, carrying the whiff of overdesign and expensive detail. The house of a man who's had money for long enough that he knows what to do with it. But the man is almost never there, except on weekends. He gives Peter a set of clothes, a haircut, says he would give him a car, but Peter doesn't have a license. During the week he drives north into Massachusetts with his cousin Alex; she's a rising junior at Amherst, majoring in political science. They take the curves slow along Route 2, in the tall pines at the north end of the Pioneer Valley. *I wanna be your sledgehammer,* the radio says. It seems to be on every station; they can't escape it. They're there to visit four friends of Alex's who are holed up in a house in Colrain for the summer; their plan is to smoke a lot of pot and play as much music as they can. Everyone's up until five in the morning; the friends have a guitar, a mandolin, and a banjo, and they stumble and laugh their way through a pile of folk-rock songs. They talk about how they want to live like that, out of a car, moving all the time. They don't have any idea what they're wishing for. *Alex, you played violin when you were a kid, right?* they say. They can't get any of the words out unless there are hard consonants in them. *Play the fiddle with us.* But Alex isn't interested in her friends, wants to know all about Africa from Peter. She hangs on every detail. Peter tells her about Rufus and him trying to stave off dehydration once when their car breaks down in Chad. They were stranded for four days with a man and two women in the shade of a crumbling building that might have been a military checkpoint, or a tiny field office for a foreign oil company. He and his father had no language in common with the other three, but they shared what little water they had, until a gas truck rattled by and they all jumped up, got in the truck, waving their arms and yelling. Even at the time, Peter didn't know how they all fit in the cab. He tells

Alex about the market in Onitsha, Nigeria, too, the maze of stalls of cloth and clothes, raw and dried meat, chicken, engine parts. A market as big as the world. Before the civil war, Peter tells her—and Alex nods, though she didn't know until then that Nigeria had a civil war—the market even had publishers. They put out pulp fiction, tracts on morality. He shows Alex one of them when they get back to New Canaan: *Learn to Speak 360 Interesting Proverbs and Know Your True Brother*, by C. N. Eze. A brittle orange cover with a Xeroxed photograph of three upper-middle-class white people on it being friendly to each other. A white guy in a shirt, tie, and sweater vest smiling on the back cover. *I enjoy myself with proverbs,* the caption reads. Alex is fascinated.

"Why are the people on this book white?" she says.

"I don't know," Peter says. It hasn't occurred to him until now that the cover is all that weird. "I think it's from the early sixties."

"Stock photos," Alex says, and chuckles. She spends an hour thumbing through the pages, reading passages aloud to amuse herself. "Chapter One," she says. "How a Brother Planned to Kill a Brother and Plunge Him into Financial Distress, God, what amazing phrasing. Chapter Four. When Do We Know Our Real Brother? Ha."

There's a faint whiff of mockery underneath Alex's glee, and Peter doesn't like it. *Why is she being so condescending?* he thinks. But then he looks at the covers of the other books in the place and realizes his paperback is cheap there, cheap and bizarre. When Henry is around on the weekend, he also asks Peter about Africa. The questions aren't like Alex's, though. They're firm, incisive, a quiet grilling. Sometimes it seems like Henry is asking about Rufus, about Peter's upbringing; he wants to know how they're doing without just saying so. Other times it seems like Henry's pumping him for information about possible investment opportunities. And Pamela—Henry's wife, his aunt—is almost never there at all. She's on the boards of multiple charities and community organizations and is always going to meetings; when she's at home, she's on the phone, speaking in a friendly and practiced singsong while her fingers snarl themselves in the telephone cord. *These people tolerate each other enough*, Peter thinks, but it's hard to tell. The entire family is encased in a shell with a gleaming surface that hides the clouds inside. Peter likes them, even trusts them, but can't believe he's related to them. He catches, then, a glimpse of the depths of his father's rebellion, though he can't see how, in the extremity of his reaction, Rufus is so much like the rest of them.

Peter stays with Henry and his family for three weeks, then flies to Cleveland. Muriel is waiting for him at the baggage claim in Hopkins, a huge smile on her face. She lets out a high squeal when she sees him and runs and throws her arms around him; and he feels small, though the top of her head is well below his chin.

"Peter!"

"How did you know it was me?"

"I'd recognize those eyes anywhere," she says. She doesn't mention the hundred other clues that give him away: the new hairdo, the borrowed clothes that say Henry, but despite them, the manner, the expression on his face, showing just how much Peter isn't from Ohio.

Muriel's house on Edgewater Drive is one of the smaller places on the block, a big colonial tucked between mansions. Muriel explains that they needed the house because they used to have five people in their family, but are down to four—her Petey is away at boarding school, she says, with a hitch in her voice; she realizes as soon as Peter does that it's a bad lie. Everyone knows it's summertime. Her other two children, Andrew and Julia, are even around, though they're out of the house all day, playing sports, riding horses, going to camps, being as overenrolled in the summer as they are during the school year. Muriel's just gotten used to saying Petey's in school now because she's tired of talking about her screwup son, and she hopes that Henry's been discreet and that Peter hasn't been following the news in Cleveland. Peter doesn't push it. He wanders through the house with his bag still hanging from his shoulder. A living room with a long, curving couch, three chairs. Nobody sits in any of them. A wide dining room table, a huge kitchen. Nobody eats there. Five empty bedrooms. Muriel shows him to the smallest one, the guest room, and as he unpacks his things, he thinks about how the house would be populated if it were in Ghana. Maybe twenty people could live here, he thinks, an extended family. The grandparents would have their own rooms, which they'd sometimes share with the smallest children. The nuclear families would be crowded into the others. The downstairs would be packed with rowdy children, the kitchen noisy with the sound of women boiling plantains and cassava, then pounding them together to make fufu. There'd be a radio playing highlife.

Muriel takes Peter to the parks in the Emerald Necklace on the weekend with Andrew and Julia; she thinks he'll have something in common with them, being almost the same age, though Peter feels more like one of their parents. To him, they seem whiny and weak, though they're just American children. They go boating on Lake Erie with Harold Anderson, his great-uncle William's nephew; Harold spent some time in the family business, only to retire at forty to devote his time to sailing. He has a forty-five-foot yacht called *Bad Break*, and he's taken it out of the Great Lakes, along the Saint Lawrence River, all the way down the East Coast to the Caribbean. *I'm not sure I ever need to be on land again,* he says. He's been to Accra, too, to Cape Town, through the Gulf of Aden and the Red Sea to Port Sudan, through the Suez Canal to Cairo. So many cities in common with Peter, though when they try to talk about them, it's like they've been living on different planets, and Harold gets a little quieter. He knows what that disconnect means, doesn't want to make the young man uncomfortable, and is also a little worried about him. At the end of the day there's a cold breeze across the water, and Muriel and her husband go below for gin and tonics. Andrew and Julia are already asleep in the wide bed lodged in the bow. Peter stays on deck, watches the sun slink between strips of cloud and into the water, below the horizon. Turns to watch how the darkness crawls across the lake, over the Five Mile Crib, up the buildings of Cleveland's skyline, chasing the pink light away. Harold watches him watching, waits until he hears the conversation below in full swing.

"You want something to drink?" he says.

"No thanks," Peter says.

"Soda? How old are you? I could get you a cocktail."

"I'm all right," Peter says.

Harold hesitates. He's not sure how to start. Then: "You know, I used to be pretty close with your dad," he says. "I think that's really why Meer had me take you guys out today. We were kind of in the same boat, so to speak, moneywise. I don't mean amountwise, exactly. But we had the same awkward feelings about it, about having so much, especially in a city like this. The same questions about what to do about it."

Peter doesn't say anything. This man is talking to him like he's fifteen years older than he is, and he's not quite ready for it.

"I know your uncle Henry and Muriel don't talk about Rufus very much, but we all miss him, you know."

Rufus, he said. Turning Peter's dad into someone other than just his dad. There's a question that's been burning a hole in Peter's head since Henry picked him up at the airport, from the inside of his car to the inside of his house, from the tilt of Muriel's accent when she speaks, to the simple fact that they're here now with a man who hasn't worked in over a decade and wants for nothing.

"How much money does my family have?"

Harold laughs. "Complicated question. Which means that they have more than most people will ever see. You must know this already, but whenever someone's cagey about how much they have, it almost always means they're rich. They've stopped counting the pennies a long time ago, maybe stopped counting the hundreds or even the thousands— and almost nobody stops counting thousands. You understand what I'm saying. Almost everyone knows how much they have because they have to. If they don't keep track of it, they might run out. But a few people don't have that problem. They might not even be sure how to count up everything they have." He takes a sip of his drink. "It makes you into a child if you let it."

"So . . . how much?"

He laughs again. "I don't know. But I can tell you this: Someone could write a book about your grandfather—the one you're named after—if anyone in the family would be willing to talk about him. The city made him, and he returned the favor in spades. He could have been a Rockefeller or a Carnegie. Instead he was like a Van Sweringen."

"I don't know who that is."

"That's what I mean. They were two brothers, and almost nobody knows about them anymore, but they pretty much built this place. They say your grandfather even had a deal of some kind worked out with them, or maybe they were just his role models. They say he had deals worked out with a lot of people. He had to have, to go from Tremont to that house in Bratenahl. I know by the time he died, he had money everywhere. Stocks, bonds, real estate, a lot of other investments. Some of it, um, maybe not as legitimate as it should have been, if you know what I'm saying. But I don't think we'll ever know for sure. All we know is that he must have made his nut. His nut and then some. He was a shrewd businessman, maybe the shrewdest I'll ever see. He had to be, to do what he did in this town. You're going to Sylvie's house, the place in Bratenahl, right?"

"Tomorrow."

"Then you'll see what I mean," Harold says. "Tell your dad I said hello, okay?"

He's right about Sylvie's house. They take the highway along the waterfront, get off in Bratenahl to cruise along Lake Shore Boulevard. Walls and gates rise on either side of the road, the houses sprawling into estates that get bigger and bigger, until they're driving along a row of places the likes of which Peter has never seen. They should be boarding schools, he thinks; they should be hotels, hospitals, government institutions. At last, they reach a low granite wall, a huge wrought-iron gate. The long branches of old trees hang over the road. The driveway meanders through a stand of enormous white oaks and a garden of flowers so bright it almost looks like it's on fire. It's in a state of controlled riot, the work of someone who knows how to manage things and when to let go. A short, neat outbuilding—a guest house, a carriage house—hides on the side of the lot. The masonry on it is too rich for its size. Not too rich for the main house, though, which Peter at first can only catch glimpses of through the trees, until the branches part at the edge of a patio of mossy bricks and the house spreads its stone, gabled wings. The place is a castle of granite and leaded glass, crawling with ivy. Sylvie is waiting on the steps, standing with her hands clasped in front of her, a small smile on her face. She gives each of them a short, soft hug.

"Look at you," she says to Peter. "I see so much of your father in you." She gazes at him with an intensity that turns Peter to glass. His past opens up to her, the present boy on the verge of shattering under the strain, though she won't let that happen. Then she blinks, and there's only kindness.

"Come in, come in," she says.

Peter's here, at last, in the place where his father grew up. The ornate woodwork, the wide floorboards. A staircase that belongs on the *Titanic*. The side of the house facing the shore is all glass, an unbroken, sweeping view of the lake and the long slope of the hill from the house down to the water. It jogs Peter's memory of Sylvie's wedding. He can still see the huge tent, the lanterns, the stage, the dance floor; the tables with white tablecloths he hid under and climbed on. The house was brighter then, in better shape, but he realizes that he never went inside, and neither, to his knowledge, did his father. They're all standing in the kitchen now, drinking lemonade. Muriel uncorks a litany of irrelevant family news. One of the Andersons was promoted to a managerial position in an insurance company. Another went to Buenos Aires last month. Her drink warming in the glass while her free hand waves in the air. Sylvie punctuates Muriel's speech with just the right interjections—*how nice, I see, that's wonderful*—then gives Peter a sideways glance. She knows he can't wait for it to be over. He's grateful to her for not calling attention to it. But she gets Muriel to wrap up the visit fast, follows them out with a large bag of gardening tools slung across her back, a lopper in one hand, a pole pruner in the other.

"You still do all that yourself?" Muriel says.

"Of course," Sylvie says.

"You know, you can get someone to help you. It's so much to maintain."

Peter is angry on Sylvie's behalf. Muriel has started to annoy him. But Sylvie smiles instead, that same small, unreadable gesture.

"I love it," she says. "I really do." And then, when Muriel's already in the car, to Peter: "Come back sometime and visit, whenever you want." She drops her guard all the way down for a second, not a trace of deception, of politicking. So unlike the rest of the family for a second, and Peter feels a little guilty for not wanting to be there. He doesn't quite see that Sylvie's way ahead of him, as she always will be. She knows he's not ready to grasp all their family history. It's a rocket that curves high in the air, then explodes into a million pieces. He's not ready to see everything he's involved in, by association, either. But that will change, she knows, and if she lives to see it, she might just tell him whatever he needs to know.

"Well?" Rufus says, when Peter comes back. "How'd it go? How'd you like the family?" He feels bad for not being able to keep the sarcasm out of his voice when he knows his boy so well, knows when there's too much kicking around in his son's head to let him speak. They never get around to talking about it.

Four times between 1986 and 1994, Peter leaves and comes back to his father. He stays away for longer and longer every time. First he just goes somewhere else in West Africa; that's where he picks up his French. Then across Central Asia to China. To Indonesia. To Central America by ship; he disembarks in Colón, Panama, works his way across the isthmus. He hears the stories of the revolutions, the things people did to survive them, the things people are still doing to carry them out, even if they lost. *Teaching math to kids in my village,* a Guatemalan man with a quiet voice and hair slicked back beneath his hat says to him, *this is my revolution.* He writes a story about this man that ends up in a local activist English-language paper. Another story he writes, about a dispute on a finca in which unpaid workers take over a plantation and end up under siege from police, even as they win a court case, appears in a left-wing magazine in the United States. He meets other journalists working in the country, who see something in him and pass his name along; he's the guy who'll get the stories other people won't get. That's when he gets his first wire service pieces. He also gets a bit of the leftist politics that it's hard to leave Latin America without. He feels an urge to do something, anything, to not walk through his entire life looking the other way. He's tempted to stay; in a weird way, the tin shacks, the roads covered in mud and paper, the loud, rattling buses, are as close to home, to belonging somewhere, as he's ever felt. But then he starts to worry about his father. He's always worried about him, though Rufus never says anything to make him think anything's wrong. *I'm in Cairo now,* Rufus says. *What a marvelous place.* But Peter doesn't believe it, feels all the more right for not believing when it's 1994, he's gone back to his father, and they're leaving again, only four months into their stay, in a car Peter still isn't sure they own.

In 1994, Rufus's idea, like I said, is to drive from Cairo to Casablanca. There's a David Lean movie in his head about it, Peter thinks, one where it's their lone car racing on a highway through the Sahara, because his father still falls for the romanticism, even after he's lived in Africa so long. But the highway itself is dusty and dry; the car's filthy before they leave the city. There's traffic. They almost can't see out the windows. Then there are the long, long delays at the border between Egypt and Libya, Libya and Algeria, while the guards try to square Rufus and Peter's obvious Americanness—maybe you can never lose it, no matter how hard you try—with the fact of their non-U.S. passports. Rufus loves it. He never quite says this to Peter, but he's at his happiest like this, like it was when Peter was a kid. The two of them skating across the surface of the world, houses and trees and people standing with blue plastic buckets by the side of the road just blurs in their eyes. His son is all he needs, all he wants.

They don't know that guerrillas invaded the Atlas Asni hotel in

Marrakech and shot two Spanish tourists dead, or that three young French Muslims from the slums of Paris will be charged for the attack. As a huge manhunt continues, the network they're a part of will seem ever bigger, and more than thirty men will see the insides of courtrooms in Morocco and France, be jailed or slated to be executed. But Morocco points its finger at its neighbor, too, right from the start, accuses Algeria of funding the whole thing. Then the border's really shut down, and reader, it will still be closed years later. So Rufus and Peter find the gate between Morocco and Algeria lowered. Two mustachioed border guards lounging outside the customs office, machine guns lying across their laps, looking at the dusty Peugeot as it drives up. They don't even act like they're going to stand up.

"Turn around," Peter says.

"Why?" Rufus says. "We need to know what's going on."

"Not from them."

Rufus nods, puts on the brakes, and backs up. The wide cafés along the road are all empty. Only two are still open, one playing faint raï from a tiny radio, which a man with a broom turns off as soon as he sees them.

"The border is closed," the man with the broom says to them, in French.

"We don't speak French," Rufus says in Arabic. Peter doesn't correct him.

"The border is closed," the man says again, in Arabic.

"Why?"

The man with the broom takes in Rufus's accent, squints at them. It's too much to explain.

"The border is closed," he says again. "Go back. And get out of this country." He knows how hostile he sounds, but he's trying to save them.

They stand in the road for a minute, the car idling. Peter leans against the hood, stares at the metal. His father walks in front of the car, looks at the border again, back at the road they came down. Then turns back to his son, smiling.

"Looks like Casablanca's out," he says. "It's just us again." And Peter takes a good, long look at his father. *I can't do this anymore,* he thinks to himself. *I just can't.*

"No, Dad," he says. "It's just you."

Rufus's smile leaves him.

"I'm not going with you this time," Peter says. "Or any time."

"Please," Rufus says. "Just come."

"Why? For the next scheme that gets us tossed out of somewhere? The next plan that falls through?"

"No," Rufus says. "Because I'm your dad and you're my boy."

"Tell me what the hell our lives mean, Dad," Peter says. "Tell me why we keep running."

Rufus has been protecting his boy so much, doing everything in his power to make sure that no harm comes to him. And it goes beyond sheltering him from the dark heart of his family, way beyond the bits of instability in his own life that Peter could see. A few times over the years, when Rufus has known that trouble is coming for them—because a deal he's tried to make goes bad, because they just aren't where they're supposed to be—Rufus has put his son to bed, then stayed awake in a darkened alley two blocks away with a gun across his lap, waiting for the intruders to come. A couple times, he's been able to talk it out with the silhouettes who appear around the corner. Most times, though, it has ended with bullets. To their legs, their arms. A couple times, their chests, their heads, when he's known there's no other way out. It's then that he's understood his own father the most, loved him and hated him, almost as much as he hates himself and what he's become. He's promised himself he'll spare Peter all of that, but it's getting harder and harder to do that and still keep him close. He doesn't know how.

"You sound just like your mother," Rufus says.

"That's just it, Dad," Peter says. "I wouldn't know."

The father is joking. The son isn't. It's just the first of a lot of things Peter says that day that he promised himself never to say. He knows he's breaking that promise even at the time, feels like the thoughts he held in for years have turned into bullets. All through this last visit, all across the highways of North Africa, it's like he's been carrying a loaded gun around, pointed at the back of his father's head, and now he's taking every shot he has. Even if the first shot is fatal, he'll pull the trigger until he's empty. It's rage, rage as he's never felt in his life, and a part of him is shocked that he can be so cruel. But it doesn't stop him from doing it. *I wish you'd left me with her*, he says. *Sometimes I wish I'd never even met you.*

And he's on the first plane out. Rufus takes him to the airport. Peter won't let him get out of the car; he jumps out almost before it stops, grabs his bag from the backseat in one quick motion. His father waits by the curb, waves at his boy, but Peter doesn't see it, because he doesn't turn around, doesn't look back. Just keeps walking until he's in the building and sure his father's gone.

It's August 1995. The street to Peter's apartment in Granada is always dark. There's a lamp mounted to the wall just two buildings down from his, but the bulb went out before Peter moved in and nobody's replaced it. It's quiet around here; the shouts from partyers and car horns feel far away. Peter's less drunk than he was, but still more than he wants to be. He smacks his lips, still feels like he's had a shot of Novocain. He fumbles with his keys for too long, drops them, fumbles again, and is in at last. He climbs the swaying stairs to the second-floor landing, screws with the keys again. In his apartment, the mattress on the floor is unmade but not messy. Neat stacks of papers line the wall. His suitcase is propped open, half out of the closet, the laundry in a canvas bag beside it. He can smell the dishes in the sink, flicks on the shuddering neon light in the kitchen. There are six new messages on his answering machine, piled on top of four old ones. The first three are from his editor. One's from an English student of his. He likes her. She's pretty and has a voice that turns upward in unexpected places, a sly intelligence and dark humor that's so soaked into her Spanish that it seeps into her blocky but effective English. In the past few lessons, she's managed to tell jokes, laugh at some of his. He tells her the old line that you know you're fluent in a language when you can argue with a cabdriver. He would ask her out, except that she's already engaged, to a man she's been dating for almost four years. They met when she was twenty. Peter has never met his student's fiancé, but admires him for knowing, even then, the kind of woman she was and would become; for knowing that he wouldn't do any better. In the last year, Peter has met a few women who have struck him, within minutes, as amazing people. *I'm engaged*, they all say. *Of course you are*, Peter thinks.

The next message has more static than usual. The voice is high and anxious. He doesn't know who it is. "Petey," it says. "It's me, Curly. I'm in Cleveland. I don't know why you went to Spain, but you shouldn't have used your real name. They know where you are, now, and they're coming after you. You got to call me if you get this, but get out of there first." The next message: "Petey, you got to call me and let me know you're all right, all right? It's Curly." The next: "For God's sake, Petey, call." The next three messages are just the sound of someone hanging up the phone, the final message with a small groan first. Giving up.

All at once, Peter's stone sober. Something rises in him, the kid who knows how to get through shantytowns, from the slums of Mombasa to the *musseques* of Luanda. His father, decades ago, walking out of Cleveland with nothing and vanishing, coming back only to vanish again. His aunt Sylvie, who knows everything. His grandfather, that survivor, that bastard, crawling up his spine. He turns out the lights in the kitchen, looks toward the stairs, wonders if he's remembered to close the outside door. Decides it's too late to check now.

Getting ready to run comes easy to him; he's helped his father do it so many times. He goes into the bathroom and kneels down to reach under the sink. Taped to the underside is an envelope, right where he left it. Inside is twelve thousand nine hundred and twenty-three dollars in a mixture of cash and traveler's checks, the last thing Rufus gave him before Peter left him in Algeria. *The rest of your money*, Rufus said. Peter also has a small blue book with a list of phone numbers in it, his passport, a folding knife with a small wooden handle. He packs three changes of clothes into a backpack. Breaks up the money, hides most of it in the packed clothes, then sticks a thin stack of the large bills in the pocket of his T-shirt, under a light jacket. He looks around the dark apartment, can't see anything well, but in his mind, the kitchen light is on and he's calm, just looking over everything one last time to make sure he's not leaving anything behind he can't live without. He isn't. Then he locks the door, wedges a chair under the doorknob, opens the window, and waits, sitting on the mattress, leaning against the wall. If he smoked, now would be the time for a cigarette.

He wants to be wrong about all of this. He wants no one to be coming for him. He wants to laugh about it in the morning. *God, could I have been any more paranoid?* But at almost one in the morning, he hears someone jangling with the lock at the bottom of the stairs who doesn't have a key for it. *So I remembered to close the door after all,* he thinks. He rises, goes to the open window while he hears footsteps coming up the stairs. He's perched on the sill by the time the intruder reaches the landing. Peter gives the situation one last chance to make him feel like an asshole. The lock rattles, rattles. Something snaps off in the keyhole and there's what sounds like a low, short curse, though Peter doesn't understand the language. Then there's a loud crack—whoever's on the other side of the door has put his foot to it—but Peter doesn't wait to see if it opens. The alley outside his window is a skinny thing, just wide enough for two bicycles. The roof of the next building is just a floor below him. He's never made the jump, but he knows he can do it. He lands hard and rolls, then has the good sense to hide on the roof, behind a chimney, instead of trying to run. He could never clear the roof without being seen, but if he hides, it'll be as if he did. He crouches again, shifts his legs to get comfortable. Figures he can wait all the next day.

It's a clean getaway, in other words, clean enough that the man looking for him, who's met Peter's cousin Petey and has a photograph just to make sure, never sees he has the wrong Peter Henry Hightower. Peter makes only one mistake—a mistake his cousin would also have made—in not erasing his messages while he had the chance. Which is how Curly Potapenko is dead within forty-eight hours, and how the body of this story is split open to spill way, way out. It's just like I said: This is about way more than Peter, Rufus's son; way more than Petey, Muriel's boy. This story is about everyone, and dear reader: There is blood everywhere.

Chapter 2

The southern highway out of Kiev shoots across open fields, vast expanses of land, but Petey can't see any of it. All he sees is what's in the headlights—blurry pavement, white dashes blinking past like a strobe light. He's in the backseat of a car that isn't his. The car's driver is nervous. He thought he was just picking up a tourist, but Petey's been getting twitchier and twitcher, and now the driver's going faster and faster to end this trip as soon as he can. The taillights of cars and trucks flutter by as they pass. The driver must be doing a hundred. The car's engine is screaming; it wasn't built to go this fast, and it's not going to last much longer if he keeps it up.

Petey keeps turning around, looking out the back windshield. Then faces forward again and points at a truck in front of them.

"Pass him," he says.

"He's going faster than we are," the driver says.

"I don't care. Pass him," Petey says. His Ukrainian is getting shaky. "You can't let anyone catch us."

The car roars, and the driver prays a little, out loud. He's doing a Hail Mary, but Peter doesn't understand enough of the language to know that. A wave of adrenaline and fear sweeps him up, and his thoughts get irrational. The headlights make him feel like the target, like the people chasing him can see him, and he wonders if he can get the driver to turn them off. If he won't, maybe he'll climb out onto the hood of the car and smash them with his shoe. He looks ahead at the red lights in front of him and thinks of an accident he heard about that everyone knows was an assassination, a head-on collision, on a road just like this, that no one walked away from. He's sure he can see those oncoming lights in the distance, also going a hundred miles. That approaching car'll swerve through all the vehicles in front of them and collide grille to grille, a dead hit. He wonders what two hundred miles per hour's worth of velocity feels like, just how much of each car will be destroyed, or how much will be left of anyone that's identifiable. *I'm so fucked,* Petey thinks. *I've fucked up everything.* It's the most self-aware thought he's had in a long time. And then: *I never should have come here. Never should have brought Curly here, or met Madalina. Never should have left Cleveland.*

Maybe you're laughing that Petey thinks that. We haven't talked about this yet, but we should: Cleveland doesn't deserve its reputation. The endless jokes. The Mistake on the Lake. *What's the difference between Cleveland and the* Titanic? *Cleveland has a better orchestra.* And everyone seems to know about the Cuyahoga River. It's true, the river's been on fire, more than once, the last time in 1969. You can find the pictures if you want. And yes, it's true that the mayor's own hair catches on fire in 1972; it's for a ribbon-cutting ceremony, except that, because it's for the Materials Engineering Congress, the ribbon is a strip of metal and the scissors are an acetylene torch. Sparks happen.

And yes, there's a lot about the city that's tragic. It's all there in print, in newspapers and history books, photographs that don't hide the way the place has looked sometimes. All that industry and all the ruins it leaves behind, all the burn marks from the riots in the sixties. It's all true, but it can't tear down what it is to visit the place, to see it for yourself. Stand on the sharp edge of the river valley overlooking the Cuyahoga, somewhere near where Lorain Avenue leaps across the river valley over the Hope Memorial Bridge. Look at the statues on it, the guardians of traffic, they say they're called. Then see how bridge after bridge jumps the same wide space over the river, highways, local roads, train tracks. Look at the streets twisting beneath the gargantuan pylons, the tiny brick buildings beneath them. Look at the river twisting, contorting, doubling back, all the way to the pale lake, a swarm of seagulls over the green water. And then take a look at the center of the city on the opposite shore, the huge stone wings of Tower City, the sleek glass office buildings beyond it, the curving federal courthouse. It's a giant monument to commerce, all of it, because Cleveland's a city built to make money and a city that money built, built and took apart, again and again. It's America unvarnished, America without reserve. When the country rose, Cleveland flew. When it declined, Cleveland crashed. And it's so easy to write it off now, to keep the jokes about the burning river coming, but somewhere in the years the city is staggering toward are the pieces of our future, too, whether we know it yet or not.

Do you see what I'm saying? Capitalism's an animal, and it eats places like Cleveland, or maybe you could say it tries to eat Cleveland, but then Cleveland kicks at the animal's teeth until it gets spat out. The people who live there are meat, and they know it. And in 1989, they can almost smell it, the blood in the air that signals a change, though into what, they've stopped trying to guess. 25th Street, in the neighborhood of Ohio City, is rough then, even for the people in the neighborhood. They don't go over there for anything after dark unless it's trouble. And that's just what Petey's there for when he runs into Curly Potapenko for the first time on the corner of Bridge Avenue and West 28th Street. There they are, two white kids looking for drugs.

Petey and Curly eye each other with suspicion; they're not there to be friendly, and they can see the differences between them right from the start. Curly's an Ohio City kid. He remembers watching the Muhammad Ali-Chuck Wepner fight in 1975 on TV, and afterward his cousins Big Joe and Mark pinning him to the floor and shaving his head, though not before Curly knees Big Joe in the balls. Big Joe writhes and screams, and Mark stands up, nodding, a look of approval on his face. *Nice shot.* He remembers watching Wepner take hit after hit, a guy from Bayonne, New Jersey, versus the heavyweight champion of the world. Wepner never stands a chance, but there he is, under the lights, and he lasts so long. *That's us,* Curly thinks, even then. *He's one of us.* He hears his parents talk about how Ohio City's slipped, how it's like living somewhere after a war, or an epidemic, where people abandon their houses or torch them for the insurance money, and then looters come to salvage the copper. But he doesn't see any of that. To him, Ohio City—the neighborhood all around them, from the edge of the Cuyahoga past the West Side Market and down Lorain Avenue to the highway exit, its low clapboard houses and its tight alleyways—are his world. It's where he's from, and he's proud of it, though not of what he's done. Petey, from Edgewater Avenue near the bluffs overlooking Lake Erie, doesn't know a damn thing about Ohio City. But each of them recognizes something of himself in the other, the same toughness and vulnerability. The marks of a strong, volatile family, of not quite finishing high school. The same sense of shame, that their parents raised them better than this, that their grandparents would be so disappointed; the same anger that they should be forced to rise to their families' expectations. The unsettling feeling hasn't kicked in yet that they're still showing themselves to be more like their own people than they know. Curly is there to buy crack, gets a shake of the head from Petey. *Come here.* Petey's buying cocaine.

By then, Petey's already what you'd call a small-time crook. That beautiful boy in the crisp suit at Sylvie's wedding is gone, or hiding. Even now, Muriel's not sure just when it happens. He's so sweet for the first few years of his life that it takes her years to realize that what she thought was just a streak of mischief in him is a lot more than that. He gets suspended from school twice by the time he's twelve, both times for stealing other kids' stuff. Then he takes his social studies teacher's wallet, spends all the money in it in an afternoon. The school calls a meeting. Muriel repays the teacher on the spot, tries to apologize. The teacher takes the money, isn't interested in the apology. *Don't you know what your son is really like?* she says. *Don't you see the things he does?* Muriel doesn't say anything, and when the teacher realizes Muriel has no idea what she's talking about—always trying to see the good in everyone has made her maybe a little too blind to the bad—a look comes over her face, a mix of pity and scorn, that almost makes Muriel cry. The principal sees that and takes a more diplomatic angle. It's the same message, just trying to avoid tears. *Look, I'm not telling you what to do with your son,* he says. *But I'm not sure this school is the best place for him. I'm not sure we can give him what he needs.*

And what is it that you think he needs? Muriel says. That's in 1980.

In 1983, Petey's fifteen and away at a boarding school outside of Cleveland that says it's all about discipline. That's where he teaches himself how to forge driver's licenses in the school's printmaking studio, first for his friends, just to see if they work, then for himself, when he knows better what not to do. He learns fast that, as far as his circle of friends is concerned, because they're all underage, it's still the Prohibition era, and they're willing to pay—a lot—for alcohol, and not very good alcohol. The difference between alcohol and small amounts of mild drugs, then harder drugs, isn't important to him. He's getting more self-aware, understands that he has a knack that goes beyond teenage bravado in cutting deals with drug traffickers: his willingness to meet them, in cars parked in empty parking lots, in the back rooms of clubs nobody goes in. He can talk straight about the big game he's chasing, meaning the kind of customer he wants. He wants to hook some future bankers and insurance executives on some pretty expensive stuff, and he wants to be the guy they keep coming back to, because they trust him not to sell them out, turn them in just because the police want to know. He argues straight for a better cut of the deal when the plan starts to work. By the fall of 1985, he's about seventeen and cocky, making a pretty nice chunk of change and still able to convince himself that he isn't doing anyone any real harm. He's using a bit himself, doesn't see the damage, just the blurry memories of nights in Cleveland with pounding music and sweaty limbs in the clubs in the old warehouses, nights ending in spins and shouts on the cobbled streets. He thinks that by selling just to his friends—well, friends and friends of friends, and maybe a few people he doesn't know at all—he's insulating himself from the things he sees on the news. Then two of those friends flip their car going around Dead Man's Curve right at the shore of the lake, the sharp bend in the interstate Clevelanders are supposed to know cold, cold enough to tell any out-of-towners they know who drive through the place on their way from Boston to Chicago to watch out. The friends are both good and high when they crash; for a few hours, neither of them knows how he ended up in the hospital, until they come down. Then they tell the doctors everything. The police, too. They point their broken fingers right at Petey Hightower, whom the police have had their eye on anyway. They're not stupid, after all. They know his pedigree. They've got a hunch about the things his grandfather did. They've been watching the rest of the family, too, because something is just not adding up about them. And Petey's not as smart as he thinks he is. Though some of the authorities are annoyed; they've been learning about Petey for a while because he seems like the kind of kid who might lead them into something bigger, something that a tenacious detective can build into a case that makes a career and puts a bunch of guys away in prison for a long time. But the accident and the outcry around it, because these are rich kids involved, you understand, forces the authorities' hand. They don't have enough to threaten Petey with to get information out of him. And they have to go to court with what they've got instead of what they think they could get if they just had the time to let it play out.

At Petey's trial, for possession of cocaine with intent to sell, the state's lawyer lays out the best evidence he can, argues for the biggest sentence he can. He doesn't say it but he means it: *We put away black kids for this all the time, and it ruins their lives. Why should the rich white kids get off for doing the same thing?* But the defense's job is easier. Petey's been careful about one thing—hiding his money—so the police don't have serious evidence beyond circumstantial testimony that he deals. The defense doesn't mind indulging in a little low-grade character assassination to undermine what Petey's friends say about him, digging up people who say they saw the two kids in the crash buying cocaine from someone in the bathroom of a nightclub who wasn't Petey, crack from someone in Tremont. The argument even taps into some high school gossip, suggesting that the kids in the crash were angry at Petey for stealing their girlfriends and wanted to get him out of the way. Why not frame him for some drug offenses? That part of the story doesn't stick; it's pretty implausible, isn't it, reader? The judge isn't impressed and tells the defense to calm down. Tells him that this is a courtroom, not a cafeteria. But the prosecution's lack of hard evidence isn't good enough for a big conviction. It's also Petey's first offense, and he's a kid, not even eighteen. The judge reminds Petey of this and takes him down a peg—it's clear he doesn't like Petey very much—and sentences Petey to nine months of rehabilitation. The state's lawyer gives the judge an accusatory look. *You let him off easy.* The judge pleads his case. *I'm on your side. But this case isn't the one we wanted in the first place.*

The conviction, though, is the end of Petey's formal education. The school's expelled him, and his family ships him off to a facility in Cincinnati, close enough that they can check on him whenever they want, too far away for him to bother trying to get out. There's nowhere for him to go. Petey's surprised by this; he's still a teenager, and not big on the personal responsibility thing in any case. He assumes that since he's going to rehab, his family will treat him a little bit like he's sick, like he's suffering from impulses beyond his control. Part of him wants to wail like a small child; he has the balls to feel like he's the victim of something, even if it's himself. It all just got away from him. In hindsight, he can see the moments it happened, the thousand ways he got sloppy. The way he started selling to people he didn't know as well. The things he sometimes just left out for everyone to see. He wants to be able to convince his parents that maybe he's a little crazy, that he needs a lot of help. *Don't you see? I don't know what I'm doing.* His mother could be convinced, he knows, if he could divide her from Terry, but he has no idea how to do that. And Terry's having none of it, makes arguments impossible right from the start. In the car on the way home from the trial, Petey says one word—*Dad*—and the man cuts him off.

"I can't believe you think you have anything to say, Pete," Terry says. "Why do you think I'd believe one word of it?"

The words hurt, though it takes Petey months to settle on how to feel about it. One half wants to become a model of upright citizenship. Get a haircut, buy a new blazer and three ties. Finish school with the best grades, volunteer at nursing homes and soup kitchens. Go back to being the kind of kid who shares his dessert with a great uncle. The other half wants to tell his father and the rest of his family to go fuck themselves. The second half wins.

He gets out of rehab at the end of 1986, just in time to turn eighteen and walk into his inheritance, the money from his grandfather Muriel set aside before he was born and gave to Henry to invest because she never imagined she'd have a son like Petey. He skulks around the house, not bothering to pretend to care about the possibility of finishing school or looking for a job. Terry doesn't know what to do; being the kind of man he is, his love for his son pulls him in opposite directions. One wanting to hand him a job, give him something, anything to do. He could just call a friend for a position in a mailroom, on a construction site. *Thanks. I owe you one.* It's still possible, Terry thinks, for a man to make himself. Eighty years ago, everyone did. Some of the rail barons around here didn't have any schooling; they were just smart, creative, ruthless when they needed to be. They hopped from sales to real estate to railroads, put it all together to build the city as we know it while they laid out estates for themselves outside of it, mansions of plaster and dark woodwork, horse stables, wide fields, deluxe versions of the farms they'd bought up and converted to suburbs and apartment complexes. You could still do that around here, still do it anywhere. Once a man has the money and has made himself, the father thinks, no one cares what else he has. But Terry doesn't want to hand Petey that kind of life. There are alarms in his head when he thinks of doing it, warning him that Petey would just squander it, squander whatever he has, and ruin Terry, too, if he were too involved. So Terry's stuck, and it makes him irritable, because he's not willing to face the guilt for having given up on his boy. He gets too impatient with Petey, too verbal about it, and at last there's a fight that starts with screaming and moves to a broken window, a sign that maybe they should all back down, but they don't. Instead, they have it all the way out.

"You aren't even my real father anyway," Petey says, because he knows how much it hurts Terry when he says it. He's expecting, then, the usual script. *But I've raised you as if you were. How could you be so ungrateful when I love you so much.* But this fight is different, because they've all reached the ends of their ropes.

"You're absolutely right," Terry says. "I'm not. I'm Andrew and Julia's father, and look at them. Such good kids. Those are mine. Your father ran off before you were born, and we haven't heard from him since, have we? He doesn't give a shit about you, just like you don't seem to give a shit about us. You're nothing like us, and do you know what? I'm glad. I'm glad, because it means I don't have to live with the idea that the fuckup that you are is part of me."

Muriel cringes, like she's been hit.

"What did you say?" Petey says.

Terry's shocked. He can't believe he let himself say something so hateful, and his shame smothers his anger.

"I'm sorry, son," he says.

"Don't use that word," Petey says. "You don't get to take back what you said."

"I know. I'm sorry."

Now Petey's just shaking his head. He wants to cry like a small boy, so that maybe his parents will comfort him, but he's too proud to do it.

"I'm never coming back here," he says. "Never." They watch him leave from the window, and something in the way the son's walking makes Terry believe Petey was telling the truth.

"Oh God," Terry says. "What did I just do?"

Petey calls home every few weeks, even though half the conversations end in arguments. He lies about where he's living. Says he's in Cincinnati with a few of the guys he met in rehab. Says he's in Pittsburgh, working as a security guard. Says he's thinking of moving to New York, and Terry can understand this. He's been on the interstate through Youngstown, seen the highway signs pointing to New York already, even though it's almost four hundred miles away. Go east, and it's the next big city; the way the highway has it, it seems sometimes like New York's the only big city, though Terry knows that isn't true. Hong Kong and Tokyo can make New York seem bucolic, and he hasn't been to Mexico City, Beijing, São Paulo, has only heard what they're like. Then there's the rest of the world, the big cities of Africa—and this is the late 1980s, when there are still more rural people than urban. That's going to change in a matter of a couple decades, it's all only going to get crazier. When the satellite images of the world at night come out, we'll all be able to see just how we light up the planet, like one big city, and quite a few places burn brighter than America does.

"Want to party?" Petey says to Curly. It's 1989, in the neighborhood of Ohio City, on the corner of Bridge Avenue and West 28th Street, Cleveland. The prostitutes are out and trying to reel in customers, but there's that charge in the air that happens when men are more in the mood for fighting than fucking. It's already a bit loud on the corner; the dealers are having a good night so far, but it's going to turn bad, end in sirens and screaming, a couple people going to the hospital and one going to the morgue, all because a man can't help himself.

"You paying?" Curly says. "I don't have the bread for that." Remember, Curly's there for crack, Petey for cocaine.

"Sure, I'm paying," Petey says. He shoves his hand in his jacket pocket, pulls out a thick wad of bills. Counts out twenty fifty-dollar bills, licking his thumb as he does it. Curly doesn't know if he looks more like a gangster or an accountant. Petey approaches one of the dealers, who seems to know him. They shake hands like old men, and Petey nods, hands him the money. Gets a big bag that he slides into his coat pocket. Walks back over to Curly, tilts his head.

"What's up," Petey says.

"That's a lot of coke you just bought," Curly says.

"They cut you a break if you do it that way."

Curly's looking for Petey's car, is already imagining what kind of ride a man like this must have. He's surprised to see him heading straight for the glass door of the apartment building on the corner.

"You live right here?" Curly says.

"Sure. Why not?" Petey says.

"You just don't seem like the kind of guy who lives around here."

"And what do you mean by that?"

"Sorry," Curly says. "Nothing."

Petey gives him a look that Curly can't read, and for a second Curly thinks he's blown it. But he hasn't.

"I'm Petey," Petey says.

"Curly."

They shake hands, each one not sure why he trusts the other so much, though they do. Curly takes another look at the cracked parking lot of the supermarket across the street, the wooden houses around him. A third of them are abandoned, and Curly imagines someone's already stripped the copper out of them. He hears that people steal the busts from the Cultural Garden on the east side now, and he always imagines the conversation at the scrapyard being awkward. How do people say they managed to come across a three-foot-high statue of Chopin? *I just found this in my backyard. It used to be my grandmother's.* The scrap dealer must be a master of deadpan. *I'll give you fifty bucks for that,* he says, knowing they'll take it and be grateful that he's not asking any more questions.

"You coming?" Petey says.

"Yeah. Yeah," Curly says.

You could say that this is the conversation that kills Curly, though it's a lot more complicated than that; by 1995, so much binds Curly and Petey together that it's too late for Curly to get out. But in 1989, it isn't. In some other version of the story, the one that isn't the truth, Curly isn't there to call Granada and warn the wrong man, and so drag the entire Hightower family back into the world some of them thought they'd left behind a generation ago. In that story, Curly lives a lot longer, and Petey dies a lot sooner. So you could say that Curly makes a trade, gives away the rest of his years for his friend's. The question of whether Petey deserves them isn't for us to judge.

So. By 1989, Petey's a small-time crook. Not as big as that roll of bills he pulls out of his pocket makes Curly think he is; some of that is his inheritance talking. He hasn't blown through it—he's smarter than that. But he's still just a middleman, connecting a few of the young and wealthy of Cleveland to the drugs they want. Sometimes he doesn't see the people involved, isn't sure what's passing between them. It's just a series of phone calls, a few lines of jargon mixed with ambiguous phrases that sound like come-ons in soul songs. *I got what you need. Your ship just came in.* All the time, though, he's thinking about how to move up in the world he's in. How to turn the cash he's sitting on and his willingness to break the law into the kind of life you only read about in books, or see in the movies. A private island somewhere. A mansion, a yacht. A helicopter pad—why the hell not? Dinners and parties, long hours in the sun. He always pictures someone with him, too, a woman, though he can't say for sure what she looks like, or how much she knows about what he does.

Curly's hanging from an even lower rung on the chain. He delivers packages, runs errands. Sometimes stands outside a door and watches the street for the cops. He never sees anything. He drives a van from Youngstown to Parma, doesn't know what's in the back. But it's all with the Ukrainians. Those are his people, that's his strength, and all of it makes the small crimes he commits part of a much larger thing. Curly spent every Sunday morning in the pews at St. Josaphat as a kid, knows how to make the food, sing the songs. He can speak the language that he doesn't know is a dialect until the fourth wave of immigration starts in 1991, and people from Kiev and Odessa arrive to tell them they're using a lot of Polish and English in their Ukrainian. *There are words in Ukrainian for all that stuff, you know,* the Ukrainians say. *Well, teach them to us,* the Ukrainian-Americans say. The speed that Ukrainians pulled English into their spoken language—*ice cream, ambulance, bootlegger, like hell, shut up, you bet, have a good time*—is just one sign of how fast they adapted, but also how much they kept. How much they've hung onto, over the decades, so that when the fourth wave shows up, it's like a meeting of long-lost cousins. A shared history, a shared understanding of the world. The same urge to spit whenever someone mentions Stalin. The same tired shrug at how hard life is. *Of course it is.* As if a hundred years were a day, though it's been a big day.

Taken apart, Petey and Curly aren't much. One's got a pile of money and no real connections. The other's got connections everywhere he turns, but no money. Together, though, they're an interesting pair. *A little too interesting,* Kosookyy thinks. He's the current big man on Cleveland's local version of a Ukrainian organized racket, the guy who's been employing Curly for years at a couple dozen different jobs of varying degrees of legitimacy. He loves Curly, you understand. About Petey, he's not so sure.

"Did you know I knew your grandfather, Petey?" Kosookyy says. Peers at them both through thick glasses that make his eyes look bigger than they already are. The hair on his head's almost gone, just a few stray strands around his ears, the back of his head. "I used to see him when he visited his brother in Tremont. I was just a kid, then, but even then I could tell," squinting his eyes, wagging a finger, "that he was someone who did things. A lot of things. I remember he was the kind of guy who could put on an accent, like an actor. He could speak that waspy English like the newscasters speak. And he could talk like Marlon Brando in *The Godfather.* But the Ukrainian his mother taught him stayed perfect, all those years. He was that kind of guy. Though I'm sure you remember that, too."

Kosookyy's trying to play up the Ukrainian connection between their families, to get Petey to feel something toward him; to feel something for Petey himself. *But Petey's two generations removed from that,* Kosookyy reminds himself. *Two generations and too much money. Give a guy too much, and he can forget where he came from, forget who he is.*

"He died before I was born," Petey says.

Kosookyy's mouth shuts tight, and he nods. *Somebody didn't raise this kid right,* he thinks. *If they did, he would understand what I'm trying to do. They throw away their culture because they think they have so much money, they don't need it anymore. They never stop to think about whether their kids'll need it later, when they're out of the picture.* "I see," he says. "Still. There's a lot you can do for us. The White Lady says I shouldn't get you involved," he says, assuming Petey knows who the White Lady is. Petey doesn't. Kosookyy goes on. "But I'm not listening to her right now. What can we do for you?" Petey just smiles at them, and Kosookyy knows he's already lost him.

"You guys do international stuff?" Petey says. "I'm looking to go international."

Kosookyy frowns. "No, no. There's plenty right here to keep us busy."

"You been reading the paper, right?"

Kosookyy thinks about smacking him, thinks better of it. "Yeah," he says. "I've been reading the paper."

It's February 1990, and the Ukrainians in America are already talking about what happens when Ukraine is its own country again, at last, at last. Goodbye and good riddance, Soviet Union. Independence is still almost two years away; it doesn't happen until December 1991. But there are so many signs. There have been hunger strikes, the digging up of mass graves in Bykivnia, hundreds of thousands of bodies, atrocities beginning to be brought into the light. Older men crying over brown bones; they've always known something bad happened, always, no matter what their leaders told them. Now the first elections in a lifetime are coming in March and Rukh, the opposition, won't go away. They organize a rally to mark Ukraine's first independence in 1919 that draws enough people to make a chain from Kiev to Lviv. It's happening, it's all happening. Independence is coming. You can buy a typewriter in Kiev now that has the three characters on the keyboard that separate Ukrainian from Russian. You see the blue and yellow flags wherever you go. And so many people are so hopeful, over in Ukraine and in the United States. Though Kosookyy isn't one of them. He can smell chaos coming. People, people and money and everything, are going to move through Ukraine, across Western Europe, to the United States and Canada, like a dam bursting. There's a serious buck to be made in that, every time a box crosses another line on a map, every time someone takes a step, and Kosookyy knows that, for the men chasing that cash, the money's going to matter a lot more than the people. And the law isn't going to be able to keep up.

So in March 1994, when Petey asks Kosookyy if he knows who the Wolf is, Kosookyy first takes a breath. *Peter and the Wolf, ha,* he thinks. Then shakes his head, nice and slow, as if by doing it, he can get Petey to see what he's thinking—*don't get involved*—and just walk out the door without a word. But Petey doesn't move.

"I don't know him," Kosookyy says. "Maybe even better to say that I know enough not to know him."

"I hear he's got a little racket going of some kind."

"I don't know how little it is," Kosookyy says.

"Do you know what it is?" Petey says.

"No," Kosookyy says.

"Come on."

"I don't, Petey."

"Don't all you guys know each other?" Petey says. By *you guys* he means mobsters. Organized criminals. He's putting way too much weight on the word *organized,* Kosookyy thinks. As if they're all in one big speakeasy and everyone already knows everyone else who comes in. The kid thinks it's a world of secret handshakes and code words, a shared history no one else knows. One big dysfunctional family. The problem, Kosookyy thinks, is that Petey's only half right. The old crime organizations are like that, and they've been like that for so long that the police and the FBI know who everyone is. They know who's a mobster and who isn't. They know who's in and who's out, even have a sense of what kinds of crimes they're committing—the gambling, the extortion, the protection rackets, the money laundering, the loan-sharking. The feds can draw a map of the United States according to the turf each syndicate covers: the United States of Crime. Kosookyy likes to think that there's a folder with his name on it in a filing cabinet somewhere in the offices of the FBI's Cleveland division. He wonders how much they've got on him, how much they know, how far back it goes, because he's been involved for a long time. But he never doubts that the folder exists, along with hundreds of others, on him and his friends and acquaintances, all the little criminals. It's like that for every organization in town, the Italians, the Irish, whoever else. A hundred tiny, squabbling families, too busy with their own problems to have very much to do with one another. They're living side by side in the same city, but they've all got their heads down, working a million little hustles. It's small-time stuff, Kosookyy thinks. It has to be. If it's a bigger deal, then what's he doing still living in Parma, right? There's no great criminal conspiracy; the only time they ever come together is on paper, in the offices of the police and feds, the people trying to bring them in.

But the new criminals are different. Kosookyy knows so little about them, has seen just glimpses of their operations. Enough to be worried, though. Enough to be scared. Which is why, when Curly calls to tell him that Petey's met a guy, that he's going to Kiev, and Curly's going with him, Kosookyy tells him not to go, even though he knows it won't make any difference.

The deal is pretty simple. Petey's got the money but can't speak the language, and Curly's the only person in the world Petey trusts to speak for him. Part of that trust involves blackmail: Each of them knows enough to put the other guy away for decades. But it's more than that. For each of them, so much has come and gone—the parties, the jobs, the girls, the dealers, the times they've both almost been arrested but weren't because they kept their mouths shut—but the truth is that their friendship sneaked up on them. Neither of them can remember when or how it was they got so tight. There was just some morning that they both knew. Each of them knows how the other likes his coffee, how stiff they like their cocktails. What brand of booze they drink. Curly knows that there's no point in discussing anything serious with Petey before eleven in the morning and that he's terrible at doing his laundry;

he wears cologne to hide the fact that he's wearing dirty clothes. Petey knows that Curly doesn't sleep very well and has something close to a fetish about keeping his shoes polished. They've shared an apartment, three different apartments, for twenty-two months, have an easy silence between them you see in people who've been together longer than that. *Why don't you check with your wife to see if it's okay,* their other friends say when they ask one of them out. Petey hasn't seen his parents for over a year, his siblings for longer than that. His extended family is a fading memory. Curly's all he's got. And while Curly's still a family man, still goes to church on Sunday mornings and dinner on Sunday afternoons, he knows he wants more, and Petey's his only way out. They know that an associate of the Wolf runs a restaurant on the East Side, a little dinner place that doesn't look like much. The meeting is quick. They talk about how Petey's interested in investing. *Good,* the restaurant owner says, in a halting Ukrainian. *We are always looking for new sources of capital.* He eyes them, waiting for them to speak. They don't.

"Fine," he says, as if they'd just agreed to something. "I can give you a good rate of return. Very high."

"What's the nature of the investment?" Curly says.

"What do you care?"

Petey laughs. The restaurant owner doesn't.

"You won't know what you're investing in, you understand?" the owner says. "None of us know."

"None of you know? Someone must know."

"Someone must," the owner says, and lets that hang in the air.

"All right," Petey says, "all right. Though we would be interested in going to Ukraine."

"Why? It's easier just to stay here."

"We want to see what we're getting into."

"You mean you want to meet the Wolf?"

"Well, yes."

"There is almost no chance you'll meet the Wolf."

"Have you ever met him?"

"Yes. Three times. It was a different person every time. You still want to go?"

Petey nods. The restaurant owner shakes his head.

"Fine," he says.

They begin to go over details, of who Petey and Curly will be dealing with when they go, how to move money from place to place, from account to account. Indications of the restaurant owner's seriousness. Petey and Curly are expecting more somehow, more of a show of being let into something, of being made members. It doesn't come, and they should see that as their first warning that they don't understand what they're involving themselves in. But they don't. Instead they're off to Kiev within a month with a phone number the restaurant owner gives him. *They'll take care of you,* the owner says, without a trace of warmth; it's professionalism and nothing else.

Chapter 3

Petey and Curly fly into the airport outside of Kiev in the early morning. It's a gray building, smaller than Petey thought it would be. Half the lightbulbs in the ceiling are out. Someone's done up the signs for the customs lines in rainbow colors. Petey and Curly have to fill out a lot of forms for their belongings to get them into the country; if not for Curly, Petey's not sure how he would have managed it. They pay a bribe. Then Curly calls the number the restaurant owner gave him from a pay phone, and they get picked up in a spiffy new black SUV with tinted windows. The driver looks and talks as if he's been awake all night. They glide out of the airport parking lot and onto the highway. All around them are sedans with dull colors that rust has faded even more, minibuses with stained curtains hanging in the windows, their mufflers coughing out exhaust. They reach a stretch of road that shoots straight through forest, and the driver puts his foot on the gas, leaves it there until the car is going about a hundred miles an hour. Through the rearview mirror, Petey can tell the driver's nodding off. Nobody says a word for a few minutes. They fly by the bus stations the Soviets built on both sides of the highway; it's easy to think that whoever in the Politburo built them wanted to build villages and towns around them, too, but never got around to it. So there they sit, monuments to the insanity of central planning—or, I guess, if you're a diehard Marxist, its unrealized potential, though there aren't many of those left. The truth confounds both lessons anyway; sure enough, there are a couple people waiting at every other station, three men walking along a trail in the woods to reach another one. Where those people are coming from, where they're going, what they're doing getting on a bus on a highway in the middle of the woods, Petey can't begin to guess. He'll never get a grip on this place. Which is why, when it decides to take him out, he won't see it coming.

They're still going a hundred miles an hour when they reach the giant sign welcoming them to the outskirts of Kiev. There's a little more woods. What looks like a tiny village by the side of the highway, all white plaster walls and tile roofs. A man in a black leather jacket strolling down the dirt streets between them, waving to a woman with a headscarf and a brown coat. Then there's a long, open field, and the city begins, the things the Soviet Union built. They pass by the outermost ring of apartment towers for what feels like miles of cold neon in the gray early morning while thousands of people wait for buses, walk to the entrances to train stations. The impossible apartment buildings rise behind them like an army of giants. The concrete's streaked with stains and every corner seems to be chipped. The tiles glued to the outside walls are coming off, the geometric designs, the modernist blocks of color put on them for decoration. All those clean, simple lines are getting more crooked every year, as if the buildings were sending a message, that the dream that all could be equal and all could be planned couldn't last. You can't make people all move in the same direction for long, no matter what you give them for a reward, no matter how bad the punishment is. It's one of the beautiful and maddening things about us, isn't it? The simple shapes are a crime against nature, an unstable state. The broken pieces lying on the ground are the natural outcome, the bodies at rest.

Then the SUV they're riding in breaks free and they're on a giant metal bridge crossing over the Dneiper, and the city spreads out all around them. The factories and refineries stick out over the low rooftops. More apartment blocks on the horizon. The river and its islands curve underneath them and away, far to the north. For Curly, it's all a little too much to handle for a minute. *You are going to Kiev?* his aunt in Parma said, when he told him what he was doing. So many emotions rolling around in her voice. A surface concern, because they all knew that the fourth wave of immigration had to have started for a reason. *What are you going over there for, when most people seem to be leaving?* But a much deeper, stronger current of something else, the pull of the mother country, even though nobody in the family has been back to Ukraine for a hundred years. *Say hello to the place for us. Tell everyone we're all right, at least for now.* Curly wishes now that he'd talked to his aunt more when he had the chance. *I'm back, I've come back. Is it like you heard?*

Because the center of Kiev is something to see. I mean, Curly and Petey are from Cleveland; they know what big buildings look like. They're just not used to seeing so many people out. The giant expanse of Maidan Nezalezhnosti, the central square, is mobbed in the morning, people weaving in and out of each other's way, dodging the orange and brown electric trolleys that crackle along their sagging wires. In the afternoons, they're lounging on the steps of the plaza in front of the Hotel Ukraina, though they're not sleeping; they're waiting for the nighttime, when the long strip of walkways and benches and trees along Khreshchatyk Street is just packed with people in skinny jeans and jackets, screwing around, chasing each other. The girls are so cool it's almost impossible. They put on sweaters and jackets with very short skirts and long stockings, and put their arms around lucky boys, kissing, kissing again, still kissing. The Americans have never seen so many people kissing in public, for so long, while the guitarist in a busking surf band revs up a battery-powered amp and, fifty yards down the street, a bunch of thin blond kids break-dance on cardboard boxes like they did in New York ten years ago. The underground passages to get under intersections, or to the metro, are lined with dozens of tiny kiosks lit by naked bulbs, and there are people selling watches, alarm clocks, clothing, flowers, fried dough, sandwiches. A man in an old army uniform encrusted with medals, his hair gelled into a shape you don't see in nature, plays a harp and belts out folk songs. Another couple does duets for voice and accordion; he's on one side of the hallway, she's on the other, and they're staring into each other's eyes as they perform. A young man plays Depeche Mode songs on an acoustic guitar in front of the entrance to the metro. All those voices echo off the bricks and tile, a mash of Russian and Ukrainian—the language of the schools and street signs and the language everyone still knows how to speak—sprinkled with a little English. At night it gets frantic. The neon from the casinos comes on; people park their cars all over the sidewalk, drive down it to get back on the road. The music starts blaring, that pulsing, throbbing, four-on-the-floor beat you hear everywhere in the northern hemisphere. Someone closes the street and sets up a stage, and there's a giant crowd in front of it, dancing with their hands in the air. It goes until three in the morning; at four there are still people out, smoking and drinking coffee in a café. There's so much energy here, the same energy that got people to vote themselves out of the Soviet Union just before it dissolved; in less than a decade, even the West will know Maidan Nezalezhnosti—Independence Square—because it'll be jammed with hundreds of thousands of people, enough of them wearing orange to give the revolution its name. They'll be there because they're tired of it, because the government that comes in after the Soviet Union falls looks too much like the Soviet Union. Maybe because it looks worse. In 1995, there's the hyperinflation, the obvious corruption. People moving to the black market just to make a living. The general breakdown in order; the creepy sense that the criminals own this place. People keep getting shaken down; people keep getting killed. At the birthday party of an oligarch on the banks of the Dneiper, there are seventy-two bodyguards, some of them water-skiing the perimeter with their Kalashnikovs in their hands. Years later, though, there'll still be the people kissing all along Khreshchatyk Street, and the musicians busking Western pop music of every era, as if they discovered it all at once when the walls came down and the country opened up, and now one beautiful note keeps getting played and the kiss goes on forever.

But again, Petey's disappointed. He expected more of a welcome from the criminals he's come to work with. Hugs, drinks, all that. A warm smile, showing their eagerness to be friends. They check into the Hotel Dnipro, a place that makes Curly think of nothing but James Bond movies from the 1970s, from the clacking buttons for the elevator to the wood paneling in the hallways, the phone and TV lines running along the tops of the walls. The industrial tiling in the bathrooms, the giant heated towel rack. It's too easy to imagine the room being bugged. He remembers a friend of the family who made good a couple decades ago and went to Moscow just a few years ago. They got into the bathroom and checked out the amenities. *Gee, I wish these towels were a little bigger,* the wife said out loud. Three minutes later, there was a knock on their door, a friendly bellboy with linens in his arms. *You wanted larger towels, madame?*

The first meeting is in a casino, where it's all about black. Windows tinted so black you can't see in. A row of black Mercedes-Benzes parked at a forty-five-degree angle on the sidewalk outside, their windows also tinted so black you wonder if the driver can see out. A huge man at the door at first won't let them in, no matter what Curly says, until a short buzz-cut man in a black leather jacket and designer jeans opens the door, gives the bouncer the nod.

"Sorry," he says in Ukrainian. "We weren't sure it was you."

He leads them through the games, the bar, fast, to a quieter back room. It's small but screams money to blow: dark wood paneling, leather chairs. A glass coffee table with marble feet. Good booze, booze from all over the world. Espresso. Cigars. Curly can see from Petey's smile what he's thinking: *This is more like it.* But Curly's nervous.

"You speak Russian?" the buzz-cut man says, in Ukrainian.

"No. Just Ukrainian."

The man smiles. "How charming," he says. Now Curly's more nervous, and he knows the man can tell. "So," the man says. "I hear you are interested in investing in Ukraine."

"Yes," Curly says.

"You didn't have to come here to do that."

"It seems better this way."

"Is it?" the man says. "I suppose it's easier in some ways. More complicated in others. But we are interested in your interest."

"Are you the Wolf?"

"Of course." Then he laughs. "No, of course not. Call me Dino."

"That sounds Italian."

"Do I sound Italian to you?"

"No," Curly says.

"You didn't have to answer that. It was a joke."

"Sorry."

"You seem nervous," Dino says. "You should be more like your friend here. He doesn't seem nervous at all. He must be the one with the money."

"You shouldn't talk about him like he's not here," Curly says. "He understands more than he lets on."

"I don't believe you. But I'm impressed. He must really trust you. Which means he's not very bright. Would you say that? That he's not very bright? I'm not judging. I'm just trying to understand the man for the purposes of entering a business relationship."

"He's not stupid, if that's what you're asking."

"According to you."

"Of course according to me. You're asking me, aren't you?"

"You're smarter than he is."

"That's for you to judge, isn't it?"

Dino laughs, and it makes Petey want to talk, though Curly knows that when he does it'll blow his cover; Dino'll know he doesn't understand a word. Curly puts his hand on his friend's knee, says in English, "I'm glad that bullshit's over." Then to Dino: "Mr. Hightower would prefer to do the rest of this in English."

For the first time, Dino frowns. "I'm not as comfortable in English."

Now it's Curly's chance to smile. He puts on his courage. "Well, isn't that too bad."

The idea is pretty simple. The organization, Dino explains in Ukrainian, is involved in a very large number of enterprises, all of them designed to take advantage of what the man says are lowered barriers to free enterprise. A certain freedom of goods, people, and currency across borders. Like any business enterprise, however, it always needs capital—or could use more—to expand its reach, to strengthen its existing operations. To make what it does more efficient and effective at bringing higher returns to its investors. Dino makes an expansive gesture, as if all the world will benefit from the things he does.

"The free market is a wonderful thing," he says. "But in our operation, there is"— he falters, then chuckles, because he's already seen enough American movies to know that what he's about to say is a serious cliché in English—"there is a *catch*, which I understand you may be uncomfortable with, because we do not operate as you do in the United States. There, buying into the organization gives you access to the organization. Here, it does not."

Curly's been translating all this. "What does he mean?" Petey says.

"I mean," Dino says, "that the way our organization works, the less you know about it—who is involved, what is being done—the better. The best scenario involves you never meeting anyone but me."

Curly doesn't translate that just yet. "Are you sure you mean to say it that way?" he says. "It sounds like you don't want our money."

"I mean every word," Dino says. "Just tell him what I said." Curly does.

"What if I want to know where my money is going?" Petey says.

"You can't. As in, we won't tell you, except perhaps in the most general terms. And I would advise you, in the strongest terms possible, not to try to figure it out yourself. It's for your own protection, in several different ways. I'm sure you understand from your dealings in the United States that certain of our operations are not, well, legal in the strictest sense. In the United States, your business associates respond to that by making a tight network, a family, where everyone knows everyone. Here, we are doing the opposite. No one knows anyone, let alone what anyone else is doing. That way, if something goes wrong and the police—or anyone else—come along asking questions, you do not know enough to implicate yourself, let alone anyone else."

"But someone must know," Petey says. "Someone must be coordinating things."

Dino smiles. "If there is, I do not know who it is."

"So if I can't see the operation, what guarantees do I have that you're not just going to walk off with my money?" Petey says.

Dino's smile doesn't break. "What guarantees do you ever have?" he says. "Newspapers around the world, every day, are full of stories of legitimate businesses walking off with other people's money. You could say that's the whole point, right? They're always just trying to get your money from you. The only question is what they give you in return."

"And what kind of return do you give?"

"It varies, of course. But the way business is going right now, I would say it's very likely that you'll be quite pleased. Most quarters, I would say we—what is the phrase you like to use?—beat the market." He says that in English. Then he's back to Ukrainian. "If you're not happy with the way things are going, you can always pull out."

"So you say, except that there's no guarantee."

Dino shrugs. "Of course not. You just have to trust us. Or maybe double-digit return rates are enough that you don't have to."

"Double digits?"

Dino nods. "For the past few years, yes."

Petey is quiet then, and Curly can tell he's not sure what to say.

"Mr. Hightower needs a day or two to think about it," Curly says.

So Curly and Petey are sitting in Curly's room in the hotel, Curly on the hard bed, Petey in a curving wooden chair. They're drunk and wired and jetlagged, and they can't sleep. It's 2:37 in the morning. The TV's on but it doesn't work very well; a man is reporting the news from somewhere, but they can't tell where. Behind the hotel, two guys are giving yet another black Mercedes sedan the washing of its life. Petey's pouring another drink while Curly looks down at them through the thin curtain. *What makes a guy wash a car in the middle of the night?* he thinks. Then Petey hands him his glass.

"Well? What would you do?"

"It's your money, Petey. Your inheritance."

"Well, pretend it's yours."

Curly thinks about that. Pretend it's his money? If he had Petey's money, he realizes, he wouldn't be here right now. He'd be back in Parma, having bought a house for himself and his parents free and clear. Maybe he'd be loaning a bit to his cousins to help them out with their places. He'd have a little store, some kind of business, he doesn't know what. He just knows that it'd be his. Something to do with the trades, something that lets him give a few guys jobs. After that, he'd see about getting married, having a couple kids. Oh, he'd travel, too, maybe come to Ukraine, but it wouldn't be for business. He'd walk around this city, get out in the countryside with his family, and tell them all the stories he knew from his great-grandparents. *This is where you came from. This is what happened here. Don't forget. Otherwise, how can you know where you're going? How will you know how to get there?*

Curly shakes his head. "No, Petey. It's your money. It's always been your money. What are you going to do with it?"

A look passes over Petey's face that makes Curly regret asking. He's an arrogant young man and a child all at once, with no sense of gravity or responsibility, the ugly side of the party boy Curly liked so much at first. This business of making big money is a game to Petey, the numbers almost meaningless to him. There's no inner monologue, no self-reflection. If Curly were to ask Petey why he wants to make all this money, he's afraid of what the answers would be. *Because it's money. Because we can. Because it's fun.* Never stopping to consider how big the numbers are, or what they mean to everyone else around him. It's Curly's first warning that he needs to watch out for himself, though even now, it's a little late.

"What do you think I should do?" Petey says.

"My honest opinion? Petey? I don't like it. I'm sorry we came all this way, but I don't like it."

"Double-digit returns is a lot of money. We could make a fortune," Petey says.

"You already have a fortune."

"I haven't made *my* fortune. I could make enough to set myself up forever. Me and you too, Curly. Don't think I wouldn't do that."

"Well, thank you so much."

"I didn't mean it like that," Petey says.

Yes you did, Petey, Curly thinks. But says: "I know. Let's drop it."

But Petey won't. "I just mean you could go back to Cleveland a very wealthy man," he says. "Isn't it worth it?"

"I don't know. Is it? I don't like not being able to see the operation, to know anything about it. They could be into some bad, bad stuff."

"Well, how bad could it be?"

And here, dear reader, is where their imaginations fail them. They just have no idea how bad it is. Which is why they call Dino the next day and tell them they're in.

For a time, Petey and Curly live like the princes to the new oligarchs do. The money from Dino starts rolling in. They move out of the Hotel Dnipro and into a string of apartments across Kiev, place remodeled only a year ago with as much going on in them as new money can buy. They go all over Europe—Berlin, Paris, Amsterdam. Change the cut of their clothes, the sweep of their hair, until they have the look of people who spend most of their time moving, on planes, in taxis, but haven't touched a steering wheel in months. They are driven around Kiev in twin black Mercedes of their own, windows tinted as dark as the metal. Their lives become a wash of vague business transactions, a certain thrill under the feigned casualness, of a stakeout, a spy movie, a bender, a wedding reception. Their tolerance for vodka climbs to heights few Americans ever reach, and they find themselves in slurred debates about the quality of caviar, the best Ukrainian rock band; Petey's developed a serious love for Vopli Vidopliassova, won't stop playing *Abo abo*, even though it's already a couple years old. And then there are the women.

It's too easy for these Cleveland boys. They're just ignorant enough, in the strange naïveté that America can breed, not to comprehend just how much money is part of—but only part of—the bargain. They don't see how a few people see them as walking, talking escape hatches out of a collapsing country, or how much their new bosses are using that image. They're not just dealing with Russians anymore, either; the contacts, the names dropped, seem to go across Asia, North Africa, Latin America. It's all very exciting to our boys, these phone calls in multiple languages that interrupt their conversations. It should be terrifying. Because their upbringing, their nation, was an invitation and a shield, opening doors and keeping them safe. They've left that behind now, and they don't see how the rules have shifted, been shaken. How dangerous it all is. Nobody cares who Petey's grandfather is. Nobody knows who either of them are, and the people who sit on the links of the chain of illegal commerce to either side of them are already scheming to cut them out after they've taken what they can get from them. A few of their associates are tapping their phone lines, reading their mail, to assess, if Petey and Curly went missing, how many people would come looking for them, how fast the search would start. These associates like what they see. Petey and Curly are a long way from the world that reared and sheltered them, and Petey doesn't notice.

Curly does. But it's only when Petey disappears that Curly starts to worry. Petey and his latest girl, Madalina, a pretty young Romanian woman with long, dark hair. They've both vanished. They said they were going on vacation; Curly saw them off from an apartment in Kiev, noticed how they talked to each other, standing close enough to touch. Her hand on his arm. His hand on her shoulder. Curly didn't realize it had gotten so serious, even though they've been together for a few months. For the first week they're gone, he assumes that they're just taking a longer vacation than usual. To the Carpathian Mountains, where Petey's always said he wants to go, or to Odessa, where he always goes. Or maybe Petey is going to meet Madalina's family, Curly thinks, to smile and speak in slow English that Madalina's parents don't understand. They'll look him over, trying to be cool, but unable to hide their joy for their daughter. That she's found someone she wants to be with, that nothing happened to her in Kiev that made them sorry they let her go.

Then Petey and Madalina have been gone for two weeks, no, fifteen days. It's too long. Curly calls Kosookyy in Parma, the weak thought in his head that maybe Petey went back; maybe he's standing right next to Kosookyy as the phone rings. Kosookyy will answer the phone, then turn to Petey. *You'll never believe who just called me right now. He never calls me. You guys are big shots now, don't need me anymore. Curly, Madalina's a lovely girl.* And then the relieved conversation. *I'm sorry, I should have told you I was leaving. No, no, I'm just glad you're all right.* But Kosookyy doesn't know where Petey is. They haven't spoken, it turns out, since Petey and Curly left for Ukraine. Curly didn't know that. Now he feels woozy. He starts to feel the loss of his friend, and with it, what little sense of safety he'd fooled himself into. As though he's been living in a town walled off from the woods outside, and every night, predators circle the settlement while he and his people sleep in peace inside. Now the gate's been left unlocked, the wind has blown it open, and the wolves are coming for the chickens.

By the beginning of the third week, Curly's in a cold panic. He'll give anything just to see Petey, imagines that when he does, everything will be better. He's wrong. It's almost four in the morning when Petey catches him outside his apartment, forces him into an alleyway, first by clapping a filthy, salty hand over his mouth, then by begging, in a fetid whisper in his ear, not to shout. He's shaking and jittery, his clothes yellowed, his shoes bruised. Like he's been homeless for days.

"Listen to me," he says. "Listen." He takes his hand off Curly's mouth.

"I'm listening."

"Things have gone bad. You're not going to see me for a while."

"Where are you going?"

"Right now? It doesn't matter to you. But do yourself a favor and drop out of all this while you still don't know anything. Go back to Cleveland. Go back to Parma."

"Where's Madalina?" Curly says.

Petey just shakes his head.

"Petey? How much trouble are we in?"

He won't answer. They just stare at each other, and Curly feels like he's spiking a fever. He can see Petey shaking through his clothes. *It's all been a goddamn act,* Curly thinks. *All that fucking swagger.* His panic breaks into anger, the divide between them fills with acid. He has a sharp and unkind thought, and their years of friendship can't blunt it. He never should have involved himself with this rich asshole, or imagined that the connection between them could change the world around them. Petey wasn't ever Ukrainian, even if his grandfather was. Fucker doesn't speak the language—still doesn't, not a word, though they've been here for almost a year. He didn't go to the schools or to church, in Tremont or Parma. His lineage mixed, and mixed again. His grandfather left Tremont eighty years ago, when Curly's family was still dodging trains. When Petey's clan moved its fingers, it knocked over houses in Curly's neighborhood. The Hightowers will come for their lost son, Curly knows, fish him out of typhoons with helicopters and lawyers, and once they have him, they won't look back to see if anyone was with him.

"I think you should go right now, Petey," Curly says.

"I know."

"And Petey? Don't screw yourself."

"I won't. I know what you're saying."

"Do you?"

"What's that supposed to mean?"

"You know. Please tell me you know."

Petey doesn't say anything, again, and Curly can tell he's angry, too. For a few seconds, they try to keep themselves from fighting it—the class war I mean—as only Clevelanders can. There's a good chance their friendship won't survive what they'll say to each other, and they both know it. Because Petey's grandfather put up the money to build a bridge that one of Curly's relatives died building. Paid for the train that crushed a great-great uncle under its wheels on the tracks running through the Flats. Petey's in the secret suite the Van Sweringens installed near the pinnacle of Terminal Tower while Curly's at the elevator doors in the lobby, polishing the bronzework. There's so much blood between them. Which is why Curly's way angrier than Petey is, why he throws the first punch and a dozen more. *You rich people,* he says. *You have everything in the world and no idea how it works. You're like babies, do you know that? If you had any idea what we really think of you. The things you get upset about, it's like a kid throwing a tantrum. And then you turn around and just ruin other people's lives without thinking twice. Boys with their toys. You're going to kill me, Petey. I'm a dead man because of you, aren't I. But hey, don't worry. Mommy and Daddy'll fish you out of whatever trouble you're in. You'll be just fine.* He's just getting warmed up. It takes him three full minutes to unload all of it, and it ends in a long chain of profanity. *You rich fucking prick. You rich fucking prick.* Petey still doesn't say anything; he doesn't have anything to say. He just sits there and takes it, and Curly understands that he's won the only fight he can win with the Hightowers, even though it also means he's lost: Losing that fight, for Petey, is yet another part of the privilege, because Petey can get his ass kicked and still walk away with every cent he has, everything he's ever had, and leave Curly to hang. Curly can see what Petey's thinking: *I don't really have to listen to this.*

"I'm so sorry," Petey says.

"No you're not," Curly says.

Petey nods again. "Let me try again. I'm as sorry as I can be, given the circumstances."

His coolness is infuriating. The hanging is coming, Curly knows. No. It's already here, he's already going down. He thought he'd at least have some warning.

"Petey, what did you do?"

"Nothing."

"Don't tell me that. If you're taking off, I'm done. You know that, and nothing you can do will fix it."

"Like I said. If I were you, I'd get as far away from all of this as I can. They won't come for you."

"In Parma?" Curly says.

"You know how to do it. You just step away. Just—" And stops himself. There's no way to say it without sparking the war all over again. *Accept it. Accept your low-wage, non-union job where you get shit on your hands all day and nobody gives a crap. The kind of job everyone always expected you to have. The kind of job I will never see.*

"Just get out of here, Petey," Curly says. "I can take care of myself." Though he has no idea how he's going to do that. So he says it at last.

"I could use a little money."

And just like that, Curly loses again. He wants to throw up. Petey nods again, reaches into his pocket. Hands Curly a wad of bills without looking at it.

"That's got to be enough to get you to Cleveland," Petey says.

It is. It's more than enough.

He goes back to Parma, where his old friends smile, to his eye, a little too much at him. Ask him how he's doing and then follow it up fast with something else—*been a while, hasn't it?*—so he doesn't have time to answer the first question. He hates himself for hating being back. And despite everything he thought when he was in Kiev, he just can't get that normal job, the one that'll let him put his time in Ukraine behind him. Part of it's that, as far as the legitimate world is concerned, he hasn't been employed since he was a teenager, and that was slinging sausages at the West Side Market; once, when he was thirteen—he remembers every second of this—he was coming up the service elevator and spilled a hundred gallons of milk across the market's floor. He watched it in awe as it washed against the calves of two ladies and raced down the aisles, sloshed against the walls of the stalls. It was like a flash flood. He had no idea a hundred gallons was so much. His boss let him keep his job, but at seventeen, he left it anyway. Thought he had better things to do. He just can't go back to anything like that now. Wearing an apron, wearing coveralls. Wearing a powder-blue suit with a shiny tie. Checking his watch. Sweaty hands on a faux leather briefcase. All the jobs the men in his family do. He knows he's being an asshole, thinking he's above all that, but it doesn't change anything.

So he goes back to Kosookyy, who at first refuses to take him on. *It's too dangerous for you now, Curly,* he says. *I don't know what Petey did over there, but it was something. They're looking for him. They shouldn't really see you, and I can't really protect you.* He's acting like an uncle now. *The White Lady told me not to get Petey mixed into this. I should have listened and I didn't. I'm sorry.* He likes Curly. Wants to keep him alive. But Curly persists, and Kosooky relents. Puts him on small jobs, the kind of thing he was doing before he ever met Petey Hightower.

"Come on," Curly says. "Give me something else."

"Start where you left off," Kosookyy says. "Then instead of going this way," jabbing his finger toward the floor, "try going this way." Pointing at the ceiling. "Let's get you into some real business, something where you pay taxes, you know? Build up some assets instead of walking around with your money in a duffel bag."

"We made good money over there."

"Is that what you're calling it? Good? Curly, you didn't make good money, you made big money. Big difference. And you know what? You let it get to your head. Now we have to figure out how to get it out again."

"You mean like you?" Curly says. He means it as a jab; he wants to hurt the old man a little. But Kosookyy just closes his eyes, shakes his head.

"No," he says. "Not at all like me. Let's just get you out of this."

But Curly never gets his chance. He's making a delivery with Kosookyy to a warehouse near the Agora, meets three men of a type he recognizes at once, which makes him understand why Kosookyy's with him. It's a rare example of the old organization working with a new one, and it's pretty obvious that Kosookyy isn't happy about it. Whatever it is they're shipping, it's important, though more important to Kosookyy than it is to the three men, who stand around with lazy expressions on their faces. They're not faking it, either; they've done this a million times, are ready to be done for the day and head over to a strip club, do something they'd be too embarrassed to do at home; *never shit where you eat,* Curly heard someone say once. He eyes the men. Multiple cars in Kiev, he thinks, just in case someone decides to blow one of them up. They have no idea who Curly is, which hurts him; he's fallen so far out of that game already. They're talking in soft Ukrainian, turning up the current slang so the old Ukrainian-American man can't quite understand what they're saying. But Curly catches every word. They're talking about a rumor going around the network, of having found someone who was from this very city, that they're going to do something about it. Kosookyy sees something change in Curly, cocks his head and shoots him a look—*don't you dare*—but it's too late. Curly doesn't like Petey very much right now, but he doesn't want to see him dead.

That night Curly calls Dino in Ukraine. *You're in deep shit, Curly*, he says. *I know, I know*, Curly says. *I want to make it right. I want to help you get him.* That's when Dino tells him they think they found a Peter Hightower in Granada, and what are the chances that it's not the same guy? They have the address, the telephone number. *Mind if I have it?* Curly asks. *I can call him. Tell him to stay put, you know what I mean?* There's a moment's hesitation, and then Dino says: *Sure. How much is it worth to you?*

Curly pays. Then makes that call to Granada that starts the whole thing. He'll never know he's called the wrong guy. And forty-eight hours later, the same three men Curly saw near the Agora throw his body, beaten with a metal pipe and shot in the face with a large-caliber pistol, into the bottom of a small motorboat they launch from a dock outside the city and drive out to the middle of Lake Erie, almost to the line across the water separating Ohio from Canada. They sit there for a minute, smoking in the dark, watching and listening for any other boats. They don't hear a thing. Then they take what's left of Curly, drape it over the side of the boat, tie a stolen anchor around the body's neck, and roll everything overboard, nice and easy. So Curly slips into the water without a splash, sinks headfirst one hundred eighty-six feet and stops, suspended in the water, when the anchor hits bottom. The body of the young man hangs there for days, trying to slip out of its noose and come up for air. But the fish get him first.

Chapter 4

You got it so far? For four days, while Curly's at the bottom of the lake, he's not even a missing persons case; he's just missing. This whole thing is under the surface. One Peter Henry Hightower has vanished from Kiev. The other's boarding a plane from Lisbon to New York after having gone by train from Spain to Portugal. At least one man has died. Well, a lot more than that—men, women, and children—and a lot more death is coming. But we're not ready for that.

The police in five countries all have just a small piece of what's going on. In Granada, they're examining the break-in at Peter's apartment, wondering where the tenant has gone, wondering what kind of man lives like he does. In Ukraine, local, state, and international authorities have noted the appearance of the two Americans, and their disappearance, too. But Curly and Petey don't seem important enough to distract them from much bigger problems, or to find out where they went. In Cleveland, the police know the most. Just like Kosookyy hoped, the FBI's got files on him and all his buddies; they have a pretty good sense of what they're all up to. It's been that way at least since the Organized Crime Control Act got passed in 1970, when the feds started being able to prosecute RICO cases—after the Racketeer Influenced and Corrupt Organizations Act, for the people out there taking score at home. See, for the FBI to bust a bunch of guys at once, it's not enough that those guys are just doing bad things. The FBI needs to show that those guys are, you know, organized. That they know each other, work together.

That there's a hierarchy, a system, people giving orders, people taking orders. So they've been collecting that kind of information for years, for at least a generation. Then they wait until the smoking gun appears, or until something big's about to happen, something big and bad enough that they can bring everyone in and put them away for a long time. They work, these RICO cases, and the Cleveland FBI office has done some good busts. They've gotten Angelo Lonardo, who started off in 1929 by killing the people who killed his father, just a year after the big Mafia convention at the Hotel Statler, and risen to run the Mafia rackets in all northeast Ohio by 1980. They got Joseph Gallo, Frederick Graewe, and Kevin McTaggart, too. Drug running, murder, a bunch of other charges. Twenty-five federal convictions and twenty state ones. Just a couple years ago, they started going international. They're investigating a Taiwanese company for stealing trade secrets from an Ohio glue factory; they'll gather enough to convict the company's president, along with his daughter, in 1999. They're doing a lot of drug cases; they'll do a lot of cyber crime. And by 1995 they've learned a couple things that don't make them very happy.

Agents George Guarino and Anne Easton have been put onto the Cleveland office's organized crime investigations, Easton because she's smart, Guarino because he's almost as smart and knows a thing or two about Cleveland; he grew up around here. We're in the days before September 11, before organized crime takes a backseat to terrorism in the FBI's priorities. So Guarino and Easton have some bureau money to spend. They've set up a nice little network of informants, they've been doing surveillance. They know the restaurant Petey and Curly visited, though they didn't see them go in there. They know the man who owns the place and have been tracing the connections—of money, for the most part, because it's all about money, right?—back to Russia and Eastern Europe, to someone, or something, called the Wolf. They know about a rival international group, whose Cleveland contact appears to be a man named Feodor. They know about someone called the White Lady, who they're pretty sure lives in town, appears to have connections to a few different organizations, including Feodor's and the Wolf's—as if she's playing a few sides at once. But they're not sure why she'd do that, or even who she is. They're just gathering their information on who's dealing with whom, trying to build up an organization in their files that matches the one in the world. Their desks, not far apart from each other, are piled with pictures and printouts—we're just at the beginning of the point where everything goes electronic—and now and again Guarino, who's better at finding things than Easton is, gives her a tap on the shoulder: *What do you think of this?* And Easton, who's better at making the connections than Guarino is, gives whatever he's holding a good stare. Starts to talk. *They must be involved. I'd say this is some kind of code, except they don't seem to work that way.* They're catching up, figuring out how the new crime organizations work. But here's the discouraging thing: The organizations don't ever seem to end. The connections lead only to more connections, all over the world. They jump from country to country, never-ending webs of people and currency that involve as many rackets as the agents can think of, from money laundering and loan-sharking to arms dealing and human trafficking. If there are real lines between them, the agents can't see them; they have no idea what the structures of these things look like on paper, let alone who's running them. So they keep having the same little confrontation between them. *Look, it's okay,* Guarino says. *We can still use RICO to get them, right? We just define the organization how we need to.* He's trying to move the case forward, put some guys away. But Easton doesn't want to do it that way. *That's not the organization, then,* she might say. *It's just something we made up. We can do it that way, but it doesn't change anything. We never get the guys who matter.* Sometimes she hauls out the tired old analogies to hydras, to octopuses—you know, cutting off one tentacle when there are a hundred more, and the one you cut off grows back anyway—and Guarino just shakes his head. They both know what the problem is: They're hacking apart the facts to make a story, and that their story's got a lot of truth in it is beside the point. Maybe that truth'll be enough to do the job, to serve some kind of justice, to do right by the people who've been wronged. But the people left out of the story—the victims and the perpetrators—are going to notice what's been done. They'll see the places the story doesn't touch, and know that there, it's open season.

Curly's friends, his family, his mother, are calling each other more and more, getting more frantic with every call. *Have you seen him? He didn't go somewhere without telling us, did he? He wouldn't do that. Where is he?* It feels like a prophecy coming true. He was such a good kid, just a little wild, but that wildness led him somewhere they couldn't follow, and they lost him. How could that ever end well? For the Hightower clan, though, things are a bit more complicated. Muriel's been too afraid of her son for a couple years to ask what he's been up to, too used to him being gone for months to know that he's in trouble. Jackie doesn't talk to anyone but herself. And Sylvie doesn't say anything. She's known for thirty years that her best chance of surviving in her family, and keeping her family alive, is to embody her mother's spirit most of the time, friendly, steadfast, quiet. To observe and wait, and act only when she thinks she can make things better. Then her father comes out of her, and man, watch out.

Henry and Rufus are another story. They both have so much of their father in them. The same fire, the same shrewdness, the same cynical understanding of laws as things to be manipulated, skirted, ignored when necessary; the same quick separation of laws from morals and values. The same desire to take care of the people closest to them, the Old World instinct that helped so many people get out of Europe when they had to, and if Rufus and Henry could ever talk about it with each other, they would lament, together, how they failed in not giving it to their children. That conversation will never happen, though, because the things that make them so similar are the same things that drive them apart.

Henry still lives in New Canaan, in the same house Peter found him in nine years ago, and it's been an interesting decade for him. In 1992, a premature heart attack puts him into semiretirement. His doctor shrugs, can't diagnose what caused it, but says maybe he should stop working so hard. His wife is more specific: She tells him he has to work on eliminating the things from his life that are causing him stress. So he divorces her. Cuts back on his hours, starts doing everything by phone, starts talking about being bought out. He's done. He throws out all his old clothes, buys new ones, dresses casual, or at least more casual. No cufflinks, no ties, blazers only when necessary, though the cut of his pants, the style of his shirts, give away that he's got some money. That's intentional. Henry's too aware of the signals himself, knows that he can't hide everything and can't be bothered working so hard to try. He's seen too many rich people try to pass themselves off as middle-class; everyone he knows, his neighbors, his former coworkers, all think they really are middle-class. It's laughable. They fail to pass and don't know they failed. People who don't have their kind of money can get the right order of magnitude of their wealth just by looking at their European-sized shoes, the angle of the collar of their designer T-shirts. Maybe that's why the rich are always building walls and fences around their houses, Henry thinks. If they didn't, everyone would be able to see right through them.

He meets Holly, a woman from Winsted, not six months after the divorce is final, marries her in 1994. Alex seems to understand. *She's nice,* she says to his father, and Henry's glad that Alex is comfortable around her. But deep down, at the time, Henry doesn't think about that too much. He's too busy putting another life together for himself, wants Alex in it only if she wants to be in it, too. He's not being callous; just loosening the rules, trying to give his daughter her freedom. When Henry was young himself, he used to think that the family bond was iron. After their father died, he never made that mistake again. He understands now that it's just a question of keeping the lights on, the door open. Doing what you can to help that doesn't kill the other's pride. Though now and again he forgets, and has to relearn the lesson all over again.

It's 1995. Henry's smiling when he sees the taxi pull up at the front of the house, sees Peter get out, squint down the driveway. The boy's leaner, sharper than he was 1986. A decent haircut, the hang of his clothes more suitable to his frame. Still not a shred of America in him. The taxi driver must have asked him some questions, or maybe he was afraid to. Or maybe he already knew what Peter was all about, being the same way himself.

"You could have called first," Henry says. "I would have picked you up at the airport."

"Your phone number changed," Peter says.

"Good thing I didn't move," Henry says.

He's in trouble, Henry thinks, but doesn't ask how. Figures Peter will get around to it. It takes five hours, after a tour of the property, the things that have changed since Peter last saw it. The first wife's office is gone; it's a study now, with a loom folded in the corner. They've filled in the pool and let the land go, let all the land go around their house. They like the way the trees are taking over. *Soon we'll have our own little preserve here,* Henry tells him, and chuckles in a loose, genuine way that Peter doesn't remember him doing back in 1986. Holly is the kind of woman who glows; she's warm and nurturing. Thick curls woven into a loose bun at her neck and tied with a colored scarf. *The kind of woman my dad should have ended up with,* Peter thinks. They make fish and rice, curried vegetables. Split a bottle of wine, open another one, and at last Peter begins to talk.

"I got a call from someone named Curly," he says. "From Cleveland."

"Curly? I'm assuming that's not his real name. Who is he?" Henry says.

"I have no idea who he is. But he says he was looking for Petey."

Henry nods. In his brain, the first pieces are clicking into place. "That's what they've been calling your cousin for years, now," he says.

"I think Curly thinks I'm him," Peter says.

"I was about to say the same thing," Henry says, and becomes very still. Takes his wife's hand. "What happened after the phone call?"

Peter tells him, about the break-in, his escape. The train from Spain to Portugal, the flight out of Lisbon. He's almost positive no one saw him do any of this.

"How'd you get the money for the flight?" Henry says.

Peter doesn't know which question Henry's asking, decides to answer both.

"I'm a journalist," he says.

Henry raises an eyebrow.

"And my dad gave me some money I've been hanging on to for a while," Peter says.

Something in Peter's voice tells Henry about what's happened between Peter and Rufus. Father and son haven't talked in a while.

"Peter," he says, "I think it's time you start to know a few things. Do you know what your father does for money?"

"No."

"Well. Maybe he does something to help support himself a little. But the money comes from me. It's always come from me."

"I see," Peter says. Henry can almost see the young man putting it together; a big part of his life that never made much sense is starting to make lots of sense. "Why did you do that?"

"Because we're family."

"Why did my dad go to Africa, then?"

"Because we're family," Henry says. "At first, I think it was disgust. But once you were born, I think he was trying to protect you."

"Protect me from what?" Peter says.

"Rufus really didn't say anything about us, did he?"

"No."

"Peter, you may be in a lot of trouble," Henry says.

"Why?"

"Because, Peter, the grandfather you were named after was a criminal. Oh, he made plenty of legitimate money. But at the beginning, it wasn't legitimate at all, and, well, what can I say? He never quite escaped."

"Did you?" Peter says.

You got some balls, kid, Henry thinks. *Good for you.* "Financially? Legally?" he says. "Yes. But the same thing isn't true of everyone. And now Petey, your cousin, is a criminal too. I don't know what kind—he's not nearly as smart or as careful as your grandfather was. I don't know how bad it is with him, either. Sounds like pretty bad, though. He was pretty bad already when you visited last, though you probably figured that one out even then. Who goes to summer school, right?" Henry smiles. Peter doesn't, and Henry feels a little chastened. Peter doesn't have the luxury of seeing the humor in it. Would Rufus see it? He thinks so. If Peter weren't caught up in it. If Rufus knew how bad it was getting, the things he would say. *This is why I left. This is why I didn't want to see any of you ever again.*

"Do you know where Petey is now?" Peter says.

"No. He's involved in something I can't see from where I'm standing. Maybe Sylvie can see it, but I can't. I haven't talked to him in years, Peter. Haven't even talked to Muriel about him."

Henry doesn't want to get into it, the last few years between him and his sister. It's 1987. Henry sees Petey at a family reunion for Easter, thinks he looks like a little thug and tells him so, before he gives it the kind of thought he should have. Petey just stands there, doesn't say a word, and Henry regrets opening his mouth. But he can't take it back now. Muriel screams and screams at him. *How dare you say that.* And then later on the phone, when Henry gets back to Connecticut, she connects everything to everything else. *Just because you have a shitty home life, it doesn't mean you have to make our home life shitty too.* Henry listens, winces, sorry all over again he said anything, but hopes to salvage some good from his mistake. He doesn't bring up the selling drugs, the sentencing, the mild incarceration. *I'm trying to help. Petey's going in the wrong direction, you have to see that.* Muriel does see it, Henry knows that, but she's not going to admit it. Henry hasn't given her a way to do it without implicating herself, and she'll be damned if she's going to admit to her brother, under these circumstances, that she made a mistake.

We're lousy parents, Henry thinks to himself—even then, back in 1987—both he and his sister. They had every chance with Petey, they had him right where he should have been, and they let him get away.

And Henry knows he can't take credit for how good his own kid is, except as a foil; Alex is good, always has been, always will be, even growing up around people as toxic as her parents, and even if she is, almost without a doubt, going to watch her father and mother say some terrible things to each other before they call it all off at last.

He gets all his information about the family from Sylvie after that. How Petey's moved out of the house, gone who knows where, though it seems to be somewhere in Cleveland. Petey shows up at Muriel's house, at Sylvie's house, a couple times a year. At first, to ask for money, but soon enough, that stops, as soon as it looks like he's come into money of his own, though it's clear it's not from working in a bank. *The young man's got a strut about him,* Sylvie says, *like he's gone a little feral.* Though to Sylvie, it's as much an act as a real transformation. *There's a part of him that's still that boy at my wedding in a little blue suit,* Sylvie tells Henry. *And I think that boy is scared to death of what the rest of him has become.* A bit of Sylvie's toughness showing, just enough that Henry realizes that if it had been Sylvie instead of Muriel raising that boy, Petey would be the straightest arrow of them all.

Peter stares at him from across the coffee table, and for Henry, it's as though the entire family is in the room with them now. His brother and sisters; their spouses, whom he has never gotten to know; all their children, some of whom he wouldn't recognize now. His own parents: his mother in the chair in the corner, knitting and humming, his father near the window, smoking in the house when no one smokes in the house. His father's brother, Stefan, who had the kindest face Henry can remember seeing in his life. He looks again at Peter and glimpses a bit of Stefan in him, the one who, if he had been the patriarch instead of his brother, would never have taken the family so far, or let them drop from so high.

Henry's earned enough of his own wealth that he doesn't think he has to justify it to anyone he sees. He hasn't let it turn him into a child or a crank, either, a man who confuses money with wisdom. He doesn't glorify poverty. He's not sentimental or stupid. But sometimes he wonders if they wouldn't have been happier with less. This thing of having too much, of not having enough; it makes people insane, he thinks, makes them do insane things. They scramble and scream, they fight and scheme. They set traps and swindle. They bring each other down, then pile up the bodies to ascend even farther, even faster. Somehow there has to be some balance, doesn't there? Of having just enough? But where is it? And why is it so hard to find?

"I think you need to go to Cleveland," Henry says at last. "You need to keep moving. And you need to talk to Sylvie." He gets up and leaves the room while Holly smiles at Peter and refills his wineglass. Then Henry comes back with a roll of bills folded in his hand. *That old habit from Dad,* he thinks, *having all this cash lying around. Have any of us broken it?*

"I want to help you get out of this," he says. "How much do you think you need?"

"I can't take your money now," Peter says.

Henry smiles. "Peter. Just take it. And get in the car and let me give you a ride to the airport. And let me pay for the ticket."

Peter stands there, just looking at him. *So smart, and so much pride,* Henry thinks. *He looks just like his father right now.*

"Are you sure?" Peter says.

"I wouldn't offer if I wasn't."

"Okay, then."

"Good. It's settled. I'll call Sylvie and tell her to tell Muriel you're coming."

"Okay."

"Call me if you need anything."

"I still don't have your phone number."

"Of course." He smiles again. Takes out a business card from his pocket and a pen from the table, scrawls the number on the back. Calls the airlines to book a flight, then drives Peter back to the airport himself.

All the way down, from the Merritt across the Whitestone Bridge to the Grand Central Parkway to LaGuardia, Henry wants to tell him the rest of it, about why nobody talks to each other anymore. His and Muriel's fight over Petey. The fight over what to do with Jackie. The big one, in August 1966, when the patriarch died and the smoke still seemed to be rising from Hough after the riots. The Cuyahoga County grand jury was pinning everything on the Communists, Henry remembers. *That would have made Dad laugh. It's always the fucking Communists with them, he would have said.* But for his family, it was something else. That there was so much—so much and not enough—to squabble over. That they all were who they were, Rufus in particular. And then the split the paterfamilias had driven into the family before they were ever born. It's not that Henry blames him for the way the family is now; he's nobody's victim, and they've all held up their ends pretty good since their father died. But when he takes in the whole of the life of his father, the first Peter Henry Hightower, from his first days in Tremont to his last days in Bratenahl, he can see how they've come to this. The family breaking apart, over him and everything he left behind. His grand and ruinous legacy. And Henry looks over at the young man in the passenger seat, thinks about the thug with the same name. Thinks of everything that both the cousins carry of the men and women who came before them. They're all caught up in their crooked family history. Maybe the two Peters together will straighten it all out, drag everything into the light, and all that's toxic will wither and die, and the things that are strong will grow. But where they'll all be by then, he has no idea.

The flight is in the evening, and it's dark by the time Henry gets back to his house. Holly's asleep on the couch, sitting up, her head back, mouth open. A book splayed on the floor near her feet. She was trying to wait up for him. He marks the page with a scrap of paper from his wallet, puts the book back on the coffee table, then goes to the study and calls Alex. It's too late to call most people, but he knows his daughter will be up, and working.

"Hello?" Sure enough.

"Alex. It's me."

"Hi, Dad. Is everything okay?"

"Yeah, everything's fine. Why?"

"You don't usually call this late."

"No, no, everything's fine."

"So what are you calling about?"

"I'm planning a surprise party for Holly's birthday," he says. "I had to wait until she was asleep to invite you."

"That's in, like, two months, right?"

"Well, yes, but I have a lot of calls to make. You're the first person I'm inviting."

"I'd love to come," Alex says, "if I can get out of work in time."

"That'd be great. It'd mean a lot to her."

"Happy to do it, Dad. Is that all?"

Henry feels like a child. Something is rising in him, overwhelming him, and it takes away his voice, makes him helpless. He wants to tell his daughter how much he loves her, how proud he is of everything she's done, of the kind of woman she's turned out to be. But there's too much between them now. The frayed wires at the end of the divorce are still sparking a little; maybe they'll never stop. The plain fact that he's never said anything like it before. *I love you so much. I'm so proud.* He's tried to show it, a hundred thousand times, it seems, but he's never sure the message gets through. Never sure that Alex isn't doing the same thing, struggling to say something neither of them has the words for, at least not for each other. Alex doesn't hate him; he knows that much. There was a time, right after Henry divorced Alex's mother, that Alex was always out of the house when he called, always away from her desk. She's around more often now, almost every time Henry tries to reach him, and it's enough, at least for now.

"Yeah, that's it, Alex," he says. "It's good to talk to you."

"Good to talk to you, too, Dad. See you soon."

"All right. Bye-bye."

My daughter is so much better than me, Henry thinks. *So much better.*

He's still standing there with the phone in his hand, the phone having cycled through the silence at the end of the call, the dial tone, the buzzing off-the-hook signal, the silence after that. Holly's still asleep on the couch. He puts the phone back in its cradle, walks over and gets his wife on her feet. Leads her to the bed without her waking all the way up, and tucks her in. Then goes to his closet, where there's a long, tall safe installed in the back. Peeks over his shoulder to make sure Holly isn't stirring, then does the combination fast. Opens it up and takes out a shotgun. He loads it there, looking at Holly the whole time; he doesn't want her to see any of this. Then moves across the carpet without a sound, goes outside to the end of his driveway. There are three men out there, guys he hired from a security agency; he called them before he left for the airport. They're big, half again as big as he is, but their guns are smaller. None of them has much to say to each other. Two of the guys are talking about sports. They wait in the dark, bored and tense.

At last, a car pulls up, going slow, and Henry knows it's not any of his neighbors, anybody just passing through the area. Nobody does that around here, not down this part of the road. They only come if they have business to attend to. It's why Henry bought the house in the first place. Even then, he was done with seeing people unless there was a reason.

"What's the move?" one of the men says.

"I'll talk," Henry says. "Do what I do."

The hired guns nod, and they all get out their weapons so whoever's driving the car can see them in the headlights. The car stops, and for one second, Henry prays. It's what his grandmother would have done, his father's mother, and what his uncle Stefan would do. Stefan taught him the Our Father, which everyone knows. Taught him how to pray the rosary. Henry stumbled over the Hail Mary as a child, blurred the words together, but it comes to him clear and strong now. *Holy Mary, mother of God, pray for us sinners, now and at the hour of our death. Amen.*

The man on the passenger side of the car opens the door and the light in the car goes on. Two young men are in there, looking at them, and Henry breathes again. It's just two local guys. Subcontractors. Someone made a call to someone else, who then made a call. Some small favors exchanged. Enough to make these two drive over from Danbury, or somewhere in upstate New York, maybe up from the city. But they're not getting paid enough to take a bullet. They just need to say they showed up. Henry takes one hand off his shotgun, makes a gesture in the air. *Turn off your engine.* The driver does, and the light goes out. They keep the headlights on.

"He's not here," Henry says.

"He got in a taxi that headed up here." The voice is from the passenger side, even and deadpan.

"That's true," Henry says. "He was here. But he didn't stay long."

"Any idea where he was going?"

"Nope," Henry says. In a narrow way, he's not lying.

There's a half minute of silence from the car, and Henry's fear returns. In the headlights, he makes a little show of tightening his grip on the shotgun, like he's ready to point it at the car. The guys he's hired do the same. They're putting on a good act. If the men in the car want to fight, they can, but one of them won't make it off this road. The engine coughs a few times, revs up. Then the car goes down the road in reverse, twenty yards, backs into Henry's neighbor's driveway, turns out, and leaves the way it came. They wait until they can't hear the engine anymore.

"All right," Henry says. "You can go."

"You bought us for the night," one of them says.

"Go home. I don't want my wife to know this happened, understand?"

One of the guys almost looks hurt, but the other two put their guns away, head for their cars. Henry takes the shells out of the shotgun, puts them in his pocket. Goes inside, back to his bedroom, nice and quiet, and puts gun and shells away in the safe. Closes it. Makes sure Holly's still asleep. Then goes to the phone again.

"Sylvie," he says.

"Yes, Henry?" She's wide awake.

"Muriel's Petey's in some real trouble."

"Yes?" she says. Her voice is soothing, almost sweet. *She knows already,* Henry thinks. *How does she know?*

"It involves Peter, too. He just showed up on my doorstep."

"I think it would be safest if you send him to me," Sylvie says.

"I already did."

"Good." *She knew that already, too,* Henry thinks. *She wasn't giving me a suggestion; she was giving me her blessing.* Somehow, every time he talks to her, he has to learn all over again that Sylvie is way smarter than he is. Always at least four steps ahead.

"He'll be at the airport in an hour or so," Henry says.

"I'll have Muriel pick him up. He can spend the night there. Then I'll have her bring him over to me in the morning," Sylvie says.

"Good." Still the businessman. *Drop it,* Henry says to himself. *For God's sake, drop the act for once in your sorry life.* A few seconds go by. Sylvie's still on the other end, waiting.

"Sylvie?"

"Yes?"

"What's going on?"

Now it's Sylvie's turn to pause. Henry can hear her let out a long sigh. Then: "I think there's just been some amazing misunderstanding, Henry. But it's okay. I think I know how to fix it."

"How are you going to do that?" Henry says.

"Well, to begin, we're going to make sure Rufus's Peter doesn't stay in the same place for long." She doesn't have to say why: *If they catch him, they'll kill him,* Henry thinks. "There's much more to it than that," she says, "but do you really think you want to know what the rest of it is?"

There were men with guns outside my house tonight, Sylvie, and they weren't police, Henry wants to say. But he knows what Sylvie's saying. The question's personal, legal, familial, all at once. She's trying to protect him.

"You're right," he says. "I don't need to know."

"Good. I might need you, Henry. If I do, I'll call. But there's a chance that, when I've fixed it, you'll just know. Okay?"

"Okay."

"Okay." He can hear her smile. "It's good to hear your voice, big brother," she says.

"You, too, Sylvie."

"I know you're always looking out for us," she says.

He doesn't know what to say to that. He wants to say so much, but it won't come out.

"All right," he says. "Take care of yourself."

"Good night."

"Good night."

He hangs up the phone, walks to his side of the bed. Strips to his underwear and gets under the covers. His wife turns toward him, puts a hand on his chest. She's snoring. He can't sleep. He's thinking about the place he's from, the people who raised him. The things he knows they did, that he did to get here, to this house. Its exquisite woodwork, in mahogany, cypress, the kind of wood you can't get anymore because we've chopped it all down. When he's at his most brutal and self-lacerating, it's all exploitation to him, people selling out other people, using them up, until there's nothing left of them. His father was so good at it. It's easy for Henry to think sometimes that it was all the man did, the only way he saw other people—how they could be useful to him—and he took everything he could get, body and soul, and threw away the rest. He never seemed to show any remorse for it, either; didn't seem to have the mind Henry has, that makes him feel guilty for his success even though it was all he craved.

Maybe it was all a question of where his father came from, though. Because the factories killed his father's father when the patriarch was a boy, and maybe his father thought he'd be damned if he let them get him, too. Maybe he thought he owed his own father that, to play the game as hard as he could. Like it was a kind of revenge to succeed as he did, and did he ever. But look at the cost. The hidden dead. The people killed inside but still walking. Henry's sure he's doing it to someone out there, somewhere in the world, every time he makes a buck. Every dollar he gets for playing with big numbers in an office in lower Manhattan is a dollar someone in a factory, in a field somewhere didn't get, right? He's selling them out until there's nothing left. Just like I'm taking everyone in this book and selling them out to you, dear reader. Cracking open their heads to show you what's inside. Telling you things about them they would never tell anyone, not their wives, or husbands, or best friends. We'll get as much of them as either of us can stomach, and when we're done with them, we'll just leave behind what remains. I hope you're satisfied.

Chapter 5

few weeks before Peter catches his night flight to Cleveland, a farmer in Eastern Europe, out already from insomnia, finds Madalina. There's a place on the map where Ukraine, Romania, and Moldova meet, and you might think that would mean something, that there'd be a monument there, like the Four Corners in the southwestern United States. You've seen the pictures, the postcards, of a girl lying spread-eagled across the spot where the borders cross, like she's been cut into quarters, a limb in each state. Her head cut in half. Her brother stands over her with the camera and takes the picture, then looks down at her, frowning. *Okay. My turn.*

In that corner of Eastern Europe, there's no monument. Madalina's lying on her back in the mud, five hundred and three meters on the Moldovan side. The mud's thick here, like paste. Where people and livestock churn it, it whips itself into peaks. It's hard to imagine it ever going away, drought or not; it'll stay like that until winter comes and freezes it all in place. It's deep enough to lose shoes in, to cake dirt on your pants up to your knees. The cars that race through here scream their way up the hill, spinning out, swinging side to side, throwing dirt everywhere. Which is why it's a little hard to see Madalina at first. She was thrown from a backseat, landed hard in the mud, so one of her arms up to the shoulder and one of her legs up to the knees are covered. Her head's thrown back and smeared with dirt, so at first it looks like her eyes are just closed and bruised, rather than gone altogether. The gunshot wound, behind her ear, is clogged with mud. But the rough stitching

91

from clavicle to pubic symphysis is impossible to miss. Her clothes are off and the incision line is a rough, swollen ridge, meandering a bit down her body, as if whoever did it was quite skilled, but in a hurry. Since they shot her in the head afterward, why they stitched her up again is a mystery. Maybe it's a mark of professionalism; they're sending a signal to the authorities that this isn't a simple murder or a serial killer; no, Madalina's been involved in an operation. Maybe it's a small nod to her family, a little shred of respect—or a mockery of respect—after the hours of brutality. What her parents were afraid of the most when she left them has happened, and if this were a different kind of story, they might have woken up in their beds at the moment of her death, or the second the stitches were done. Woken up and wandered around the house looking for their daughter, swearing they heard her come in. But this isn't that kind of story. Her parents are just human beings and they sleep through all of it. In just a couple days, though, they'll learn enough to know they'll never see her again. They'll see how her life can be described as a loop, first rising away from the border of Ukraine and Romania, pausing over Germany, then falling again, over Kiev, to come back to earth in Moldova. The farmer who finds her is terrified. He doesn't trust the police, doesn't trust anyone except his brother with what he's found. He runs to his brother's house and wakes him; they get Madalina off the hill before the sun's all the way up, bury her that night in the back of the farmer's own field, with as much dignity as they can give her. He feels terrible for her, for what she must have gotten mixed up in. But he'll never tell anyone what he's done, or where she is.

You need to know a few things now, dear reader, if you don't already, about Romania, just like you needed to know a few things about Ukraine before. You need to know because it's hard for us over here in the United States to see just how chaotic, how desperate sometimes, things get in Eastern Europe just after the Soviet Union collapses. We see them taking apart the Berlin Wall on TV, we see the big protests in the streets. But it's a lot harder to see the lawlessness that comes with it. Harder to see what a few people with money and means and not much in the way of morals can get away with—and how—when the old order falls and the new one takes too long to build. For a while, the cages are open and things run wild. That's what I'm trying to show you. I'm not trying to tell you what it means; I'm just trying to tell you what happened, and I'm trying to do it so you see for yourself, in the end, why you should know.

Madalina is born in Negostina, just outside of Siret, near the border with Ukraine. It's 1970. Siret's down in the valley of a small river, a little pocket of the country far from the capital, but on some days it can feel like a snapshot of all Romania: the houses with chipping plaster walls, the crowded little market in a tight intersection. An old woman trying to sweep the sidewalk in front of her house, while the wind blows the dirt all around her. Then there's the weight of the past. Siret has two Jewish cemeteries. One of them's centuries old and looks it: It's on a craggy hill so steep that some of the graves are almost horizontal. It's all walled off. The house next to it raises chickens. The newer cemetery is bigger, a little tidier. The neighbor will give you a little tour, for a small fee, if you ask. She'll show you the oldest graves, from a couple hundred years ago, the newest ones from a half century ago. The monument for the Holocaust at the gate; underneath it, they buried some of the soap they found in the camps when the war was over. You don't always think of Romania and the Holocaust, but the Antonescu regime, which sided with Hitler during World War II until a coup took it out, killed hundreds of thousands of Jews. And that means that, in some towns— like Siret—there isn't a single Jew left. The last ones died or left in the mid-1950s, though in the center of town, the synagogue is still there, chained shut for decades, to remind everyone else what happened.

You climb out of the valley and up to the plain to get to Negostina, and even though Siret's a little closer to the border, it's out of the valley where you start to see Ukraine coming. It's not just the signage in both the Roman and Cyrillic alphabets. It's the land itself. The hills flatten out, the wind picks up. The sky gets bigger. It's a little glimpse of the vast steppe that covers almost half of Ukraine, the land the Soviets wanted, that Hitler was willing to kill everyone there—not just the Jews, but everyone—to get. The place that could feed Europe, and where millions starved. Negostina's huddled down against all that vastness. It's been there for a long time, though it feels almost temporary, a concession to the borderlands, the waves of history. The town is just a few roads, some of them not so much roads as a set of dirt tracks that wind through the town, the paths where everyone's agreed it's all right to drive a car. The houses there are tidy, cozy, though even a tourist can almost tell the Romanian and Ukrainian houses apart. The Romanian houses are a little breezier, the Ukrainian ones more like compounds, as if the Romanians are living for the summer while the Ukrainians are getting ready for the winter. Things are easy between them, though. There's a bust of Taras Shevchenko, orphan and serf, political dissident and conscripted soldier, exile and blasphemer, writer and artist—the founder of modern Ukrainian literature, the voice of Ukraine's written language; part of the blood, now, of the Ukrainian nation, though if you've lost your Ukrainian, you'd never know it.

So Madalina—a Romanian finding herself a minority among Ukrainians—learns both languages. Her Romanian is perfect; her Ukrainian's only a little off, but you'd only notice after an hour of talking to her, a slight hesitation sometimes to look for a word she has in one language but not the other. She's very bright, and from a very early age, everyone knows it. But she's born under Nicolae Ceausescu, like the rest of Romania, and though we in the West have heard some of the stories—a little Stalin, a little Mao, a little Kim Il Sung—maybe we're still not paying enough attention. Not enough for Ceausescu to spook the West the way other Communists did during the Cold War. The Conducator puts some space between himself and the Soviet Union, recognizes West Germany. Richard Nixon visits him in 1969; you can find the picture of them standing together in front of a bank of microphones, waving at what might be a crowd. Nixon's got his arm around Ceausescu's shoulder. In 1983, when the first George Bush is vice president, he calls Ceausescu one of Europe's good Communists.

But if you're living under him in Romania, it's probably hard for you to agree. There's the development of a massive, paranoid cult of personality, pretty much at the same speed that the personality itself loses touch with reality. There's the repression, the terror, prosecuted through a huge secret security apparatus. The willful ruination of his people, making them go hungry to pay the country's debts. The building of gargantuan projects—herding farmers off their land into apartment complexes with forty-watt bulbs and terrible heating—for no useful reason, except maybe control. Ceausescu turns life in Romania into a knock-down, drag-out struggle to survive; infant mortality gets bad enough that they stop counting babies until they're a month old. Meanwhile Ceausescu goes hunting for bears. He makes hundreds of men go up into the hills and drive the bears down into a valley by hollering and firing into the air with semiautomatic rifles and shotguns. He himself sits in a treehouse with a pair of Holland & Holland .375s someone else loads for him. By the time the bears are in the valley, they're almost shoulder to shoulder. Ceausescu can't miss, and doesn't. He kills twenty-four bears at once and has them dragged back to a hunting lodge to be laid out so he can be photographed with them. The forest rangers still remember it years later. They call it a massacre.

In hindsight, his death seems almost a foregone conclusion; by the end, it's obvious to everyone in Romania but him. A protest over the eviction of a pastor in December 1989 turns into a demonstration against Nicolae, who leaves the country to visit Iran while his security forces fire on the protesters. His power in Romania has been almost absolute since the late 1960s. *This little uprising,* he must think, *it's not such a big deal.* On December 21, Ceausescu stages a rally, a speech. It all seems to be going so well. He speaks; people chant and clap. And then, from out of nowhere, a scream rises and won't stop. It's the sound of a predator coming for Nicolae, the sound of a regime dying, though even then, the dictator doesn't understand what's happening. His voice falters. His hand rises, feeble, shaking a little. On the balcony he's speaking from, there's confusion. *Someone's shooting,* his wife Elena says. *Earthquake?*

Stay calm! What's wrong with you? It's unclear who she's talking to. Then Nicolae himself: *Alo! Alo! Alo! Sit down and stay where you are!* They don't. On Christmas, Nicolae and Elena Ceaucescu are executed in Targoviste, a hour from Bucharest, sentenced to death after a fifty-five-minute show trial and five minutes of what can't be called deliberation. Against the wall, their hands tied behind their backs, Elena screams at her executioners while Nicolae sings from "The Internationale." There's no order to start shooting. Fifty rounds later, there's an order to stop. The whole thing, except for the very beginning of the shooting, the moment of death itself, is videotaped and released to the Western news; in Romania, it's played on national television over and over, even as pro-Ceausescu forces keep shooting more people before giving up. It looks at first like the natural end of a popular uprising. There's that humming sense in the media that for Romania, the hell is over. But later it seems clear that it's not that simple. Maybe under the robe of the revolt was just another coup, a chance for someone who wanted power for themselves to put a bullet in Ceausescu's head and say it was what the people wanted. And maybe the people did want it, this tyrant's death; though it's hard to be sure that what comes afterward was what they had in mind to replace him. The crime. The instability. The long, hard road of recovery.

Madalina's twenty when they put the old regime in the ground. In December 1990, she leaves Negostina looking for work in journalism. Her father doesn't understand why. *The same people who controlled the papers under Ceausescu control them now,* he says. *Why would you want to work for them?* She shakes her head. *Things will change soon,* she says to him. *Don't count on it,* he answers, but sees there's no talking her out of it. He gives her money, a long hug at the door. *Good luck, my best girl. Be safe.*

She has a room in Cluj for a year, a small place near a stretch of apartment blocks. Every morning, a man with a shopping cart rattles by, filling it with cardboard. At the market that stretches along the train tracks that run into town, they're selling scraps of wood, scraps of metal, shoe leather, salvaged pieces of fabric, the kind of stuff we'd throw away; but there, people will use them to patch their jackets, seal up a loose seam, prop up the walls in the buildings that were built in the 1980s and are already starting to crumble. Every night, Cluj's stray dogs stage gang wars outside her window. It becomes a joke she has with the neighbors, that they're living in a battle zone even though the revolution's been over for years. One day, two men slaughter and butcher a pig on the sidewalk; they take what they can use and leave a huge smear of blood and offal on the ground. The dogs take sides around the carnage before nighttime, and the fighting draws the neighbors to their windows to watch. Some of them make bets, on bottles of beer, a plastic bucket. A ride to the next town, because someone knows someone who can borrow his cousin's car, and favors are owed. They look at Madalina. *What are you doing here?* they say.

Things are better in Iasi; she finds work in a used bookstore that runs a kiosk on Pietonalul Lapusneanu, a narrow tree-lined street that runs downhill from Bulevardu Independentei to Strada Arcu. It's late April 1992, and the weather is pleasant; people are starting to get out again. Madalina's outside all day. In the morning, two men dig a ditch down the middle of the street, lay in a drainage pipe, fill it with gravel, then cover it over with cement and leave it to dry. Seven minutes later, two American visitors on the other side of the street spy her kiosk open and cross. One of them steps right in the wet cement; *son of a . . .* the tourist says. Constantin Radalescu, sitting on a bench near Madalina's kiosk, tries not to laugh, decides not to hold it in. He's still smirking when the Americans are within earshot.

"We're looking for . . ." the American says in pretty bad Romanian. Then stutters, trying to find a phrase he practiced before but can't remember now. He gives up, resorts to pantomime. Holds up a book, pretends to play an instrument while staring at it.

"Sheet music?" Madalina says. Pronouncing the Romanian so he can learn the phrase.

"Yes, sheet music."

"You should try up the street. Anticariat D. Grumăzescu." She points to an antique store maybe ten doors up, on the other side of the street. The American peers up there and nods. Behind him, a university student running to class puts a deep footprint in the cement and hops away, cursing. A bicycle follows thirty seconds later, leaving long snaky trails.

"Thank you," the American says, or at least Constantin and Madalina think he does. Constantin waits until the Americans are halfway up the block.

"Imagine that," he says. "An American speaking Romanian."

"Mm-hmm," Madalina says.

"You ever think about going to America?"

"No."

"How about Germany? When are you going there?"

They've talked about this before. She holds up the book she's had in her lap for the past few weeks, a German-language textbook.

"As soon as I've mastered the language," she says.

Constantin laughs. He knows she's half joking. "You don't need to master the language to go to Germany," he says. "You just need to be able to stumble around it like a drunk at a wedding reception."

"I think I should be a little better than that."

"Why? It's not stopping the Americans."

"Nothing stops the Americans," Madalina says.

Constantin smiles. "Give it time."

By the time the Americans weave out of Anticariat D. Grumăzescu, drunk, full, and caffeinated, the cement in the middle of Pietonalul Lapusneanu is full of footprints, bicycle tracks, the deep trench left by a wheelbarrow tire. A record of every unlucky person who crossed the road that beautiful spring day.

"You know," Constantin says to Madalina, "you really should get out of here."

"But Iasi is such a nice town," she says.

"Sure. But people don't teach themselves German just for the hell of it. Please tell me you have bigger plans for yourself."

She decides to be honest. "Journalism," she says.

Constantin nods. "Be seeing you," he says. But after she leaves Iasi, a few months later, he never sees her again.

You may be wondering why all this matters. Hang in there, reader. We're getting there.

Madalina's in Berlin from 1992 to 1995. Her facility with languages applies to German, and she finds work as a translator, both writing and speaking. She gets involved with some serious journalism, too. Because she can speak both Romanian and Ukrainian—and because she's a woman—she helps a few investigative reporters interview women who have escaped the sex trade. It's hard to hear, hard to make them talk about it. They all thought they were coming for legitimate jobs. Someone told them they could work as maids in hotels, as housecleaners to wealthy clients in Berlin. Someone got them passports and working papers, covered the travel expenses. The women took the offers without asking a lot of questions; they couldn't afford to. They came to Berlin by car, by plane, never realizing anything was wrong until they were led to an apartment somewhere that didn't seem legitimate at all. Then the stories all turn horrible. The constant raping. The beatings. Some of them watched while women who tried to get out were caught and killed, by stabbing, by strangulation. Half of the survivors are sick now, so sick that they don't want to get tested. They know what the results will be. For the first few days of this, Madalina goes home and cries. She has nightmares, a collage of the things she's been told. It's too easy to imagine, to picture herself or her friends from Negostina where those women are now. In the morning, she talks to the reporters. The ones who are men are ashamed of their sex. They know that if there weren't men willing to pay for it, nothing they're investigating—that brutal chain of illicit commerce stretching across Europe, the world— would exist. And it's hard not to notice that it doesn't work the other way around. There's no male sex trade. It's just men brutalizing women, raping and killing in the service of their pleasure, and that horror seems to reveal something: that the long conversation about how there's no real difference between men and women is only half right. When we're at our best, boys, maybe there's no real difference. But at our worst?

Then there's the glimpses the reporters get of the organization that does the trafficking—the same shadows of movement that Kosookyy sees, that the FBI's taking notes on. The chain of sex trafficking is one of many; there's a web, a network, a cloud of connections. Money laundering, pirated goods, fraud, grift. Parting people from their money. Trafficking in drugs, in arms: All those guns the Soviet Union made have been sold off, and now they're spilling across the world, to Africa, to Latin America, ending up in the hands of drug cartels, private militias, revolutionaries, child soldiers. Making the world a more dangerous place. And somewhere underneath all that, organ harvesting, the shadow of a shadow. The reporters know about the documented cases. The organ bazaars in India, local brokers paying people in shantytowns a few thousand dollars to give their kidneys to patients traveling from Oman, the United Arab Emirates, other places in the Middle East; by the early 1990s, it's up to two thousand transplants a year. A law India passes in 1994 makes the organ bazaars illegal, but that just means that it's taken over by organized crime syndicates. They say the trade is as thriving as ever. In 1995, it comes out that China's government has been harvesting body parts from prisoners: kidneys, corneas, liver tissue, heart valves. Sometimes just after they execute the prisoner. Sometimes just before. The organs go to people in China with good political connections, or they're sold somewhere in Asia, for as much as thirty grand. Chinese officials, of course, deny the whole thing, but that gets harder to do in 1998 when two Chinese citizens are caught on videotape offering to sell body parts to doctors in the United States. It's all over the papers, but that doesn't mean it stops.

The stories will continue for years, multiply all over the world. In Brazil, a São Paulo police investigation reveals that the local morgue has taken several thousand pituitary glands from the bodies of poor people and sold them to American medical companies. An anatomy professor in Recife has sold inner ear parts to NASA. A couple German and Austrian medical centers get heart valves taken from the corpses of paupers in South Africa. A clot-dissolving drug has been developed from kidneys taken from dead newborns in a hospital in Colombia; it's unclear whether the parents know, let alone consent. A South African doctor tells a researcher that there's a broker in Southern California who delivers fresh organs, as he calls them, to anywhere in the world in thirty days; clients place their orders by email. In 2002, it's discovered that local kidney hunters recruited three hundred men from poor rural villages in Moldova to sell their kidneys. They're trafficked to Turkey and the United States to do the operation. The men are destitute, don't have what you'd call proper shoes, don't have enough to eat. Nothing left of value but themselves. And then there are the rumors, of people—children—kidnapped and murdered for their eyes, their hearts, across the southern hemisphere and into Eastern Europe. The stories are wild and terrible, hard to prove, but so persistent. There's a market out there for bodies, parts of bodies. Parts of us. It's capitalism taken to its logical end, our complete rendering into a commodity. A dollar amount on just how much we're worth. The market is an animal, and when you let it run free, it eats us. And Madalina, in time, reports on it herself. First she shares bylines with other reporters, but when they, and their editors, realize she can get the story herself, they hire her to do it.

She's written twelve pieces already, under her own name and no one else's, for newspapers, magazines, and advocacy organizations, by the time she goes to Ukraine. She's there because she's been translating for a German telecommunications company that's interested in moving into the Eastern European market. A junior executive there sees that Madalina's more than a word machine. She's smart, and knows things about Romania and Ukraine that he doesn't. So when he gets the account to start business in Kiev, he says he won't go without her. That's how she meets Petey Hightower.

She's in Kureni, a restaurant overlooking the Dneiper. On the table are plates of duck leg and rabbit liver, pike and salmon. She and the junior executive are entertaining a client, a large Ukrainian man with an interest in being a conduit for German investment into Ukraine. He already has a cell phone himself—one of the sleek, new-generation ones that, for 1995, is pretty sophisticated—and he makes a show of having it, leaves it next to his plate while they're talking, has a habit of picking it up and tapping it on the table every time he says the German word for it—*Handy*—which he insists on using. He's still smarting from not being in on the Mobile TeleSystems deal that went down in 1993. He should have been there, he says. He should be raking in the cash now; and Madalina looks again at the cut of his Western European suit, his custom Italian shoes. A man who doesn't want for much. But he wants, she thinks. He wants everything. Then she sees Petey, over the businessman's shoulder, a young man sitting among older men in expensive suits in the VIP section. Everyone at that table's having what even for Ukraine is a little too much vodka, and they're all yelling at each other as drunk men do, in a mixture of Ukrainian, Russian, and English. She's repulsed by them, but not by Petey, his lightning-blue eyes, dark hair combed back like the two photographs from the 1920s of Madalina's relatives that her parents have on the walls of their house in Negostina. Then he sees her and stares back, stops paying attention to everything else around him. She breaks eye contact, returns to her meeting, but when it's done and they're leaving the place, she notices the young man excusing himself from his table, following her out the door from a distance. She pretends that she forgot something in the restaurant she has to go back for. She shakes hands with the Ukrainian businessman, who tells her it was wonderful to meet her and then says something awful to her—*when we close the deal, tell the Germans to send a man.* She doesn't flinch. *Why? Have I misrepresented you? Because one more remark like that and I can start.* The junior executive smiles through the whole thing; he doesn't understand a word. She nods, turns, walks back into the restaurant, and stands in the vestibule. In three seconds Petey is there, a little hazy around the edges, but still looking at her with the same intensity, as strong as it is opaque.

"Do we know each other?" she says in Ukrainian. She's wondering if his interest is romantic or criminal. He doesn't say anything at first, which puts her on guard. She goes through the small conversations she's had with strangers in the past few days, maybe the wrong things she might have said to the wrong people without knowing it. The things she might have been an accidental witness to.

"No," he says at last, and in that single word, she can already hear his American accent, tell how much he doesn't know the language. It's endearing. "I wanted to see you," he says. Extends a tentative hand. "I'm Peter."

"Madalina."

"Can I see you again?"

She smiles, wants to tell him something nice, but is afraid he won't understand what she's trying to say, because his Ukrainian is so bad. So she just digs into her pocketbook for a business card and a pen. Writes her phone number on the back of it and hands it to him.

"Call me," she says. "I like coffee."

He smiles back at her, and she leaves then. Later that night, falling asleep, she can't say quite why she decided to give him a chance. *Look at the kinds of friends he has. Look at the people he's with*, her father would say. *Too ambitious.* But she sees a thing in him that, so far in Petey's life, only his mother and his aunt Sylvie have seen. She looks right through the swaggering, angular young buck, sees the good boy Muriel tried to raise. Just prone to mischief, that's all. She's sure enough of herself to think that she can handle it. He calls the next day.

You know how the story goes. It's first love, for both of them, and it happens fast. Within weeks, they feel like they've discovered a new continent, a new ocean. They've been let in on a giant secret; something about the world has been revealed to them that no one else seems to know, or maybe they've all just forgotten. They look at their friends with pity, because nobody they know can be as happy as they are. By the end of the second month, for each of them, the other seems to give off light, and they transform the city wherever they go. The colors heighten, run together, like it's all a carnival and they're spinning around in it, screaming, laughing, their hands in the air. They're impregnable, they have superpowers. They could jump from the roof of her apartment building and land on their feet, right on the sidewalk, walk to the curb, and hail a bus. They could turn knives into paper, bullets into steam, but they don't have to. No one would dare touch them.

It's only when Petey's Ukrainian gets a little better that Madalina realizes how deep in he might be. Like I said, reader, Madalina's not stupid; it's just that she doesn't imagine that whatever Petey's involved in could be so terrible. She's thinking it's just about money. A little graft, a little corruption. Getting government contracts to do construction, putting up money for a bunch of guys to do half-assed work building fancy new apartment complexes on the highway out of Kiev. The returns come in when the units are sold to foreign corporations for a price that's too high. Or maybe there's a favor called in to someone in the finance ministry in return for a business arrangement in Lviv so exclusive that it amounts to a monopoly. The kind of thing that, as a friend of her father's was fond of saying, is illegal but not a crime. Just the way of the world, the way things get done, among those who understand that the size of your bank account and who you know just might be all that matters. This is what legitimate market economics looks like, right? Government and business working so close together that it looks criminal. The market looked like that when it *was* criminal, she reminds herself, under Ceausescu, under Brezhnev, even under Gorbachev. That was the big lesson of the planned economy, that you can't stop people from buying and selling things how they want to buy and sell them. Telling people how much a loaf of bread is worth from on high is just asking people to walk down the street to buy their bread from a guy selling it out of a van—the guy who bought it all up quick, maybe before it hit the store, because he knew it was worth more than the government was saying. He knew it and he was right. The farce went on for so long that the black marketeers got really good at their jobs. It shouldn't have surprised anyone that they grew so fast when the collapse of communism set them free. It doesn't surprise Madalina. But she isn't prepared to accept that it's gotten so bloody, or that her sweet Petey has it all over him.

She only realizes it after he says the smallest thing. They're in Kiev, in a café with dark wooden beams and strong coffee, and he mentions that he has to get some papers for a shipment his business is conducting. She starts talking about the customs house, about imports and exports—it's her line of work, too. Tariff schedules. Changing regulations. All that sort of thing. But she sees fast that Petey has no idea what she's talking about, none whatsoever, and he can't hide it. He loves her too much, and his Ukrainian isn't good enough to hide his ignorance.

"Petey, what are you investing in here?" she says.

"Import-export stuff," he says.

"But that's what I'm talking about, and you don't seem to understand it."

For a tiny moment, the Petey she's gotten to know is gone. He has a look on his face that's small, and scared. Asking her to leave it alone.

"I don't need to understand everything about it just to invest in it," he says.

"I know that. But don't you feel like you need to know more than you do?"

"No. That's not how it works."

"What does it work on, then?"

He's looking for the word and, this time, finds it. "Trust," he says.

"That's it?" she says.

"That's all market stuff ever is, isn't it?"

He's confident again, smiling. But she can't get that look out of her head. For a few days, she tries to ignore it, to not think all that much about where Petey goes when he's not with her. But it's too much. She's thinking of that man in Berlin. All the girls she interviewed in Berlin, all the girls she knew in Negostina, the ones who weren't as lucky as she was, to be so clever, so quick with language, to have parents like hers. To have anything. There are so many of them, she thinks, all along that border of Romania, Ukraine, and Moldova, and she's heard way too many stories from there to not know how bad things have gotten there. How the open gates to Chisinau, those apartment blocks built as though they were the entrance to a palace on either side of the highway, are more like a broken dam, and the current is raging, pushing people westward. Some of them riding the tide. Some of them being dragged, screaming, under the water. Coming apart against the rocks.

So Madalina tells Petey that she has a day off, says she's just going to spend it at home, but then follows him instead. It all seems innocuous. Lunches, coffee, dinner, vodka. Petey doesn't seem to do much of anything. Then there's a conversation with a man who moves his hands as he speaks with great deliberation, as if meaning's a solid thing, a weight resting in his open palms. Petey leaves this last appointment weaving a little—the vodka's still a little much for him—and he and the man exchange a slow handshake that gives Madalina the impression that maybe Petey's not sure what kind of deal he just closed, but the other man is under no illusions. Her poor American boy. One too many generations, a little too much money and capitalism, too many pop songs and TV commercials, between him and the place where his family is from for him to read the fine print written all over the streets, the movements of limbs, the pursing of lips, the long silences where people just breathe. We're a wolf, she thinks, and you're just a small boy.

She's about to go home when she feels a hand on her shoulder, not warm. She flinches and wheels. It's a man with a close-cropped haircut, a leather jacket, slacks. The gangster uniform. His eyes travel over her, linger at each part, before he nods a few times. A faint smile, approving. There's nothing sexual in his gaze at all, and that makes it worse.

"You're the American's girl," he says in a hitched Ukrainian that suggests it's his third or fourth language.

"Who are you?" she says.

He goes by the nickname Pocketknife, because he does a little of everything. But he's not going to tell her that. He switches to a more, but not quite, fluent Romanian. She realizes she has no idea what nationality the man is, which means the costume isn't just going along with the crowd. He wants her to know what's up.

"Did he forget something at home today?" he says.

"I'm not going to play this game with you," she says.

"Good. Then I can just tell you that we are going to kill you. You and your American boy, because you have connections to journalists that we do not want to be that close to. You are even a journalist yourself. So you are as good as dead already. Maybe we will kill the other man, too, his friend, if he talks. Would you like to know how we will kill you?"

"No."

"I think you will be very interested to know. Because there is a lot on you—*in* you, in fact—that can be very useful for us. That we need to kill you is a matter of course. But since you appear to be in excellent health—do you smoke?—we will be able to get excellent prices. Your lungs. Your liver. Your kidneys. Your eyes. Perhaps even your heart. It has many more years of life left in it."

He says it like he's just passing along information, something that's been decided somewhere else. She doesn't know why he's telling her, when he knows she'll have to act on it. *Why is it better to have told me?* she says. *Why do they want me to run?* She's hoping that maybe all they want is for she and Petey to disappear, that being out is as good as being dead. She can't see the whole scheme; it's a huge machine that stretches far and away, too far for her to take it all in at once from where she's standing. But she understands she doesn't have a choice. Staying in Kiev is now a kind of suicide, and there's only one place she can go.

"You're very pretty," the tall man says. "Even in my line of work, I can still appreciate such things."

Petey comes to her apartment well after dark, finds her packing a few of his clothes into a backpack. A small bag for herself already on the floor.

"Why did you come here?" she says.

"To your apartment?"

"No, no. To Kiev. To Ukraine. Why did you do it?"

She's so angry. The man is right: She already knows the answer. But she wants the question to hurt, to carry all her shock, all her disappointment. Her terror at what she's gotten involved in.

"What are you talking about?" he says, but his voice is already shaking.

"Do you really think I'm that stupid?"

"No."

"You must think I'm an idiot to say something like that."

"No, I don't. I love you, Madalina. I love you."

"Those two things have nothing to do with each other."

She sounds like her own father, Madalina thinks, at their last dinner in Negostina. She sees it now, in her head: her father, Claudiu, trying so hard not to show how scared he is that he comes out looking angry. His hand shaking when he lifts a fork. He drinks too much to try to steady his hand, but it only makes him sloppy. Soon they are yelling at each other. *This world,* the father says, *will eat you alive now.*

Yes, she says, *because everything under Ceausescu was so much better.* She winces as she says it, knows her father doesn't need the history lesson. He has the dead friends to remind him of it all the time. Her father gets quiet, and she's more scared of him then than she's ever been in her life. But he's just trying to warn her.

At least under Ceausescu, he says, *you knew how you were getting fucked. Now, you will never know, until it's far too late.*

Petey just never looked that hard at what he was doing, Madalina realizes. But now she's prying his eyelids open, forcing him to take a good long stare. And he has no idea what to do.

"We have to leave," she says to Petey. "We have to get out of here."

"Where are we going to go?" His voice rises and falls like a little boy's. It's something she's doing, how she's holding herself, a tone she's taking. He's shocked all over again, the same shock she's seen a hundred times in the backpackers and college students from Western Europe and America who come here. Some of them, of course, are oblivious. They're here just for the cheap alcohol, the license for debauchery that they seem to think being in a foreign country gives them. Or they're here because they're fascinated. They want to know just what on earth went on here during the Cold War, which, she understands, the hipsters are already turning into kitsch. Or maybe they don't have anything in their heads but fairy tales and monster stories. They know about Transylvania only because of Dracula. Imagine that maybe, just maybe, the Roma are dressed like the pirates in children's books, riding around in caravans drawn by donkeys, telling fortunes and doing tricks with knives. They're imagining craziness, absurdity. They read Bulgakov and get some of the jokes, but don't see the darkness for what it is. She doesn't know what they think. But whatever it is, it doesn't prepare them for what's here. They spend the first day inside, on their beds, staring out the window. Come out the next day trying to hide the guidebook they've shoved in their pocket, their lips moving in silence. They can't get through the easiest phrases. Can't say a word. Can't get their heads around what it is to be there, to see what history has done, what the people are doing now. And her Petey, who she thought knew a little more than that, is turning into one of them, right in front of her.

"Madalina?" he says. "Can you get me out?" In a voice so tiny that she wants to take him in her arms, put his head to her chest, and tell him everything's going to work out fine. Either that or bury the claw end of a hammer in his skull.

"We just have to leave," she says. "Tonight."

She's getting even angrier. *I had plans,* she wants to tell him. *Good plans.* It was going to be just a few more years of business translation, to save up enough to live on for a couple years if she was careful. She was more than halfway there. Then she was going back to school to do journalism, to be the people she was translating for back in Berlin. She was going to show the world what a few bad men were doing, and maybe get them to stop. At least alert them that the days of impunity were over. That someone was watching them, and had a big megaphone.

But it's more than that, because the truth is that, here in Kiev, with Petey, up until today, she was happier than she's ever been; happier, maybe, than she ever thought she'd be. And it isn't just Petey, but the city. The sense of a giant, waking up. She sees it in the way they're renovating the old parts of the city near the center, blasting the paint off the brick and putting a new coat on, gutting the insides and rebuilding them. Recobbling the streets. In the heart of Kiev, Stalin pulled down the twelfth-century church and monastery of St. Michael's in the 1930s, but they're putting it back together already; the money came together so fast, and in just a few years, it'll be back, as though nothing had happened. Even if it's only a symbol, it's Ukrainians undoing what Stalin had done. They can't bring all the people they lost back to life, but they can bring back some of the things they loved.

But Madalina also just loves the city for what it is. The bright, bright days that turn the dust in the air into light. The beaches along the Dneiper at the Hidropark, where men fish in the early spring before the summer starts and the sunbathers come. The merry-go-round perched on the edge of a cliff high over the river, under the titanium Friendship Arch. Her own neighborhood, beyond the university. The old accordion player in front of the Taras Shevchenko metro stop, across the street from the lawn of a blue factory three stray dogs have claimed as their own. Her little apartment on Mezhyhirska Street. In the square in the middle of the apartment complex on Shchekavytska, there's an old, abandoned building there that's already lost its windows and its roof, and the apartment buildings themselves look like they're rusting where they stand. But in the square, families relax in the sun, pushing babies back and forth in strollers. An old man struts by in a neon gym suit. Another man in a dirty T-shirt plants trees. Children in green and orange coats climb on a red and yellow playground. A mom hoists up a kid in a pink suit so she can grab the monkey bars. Orthodox Jewish kids in black and white clothes dart in and out among the hip young things in leather jackets, tight jeans, striped scarves. The air's filled with the smell of roasting meat, as though the square were a village; maybe it is, and she just didn't stay long enough to meet everyone. In another park, the basketball court's asphalt looks like a flash-frozen ocean; it bucks from erosion and frost, and the square on the backboard of the basketball net is hand-drawn. But kids are playing the game all the same. At the trolley stop on the corner, the concrete slabs of the sidewalk are tilted at insane angles, like they've been hit by an earthquake. Two teenagers are skateboarding on them, having the time of their lives. In the huge market building on Verkhnii Val Street, the side stalls are filled with clothes, linens. People grind keys, sell power tools and leather belts, woven baskets and flowers. In the middle, the air is rank with meat, poultry, and fish, cheese and onions. Men and women bark out numbers, haggle over prices, while pigeons roost in the rafters above them. The electric trolleys squeal as they spark around corners, wheeze with every stop and start, and there's scaffolding over everything, offices and apartment buildings, so that you're never sure if they're fixing things or taking them out. She'll miss all of it, and doesn't want to leave, but she doesn't have any choice. And Petey is to blame.

"Tonight, Petey," she says.

"I need to see Curly first."

She glares. "How long?"

"A day."

"Two hours."

"Okay. Okay. Two hours."

He's back in three. She's just shaking her head at him.

"I came this close to leaving without you," she says.

"I couldn't find him. Also, I got a little lost," he says. His first impulse is to smile, but then she looks at him in a way he's never seen before. *Did I just lose her?* he thinks. *Will she ever love me again?* Concerned, all of a sudden, about the future of his heart. Not hers. He tries to kiss her, but she pushes him back.

"Are you crazy?" she says. "We have to go. Now."

But they've already waited too long. There are two cars on either side of the block, idling. Three men each inside. They all watch Petey and Madalina come out of her building; their eyes follow them to Madalina's car. She gets in on the driver's side, Petey on the passenger side. She starts the car, turns east. One car pulls out so it's in front of them. The other comes up behind. They wait until they're on a smaller street, just a couple blocks from the road that skirts the river. Then the car in front stops short, the car in back pulls up quick. Petey sees what's happening a second before Madalina does, and reader, he does something then that will be almost impossible for him to live with afterward. He doesn't say anything, doesn't give Madalina any warning: Before she can stop the car, he opens the door, jumps out, and is off, down an alleyway, into the dark. Two of the thugs who see him bolt run after him, but they can't find him. They have Madalina, though. She doesn't so much scream as shout. *You sons of bitches. You fucking animals.* She lunges and bites one of them when he gets too close, hard enough to take out some of the muscle at the base of his thumb. His hand won't work right ever again after that. Then she spins around, digs her nails straight across a second man's face. Those stripes will still be on him when he dies. But there are four of them and one of her.

Madalina's alive after that for longer than you might think, but not much longer. Too long for what they make her live through. They've got a truck parked on the outskirts of the city, rigged up to be a mobile operating room. When she sees the inside of it—the table, the straps, the set of tools, the coolers and ice lining the wall—she knows what they're going to do. She defies them to the end, screaming, cursing, kicking, turning every shock of pain into anger, until at last they have to shoot her to finish the job.

Chapter 6

Sylvie is in her garden, hands in the soil, clearing out the overgrowth from last year before it comes back, when she spots Muriel's car on the gravel driveway. *Driving a little faster than usual,* she thinks. She stands and claps most of the dirt off her hands, wipes the rest of it onto her gardening apron. Walks through the garden to meet the car at the front door of the house. Watches Peter get out on the passenger side, give the house a quick, cool appraisal. No more gaping at the wealth like he did years ago. *The boy in him is just about gone,* she thinks. *There's no fooling him anymore.*

"Peter," she says. "So nice to see you."

"Hi, Aunt Sylvie."

"You're grown up now. It's just Sylvie. I'd give you a hug but I'm a little dirty. Why don't both of you come inside? Then give me a minute to change."

The parlor overlooking the lake looks the same as it did when Peter was there as a child, as a teenager. Just older. Faded flowers on the upholstery, a web of cracks in the ceiling, the paint pocking outward, chipping away. Sylvie comes back downstairs, goes in the kitchen to make tea. Muriel's going on about things that happened in the parlor when she was a child. A fight between her parents over a family dog. Her father saying the dog was too small. *It's not a real dog,* he said. *It's half a dog.* Her mother wanting to keep it. Another time they were having a party, and she spilled raspberry sauce all over the carpet, and the stain wouldn't come out. *It looks like we shot someone in here,* her father said. Her mother just putting on a smile and shaking her head. *You shouldn't say things like that around the children.* Loving the whole man, but hating so much about him. A game of pirates among all the siblings, even Jackie, that broke a leg on the couch after it was boarded one too many times. The very same couch Peter's sitting on right now; if he were to push on the armrest closest to the kitchen door, he could still make the leg creak. Muriel thinks she knows what Sylvie's going to tell him after she leaves—though she doesn't know the half of it—and she wants to give him this one simple idea, that they are family, still, no matter what. She hopes that it survives after Sylvie's finished.

"A lot of ghosts in this house, Peter," Muriel says.

"Memories, Muriel," Sylvie says. A tray in her hands, tea and small sandwiches. Correction in her voice, swathed in so much gentleness, but there's no mistaking the hardness underneath. "Memories. We can't be ghosts if most of us are still alive."

That's Muriel's cue to go; she doesn't have to look at the tray to know that there's only enough for two on it. She makes a small show of how busy she is, how many errands she has to run. She'll be back before dinner, would that be all right?

"I'll call you," Sylvie says. Shows her to the door. They give each other a long hug on the threshold, Sylvie patting Muriel's back. Muriel thinks Peter can't hear them from the parlor. Sylvie knows he can.

"It's never going to be all right," Muriel says. Muffles a sob on Sylvie's shoulder.

"There, there," Sylvie says. "We'll find out where Petey is." She comes back to the parlor looking the same as she did when she left—none of Muriel's tears, or even Henry's caution—and Peter, there on the couch, realizes that maybe Sylvie, who never seems to leave her house, to interact with the world in any real way, is the toughest one in the family. Tougher than Muriel, than his father. Tougher even than Henry. As if her brothers and sisters have done so much because Sylvie lets them.

She sits on the sofa across from him, back straight. Picks up her tea and takes a sip. Then looks at Peter and doesn't blink.

"Now," she says, "you and I both know Petey's in a lot of trouble."

"Yes."

"And how that means you are, too."

"Uh-huh."

She shakes her head, looks up at the ceiling. "Oh, Rufus, Rufus," she says. Then back at Peter. "We have a lot to talk about. A lot. But business first, yes?"

Yes? She lets that last word fly on purpose, lets the accent come out, the transformation begin. To Peter, it's as if the room has darkened, and Sylvie's calm moves from solace to menace. All those things she knows but doesn't say. The people she could destroy, Peter thinks, just by telling someone else what they told her. Just by speaking.

"First of all," she says, "Petey's in Ukraine. Or at least he was as of a few days ago. Maybe he's somewhere else now, but I'd bet he hasn't gotten far. I'm sorry you came all this way, because if you were hoping to find him, I can't imagine he's come back here. What he's involved in, Peter, is about as bad as it gets."

Peter takes a breath, and then asks.

"How do you know?" he says.

Sylvie glances toward the window, as if to make sure that nobody else is there, though she knows they're alone. "Because, Peter," she says, "I am involved myself, and have been for decades. I took over from your grandfather before he was dead. Do you want specifics?" She's expecting him to say no. But he nods instead.

"I don't know whether I should be proud of you or think you're an idiot," she says. "Once I tell you, you don't get to go back, do you understand?"

"Tell me," Peter says.

"Fine. It begins with money laundering—the same amateur bullshit your stupid cousin started with—but moves quickly to financing, and a lot of it. On the domestic side of things, it's not so bad. It's graft, extortion, real estate swindles, bribes. A little drugs. A little prostitution."

A little prostitution? But Peter holds himself together. "What about the international side?"

"Ah yes, Eastern Europe. Well, there things are uglier. You hear some big-shot investment bankers saying it's like the Wild West over there? It's way wilder than that. The shackles on the market—the market for everything—are off. The animals are loose. Buying the government and industry, what they used to call the commanding heights of the economy, is just the beginning of it. It ends in drug running, arms deals, a flood of weapons from Eastern Europe and the former Soviet republics to just about everywhere else in the world. Human trafficking." She waits a second to say the last thing. "Organ harvesting."

She can tell Peter's shocked. She keeps going. "I got in early and made the right friends," she says, "friends on all sides of every deal, and Peter, I have made a fortune, more than I ever thought possible, though you'd never know it to look at how I keep this place up, I know. Must keep up appearances as an aging dowager, someone who's not sure what she's doing. And I've been keeping it for other things. Perhaps, as it turns out, this thing."

She takes a sip of tea. "Your cousin got in later and is, to just put this in plain English, a dumb fuck. The dumbest fuck. He's gotten us all in more trouble than I can contain. I tried, but I can't do it. It started just because Petey fell in love with a woman who was connected to journalists, researchers, people who were investigating the activities that he himself was involved in."

"That seems like a flimsy reason to want someone dead," Peter says.

"It does, doesn't it," Sylvie says. "But life? It has a different value over there right now. And Petey should have known that. But he didn't, so he handled the situation very badly. If he wanted a girlfriend so much, he should have checked up on her before he decided to get involved, or at least very soon after, and he should have dumped her as soon as he found out what her past was. But he didn't. Then, when they came for her, he should have had the good sense to die with her—I'm sorry, does that sound harsh? It's the game they're playing, Peter, and nobody forced your cousin to join in. If he had just let them kill him then and there, for his mistake in letting some journalists, and therefore the authorities, get too close, we would all be able to go about our lives. But he didn't, and because they don't know where he's gone and don't trust him to keep his mouth shut, at all, they're not taking any chances. They're coming for all of us now, it seems. Which means I only have a couple of moves left."

Peter's scalp is blazing; the hair on his neck and arms is standing up. It pulses through him in wave after wave.

"Do you want something to drink?" she says.

"I want to call the police," Peter says.

"For what?" Sylvie says, and Peter flinches inside. It occurs to him that he's just threatened a dangerous criminal. Then realizes that Sylvie's just asking; she's way too smart to have told him anything she doesn't want him to know. "There's no case yet," she says. "Right now, all there is to the authorities are people who have been lost track of. They're not considered missing yet. There are Petey and his girlfriend in Ukraine." She softens. "I don't even know her name. Then there's a friend of Petey's, Curly, whom no one has seen in a few days. He's missing here, in Cleveland. I suppose you would be missing too, Peter, if anyone were sure you existed in the first place."

"But I'm here."

"I know that, honey." She's getting a little meaner again now. "But almost no one else does. Just your family and whoever's been put on the case of tracking you down since you left Spain in such a hurry."

"So what do we do?"

"Well," Sylvie says, "if I were you, the first thing I'd do is find your father. If they can't find you, they'll go after him to try to get to you. You might as well be a step ahead of them, to give Rufus time to get ready."

Now Peter doesn't say anything.

"What?" she says. Then the ice-cold criminal who was just sitting there, the one who rules an empire of carnage, disappears, and the aunt, the one who gardens and makes tea, comes back. "Oh. Oh, Peter. How long has it been since you've seen him?"

He still doesn't know what to say.

"You know where he is, right?"

"Yes," Peter says.

"That means they know where he is, too."

"Don't be so sure," he says. He knows he's out of line as soon as he says it. Sylvie gives Peter a look that makes him wish she'd shot him instead. It might have been better that way.

"I'm sorry," he says.

"You're sorry?" she says. Now she gives him a tiny smile. "That's the first time I've ever heard a Hightower man say that. Maybe there's hope for us yet."

She takes a sip of tea. "You know that a few men with guns visited your uncle Henry last night?" she says. "Oh, don't worry, he's all right. But he's all right because he convinced them that you weren't there. Which is why you should leave tomorrow. I can't protect you from the people I think are coming for you, at least not here. I think you can stay here tonight. Please do. But be out by morning. Get to your father."

"How much does he know about this?"

"Not everything," Sylvie says. "But enough to know what kind of trouble we're in."

"About that," Peter says. "You said you only have a few moves left. What are you going to do?" he says.

She looks at the ceiling, and the expression on her face, so cold, capable of such manipulation, makes Peter as scared as he's been since he left Granada.

"Tell me again why we aren't just calling the police," he says.

She turns to him, her voice sharp. "We are, Peter. Just not quite yet. Because I want to fix this. Fix it for good."

"What are you talking about?"

She smiles. "You'll find out."

In the morning, she gives him a stack of bills—*don't argue with me, just get to the airport,* she says—and calls Muriel.

"Drive fast," Sylvie says to her. Peter's in the car already.

"This is going to ruin us," Muriel says.

"Muriel, honey. We're already ruined." She doesn't have to say what she means; Muriel wants to act hurt for bringing it up, but thinks better of it and nods. Because for all the children of Peter Henry Hightower, the past is always crashing into the present. Like I said before, it's what binds them all together and what drives them apart. Over the years, each of them has thought that's a little unfair, that what happened before can still affect them so much, when they can't go back and change it, and none of the five siblings have been able to talk about it. But over dinner and after it, before Peter's left, Sylvie's told him everything. All the things his grandfather did, and how the family staggered away from his death. By now, dear reader, you should know it too. Ready?

It's 1966. The riots are over in Hough, but the National Guard hasn't pulled out yet. Everyone's waiting for Cleveland to catch fire again. Peter Henry Hightower, the first, the benefactor, the rat bastard, has been dead for a week. A tiny funeral. A burial. Not in Lake View, where the Van Sweringens ended up, along with James A. Garfield, Eliot Ness, John D. Rockefeller, and those poor kids from the Collinwood school fire, all in a mass grave together. Not in the Ukrainian Catholic cemetery in Parma, either. No, in accordance with his will, he's put down in Riverside Cemetery, as close to Tremont as he can get. Next to his mother, in the plot he bought for them all years ago. An uncommon sunny day, one of the twelve of the year. The hospital's visible through the trees, just across the highway; the traffic is far enough away to sound like the ocean, like wind. It's an unassuming grave, no more elaborate than the stones around it. A man coming home to his people, whether they want him or not. The priest says the prayers right, has some nice words to say, almost as if he knew the guy, but he admits that Peter Henry Hightower didn't make it to church very often in the twentieth century. Just three of his children are there—Muriel, Sylvie, and Henry, who flew out to see his father pass. Rufus said he would make it, but he didn't, and they think it'll all just be too upsetting for Jackie to be there, though in hindsight, maybe they should have let her come. Michael Rizzi, Sylvie's future husband, accompanies the family; four men no one in the family knows are also there, who don't say a word. They stand on the other side of the grave while the priest speaks. Put their fingers to their lips, then to the coffin, before they lower it down. Then there's Stefan, Peter Henry Hightower's brother, whom Henry doesn't recognize; he hasn't seen him in decades, though Stefan's been caring for Jackie for years. But Stefan recognizes him at once, him and everyone else. He tells them how good it is to see them all, then stands on the plot next to where Peter Henry Hightower is buried, where he knows he'll be soon enough.

Afterward, the children of Peter Henry Hightower assemble at the house in Bratenahl to read the will. Henry, Muriel, and Sylvie get there first. Sylvie's bustling around the house, getting the dining room ready; she's the only one who knows where anything is anymore. Muriel's trying to be pleasant, but it's too awkward to work. She keeps bringing up small topics that go nowhere. *We're thinking of moving to the West Coast,* she says. *Maybe San Diego. They say the weather is perfect there.* Sylvie just wants to go to her, take her hand. *Our father's dead, dear, and now we have to carve up what's left of him. It's okay not to pretend it's okay right now.* Henry doesn't have a problem with not pretending. He's been living in New York for a few years, works in finance. He's picked up a cigarette habit that's inches from chain-smoking; he switches between pacing the parlor, shooting glances out the window—*when is Jackie going to be here? Where's Rufus?*—and going out to the long porch overlooking the lake to light a cigarette, smoke it fast, and with one hand, flick the butt into the ashtray on the metal coffee table while the other goes for the rest of the cigarettes in his jacket pocket. Sylvie watches him smoke two cigarettes that way, then come back in again, stare out the window for the car that isn't coming.

"Where the fuck is Sonny Bono? Where the fuck is he?"

"Remember where Rufus is coming from," Sylvie says.

"He missed his own father's funeral, Sylvie. Of course he'll show up to collect his cut of the winnings, but he doesn't even have the decency to be on time for it."

"That's a little harsh, isn't it?"

"I don't know. Is it?"

"He's not late yet."

"No, but he will be. And why do you have so much sympathy for him, anyway? I've never understood that."

"Henry," Sylvie says, "maybe you should stop talking before I'm forced to say something uncharitable."

He turns to her, his eyes sharpen. *Uncharitable?* She can smell the cigarettes on him, read in the way he stands how much stress he's under. A man who works eighteen hours a day, makes so much but has to spend so much too, it's what the job demands, the English collars, the Italian shoes. *Dad never had to do this,* Henry can't help thinking. He's feeling a little sorry for himself, and it's making him a little sloppy. He goes on. *The money he made was his, not theirs*—you know, *them,* the owners of this place—*but we don't live in days when quick fortunes can be made.* That was their father's life, he thinks, and maybe it will be the lives of their children, their grandchildren, but it won't be theirs. That's the price of affluence and stability now: You decide to make your money yourself instead of just living off what you already have, you try to do the honorable thing, but it's so much harder than it was that you'll never measure up to what your parents accomplished. And Henry resents it, resents how he feels like he has to apologize to his father, as if the reason they couldn't see eye to eye was because the son didn't make as much, couldn't build the empire his father did. Henry never saw the respect behind his father's abuse, the taunts, the goading; only felt the hurt. Peter Henry Hightower made his namesake the executor of his estate because he trusted his oldest son to do it right. But his son only feels the burden.

Jackie arrives in Stefan's care; he pulls the car up to the front door, lets the engine idle for a moment before turning it off. Opens the back door for her to get out, then takes her by the arm. She's a little unsteady walking through the door; *it's her medication,* Stefan says. *It's making her a little confused.* He doesn't say how confused she'd be without it. Sylvie takes her other arm and they lead her to the couch. Take off her shoes, put her feet up on a sun-bleached floral ottoman. Stefan still hasn't lost his Ukrainian accent. Never will now.

"I need something to drink," Jackie says. "Water. Or juice." Henry takes a look at her and goes outside on the porch, where he vanishes in the growing dark; then there's just the spark from his lighter, the pulsing glow from the latest cigarette, being dragged to a column of ash before he drops it to the patio. His foot mashes it out while his fingers fumble for another one. It's been dark and raining for an hour when Rufus arrives at last, his hair slicked onto his head, his shirt soaked enough to see the stained undershirt he's wearing below it. A pair of pants so heavy with water they're sliding off his narrow hips.

"I'm so sorry," Rufus says. "So sorry I missed everything."

He staggers a little and it occurs to Henry that he might be high. Then Henry sees how much Sylvie beams, so happy to see him, high or not, and all the old resentment, the jealousies of childhood, come back all over again. Henry, always the oldest and acting it. A little adult by the age of six, when the next one, Sylvie, came along. Rufus came less than two years later, Muriel a year and a half after that. Henry was thirteen by the time Jackie was born, his voice dropping already. He could see that Jackie wasn't just eccentric. Everyone could. There was something in her, going on in her head; she walked like the ground was always moving under her, screamed for no reason they could see. She talked to people who weren't there, and she wasn't pretending. Her favorite doll went missing and she swore it was the birds who took it; they found her in the yard, angry, throwing rocks at them, yelling at them to give it back. *I was too old to have another child,* he remembers his mother saying afterward. Muriel screamed, too, but with her it was always something. A friend had said a mean thing, or a boy had done a mean thing. Henry can still remember her sharp voice in the hallway upstairs—*I am never speaking to her again*—and then her feet stomping down the hall, a door slamming shut. Then the crying, angry crying, though of a kind that burned fast and wiped her out. He can remember her bright blue coat against Joe Rizzi's arm, there in the front yard. That night she slept for twelve hours, and his father's rage was like a razor, quiet and precise. Someone was going to pay.

But what Henry remembers most are Sylvie and Rufus out in the garden—it looked so different when their mother tended it, a little deeper, a little darker. The two children chasing each other around down the paths their mother had made, playing hide-and-seek, then stopping their running to just talk to each other. Rufus standing in the middle of the path, the sun in his dark hair. Sylvie leaning against a huge old tree. At first yelling to each other. Then Rufus would walk closer and their voices got quieter. In the end, they would be crouching in the myrtle, side by side, their hands in the dirt. Far away from the rest of them. Or they would go out of sight of the house altogether, and their worried mother would send Henry out to fetch them. He'd find them in the carriage house, or at the lakeshore. Always close together, talking in low voices. Stopping whatever they were doing as soon as they heard him; he never saw what they were up to. It was like that for years between them, and when they became teenagers—Sylvie stayed in more and more while they had trouble keeping Rufus from hopping buses to the next state—they had a connection no one else in the family had. As if they spent so little time together because they didn't have to anymore, to be that close. Henry envied that bond so much, still envies it today, even as he winces with the memory of the rancid self-pity that made him think he didn't have that with anyone because he was the oldest, always having to act even older than he was. He knows now that it's not that simple, that maybe he's not built to be so close to anyone. But it doesn't take away the sting.

They sit at the family table in the dining room, and except for Henry, they all take the chairs they had as children. Stefan takes the foot, where their mother used to be, next to Jackie. Henry takes the head. He looks them all over, all that's left of this family. None of his siblings are married, maybe never will be. *For Jackie, it's almost certain,* he thinks. *Who would volunteer for that? Who will care for her if she goes last?* Just the sort of thing that, if he said it out loud, Sylvie would shake her head over. It doesn't matter. He looks down at the papers in front of him and begins.

"Thank you all for coming," he starts, already wishes he hadn't said that. *You're not at a goddamn board meeting.* "It's so good to see you all, even though it's grief that brings us together." His internal critic raging now, because he hates it when people talk like that to him, doesn't understand why he's doing it to them.

"As you all know," he says, "our father has left it to me to be the executor of his last will and testament, and I'll try to carry out what I think he wanted to the best of my abilities." He can see how Rufus is already looking him, a little concerned, a little amused. Like a boy watching a mouse try to sneak up on a trap. He thinks it before he can stop himself: *Asshole. If he says a word.* "In his final months, weeks, and days, Dad and I talked a lot about how this might go. About what he wanted for all of us. There was some discussion," Henry says—and here he looks at Sylvie; *please don't contradict me now,* his eyes say, *we just need to get through this,* and Sylvie nods—"some discussion, in his final weeks and days, about whether the assets remaining to him should be made, um, more liquid, so as to carry out his wishes with greater ease. But in the end it was determined that perhaps it was better to leave everything as it was, so that, once the monetary lots were established, those of us who were more interested in things other than strict money could perhaps put their, uh," he looks for a better word, can't find it, "allowance toward, say, one of Dad's cars. Or his liquor collection."

He's hoping to get a laugh from that. Nobody gives it to him.

"How are these lots, as you call them, determined?" Rufus says.

"I'm getting to that, I'm getting to that." He's thumbing through the papers, can't find the one he wants. He's more nervous now than he's ever been at his job. The editor in him notes that, if he acted like this in front of one of his clients, his boss would fire him. At last, he finds the numbers he needs.

"Considering how we all grew up, um, the opportunities available to us as children, it may surprise you how much is left. It's a substantial amount, but not as much as you might expect."

"How much?" Rufus says.

Henry's eyes meet his brother's; he puts everything he has into that look and says the number in a voice that makes his brother look away.

"Is that all?" Muriel says.

"The last decade was unkind to the estate," Henry says. "As you know, so much of the money was tied up in the city. And look at the city right now."

"That's not funny," Muriel says.

"I'm not laughing," Henry says. With the numbers in front of him, his home turf, he's on the offensive now. "And on top of a number of investments that could have performed better, there were the medical expenses to consider." Nobody asks for clarification, whether he's talking about their father's illness or Jackie's.

But Jackie doesn't understand how they're trying to protect her. "I haven't taken any family money since last year," she says, "and that was just for—just for . . ." She's lost the trail of her sentence, lost herself in the woods. Her uncle lays a hand on her shoulder. She's been in and out of institutions since 1961. She hasn't been put away for good yet, but she will be soon.

"It's okay, Jackie, nobody's blaming you," Muriel says.

"Blaming me for what?" Jackie says.

"Um."

"For what?"

"Nothing, sweetie," Sylvie says. "Your sister misspoke."

"No she didn't," Jackie says.

"Yes, I did," Muriel says. "I did."

"Who's Miss Spoke?" Jackie says.

"Can we continue?" Henry says.

"Yes," Sylvie says. "Let's."

"Excellent," Henry says. Turns to another sheet of paper. "The most important aspect of our father's holdings is that, due to our decision to retain them in their current forms, the estate is quite illiquid."

"What does that mean, Henry?" Muriel says.

"There isn't a lot of cash involved, Muriel. It's all tied up in things. Bonds. Cars. Art—that's from Mom. Ahh. Real estate. And some of that is spoken for already. There's a series of trust funds set up for our children and future children, which they'll come into when they're eighteen. There's more in that pot than you might expect, and I'm assuming none of you would begrudge our father for that. But it makes dividing up our own share of the inheritance a little complicated. It doesn't sound that way in the documentation, though, which reads, quote, I wish what remains of the estate to be distributed to my surviving children in as equitable a manner as possible, unquote."

He waits. Takes a breath. He's feeling pretty good, like he has the room under control. Entertains the idea that maybe if he says what he needs to say in just the right way, they'll have this wrapped up in less than an hour, and then they can all go home. He says: "Now, *equitable* is an interesting word, but I think it's reasonable to say that, given the kind of man our father was, what he meant was *equal*. Such an interpretation would give each of us around one-fifth of the estate—after fees and taxes, of course, and depending on the market value of so many of the assets—which we would best arrive at by making the estate liquid and just dividing it by five."

"Again, Henry," Muriel says.

"He means sell everything and take the money," Rufus says.

"Well, I wouldn't put it quite like that," Henry says.

"I know. You didn't." Rufus says. *You must love this,* Henry thinks. *So many opportunities to be clever.*

"Do you mind if I ask you a few questions?" Rufus says.

Yes, Henry thinks. *I mind. I mind a lot.* "Of course not," he says.

"Well, first of all, how much is this house worth now?" Rufus says.

"Well," Henry says, "we've done a few appraisals, and research into comparable properties, so how much the house is worth isn't as clear as I'd like it to be."

"Ballpark," Rufus says.

Henry gives him the number.

"That's more than one-fifth of the part of the estate we're dividing among us, right?" Rufus says.

"Yes."

"So the first thing that happens under your equitable plan is that we—"

"Yes. Lose this house," Henry says. He won't let Rufus say it, however he would have put it. *Sell out our sister. Put Sylvie on the street. There's still time to salvage this,* he thinks. *Still a chance to bring it around.*

"And the second thing is that this means you get as much as Jackie does," Rufus says.

Henry glares at his brother, hates him now like he did when they were kids. Hates how Jackie's such a convenient proxy for himself. *At least Jackie has an excuse for being so down-and-out,* Henry wants to say. *She's insane. What's your excuse, Rufus?* It's the same shit all over again, he thinks. Henry always has to carry the burden, and there's Captain Kangaroo in his linen shirt, pointing and criticizing. Never bothering himself to help.

"Well, yes. That's what equitable means," Henry says. "In this case."

Rufus looks around the room, and Henry, in his anger, could swear he sees his brother smile, though it's not clear that's what happens.

"Raise your hand," Rufus says, "if you think equitable doesn't mean equal, but fair."

Muriel raises her hand. "I think we need to talk about this," she says.

Henry tries one last move. "What do we need to talk about, Muriel?" he says.

"Why did you just say my name like that?"

"I'm sorry. What do you want to say?"

"That Rufus is right, it just doesn't seem fair somehow to split everything even-steven."

"Why?"

"Because of how things are," Muriel says.

"What do you mean?" Henry says.

"She means," Rufus says, "that's it's very easy for you to say that everything should be even when you have so much more than everyone else. What's wrong with you, Henry? Don't you ever see regular people anymore?"

In that next second, Henry would do anything to go back to the beginning. To have them all sitting at the table, and him walking into the room, the papers under his arms. He would start everything over. Say different things. Maybe offer a different deal. No: He wants to go back even farther, to the days when he first started making serious money—not serious money by his father's standards, but by anyone else's standards, very serious. He wants to take his younger self by the hand and force him to be more generous. To send money to Jackie. To at least call, call more often. To ask after Rufus, let his brother know that if there's anything he ever needs, any way Henry can help, he's there. He wants to tell them he's sorry, he wants to try again, all of it, all over again. Because in the back of his head, he always knew this day was coming. That they would be at this table, slicing up what was left of their father's body, and there was no way it wasn't going to be bloody.

By the end of the night, it's all out. Things with Muriel and her boyfriend aren't going so great. They need money. Neither of them can think straight anymore. Sylvie doesn't say a word, but Rufus is doing all the arguing for her. *How can you take this house away from her?* Henry's not about to put up with any of that. *That's funny,* he says, *you talking about responsibility. Look at you, Pancho Villa over there. You just traipse off to Africa, leave us all behind, without a shred of responsibility to anyone, and then come back here just in time to tell everyone else how wrong they are.* Henry's gagging on the superiority. *How dare you come in here and talk to me about regular people. When's the last time you even had a job?*

He knows how to hurt his brother and does it. *I don't need to justify my lifestyle to you,* Rufus says, mustache quivering. *You don't?* Henry says. *Then why do I have to justify mine to you?* Their uncle is there, shaking his head, trying to calm them down, trying to stave off mayhem. But they're all way too far gone for that.

Later, nobody will remember how Jackie's pulled into the fight. Maybe it's Rufus who does it, or Henry, or Muriel. But before anyone knows it, Muriel is describing, in lurid detail, the state of Jackie's apartment in Tremont. *You should see the way she's living,* she says. *You should see it.* It smells like a garbage dump; any food that comes in there spoils. There is laundry everywhere. Underwear in the toilet. There's oil paint everywhere, some on a few half-finished canvases, of churches covered in soot and fire. But most of it's on the floor, on the furniture. There's some on the ceiling, on the sheets of her bed. A horde of cats; the last time Muriel visited, one of them was dead and Jackie had it in a shoebox under the coffee table, where it was starting to reek. Jackie yelled and moaned when Muriel told her she had to throw it away. And then there were the dirty dishes, piled in the sink, across the counter, in stacks on the floor. *When they get dirty, I just buy new ones,* Jackie told Muriel, though there was no evidence of that. Swarms of flies, hordes of maggots, ants, roaches. The kitchen was revolting.

"She can't live by herself anymore," Muriel says.

"Yes I can! I'm an adult! And I'm right here! Stop talking about me like I'm not right here! Like I'm insane!" Jackie says.

Henry knows he shouldn't say what he says next, but to him, it's right across the plate. *What the fuck,* he figures. *This is the night where we're all saying the things we shouldn't say. Might as well say them all.*

"But you are insane, Jackie," he says, "Batshit crazy. You should be in an institution."

And Jackie lets out a wail the likes of which no one in the room has ever heard. It's inhuman, a sound stripped of sense. The sound they imagine their mother might have made, had she been alive to see their father die. Full of heartbreak and rage, at herself and him. That she could have loved a man like that so much, that she let herself do it. That he could have let her, after everything he did, everything he did to them.

It's almost one in the morning by the time they shout themselves out. They all go to bed, try to sleep, get up after they fail. Sylvie makes them eggs and sausage as if she were a short-order cook. They eat without looking at each other, speak just enough to move the salt, pepper, and coffee around the table. Then Henry goes upstairs to take a shower. Through the bathroom window he can see Sylvie and Rufus walking side by side in the garden, their hands behind their backs. Now and again Sylvie crouches down and Rufus crouches too. She's showing him plants, the things she's been growing. They're out there for a long time, and it occurs to Henry that maybe Sylvie's saying goodbye to this place, taking the farewell tour, and there in the bathroom, he feels dirty for watching. Closes the curtains and starts the water. He's in there a long time, takes even longer to dress. His mind working the problem over and over, trying to see a new way into it, because he can't see any way out.

When he comes back into the dining room, they're seated almost like they were before; Muriel tells him before he has a chance to see it for himself.

"Rufus left," she says.

"What?"

"Yup. Gone out to the airport."

"When did he leave?"

"Just five minutes ago."

It's too much. He almost laughs. "That's ridiculous."

"He didn't say goodbye to me either," Muriel says. "But here's this." She hands him an envelope, a letter. To Henry, from his brother. Signing over, in almost perfect legalese, his portion of his inheritance, for Henry to execute, with the intention that half is to go to Sylvie, so that she can keep the house; the other half is to go toward Jackie's care. *I trust this will resolve the problem*, the letter's final sentence says, *that our father's unjust equality created.*

You bastard, is all Henry can think. Detests himself for not being grateful, or grateful enough. He can't tell the difference yet. Can't tell how much is about Rufus and how much about their father. He sees his brother only once in the next decade, and then never again. But after

Sylvie's wedding, when he knows Rufus has a son, he keeps sending them money, as often as he can, his own money on top of the trust fund disbursements; after a while, just his own money. *It's all for you and your boy,* he writes, and thinks to himself but doesn't write: *He shouldn't be cheated by your financial drama.* Rufus is gracious and writes back, thankful for the money. Always takes it. But he never tells Henry what he's doing with it. And he never tells Henry when he's moving, or why. A couple years in, Henry risks an annoyed note—*just tell me when you're switching cities so I know where to wire, is that so hard?*—and Rufus almost stops communicating altogether. Months go by where Henry's money just piles up, waiting to be collected, and Henry worries, then, that something's happened to them both, to Rufus and his boy. He starts skimming the international section of *The New York Times* for news of coups, wars, riots in Africa. Things to feed his anxiety. Then the money disappears from the account with a two-word reply, *thanks, Rufus,* and Henry sleeps better. Though he doesn't know how to get Wyatt Earp to say more, either. Or how to get him back.

It's been like that for years, now, Sylvie thinks. It's 1995 again, and Peter's been gone for hours; the afternoon's turning into evening, but the memories of 1966 are brighter than ever. The family was a handful of seeds that night, Sylvie thinks, tossed into a hurricane that howled through the house. Now Henry and Rufus are far away. All the girls still in town, but they almost never see each other. And Jackie's been put away for so long now, she might not know who she is anymore, let alone them.

But all their children. If Sylvie concentrates hard enough she can almost feel it, the way the past is blowing them all in again, forcing them to come together. The shape of the thing is there, in her head. The storm is still out there, maybe worse than ever, but she understands that maybe, if she closes the right doors, opens the right windows, they might all whirl in again, roll across the floor, then wake up, blinking and smiling, as if they've come out of a long dream. She can hear her father spit then—*people always do what they want, Sylvie, never forget that*—and she knows, she does. There's no telling what any of them will do. But she can begin to move them all, and all she has to do is make a couple calls. Because she knows, she knows, what happened to Curly. And she knows what she has to do to fix things.

Kosookyy sounds groggy on the other end of the phone. She says his real name, and at once he's clear.

"Sylvie," he says. "It's late."

"I know. I'm pulling out my investments, Kosookyy. As soon as you can do it. And I'll need it in cash. Something portable and liquid that the FBI can't also trace, at least not right away."

There's a long sigh. Then: "You're sure."

"Yes. I'm liquidating everything. Cutting it loose."

"Everything? That's a lot of money you're going to end up with."

"I'm aware of that. But there won't be too much of it left when I'm done."

"What are you planning on doing?"

"I'm going to bring down the Wolf."

"Because of Petey."

"That's right. Petey and the rest of my family."

"You're crazy," he says.

She says his real name again. "I have the money."

"Your father would disapprove," Kosookyy says.

"My father's been dead for almost thirty years. Things have changed since then."

"That's weak, Sylvie. Your father would understand today better than either of us."

"So what. He's still dead."

"A lot more people are going to join him if you do what you say you're going to do."

"A lot of them deserve it."

"A lot of them don't," Kosookyy says.

"Name one," Sylvie says.

"How about me?"

"You think you're one of the good guys, now?"

"Don't be so cold. It doesn't suit you."

"Duck and cover. It's all coming down. And besides, I think I can rig it so they don't touch you."

"You think you can. What if you're wrong?"

"It's a calculated risk," Sylvie says.

"You're not being fair," Kosookyy says.

Sylvie laughs. "Fair? You know what my father would say to that."

Kosookyy sighs again. "Yeah, I know. But he would never do what you're doing. He'd just let his grandson hang."

"Two grandsons?"

"Without thinking twice."

"Like I said. I'm not him."

"One more thing," Kosookyy says. "I'll be amazed if you live through it yourself."

"Watch me," Sylvie says.

Now Kosookyy laughs. "That's your father talking."

"You better believe it."

"Sylvie?"

"What."

"I was wrong just now. Maybe he'd be proud of you."

"I think you were right the first time," Sylvie says. "He'd say I was being a dumb bitch. But I never liked him much anyway."

"Good night, Sylvie."

"Get out of here, now, okay? Lie low for a while?"

"Oh, honey," Kosookyy says. "Those days are over. I got nowhere else to be than where I am. Just do it already, all right? I'll take care of me and mine."

"All right. Good night."

"Good night."

Kosookyy hangs up. Sylvie doesn't put down the phone. She dials again. The voice on the other end is thick with a Russian accent.

"Feodor," she says. "It's the White Lady."

"Good evening. Are you calling about your investment?"

"Yes. I'm pulling it out. In cash."

"I see."

"Though not all of it. I want you to keep a sizeable amount."

"For what?"

"To kill the Wolf."

Feodor laughs.

"I'm serious," Sylvie says.

"You invest with him, too, don't you?" Feodor says. "I've always admired that about you, the way you don't take sides. Why are you taking one now?"

"It's not in your interest to know, is it?"

"Well, we aren't interested in going after the Wolf, then," Feodor says.

"How much would I have to pay you to become interested?"

"A much larger percentage of your investment than you would be comfortable with."

"How much?"

He gives her the number.

"Done," she says. "And I'll be able to make the job easier for you. Much easier."

"How."

"That's my business."

There's a long breath on the other end of the phone. "You are serious."

"I'm serious."

"When do you want this done?"

"You'll know when. I'll give you everything you need. Also, I have a message—no, a series of messages—that I want you to help me deliver to his organization."

"I will make the calls. But I have to warn you, whatever you may be planning, there is no way to make it clean. You will need plans. For you and your family."

"I have plans," Sylvie says.

"I hope so, for their sakes," Feodor says.

"So we have an understanding?"

"Yes."

"Good. We'll talk again soon. And Feodor, after this is done, we have no more ties between us, yes?"

"That's right."

"I'll make no more trouble for you."

"Nor I for you. Unless you give me a reason."

"Understood."

"It's been a pleasure doing business with you, White Lady."

"And you, Feodor. It's morning there now, yes? Have a good day."

"And you have a good night."

She looks at the clock. It's late. *The day after tomorrow I'll talk to the FBI,* she thinks. She goes out on the patio. It's already dark, colder than she thought it would be. The lawn runs away, fast, down to the lake she can't see, though there are lights on it, boats moving across the water. Curly's down there somewhere. It doesn't matter whether they find him or not. She knows the police and the FBI have always had half the story, always knew they were looking at pieces of a scattered body. They'd found fingers in a field. A leg. A toe. All she has to do is show them where the rest of it is. Where to go, around this town, everywhere between here and Moldova.

She thinks, then, about the bonds of flesh and blood that lead back to her father, her father and the people who are still living with his ghost. *We're ready,* Sylvie thinks, *at last we can get out and be free of him, him and all he did.* But what will she do then? It's a trait Sylvie inherited from her father, to stay practical, to not think too hard about the bigger questions that lurk behind the choices she makes. From what Sylvie can remember, Peter Henry Hightower was a master at it; in all her years with him, she never saw him flinch, or take back a decision. *We all play the hand we're dealt,* he used to say. *We all do what we can with what we have, and we can't be blamed for it.* But Sylvie's fifty-seven now, only ten years younger than her father was when he died, and it's hard for her not to think about what his life was like then: his financial empire stagnating, his family in ruins. *You never said anything, Dad, but you must have started thinking about your legacy,* she thinks. *How things might have been different.* She's started to think that for Peter Henry Hightower, his ambitions, strategy, and practicality were the walls of a fortress. All the carnage, the people he hurt and killed—the things that would force him to come to terms with the things he did—lay on the field beyond, and if he ever looked outside, he never let on.

Sylvie has lived inside the walls her father built all her life. Now her hand is on the gate and she's about to open it. She doesn't know what she'll see, but she can picture it. The staggering multitudes, the poor, the destitute, the starving, the people who weren't given their share so that two generations of Hightowers could draw their profits. Among them, the bodies of the dead. Two of them are old and mummified: a man in a suit with his throat slit, a yellow handkerchief dangling from his pocket; a mobster's son. But there are piles of fresh corpses, all Sylvie's doing. Raped to death and shot in the face. Slit down the middle and emptied out. No livers, no kidneys, no hearts. No eyes. And there are predators out there, the animals of commerce and its consequences, feasting on the living and the dead. If they find Sylvie, she knows, they'll rip her to pieces. After that, the only difference between her and the rest of them will be that she'll have deserved it.

Part 2
1896–1966

Chapter 7

So you're starting to see the blood, the pieces all around, of the body of the truth. There's no other way to tell you what happened without lying to you. But every body has a spine; every story has a line. The spine of the Hightowers curls back decades, from 1995 to the end of the last century, and you need to see it, too, to know how the pieces used to fit together.

Petro Garko is born in 1899 in a house in Tremont, the neighborhood on the west bank of the Cuyahoga River, with a midwife in attendance; Galina, his mother, cleans up after the birth herself the next day. It's June, just in time for the streetcar strike, the riots and smoking wreckage of machinery, the National Guard patrolling the city. That's Cleveland all over, what America looks like when it's angry. There's a small crowd of their friends and neighbors in the church when Petro's baptized, dressed in their best while Father Tarnawsky, of St. Peter and Paul's Catholic Church, traces the cross on the baby's forehead with oil. A larger crowd is waiting back at the house. Mykhaylo, Petro's father, gives each man a shot of whiskey and a cigar as a favor, and there's more where that came from. There's beer, too, that the guy on the corner made in his basement and rolled down the street in a dark barrel. Homemade root beer for the kids. The musicians tear through all the songs they know the people want to hear, and couples whirl in lines and circles, the music whips them faster and faster, and just when it can't get any more frantic, the musicians go on strike, won't play another note until someone stuffs a five-dollar bill into the bass's F-hole. Some of the guests complain, say it wasn't part of the deal, but they pay anyway, because nobody wants the party to stop. This happens a dozen times, and three days later, when the guests at last can't drink any more and are asleep on the steps outside, the band packs up and goes around the corner. Once they're out of sight, the bandleader puts his violin down, opens a trapdoor on the bass's back, and divides up the earnings in the middle of the dusty street. By then, two of the men Mykhaylo works with in the mill are lying in the grass in the backyard with bloody faces; they started a fight with each other for a reason neither of them can remember later. *It must have been the booze*, the godparents say. *It wasn't the best.* The godparents say they'll do everything they can to protect the boy, and they have the best intentions at the time. But they end up moving out of Tremont within the year, and Galina never hears from them again.

In 1912, Mykhaylo, who loved to dance, who got a kiss from Galina the first night they met in a social hall, after he spun her across the floor, dies in an accident at the mill. You can see it in the insurance claims for the Ruthenian National Union of America, soon to be called the Ukrainian National Association. Mykhaylo was killed by a train—that word, *train*, spelled out in Cyrillic on the form, but in phonetic English, those small but important signs of how the Ukrainians in America are becoming something else—down in the Flats, in the Cuyahoga's floodplain, in the black soot of a dozen steel mills and crisscrossing rails. Nobody knows how it happened. Nobody ever seems to know how any of these things happen anywhere: the deaths in the mines in Pennsylvania, the lost eyes, a man crushed in an elevator shaft. But it happens. One minute Mykhaylo's heading home from his shift, out of the river valley. Maybe he doesn't realize quite where he is, or maybe he doesn't hear a signal he's supposed to. Maybe there isn't any signal. The next minute, he's under the wheels, and a union representative is helping the grieving Galina make funeral arrangements, cashing out the policy she has on her husband. Trying hard not to look too much at the two sons. Petro is thirteen then. His brother Stefan is nine.

Galina remarries fast, some say a little too fast, even for her. Her new husband is Polish, which makes a little stir, but Galina doesn't care. *The hell with them,* she thinks. *They don't have no husband and two boys to feed.* The new husband isn't bad. He likes the boys' mother well enough. He works in the mills like Mykhaylo did, provides for them, but isn't around very often, doesn't talk to them very much when he is. Even less when Petro lets the man know how much he hates him. Father Tarnawsky is the closest thing the boys have to a real father now, and for Petro, that means not very close at all; for Stefan, it's closer. But it's Tarnawsky who puts them on the paths they follow. He sees the kindness in Stefan and tells him so. Sees how sharp Petro's ambition is and tells him to be careful. *Oh, I will,* Petro says, and Tarnawsky, who has dedicated his life to helping children, assumes the best. He shouldn't.

On Easter 1917 all the bells in all the churches in Cleveland, a city of churches, churches and factories, are ringing everywhere, all the notes in the scale at once. They've been ringing since seven in the morning, and they'll still be ringing into the afternoon. The churches are packed, like they are every Sunday, but today's the big one: The three-hour mass has just let out at St. Peter and Paul, and you could say this story's born here, on this sacred ground, because everyone's there. There are the factory workers and their families, the mothers and children in smart outfits they bought just for today, the fathers in the same suits they've been wearing to Easter for years. They've got baskets of food they put in rows for the priest to bless, sausage and eggs, ham and bread and cheese, cloves of garlic, the makings of the giant meal that's coming. There are the factory managers in finer clothes, too, the guys who made it that far up and live along Lincoln Park now, but come out on the lawn to hear the bands in the gazebo in the evening, just like everyone else. The shopkeepers and the grocers, the local politicians, they're all there, too. In the middle of it all is Father Tarnawsky, spectacled and balding, but with so much life still in him. He's building schools, starting businesses. Doesn't worry much about the conflicts of interest among business and church and politics; he just wants to get things done. He'll meet with the president in a few years, still speak his native tongue as well as ever. Next to him are two of his altar boys, the Garko brothers, Petro and Stefan. Stefan's fourteen and small, a little fidgety, hiding in the robes. The look on his face is too open, too earnest, for this place. *What a good boy,* his teachers in school say. *What a good mark,* say the kids in the gangs who intercept him on the way home. Petro's almost his opposite, just this side of eighteen, and if you look at him the right way, you can see how he doesn't belong in those altar boy clothes anymore, because the beyond he's contemplating doesn't have much to do with heaven. *Watch out for that kid,* the teachers say. The kids in the gangs say the same thing. Both with admiration and fear, because the thing that makes him so strong—untouchable, some people say—makes him dangerous, too. One of these days, Petro's going off like a firework. And everyone who wants to be near him is trying to figure out if they can go for the ride without getting scorched, or losing their fingers, or worse.

But the trouble takes some time to start, because for a while, Petro can't see any way out of the South Side, out of Tremont. The streets are a labyrinth, tangling into alleys too narrow for two carts to pass each other. For the people who don't think of leaving, it can seem as though all the world is on Professor Avenue, with its bakeries and candy stores, used furniture and appliance places. A photo studio. A bowling alley. A bank building like a tiny temple. Two funeral parlors. Kids following the pie man down the street; when he opens the back door to make a delivery, they all get in close just to smell it. The streetcar, the dinky, running down the middle to Starkweather Avenue, the women going to the West Side Market in Ohio City asking for a free transfer. The street peddlers shouting out their wares. Boys making small change any way they can. They pick up cigarette butts that still have some tobacco left, fill a cigar box with them, and sell them to some addict for a penny. They sell empty booze cans, shell peas at the market stalls if they can get over there, beg for chicken feet from the poultry house, fill a sack with them, and run them home so their mothers can make soup. They collect scrap metal, iron and steel, copper and aluminum if they get lucky. They wander around on the tracks of the Erie Railroad with burlap sacks, looking for any coal that might have fallen off, because the house doesn't stay warm by itself. When the railroad cops aren't looking, a couple of them climb into the cars and throw the coal down, and for the children on the ground, it's like black hail, until they get chased away. They gather rags to sell to the paper and rag man who comes through the neighborhood on a horse and wagon, shouting *paprex, paprex*. A band of little criminals tails the man down the tiny streets; the kids raid his cart when someone lures him into a house with the promise of a big stash. Or they ambush him on the Central Viaduct Bridge when he's going back to the East Side, beat him down and sell what he's got at the junkyard before he wakes up again. At home, Galina makes curtains out of wallpaper and beads, hangs a cardboard triangle in the window when they need more ice from the iceman, who carries a fifty-pound block on a leather pad draped on his shoulder while the kids in the street suck on the shards that drop off the back of the truck. The stepfather takes a shot of booze before work, a shot of booze when he gets home. Galina doesn't say anything; Mykhaylo did the same thing. On Sunday evenings there's a party, and they bring out the good stuff, have a shot of it chased with a mouthful of black pumpernickel bread they tear off the loaf with their hands. They're there long after dark, the boys slaughtering songs new and old on ocarina and ukelele, beating on the bottom of a booze can for a drum. There are fights between people who want to hear obereks, the Polish dances, and people who want to hear the Ukrainian songs. The boys can't play either very well. Then all the guests stagger home, or almost home. The stepfather doesn't always make it to the bed. They go to a wake of a friend's cousin, see the wreath on the front door of the house of the deceased, the open coffin in the living room. Men sitting around playing cards and drinking, again, telling each other all the good things the dead man did. Everyone looks at the coffin, at each other. *None of us is ever getting out of the South Side alive,* they think. It's an island in the middle of Cleveland, surrounded by fire. The trains howl in and out along the tracks, day and night. When the wind blows in from the north or the east, the smoke from the mills and the freight yard, the tar and asphalt plants, the stink from the slaughterhouse, covers everything in the neighborhood. The church steeples are black with it, and the South Siders who go downtown that day can't get the smell off their clothes. No one will ever swim in the river again. But so many people who lived there will be proud they did, until the day they die.

When Petro and Stefan are older boys, Galina takes them to the edge of the neighborhood with her and tells them a thing or two. *Look behind us,* she says. Takes all of the South Side, everything they've ever known, in one gesture, with one hand. *Now look ahead. Look how big this city is,* she says. Opens her arms wide. *Now think about the world.* And Petro starts sitting on the edge of the ravine to the Flats, too, trying to take it all in. Below him, the slope is tangled with weeds. He can see the bobbing heads of a few boys harvesting the marijuana; in a few months, the police will come and burn it all, but it'll just grow back again. In the valley, a freight train heads out of town with a hobo on the roof. He's tying himself down so he can sleep. Across the river, Petro can see the great lit arc of the city, from the opposite bank of the Cuyahoga to the shore of the lake. He's going to get out of Tremont; he can feel it. He's going to rise above it, so far that they won't be able to see him. Just the trail he left in the air.

It's when Prohibition starts that Petro gets his shot. It's 1919. They read in the paper that alcohol's illegal, hear about it on the street. At first, it doesn't seem like that big a deal. It's just another rule that people in the South Side can ignore, and they're almost cheerful about it. They're ahead of the rest of the city; they start making booze themselves about as soon as they can't buy it from the store. Soon every fourth house is making beer or liquor and selling it to the other three. On Saturday night, they go out to the dance halls, where the bands play loud and the singers use megaphones to be heard above the music. They can't drink there because the police make sure they don't, ruining a good time. But when everyone gets home, after the band sends them off and the dance halls close, everyone drinks as much as ever. It's just that the stuff they're drinking is a lot worse. Some of it's bad enough to cause seizures. Some of it'll put you away for good.

And everyone gets a little too used to seeing guns when the bootleggers come around, people from the East Side. They have good wine that the Italians are making—Dago Red, they're calling it. Whiskey from Canada, the real thing; they bring it right across Lake Erie into Cleveland at night. They fight with each other over who gets to control Tremont, and now and again that ends in gunfire. A couple people end up under the ground. But they're nice as anything to their potential customers. A gangster named Cesare, who can't be much older than Petro is, does a deal with a man who lives just down the street named Bogdan; Bogdan's daughter's getting married, and he wants to have something for his guests as a treat, to express his happiness and gratitude. The neighbors gather around when the transaction happens; they want to see how good the stuff is. Almost everyone's eyes are on the alcohol. Petro's are on the money. He sees just how much more Bogdan's willing to pay for the quality—a quarter a pint—than for the rotgut his neighbors are making, which doesn't taste like anything good. And Petro sees where the money's going. It starts with the clothes Cesare's got on, the tailored suit, the tilted hat. He saunters up the road in that, and all Petro's neighbors, all at once, look like they just got off the boat, like they can't speak a word of English. For some of them, that's the truth: they've been here for two decades and English is as far away from them as ever. Petro's own mother struggles with the language, has trouble getting her tongue around some of the phrases that have crept into American Ukrainian—*receipt, umbrella, strike breaker, smart man.* Stefan's not much better; his English is okay, but he speaks it with such a thick accent that people outside of the South Side have to use their imagination to comprehend him.

"So this is the best you have right now, yes?" Bogdan says, in English.

"Speak English, pal," Cesare says. "I don't understand a word you're saying."

And what is the point of speaking English if you can't use it outside the neighborhood? Petro thinks. *What is the point of speaking it if they still think you're just a dumb Slav?* He thinks about his little family, his friends, his neighbors, and is embarrassed; and that makes him loath himself, that he can't stand to be around his family outside his house. That his own accent is still so sharp. That he can't talk anything like the people he sees downtown, who speak English with the careful, lilting ease he associates with actors, singers, voices on the radio. *That's the key to all this,* he thinks to himself. *Knowing what to say and how to say it. That and money. The rest is just appearances. Disguises.*

Which is how, in 1921, Petro and Stefan have the first conversation that starts to drive them apart. It's after dinner, and Galina and her husband have gone to bed. Petro and Stefan are in the living room; the parlor, as Galina likes to call it, half joking. Petro's twenty-two. Stefan's eighteen. They've broken out a couple beers, some semi-flat stuff they bought from their neighbor neither of them likes, but it's what they have.

"This house is really too small for the four of us," Petro says.

Stefan shrugs. "It works well enough."

"Does it?" Petro says.

"Sure it does."

Petro takes a gulp of his beer. "I'm leaving, Stefan," he says.

"What?"

"You heard me."

"Where will you go?"

"It's not so much where," Petro says, "it's what. I've been watching those bootleggers, how much money they make, and I'm going to get a piece of that. A big piece. Enough to get us all a bigger place."

"Like the places on the park?" Stefan says. His voice is weak.

"Are you kidding?" Petro says. "Those aren't big enough."

"They're the biggest places on the South Side."

Petro just looks at him for a couple seconds. Then he says, "Screw the South Side."

They're both angry young men, and maybe if they weren't, they'd know how to say what they need to say without tearing everything down. But they are, and they don't.

"I'm glad Ma isn't here to hear you say that," Stefan says.

"You don't get to talk to me like that," Petro says.

"Someone has to," Stefan says. "If Pa were here, he would."

It's been almost a decade since their father died, and he worked so much in the Flats that Petro and Stefan didn't see him very much at all. But they miss him every day, so much, and they've lived with the grief for so long to know that they'll never get past it. They see a father playing with his son, throwing him in the air, spinning him around, playing chase, and remember when Mykhaylo used to do that with them. They remember him on the couch, and both of them on top of him; he used to pretend to be a bear, and they would capture him and try to tie him down, but he would always get away from them, roaring and laughing. They remember him kissing their mother on the forehead in the kitchen every morning, then patting her on the back just before he left the house. The only thing they have trouble remembering is his funeral, and the gigantic party it became, because so many people liked their father and were shocked to see him go. There was a coffin, but it was closed. So for them it's almost like he's still alive, alive and out there, watching them somehow, always asking how they are. Trying to keep them in line, raise them right, even though they can't see each other anymore. It makes what Petro says next more hurtful.

"Pa was a sucker."

"Take it back now," Stefan says.

"The hell I will. He let them work him to death."

"He was killed in an accident, Petro."

"That wouldn't have happened if he'd had any ambition at all," Petro says. "If he'd wanted more than to work in a factory and go dancing on the weekends, he never would have been anywhere near that train. He'd be working somewhere else, and he'd still be here with us, and none of us would have to be here, in this fucking place." He waves his hands in disgust at the house, the street, the entire neighborhood.

"How can you be so ashamed of us?" Stefan says.

"How can you not be? Look at this place. Look at yourself."

In the backs of both of their minds, a small voice is screaming at them, telling them to stop talking, wondering how the hell the conversation went so sour. But they don't know how to stop. They're both buzzing, shaking, and it's Stefan who lunges first, throws the first punch, hits Petro square across the jaw. Petro doesn't hesitate; he kicks Stefan in the stomach, sends him flying back across the room, and then jumps up and closes in. Stefan manages one more good, solid hit, a punch that gives Petro a gushing nosebleed, before Petro, who's still bigger and stronger, has him pinned to the floor. He punches his brother four times in the stomach and then stands up and kicks him. Stefan's yelp sends Galina rushing from her room in her nightgown. *Stop! Stop, both of you,* she yells. *If your father could see you like this.* They skulk off to bed, don't say a word to each other the next day. The day after that, they seem fine. But they're not.

So, in 1921, for Petro's family, it's as if Petro vanishes. For a little while, he's one of those same-old-stories, the one about the guy who goes out for a pack of cigarettes and is never seen again. His mother and Stefan ask around, but nobody knows where he's gone. Stefan goes to the police, but that doesn't go anywhere; the police have other things to do. Petro Garko is a missing person case that, in a way, never gets solved. Because when the man turns up again, his family doesn't recognize him.

Chapter 8

It's March 21, 1921. Petro's walking home when he happens to cross paths with Cesare. Like I said, Cesare and Petro are about the same age: Cesare still has a bit of the boy about his face, which is even more obvious because he doesn't work in a mill, doesn't work on the Flats at all. Doesn't have all that oil and smoke driven into his skin like everyone around the South Side does. Petro's seen Cesare a dozen times since he sold the whiskey to Bogdan, moving from door to door down the alley where the Garkos live, passing out bottles, taking orders for more. Petro's been wanting to approach the guy for a few months now, but it's never the right time. Cesare looks like the kind of guy who doesn't like his business interrupted except if it's for more business, and Petro respects that, knows he doesn't have anything to offer Cesare, at least not yet. Right now, it's all favors, what Cesare's willing to do for someone he doesn't know. What Petro might be willing to do in exchange for what he wants.

Cesare's in the passenger seat of a car, parked on the corner of Professor and Literary. The ride's an Ogren phaeton, though Petro doesn't know that; he just knows that it's nice. For about one second, Petro hesitates. You could say he starts to wonder if he's about to do the right thing; you could say he thinks about Father Tarnawsky, about his mother and brother, about his dead father, what he might say. About his grandparents, somewhere back in the Austrian Empire, in Ruthenia, in whatever name you stumble to call it, because that word, *Ukraine*, that identity, *Ukrainian*, is still forming. You could say all that, but you'd be wrong. Because it only takes a second for Petro to decide. Then all self-doubt is gone, and he walks up to the car with a certain strut, as if he doesn't look or talk like he's the son of a factory worked killed in an industrial accident, whose brother is still an altar boy, whose mother still has problems with English. As if he already thinks he's better than the man he's about to talk to, even though that man is sitting in a car worth more than his family's ever seen.

"Hey, Cesare," Petro says. "I think you should take me on."

It doesn't throw Cesare that Petro knows his name. A lot of people around Tremont know it, now, and he's proud of that. It's a sign that he controls the territory. That the single bullet he took in the leg, the couple bullets he gave back, were worth the trouble.

"Yeah?" Cesare says. "Who the hell are you?"

Petro's voice doesn't waver. He says: "I'm the one who's going to make your boys a million dollars."

Cesare gets a good laugh out of that, as good as a guy like that can get, anyway. It comes out in a chain—*heh heh heh heh heh*—while his eyes crinkle. The cigarette jutting from his mouth dangles, almost falls out. He leans back in his seat, puts a hand to his brow, a gesture older than his years. Then squints back out at Petro, looks him up and down.

"You're not fooling anyone in those clothes," he says.

"Think you can do something about that?" Petro says.

He looks away, drags on his cigarette. Throws it in Petro's direction to see if he jumps. He doesn't.

"Just wait a minute," he says. "It ain't up to me." Two men are coming out of a bakery down Professor, both wearing jackets and fedoras, the kinds Petro sees downtown. One of them's rubbing his hands together inside a yellow handkerchief. *For the car,* he says, when the other gives him a funny look. *I'm trying to keep it nice.* He stops when Cesare nods at him. Looks at Petro.

"Who's the peasant?" he says. "Friend of yours?"

"No, no," Cesare says. "Kid says he wants a job."

Kid. Petro gets angry at that. *I think I'm older than you are,* he wants to say. No, more than that. He wants to punch Cesare in the face, or better yet, smack him, as if Cesare were his son, a little boy. Maybe mess up the car a little. But he fights it down, because right then, this feels like the only shot he's going to get.

"He also says he's going to make us a million dollars," Cesare says.

"Yeah?" the man says. "Pleased to make your acquaintance, Mister Millionaire." He looks Petro over once, an expression on his face like he's doing a lot of math in his head. Then he opens the door to the backseat for him. "Get in."

And just like that, they're in the car, speeding on the long arched bridge over the Cuyahoga, from the west side to the east side. For thirty seconds, the river valley's what a religious man might consider a vision of hell: all flame and black smoke, the water made of bright rust, giant machines screaming along tracks, while the shadows of men try to work, try to survive. But it's not hell; it's just industry. They know they've ruined the Cuyahoga. But the rust in the water means the mills are going, and those mills built this town, built parts of this country; built both the phaeton and the bridge that the phaeton gets to soar over right now. The downtown they move through after that isn't yet what it'll become. Tower City, the Terminal Tower and all the gold and marble to go with it, are still just talk. They haven't built Severance Hall yet, either. But Public Square is already something to see. The green is a big nod to New England, a reminder that Connecticut had once laid claim to this part of Ohio, drew lines from its northern and southern corners and stretched them across the map to the shore of Lake Erie to take what they thought could be theirs; the Yankees imparted just enough of that old New England hierarchy to turn Cleveland into a little version of itself, with a few old Protestant Brahmin sitting on the money, pulling the strings, while the rest of us whirl around them. You can see it in the architecture, the office buildings with florid stonework, arched windows, as grand and committed to its intentions—to make money, and lots of it, to become powerful, very powerful—as any place in New York. Public Square's the kind of place where politicians hold giant rallies. Where there are parades on major holidays, and people line Superior Avenue fifteen feet thick while the floats go by with city representatives in paper hats waving from them over the din of a dozen marching bands, the flash of a dozen color guards. Amid all that commerce is the Old Stone Church, on fire twice already in the past sixty-five years and now blackened by the soot from the factories. But it's still there; the Presbyterians still show up every Sunday to worship. By 1930, the square's grander still, when the Van Sweringen brothers open Terminal Tower and the train station beneath it, and everyone's blinded by the metal and stone, the bronzework on the elevator doors—just as the markets decide to crash all around them and ruin the brothers, ruin anyone who doesn't see the market coming to feast on them. Petro Garko is Peter Henry Hightower by then. But that's still a ways off.

The phaeton flies by the square in seconds, turns north and gets onto Euclid Avenue. Farther east is Millionaires' Row, or what will become it when the millionaires are there to build the places. Down here, in the city, there's already the Arcade, that icon of glass and metal that turns business into religion; it's a church of commerce in there, as if the people who built it in 1890 knew what was coming, knew the marketeers needed a place to pay some respects to their gods, too. The car slows down as it passes, pulls over. Cesare and the man with the yellow handkerchief get out, leave the door open for Petro to get out and close the door behind them. The car drives off and they walk into an alleyway. Petro's trying hard not to break his stride. It's the sort of place where he's used to people trying to jump him, but he's not scared, and he doesn't want them to think he is.

"Didn't hear what your name was," he says to the man with the yellow handkerchief.

"Is that right?" he says. Doesn't give him the dignity of looking at him. "Here's an idea for you. Start figuring out how to keep your mouth shut. Don't open it until you got something to say."

They come to the end of the alley, where there's a steel door that looks like it goes to a boiler room, an incinerator. The man with the yellow handkerchief knocks and it opens, much faster and with much less sound than Petro expected. A guy's there with suspenders and a pistol. Gives Cesare and the yellow handkerchief a nod. Looks at Petro and doesn't move.

"He's with us," the man with the yellow handkerchief says, with a hint of shame. "Or at least he wants to be." Then down the stairs they go.

It's not the boiler room or the incinerator, but it's hot enough to be. The cigarette smoke attacks them at the door, makes Petro's eyes water; then it parts like a curtain, and he can see dim electric lights, suspended by wires from the ceiling, put up fast and sloppy, as if they're not planning on keeping them there very long. The voices of what seems like a hundred people, two hundred, almost all men, laughing, joking, threatening. A lot of trash talk. The clatter of roulette balls, the slip, slap, and shuffle of cards. Then Petro's eyes clear and he can see the tables, how small and packed they are. Glasses full of liquor are squatting everywhere. At the end of the room, there's not so much a bar as a counter, something that two guys could pick up and haul away. The place is designed to be dismantled, quick, as soon as they know the police are coming. It's so easy to imagine: There's a shout from the top of the stairs—*the cops are here*—and everyone scrambles out the back door while the guys who run this joint run from table to table, folding in the legs and then tucking them under their arms. Then they flip the counter over, throw the bottles in a bag, and take off. The police come down and the smoke is still in the air, the lights swinging a little; the officers can smell the booze that spilled on the floor, but there's no other evidence that anything illegal happened. It's not the Harvard Club, which by the mid-1930s'll be five times as big, moving from address to address out on Harvard Avenue in Newburgh Heights, with roulette and poker, craps tables and slot machines, its own fleet of limos to pick up the clients downtown. That place'll survive raid after raid; not even Mister Eliot Ness'll be able to close it down. This place isn't like that. They don't have a name for it yet. But Petro can tell it's the kind of place they'll be writing about in the papers for years, right next to the stories about the Coast Guard intercepting a boat full of liquor trying to waltz in from Canada. But so many more boats get through, the Coast Guard can't catch them all, because the booze they carry—like the stuff they're selling in this place—isn't something a guy on the South Side made in his bathroom, and the people in this room aren't his neighbors, either. Petro can see it in the angles of their suspenders. He looks at that back door again, wonders if it doesn't lead right up to the Arcade, so that, when the cops come, the clientele can run for that back door, through a long hallway under the sidewalk, then get to the end and stop, straighten their clothes and hair, and open a door to that glorious building's polished wood and gleaming metal. Stroll into the thoroughfare as easy as you please under the ceiling of shimmering glass high above, as though they've been there all along, buying jewelry, meeting someone for the afternoon; and it works because, when they're not breaking the law, it's what they're doing anyway. Everyone who works in the Arcade knows who they are. Nobody's surprised to see them there. If they notice that the escapees smell a little more like cigarettes than usual, or seem a little out of breath, they don't comment. They know better than to ask; they know that the only business they should mind is their own, if they're interested in making a living—maybe living at all—in this town.

The man with the yellow handkerchief puts his arm around Petro's shoulder like they're best friends, talks into his ear.

"Anyone in this room look familiar to you?"

"No," Petro says.

"It figures they wouldn't," the man says, "because the young men assembled before you represent the most recent generation of some of Cleveland's wealthiest. Some of the money in this room got here a hundred and fifty years ago. Some of it was made yesterday. New money, old money. We don't care which, as long as they got it, you know what I'm saying?"

"Yeah."

The yellow handkerchief man frowns. His fingers are digging a little too far into Petro's shoulder.

"No you don't. You don't have the first fucking idea what I'm saying."

He leads him through the smoky room, through a door behind the counter. Now it's like they really are going to a boiler room. A door closes behind him and it's dark. Too dark to see anything.

"Jesus," the handkerchief man says. "Somebody light a match or something."

Somewhere in front of them, someone says *sorry,* and at the end of the hallway, where it bends to the left, an orange light fires up. They follow it until they're in a small room with brick walls. A man in a green suit is standing there with a candle.

"Romantic," the handkerchief man says.

The man in the green suit shrugs. "It's what I had, okay?"

There's a boy, maybe eleven years old, in the corner of the room, crouching, cringing. He's wearing shorts, a stained shirt, a thin jacket. A little cap. The same clothes Petro and his brother wore when they were his age. *A South Side kid,* Petro thinks. *Has to be.* Leaning against the wall nearby is a short, neat length of metal pipe, which the handkerchief man picks up and hands to Petro.

"Okay, Mister Millionaire," he says. "I want you to beat this kid with this pipe until he can't sit up no more."

The kid doesn't move or say anything. But he does pee himself.

"What?" Petro says.

"Okay. We'll drive you right back over to the South Side."

"No, no, wait."

"What."

"He's just a kid."

"So what. So are you. Don't tell me you've never beaten anyone up before."

He has, a few times. When he was about this boy's age, there were three older boys—Polish kids, he thinks—who used to harass him and Stefan whenever they saw them. Push them over and take whatever they had, some pocket change, a hat. Once, their shoes. Until the day Petro followed them home, learned where they lived. Waited around the corner the next night with a long stick and smacked one of them so hard with it that his left ear bled. The older boy fell, curled up on the sidewalk and cried. *Like a little baby,* Petro thought then, with some satisfaction. The other two boys backed away, their hands out, and Petro raised the stick again. *I'm going for the other ear,* he said. *No, no, don't,* one of the unhurt boys said. *Then leave me and my brother alone, got it?* It was the beginning of Petro's simmering reputation. When it boiled up high enough to reach his mother's ear, she approved. *Because there was justice in it,* Petro thought, a reason for the violence. He was standing up for himself, him and his brother, his family. His people.

"What'd this kid do?" Petro said.

"Fuck you care?" the handkerchief man said. "You want to make us a million dollars or not?"

"What did I say?"

"Then you know what to do."

Petro doesn't want to do it. He takes a gamble. "This is beneath me," he says, and the other two men can tell he means it. The man in the green suit smiles. The handkerchief man doesn't.

"Not yet it isn't," he says. "You work hard for us? You do what you say you'll do? You won't have to do this more than once or twice. Maybe three times." The man narrows his eyes. He's a good Catholic, can't help running through the moral implications of what he's suggesting. He amends his statement: "Well. Not yourself, anyway."

Petro looks down at the boy. The boy is looking at the ceiling.

"Go ahead," the handkerchief man says. "If you're good at this, it won't take more than four shots."

It takes three. Then the boy has fallen over on his knees, head to the ground. A huge welt rising on one cheek. Blood seeping from his mouth. And Petro looks down at him, back at the men in suits around him. He has never been angrier in his life; it's moving through him hotter than it ever has, faster than he thought it could. He feels like the pipes around him are shaking, bursting, like the whole building's shuddering. It's going to come down around him. He'll bury these men, he swears to himself. He'll be their boss within a year, the boss of their boss. He'll put them in the ground and then rise, up, up like a shot. He has the nerve to think that where he's going, there'll be no more blood.

The handkerchief man, at last, is smiling. He puts out his hand. "Allow me to introduce myself," he says. "Rinaldo Panetti." Petro doesn't want to know his name now. But he composes himself and shakes the hand.

"It's very good to meet you," he says. "Now how about some new clothes?"

You don't need to know what happens between March and September, do you? Peter starts making good on his promise to himself. Starts getting somewhere—not where he wants to be yet, but he's got his strategy all mapped out. His first big move plotted. But first, he's got some people to take care of.

It's September 25, 1921. A warm Sunday evening on the South Side. Everyone's out on the sidewalks, in the streets. Children hollering up and down the alley. Boys playing the whip, run sheep run. Riding on scooters they made from old cheese crates, the wheels pried off a couple of old pairs of roller skates. One of them's tooting on a trumpet made from a toilet paper roll. Another of them's still whining about the knife of his that got ruined when they tried to play baseball with it. A third sits down, pulls a harmonica from his pocket and plays; he's got a chromatic and he's pretty good, so nobody tells him to stop. Three girls do hopscotch. The men gather in drunk, loud little clusters, shooting craps, talking about the shit they got into and out of back in Europe, some new foreman at Otis who's a complete pain in the ass, a man who got his nose broken in a bare-knuckles grudge fight on the West 7th Street hill an hour ago. *He should go to the hospital,* one of them says. *He ain't going to the hospital,* says another. Then they find something they can agree to complain about together: the goddamn Communists and their little parades. Don't they understand that everyone around here knows the difference between communism and socialism? That the most recent arrivals left Ukraine to get away from communism? It's something the Ukrainians are proud of decades later, a pride born of horror and rage, that even the socialists among them never fall for Stalin, always see through the flimsy progressive veneer to the paranoid mass murderer behind it. How could they not, after what Stalin does to them? It skews their politics, poisons their love of democracy with distrust for the politicians themselves. They vote Democratic because it's better than the alternative; they want to keep what unions they've got and are pretty sure the Republicans will take them away if they get the chance. But they'll never shake the feeling that anytime a politician comes around, shakes your hand, it's because he's sizing you up. Trying to see what he can get out of you, and just how hard he can screw you before you and your buddies riot.

Stefan's sitting on the front steps of his house. The windows to the house are open, and he can hear his mother bustling inside, singing a song in Ukrainian. The son knows the melody, but can't remember the words. Then he sees a man coming down the alley who—well, he can't tell who it is until the man gets close, because the transformation is so complete. The clothes. The shave. The cut of the hair. The walk, angular, jaunty. As if a certain part of the man's personality slit the throats of the other parts, and now the edge of that knife is all that's left. Even the voice is hard to place, because there's not a trace of a Ukrainian accent. If not for the fact of his body—those are still his limbs, his muscles and bones, his eyes, pale and bright—you'd say there was nothing left of what he was.

"Hey, baby brother," he says, in a sharp, city voice Stefan associates with Italians. With mobsters.

"Petro?" Stefan says.

"It's Pete now. Pete the Uke. Petey Ukulele, if you're in the mood," he says. Then changes his accent again, to one Stefan only hears on the men and women who shop downtown, who have other people carry their bags for them: "Or Peter, if you prefer." The accent is flawless. Stefan almost can't contain how happy he is to see his brother, to know he's alive. He wants to shout, to jump up and hug him, as if they were both boys again. He wants to call back into the house, *Ma, Ma, come quick, Petro's home, he's home, he's home.* But he doesn't do any of those things, because looking at his brother, the way he holds himself, the way his speech has changed, Stefan's scared to death of him.

"Where have you been?" Stefan says.

"I don't have time to tell you," Pete says. He's back to that street voice, the gangster, the hit man. Their mother's still singing inside the house; then they both hear the back door slam shut, a screen door on a hinge. She's out in the backyard now.

"You got chickens back there now?" Pete says.

"What have you been doing?" Stefan says. "Where did you get those clothes?"

"I told you, no time," Pete says, "and don't call Ma, either. I wanted to give you this." He hands him a brown envelope. "Don't open it until I'm gone."

"Why?"

Pete's already turning to go, already a foot away. Over his shoulder: "Because I don't think you'll take it if I'm still here. Just know you're taken care of, okay? I'm still your brother."

There's a thousand dollars in that envelope, in neat crisp bills. Stefan takes it into the kitchen, sits at the table, opens it up and counts the bills. Doesn't believe it. Takes out all the bills and fans them out on the table, and just sits there, looking at them. He's still there when his mother comes in from the backyard with a bag of coal for the stove; when she sees what's on the table, she stops and gasps, and her son looks up.

"What did you do to get all that money?" She says it in Ukrainian; her English can't convey everything she wants, her excitement and her fear.

"Nothing, Ma, nothing," he says. "It's from Petro."

"He was here?"

"He says he's coming back," Stefan lies.

She nods to herself, and Stefan sees something in his mother then, some of the bile that got her out of Europe, that married a man from Poland, that still wants something better for her family than she's got right now.

"Hide it before your stepfather comes home," she says. "We'll figure out what to do with it later. You and I." As if they'd reached that decision together.

Chapter 9

Y ou see how fast it happens, Petro Garko becoming Pete the Uke, on his way to becoming Peter Henry Hightower. It happens in less than a year: It doesn't even have time to snow, and this is Cleveland we're talking about. It's spring, and the young man is a factory worker; it's the fall, and the man is a tony dandy, on the eve of his ascent to become a dark star in the city's firmament. *But wait, wait,* you say. We've heard this story before, haven't we, the one about the immigrant who makes good, really good, but at such a cost. It's the story of the era, isn't it? Sure, of this and every other; the names change, the languages, the cities, the jobs, the crimes, but the story's always the same. It's in every other book, in every other movie, and you might call it the story of America—a swath of the fabric of the American myth so worn out that there's no patch big enough to repair it—except that it's so old it's in the Bible, too, right? *For what is a man profited, if he shall gain the whole world, and lose his own soul?* That's the way we always hear it. Everyone knew that story even then, and knew they knew it, too, because whoever wrote down that line had already read this one: *What has been will be again, what has been done will be done again; there is nothing new under the sun.* But we keep telling it, too, because it's not really about the story, the history. It's about that awful inevitability, the blood we know is coming. It's about us.

But there's something special, too, about how well Peter Henry Hightower does it. How far he goes in transforming himself. He does it first by being invisible. Doesn't give the speakeasy's customers any reason to glance at him, notice his existence. Never makes eye contact, never says a word. Wears clothes that look like the walls of the basement. Just watches everything: the way the patricians of the city carry themselves when they walk, how they open doors and close them, where they put their arms when they lean against a table, the angles of their wrists when they offer each other cigarettes. And he listens hard to the way they talk. The lengths of their sentences, the vocabulary they use. The way they talk about business, about women, when the gals are around, when they're not. The sense of humor they have, a caged cleverness, breezy and lethal. Their almost tonal language; their syllables rise and fall in different cadences than anything you hear on the South Side, or from the mobsters who run the place. He understands, then, how much he's been at the edge of English, even though he's spoken it for as long as he can remember. In his old neighborhood, the language is shouting and ragged. It's an old car, a house falling down. Words are always breaking, idioms flame up and die out like coals jumping out of a stove. Your speech slips away from you, runs you down, runs you over, until you learn how to catch it and bring it down, and even then it still bucks. But these people in front of him are at the language's quiet center, where English is a glorious bird, and they're all mimicking its call. They've all read the same books, had the same teachers, and now they're pretty much doing the same jobs; they see each other all day. They've got in-jokes running for so long that they can piece together the last decade just by remembering who said it when. It's just one happy little club, and Peter wants in.

He stays up all night, listening and watching, then sleeps for a few hours in the basement somewhere, anywhere but the room where he hit that boy; then, he stands under the dim light and practices. It's not *howarya*. It's *how are you?* It's not *I'm good*. It's *I'm fine, I'm well*. He stands in front of a mirror, making sure he's holding himself up right. Checks his walk, checks the way he gets something out of his pocket. Practices combing his hair. It takes months to get every detail in place, and get them to where he doesn't have to think about them every second to keep up the appearance, to fight so hard against who he was. And he doesn't show anyone what he's doing, not Cesare, not Rinaldo Panetti. The first one who sees it is his brother, that day in September 1921, and Peter revels in the look on Stefan's face. Because his brother is so transparent to everyone. He can't hide his surprise, his fear, and it's then that Peter knows he's ready.

He's got his history all plotted out. Peter Henry Hightower is from Connecticut. Attended Cheshire Academy—it's the Cheshire School then—just before it becomes a straight-up prep school for Yale, but he goes to Yale anyway. Gets through there in three years. His teachers tell him he should become a scholar, a professor, but he's always thought he has more of a mind for business. So here he is in Cleveland, because he knows Rockefeller was here, Carnegie was here. It's a place where a man can make the kind of money he wants to make. And he's an orphan. Which is only half a lie, though it's the kind of half-lie, he knows, that hurts the people who are still alive.

It's not a perfect story, and there's not enough of it. If he's unlucky and he meets just the wrong guy who blunders into just the wrong questions to ask, the whole thing'll come apart on him, because he doesn't know quite enough about Connecticut, Cheshire, or Yale to pull off a long conversation about them. But he's betting nobody'll ask. Not in the speakeasy, where they're not in the mood to interrogate anyone about their past beyond knowing what school you went to. The talk'll just be about business, and business, at the beginning for sure and maybe even later, is all about not digging too deep, isn't it? About staying just a little bit ignorant, maybe more than a little, knowing just enough that what you're doing seems risky and fun instead of stupid. Because if you know more than that—if you do your homework, work out for yourself on a piece of paper just how bad it can get—you never do anything. Besides, in the end the disguise is just a front to get them to trust him. As soon as they see how much money he has, no one will ask him anything.

About that money, though, and the things Peter has to do to get it: If you've been paying attention, you'll notice that, between working at the speakeasy and becoming someone else, there are still about four hours of every day left. Those four hours are the time Pete needs to put in for Rinaldo Panetti. There are people who end up in the hospital because of those four hours. People who don't get to live out their allotted time on this earth. Until, at last, in May 1922, Pete figures out enough about Rinaldo to do a job on him.

For a few days, the official story—the one the police know—about Rinaldo Panetti is that he's missing, leaving behind a wife and three kids that the rest of the family and the organization takes care of until they don't need it anymore. There are a lot of stories running around about why Rinaldo Panetti leaves. Some of them are financial: He stole money from his boss, or got into a side racket that started making serious money. Some are romantic: He found another lady and ran off with her. That story's closer to the truth, but to get to it, it's better, maybe, to tell it backward.

Rinaldo Panetti's corpse washes up a few miles south of Cleveland; they're able to identify him by his fingerprints on account of a little petty theft he did once when he was a younger man that put him in jail for a bit. If he were a bigger deal, a bigger criminal, they would have been able to match him to a photograph, because apart from the slit throat, the body's in pretty good shape. Pete gets three bigger guys to dump Rinaldo's body in the lake, but it's his own hand that slits Rinaldo's throat, and right before he does it, he's surprised at how calm he is. How easy it is for him to do it. Rinaldo's sitting in that same speakeasy basement, in a rickety wooden chair. He doesn't quite understand why he's been brought there. Doesn't say anything until he sees Pete with the razor.

"You son of a bitch," he says. "Who ratted me out?"

"What business is it of yours now?" Pete says.

Rinaldo's so angry. Pete takes off his jacket and walks around behind him. Puts his hand on the man's shoulder like he remembers Father Tarnawsky doing. As if he's blessing him, trying to comfort him. Then that hand moves to the top of Rinaldo's head to hold it in place, and

Pete the Uke draws the razor into the skin, easy as you please. The man just sits there, bleeding out, almost as if it doesn't hurt. He looks so tired.

"Get this guy out of here," Pete says. "And make sure you bury the handkerchief with him."

That's how Pete moves up. He sees how the operation he's involved in is based on loyalty. For some of the guys, it's loyalty based on family, on long friendships. It's almost sentimental. For Pete, though, loyalty's just another kind of currency. He sees how he can save it and spend it to make himself more valuable, and devalue the people in his way. It doesn't take him long to see who's screwing who; it takes him just a few weeks to discover that Rinaldo Panetti's not only skimming some money off the top of the speakeasy's nightly earnings, but fucking his boss's girlfriend besides. His boss: Lou Rizzi, who's a capo in Big Joe Lonardo's operation, which is just getting started in Cleveland, though Big Joe's already made it pretty big for himself.

In 1922, all the liquor everyone has left over is starting to go dry—I mean, for people who weren't already making it in the first place, which is most people. Now a lot of people want to make it for themselves, and Big Joe's got just the thing. He's already been bringing corn sugar to Cleveland for years; people use it as a sweetener because it's cheaper than cane sugar. Corn sugar is legal. After you get six pounds of it and distill it into a gallon of whiskey, it's not legal anymore. But a lot of people around Woodland Avenue—that's Cleveland's Little Italy—aren't too worried about that. So Big Joe gives a bunch of them stills, sugar, and whatever else they need to make corn whiskey, which they say tastes more like rum, but who cares? It's alcohol. When it's done, Big Joe buys it off the distillers, a kickback for being involved in the racket. Then he turns around and sells the product at a markup. He clears five thousand a week that way, and that's in 1922 dollars, the same as making somewhere north of $65,000 a week now. They say you can smell the fermenting hash all over the neighborhood.

So Big Joe Lonardo's operation is pretty big, and bad, because Lonardo doesn't just beat his competitors; he kills them. The first bootlegging murders happen right at the beginning, in January 1920. Two men found in a snowdrift, shot in the head. One of them is carrying a letter from his father. *I understand the situation in which you are but you must have courage and face things as they come. There is no advice I can give that will save you.* A third one gets away, leaves his hat in the snow, a kernel of corn stuck to the inside brim with dried blood. People say it's a sign. Cleveland's murder rate starts to rise. In November 1924 Louis Rosen and his brother-in-law, Adolph Adelson, are killed with handguns and a shotgun in Rosen's garage, Rosen for having the nerve to steal corn sugar from Lonardo after Lonardo stole from him, Adelson just for being in the wrong place at the wrong time; he's an accountant from Pittsburgh, just in Cleveland for a wedding. In June 1925, August Rini gets seven bullets to the face on the sidewalk in front of his office on Woodland Avenue. Salvatore Vella is shot in his car in front of a funeral parlor on the same avenue in 1927. You could say the violence creeps up the chain of command, because early in 1927, Big Joe goes back to Sicily for a few months to visit his mother—and, they say, have an affair with a Sicilian girl, another affair—and when he comes back to Cleveland in October, he and his brother John are shot to death in the back of a barbershop. They say Salvatore Todaro, Lonardo's right-hand man, orchestrates the whole thing while Big Joe's away, because when Lonardo dies, his main competitor, Joseph Porrello, who also goes by Big Joe, takes his place. Which is why Angelo, Big Joe Lonardo's son, shoots Todaro in 1929. It's the son avenging the father, and dooming himself.

The whole thing is a massacre for anyone involved in it; it's pretty obvious to anyone on the outside looking in. You don't have to look any farther than the thick stripe of blood John Lonardo leaves on the sidewalk when he staggers out of the barbershop and dies on the steps of the meat market, twenty yards away. So it can seem just as obvious to ask, if Pete's so smart, what makes him go in; or once he's in, how he ever thinks he'll get out again. That's an easy question to ask now. We have the luxury of asking it. But Petro Garko can't afford that, not when he's starting from the South Side. For him, there's just the way off the South Side, across the river, the way forward. He's not blind: He can see the carnage on either side, the corpses on the ground. But he can't see where it all leads to, and neither can anyone around him. We couldn't have, either, if we were there with him. Don't fool yourself into thinking otherwise. In 1922, Petro Garko, Pete the Uke, Peter Henry Hightower thinks that maybe if he's careful, if he stays sharp—if he moves when he can, when he has to—and if things can just fall into place around him, he can escape. Dodge all the bullets and knives Cleveland points his way and end up with just a little blood on his shoes. He's got a good plan, after all. He thinks it should get him out within a decade. It's only years after that, many years, in his big house in Bratenahl with his wife and children, and the avenging angels of his past closing in on him, that he can see what we see now: that maybe it was possible to do what he set out to do, and maybe he was lucky, and maybe he was smart; but he wasn't lucky or smart enough.

Rinaldo Panetti's funeral happens a couple days after his wife goes down to the morgue to pick him up. It's not as grand as the Lonardo brothers' funeral will be, but it's a pretty big deal. A small procession of cars down Woodland Avenue to Calvary Cemetery. A brass band. The wife and mother in clothes of black silk. A couple of open flower cars. Everyone from the organization is there, including Pete the Uke, who buys Rinaldo a wreath for the grave. At the edge of the street, he sees a gaggle of South Side boys, who have come to gawk. They're talking a little too loud for a funeral, loud enough for Pete to hear. *Looks like a pretty swanky life,* one of them says. Another of them turns and shakes his head. *Yeah, but what's the point if you don't live to enjoy it?*

"I want to thank you for what you've done for this organization," Lou Rizzi says later. They're in the back room of a bakery, playing cards.

"It was nothing," Pete says.

"Oh, don't say that. Killing a man isn't nothing."

"You know what I meant."

"I do. You're smarter than most of the guys I have, Pete. Way smarter. My mother used to say that if you can't tell how smart someone is, then they're probably smarter than you."

"That sounds about right," Pete says.

"It sure does. Which of us would you say is smarter, Pete?"

Pete looks at his cards.

"I can't say," he says.

Rizzi laughs. "Me neither," he says. "So. Tell me about this plan you got."

"Well, it's more of a con."

"Who's the mark?"

Pete looks up.

"All of them," he says. The way he says *them*, Rizzi knows who he means. All those rich fucks they fleece every night. The Lonardo operation has gotten rich off of them. Lonardo himself is going to buy a nice place in Shaker Heights for his family. Not Millionaires' Row nice, but nice. His wife's got a fur coat, some pieces of fine jewelry. Rizzi's got some fine suits. His kids'll be able to go to college. They want for nothing in the material realm. But for Rizzi, it doesn't take away the bitterness of knowing that he and everyone else he knows are still the puppets of the people who own this town, the people with real money, real connections. The ones politicians court. The thing that Rizzi depends on for his livelihood—the thing that his people shoot each other over—is only stuff for their amusement. His people live and die on their largesse. Maybe Rizzi's got some power inside the Lonardo operation, and in the neighborhood, people cross the street to shake his hand. But the young men who drink his booze every night could turn him in and send him to prison for years if he ever crossed them. Or they could just ruin him in secret by deciding among themselves, one day, not to come anymore. The capriciousness is built right into the arrangement; it's so obvious none of them have to talk about it. Maybe that's what gets Lou Rizzi the most, that he can't do anything about it. He has no way to hurt them that doesn't make him ruin himself, too. It offends his sense of common decency. He doesn't begrudge them screwing him. He does plenty of that himself, to other people, and he's no hypocrite. But he believes people should be able to talk about it, to argue, to fight back. *It's the only dignity we get,* he thinks.

Now Rizzi looks at his cards.

"Tell me more about this con," he says to Pete.

"Maybe I should just show you," Pete says. He puts his cards down, leans back a little in his chair. And in a second he switches personalities; Petro and Pete are gone, and there's Peter Henry Hightower in all his Protestant, patrician glory. Rizzi can see it before Peter says anything.

"Because," Peter says, "I can become one of them."

"You don't have the history."

"That's right. But I don't need the history if I have the money."

"What's the con?"

"The con," Peter says, "is that we get to enter legitimate business. We get to leave our little game and play their big one. I just need enough money to become an investor."

"In what?"

"Construction."

"We're already in construction."

"Only on the labor end," Peter says. "Not the capital. I don't want to build the building, Louis. I want to own the building. And then another. And another. Then to diversify," his hands fan outward, in a gesture Pete the Uke would never make, "into railroads, the stock market." He takes a breath. "Everything."

Rizzi believes Pete can do it. The ambition seems to warp the air around him. He's a fire in a closed oven, and in that moment, the boss sees just how big it could get if he opens the door.

"You know better than I do how huge the money is on the right side of the law," Peter says. "A hundred times as much as what you can make now. A thousand times as much. And no more need to hide it, or launder it. No more pretending. Just money as far as we can see. And all we have to do is tell two little lies to get it. Two little lies that make one new man. In person and on paper."

He leans forward. "I'm the person."

Rizzi is smiling. "And we're the paper."

"Right."

"So how much are you asking for?"

Now Peter's smiling, too. "How much do you have?"

He lies low for another month, just to make sure that nobody in the speakeasy will remember him. Does a last liquor run across Lake Erie for the boss. The money's in a satchel in his lap on the way over. The boat chews through the water. On the other side are four guys on a dark dock with cases of booze and their hands in their pockets. Nobody says much more than a couple words. They've done this all enough times by now that everyone knows what to expect; they only speak up if something goes wrong: a crate about to tip into the water, someone's hand about to get mashed, the police coming. Peter gives them the money, tips his hat to them, and they're off again, back over the water.

They cut the engine when they get close to Cleveland. The Coast Guard's been getting better at nabbing the runs, so they don't go right into the port anymore; a half mile offshore they turn east, heading toward the edge of town, a waiting truck, and Peter gets a good long look at his city. It's always harder to see at night than he expects. But he can see how the place is growing, the buildings climbing into the sky. They say the town's booming, it's the best it's ever been, but Peter knows—he can hear it in the way the customers, the marks, at the speakeasy talk—that the city's forces are still gathering. It's all latent power, something about to be unleashed. Peter promises himself that when it crests, he'll be at the top of it. Then for some reason he can't explain, he thinks of his father. Petro Garko, five years old, is at the front window of the house, waving outside to his dad, who's being silly, walking backward through the front gate on the way to the street so he can wave back to his son. *It's not that easy, kid,* his father says. Peter tries to ignore it.

Chapter 10

*C*aroline Anderson is only fifteen in March 1922. She's the youngest of three. Her sister Cecily is twenty-three, outspoken, progressive, a member of the League of Women Voters of Cleveland; is still, now and again, talking about the election of 1920. She voted for James M. Cox, newspaperman, Democrat, former governor of Ohio, and has decided she hates Warren G. Harding, even if he's from Ohio too, and a newspaperman, and a very popular president who won in a mammoth landslide. *There's just something about him,* she says. *Too much of a man.* A month later, when *The Wall Street Journal* breaks the story that one of Harding's boys, Albert Fall, secretary of the interior, leased some land in Wyoming to another of Harding's boys, Harry Sinclair, an oilman, Cecily smiles. *See, I told you. Too much of a man.* It's a gutsy thing to say at the time. Nobody knows about the kickbacks yet, and nobody's asking how Fall got so rich. Jess Smith is still alive—he'll be found shot in the head eleven months from now, with people haggling over whether it's a murder or a suicide—so there's no talk about just how Smith's boss, Harry Daugherty, Republican party hotshot made attorney general, is connected to bootlegging. Teapot Dome isn't a household word yet, or the Little Green House on K Street. *Smoke-filled room* hasn't become a cliché instead of just referring to the room in the Blackstone Hotel in Chicago, where, they say, a bunch of senators got together to arrange Harding's nomination. Even after all these things have happened, people won't decide Harding was a lousy president for years. He'll be long gone by then. His own sudden death in San Francisco—in mid-sentence while talking to his wife, some will say, though it seems nobody's really sure what happened to him—is only seventeen months away. But when it all comes out, Cecily smiles, raises her eyebrows, shakes her head, a heady mix of disgust and smug satisfaction. *I told you all he was like this, and you didn't believe me.* She doesn't see through Peter Henry Hightower, though.

Their older brother, William, brings Peter to the family's house for dinner in April 1923, after a few months of talking about him. This charming man, a little roguish, from Connecticut, William tells the family. Seems to have gotten through Yale without anyone knowing who he was, which is a little hard to square with his ambition, though not with his intelligence. A very intriguing man, savvy and wary, but willing to take some risks; also, he seems to be sitting on a rather large amount of capital, which, as William puts it, isn't being exploited to its full potential.

"I would very much like to go into business with him," William says. He doesn't say that he met Peter in a speakeasy.

"You're saying he's your ticket," Cecily says.

"I wouldn't put it that way."

"I know."

Cecily teases William because it's so obvious how much he wants to be rich. It's also obvious that he can't do it by himself. He just doesn't have enough: enough smarts, money, daring, intuition. The one thing he does have is connections, to people Peter has told him he would love to meet someday, his voice carrying the strong hint that wherever those introductions take him, he'll let William follow.

"So he's using you," Cecily says.

"It's not as cynical as that," William says. He fumbles a few words before saying: "It's more like we're using each other."

"That sounds so much better."

"You know what I mean."

"No, William. I don't."

"Don't hate the man before you've met him."

"It's so hard not to, after everything you've said."

But Peter wins Cecily over on the first night. He's charismatic and clever, like William said, but not in the way Cecily was expecting. She had already made him into just another of the guys his brother knows. They're a little too confident and a little too loud about it when you see them in a speakeasy or on the street. There they pretend they're the next Lorenzo Carter, the first white settler of Cleveland, who settled disputes with knives, guns, and sheer bravado; they pretend that those pioneer roots or some distant middle-class ancestry aren't so distant. And then they're a little too deferential when you see them at social engagements, weddings, the theater. Those times when they cover over the smallest hint of their individual personalities with a thick cake of breeding.

Peter isn't like that. He's got the moves down, says all the right things, but in his hands the rules seem more like tools. He's made them his servants. He's not confident, he's strong; not deferential, but disciplined. When he walks across the rug in their living room, it's as though he's cutting it in half. The kiss on her hand is firm, European, though somehow not an affect, either. His eyes close when he does it, then look straight at her, as if taking all of her in at once. Giving her his full attention. For the time when they talk, nothing can distract him.

"It's very good to meet you, Cecily. I hope you don't mind me borrowing your brother so much these days."

"I think he's happy to be borrowed."

"Not as happy as I am."

He says it like he's flying a kite, but she can tell how serious he is about it. She's never met anyone so forward, and yet so good at staying in the lines; it seems so natural, like he's been doing it all his life. He's got her fooled.

Peter doesn't fool Caroline. Part of him doesn't want to. She sees that it's an act because she does it herself. Caroline's never been too comfortable being comfortable, and it's not just because she's a teenager. It's what she is, it's a sharp point in her personality. Her life in Cleveland is all oak woodwork and private schools, friends who take riding lessons, though they don't have enough to keep horses themselves; just for a nice address in Cleveland Heights. Fashionable clothes every season. They can dabble, just a little, in politics and society. It's easy for the rest of her family to look toward the center, at the inner rings of power in Cleveland, the families and the big money that make the city run, and feel how excluded they are. But Caroline's looking outward, at everyone else. To her, it's like they're just inside the walls of a castle, and nobody else notices that the walls are made of glass. She's always noticing the newspaper boys on the corners downtown, freezing in their shorts and cotton clothes in the winter. She's always looking out, when they're in the car, at the neighborhoods on the East Side where the houses are much closer together. She sees how many more people are out on the street, sharing their space with each other because the places where they live are small enough to feel like coffins. When she's downtown, she looks over the river and sees how much smoke there is in the air; for the people living under it, she thinks, it must be like they're living in a thunderstorm. If you were the sentimental type, you might say that Caroline Anderson and Galina Garko are mirror images of each other, the same kinds of women, just in different circumstances, sitting on opposite sides of the Cuyahoga. One in a smart dress she just bought for school, the other in clothes she's been wearing for ten years. Each one seeing the other shore like a foreign country, a continent to explore. But this isn't that kind of story.

Let's say it like this: When Caroline and Peter meet, they both can't breathe, because for each of them, it's like the other one split them open, and now they can see everything inside: the contents of their hearts, their lungs shaking in the open air. All the secrets they've ever kept, the doubts they've locked in cages in the backs of their heads, because they'd eat them alive if they got out. It's carnage, terrifying and thrilling, and when Peter takes her hand, he can't bring himself to kiss it. Cecily takes it for lack of interest—how could a man like that be interested in Caroline, still just a girl? She's only sixteen. Cecily doesn't know, as Caroline does, what he's thinking.

"Peter, right?" Caroline says.

"Yes. And you're Caroline?"

"That's right."

"How do you like school, Caroline?"

"That's a complicated question."

"I felt that way about school myself. I didn't realize how much I would enjoy being done with it until I was."

"It's good to hear an adult say that."

"It's easy for me to do it. I don't have any responsibility here. No need to make you think I have any authority over you."

"None of my brother's friends has ever talked to me this way before."

"Have they ever talked to you at all?"

"No. Not really."

She reminds him of some of those South Side girls, the ones forced to be adults before they hit puberty. They know how to start coal fires when they're five, how to care for babies when they're eight. They've got all of grandmother's recipes memorized when they're nine, the ways to cook meat when you don't have much of it and there are a lot of people in the house, expecting to be fed. He's caught himself thinking about what will happen to those girls. How many of them will stay in the neighborhood, have enough kids to be able to work a farm, though there's no farm in sight? How many will speak more Ukrainian than English, talk about a fight with the Poles as though it were headline news, international affairs? How many will wander away from their history and become Americans instead? And then what does that mean? To be American? The people he thought were Americans on the South Side are always saying they're something else. Irish. Italian. Methodist. Episcopalian. Anything but allegiance to the country they live in. To Peter, being American is an idea, not an identity. It means you're rising, progressing, moving forward; but for all the talk of God and country, prosperity and destiny, there's no destination Peter can see. Just movement. For some people, it's a mad scramble. Others just go around and around. For a few, it's all much more deliberate; they have a place in their head where they want to be, and they're figuring out how to reach it before they die. And there's a lot of elevated language about that, words that approach the religious. It has the rhythms built into it that Peter heard Father Tarnawsky say in church on Sundays. But as far as he can tell, it's really just about money. Money and fucking people. Maybe fucking people over. He thinks he understands it so well, and it gives him a dark confidence that he knows how to use it. Even as he can hear what his family would say. His brother, wondering why he can't be nicer. His mother, telling him he's getting too big for himself. She doesn't begrudge him leaving the South Side, but does he have to go so far? One of those big houses along the lake he wants, their gardens, their driveways—it's just more furniture to buy, more carpets, more trees to trim, more cracks to fix. People to hire, because it's more than one family can manage, which should tell him something. Why does he need all that? Who is he trying to impress? What is it inside him that can't be satisfied? And then there's his father again, picking himself up off the tracks in the Flats, with his sooty clothes and blackened hands, to remind him that death comes when it comes. You think you're going to live long enough to be a great-grandfather. You think that death will approach you from far away and take years to reach you, that the warning bells will sound one by one. That you'll have time to prepare. You'll go blind, you'll go deaf. You won't be able to taste the food in your mouth anymore, or feel your toes. Your bones'll get so brittle that you'll crack ribs when you roll over in your sleep. At last, the old heart'll slow down, way down, until the last beat is like a surprise, because you'll think it stopped already, a couple seconds ago. But it doesn't always happen like that. You'll spend so many years, his father says, amassing your empire, assuming that you'll be alive to see the end of it. But you might not be. Then it'll just be years of spreading misery, across the world and across your soul, until you're cut off by a train, a speeding car, a piece of falling masonry, a spinning bullet, the sharp side of a knife, a burst artery. And then think of all the parties you didn't go to, the girls you never danced with. The people who'll never miss you because you never met them. What'll all that you've done be worth then?

Peter gives Caroline a good, long look, like a favorite uncle.

"Your brother's friends are missing out," he says. Looks at his watch. "Be good, all right?"

He lets it slip and she catches it. "Be good? That's something the kids on the South Side would say." But he's back in character by the time she's done talking.

"And how would you know what the kids on the South Side sound like?"

"I go downtown," she says. "I've got ears."

"You're onto me, Caroline," he says.

She doesn't see him again for two years. She doesn't see much of her brother, either, because he's busy. She's not interested enough in Cleveland's business world to follow a lot of what he says to his parents when he comes by, but she notices other things. His new suits, the cut, the fabric, the colors. The way he combs his hair. The cuffs on his shirts. The big one: his shoes. You can always tell a man by his shoes, and William's got some beautiful ones. Soft, light brown leather, an elegant curve of stitching up the side. Almost like a slipper, a lady's shoe, except for the strong block of a heel, the wider taper at the front. The shoes of a man who's not stepping in anything he'll regret; a man who's doing better than he expected, who knows he's getting away with something. He's bought a house a few blocks away from them, bigger than the one he grew up in, though he lives in it by himself. Someday when it all goes south, he might have to sell that place and the car he bought to go to work from it. Might end up in the same kind of apartment he was in just a few years ago. But he'll still have those shoes, and when he puts them on, they'll remind him and everyone else where he was at. *When times were good, I was a player. When they're good again, I will be, too.*

But Peter. Well. When Caroline sees him, she can tell that Peter puts her brother to shame. He's not flashy like William is. His hair is the same as before, his manner just as forward and subdued. He's not letting anything go to his head; if anything, it seems like he's trying to hide how much he has. She hears that he lives in an apartment somewhere—*downtown* is all he'll say, and she'd believe anything. That he lives in a tiny, tidy little flat in an unassuming building, almost ascetic, so every cent is going into something productive, every dollar's making three more. But it's also possible to imagine that he means the word *apartment* like Louis XIV meant it: There's a place in downtown Cleveland somewhere that looks like an office building, but the top three floors are taken over by parlors and libraries, a grand ballroom, bedrooms with crystal skylights, a staff of seven just to keep the place in shape, all invisible from the street. But he can't hide everything, because when Caroline looks him over, one word enters her head: *flawless.* In the last year and a half, several boys have been interested in her, and she's returned the favor to one or two—isn't that teenage girls everywhere? It's as if they've got everything figured out and don't know it—but in the back of her mind, she can't get away from the straight fact that those boys are boys. Kids. Peter's not a kid, and she can still remember how he didn't treat her like one, either.

"You must be close to graduating now," Peter says.

"In June," Caroline says.

"What then?"

"I don't know." She doesn't have to tell him what he already knows: college, because she's done so well in school, but then it's either teaching, or nursing, or being a secretary, or nothing. Caroline isn't like her sister; she's not angry about it. Cecily's giving her father lectures at the dinner table these days about how she's at least as smart as some of the men her father works with. She's met some of them and isn't impressed. Her father sits there and takes it, at least for a few minutes. He knows she's right, but also has the luxury of not caring. When he decides he's had enough, he stops it with a single sentence: *What are you going to do about it?* Or: *You could always just get married already.* That makes her even angrier, because it's so easy for her father to shut her up. Reminding her that what she thinks are her rights are an extension of his privilege. One of these days, she wants to have the real talk, cut right down to the bone: *What are we to you really, Dad? Mom and Caroline and I? Are we people or just meat?* But she has to be ready to leave the house after that one, and she isn't.

Caroline's more subtle; she sees how futile it is to be direct. To Caroline, Cecily's taking a hammer to a wall that won't come down. But there might be a way around it, or as Caroline likes to think, over it. She imagines herself standing next to her sister, who's swinging over and over again, sweat running down her arms, crying out at each blow. Meanwhile, Caroline collects balloons, one after the other, until there are enough to carry her off. She checks the wind, and over the wall she floats. Then she lets a few of the balloons go, comes to a gentle landing in another country, where she's free.

"It's a waste, isn't it?" Peter says.

"What is?" Caroline says.

"That you're so bright. You're smarter than your brother. Smarter than your sister, too."

"I wouldn't say that," Caroline says.

"But you must have thought of it."

"I don't like saying mean things about my family."

"It's not mean if it's the truth," Peter says.

"Yes it is. And besides, what makes you so sure it's true?"

Peter laughs. "You're right. It's just a hunch. But it's a hunch I've had for a while and nothing I've seen in your family has led me to believe otherwise."

"You haven't seen me for years."

"I've seen enough."

"You're a very interesting man, Peter Hightower."

"And you have become a very interesting young woman, Caroline." He manages to say this without setting off alarms, a warning that Caroline might be prey. She hears only admiration, the beginning of affection. Decades later, when her life is unraveling all around her and she fights with Peter for a solid year, she'll wonder if he ever meant any of what he said. If even then, he was playing hard, gaming her and her family for as much as he could get out of them; or if he was telling her the truth when he said he loved her.

"There's no chance I could see you again, is there?" Peter says.

"In the next three years?" she says.

"I'd like it to be sooner than that."

"Well, Mister Peter Henry Hightower," she says, "you know the rules."

They start seeing each other at parties, because they're running in the same circles now. Each one acts surprised to see the other one, when each of them showed up hoping the other would be there. Then it's a night out to the Allen Theatre, with William and his current girlfriend—by the 1920s, girls are dating, or at least these girls are. The intersection at Huron and Euclid in 1925 is all hazy light, one sign for the Allen vertical over the sidewalk, the other high above their heads, the sign for the Loews State just a few doors away. The streetlights making stripes all the way down to Public Square while cars zip over the tracks for the trolleys. They watch *The Phantom of the Opera* with Lon Chaney. Before and after, the Allen Theatre Orchestra plays, Phil Spitalny conducting. Spitalny was born in Odessa in 1890, was a prodigy on the clarinet, and he's all about jazz now. He conducts a dance band in the city that cuts records for Victor, good ones; by the 1930s he'll be out of Cleveland, doing the Hour of Charm for radio in New York with his All-Girl Orchestra and Evelyn and Her Magic Violin. He'll marry Evelyn in 1946, retire in 1955 to Miami Beach, where he'll write music reviews for a local paper. Cancer will get him in 1970, and though he'll have worked with Gus Kahn and gotten a star on the Hollywood Walk of Fame, he'll be buried back in Cleveland, to be close to his family. By then, Peter Henry Hightower and Caroline Anderson, watching him now from the balcony, will both be gone, too, though they were born after him. But we're getting ahead of things.

There are only a couple more dates with other people before they're going out alone, just the two of them. A lot. She hasn't seen where he lives—she's more cautious than that, still has a sense of propriety—but they're starting to develop their own language, the things every couple have that they almost never let anyone else see. Nicknames for each other, certain words given bigger meanings than they have for other people. They're quiet about it, discreet, but they can't stop everyone from noticing, and the Andersons are talking about it.

"We like Peter," the mother says, "but we don't really know anything about him. Can we trust him?"

"Mom," William says, "Peter is the straightest shooter I know." Which, for all of Peter's fabrications, might still be true. But William has no idea that, before Peter talks to Caroline's father, he needs to talk to Lou Rizzi, who sighs.

"We've all been very happy with you, Pete. We've all done so well by you. You know that."

"Yeah," Pete says. He's playing the gangster now, though he's been doing it less and less. Like I said: It's so much more lucrative when you're on the right side of the law.

"You haven't made a mistake yet," Rizzi says. "I just wonder if this isn't your first."

"Because I'm making my business personal?"

"Of course not. We don't care about that. It's more that the closer they get to you, the easier it'll be for them to figure out that you're not who you say you are. You have to think hard about that. About what you're going to do about that."

"I have, Lou. I have."

"You're sure? There are so many things to think about. You got to be ready."

"I'm ready."

Lou Rizzi gives him a long hard look. Frowns, rubs his chin. Pete can tell he's thinking about killing the whole plan. Then he shakes his head, not in denial. More like, *ah, fuck it.*

"I'm trusting you that you know what you're doing," Rizzi says.

And then Peter has to talk to Caroline herself. *We have some things to discuss,* he tells her, with an intensity she's never seen in him before.

All right, she says. They go for a drive. He picks her up at her parents' house and they head toward the lake, out of the greenery of Cleveland Heights, through Forest Hills, until they've arrived in Bratenahl, turn onto Lake Shore Boulevard. Its walls, its dark trees, its wide lawns. They pass a couple pieces of land where houses are being built, grand things that are still skeletons with no flesh on them. *It must be business,* she thinks. A real estate development deal he and William are involved in, maybe, though he's talked about business so little with her; just vague conversations about money and loyalty. She's never been sure if he's serious or just making small talk. William and her father talk about money all the time, with an air of precision that suggests that they think it's all very important. Peter's talk is different, somehow lighter and heavier at the same time. A tone of voice, she's thought to herself, that you might use to tell jokes at the bedside of someone who's very sick, and you're trying to cheer them up. The substance of the conversation seems so light, but there's no denying the real conversation happening below it, as if big decisions are being made.

"Why are we here?" Caroline says.

"I need to show you something," he says.

They slow down before a long stone wall with iron spikes driven into the top, turn into the curving driveway. Wind their way through large trees, a broad expanse of ivy, because the owners—rail barons who made good enough that they're moving to New York, and all the way into finance—aren't half the gardener Caroline or Sylvie will turn out to be. She thinks maybe they're in a park until she sees the house. Its garrets, its long windows, the lawn rolling down to the lake. It's so grand it's hostile; it makes the central myth of our country's founding seem like the longest, biggest con of the past two hundred years. Because if we're all created equal in this country, then how does a place like this come to exist here? It's beyond luck and wealth, beyond privilege. It's the building of a new aristocratic class. You go in there and shut the door behind you.

"Why are we here?" Caroline says.

"I'm buying this place," Peter says. Takes a breath; that was the easy part. "And I want you to be in it with me. My partner, in life and in business. But I need to know something first. Can you keep secrets?"

"You know I can," she says.

"How many?"

"How many do you have?"

"Well," Peter says. "To begin with, I am very, very wealthy."

"You and William have been doing very well the past few years."

"You're right, William has done well. But I've done much better than he has."

"I thought you were partners."

"We are. More or less. First more. Lately, less. Because there are certain investments I've decided to make without him."

"Since when?"

"A couple years ago. I decided to branch out."

"I see," Caroline says.

"And some of these deals, I made with people who William introduced me to. I wouldn't ever have been able to meet them without him. But, as it turns out, business couldn't move forward with him."

"And does he know this?"

"No," Peter says. "If he found out, he would be right to accuse me of using him."

"How much more do you have than him now?"

"It's hard to say, because I don't know how much he has."

"Take a guess," Caroline says. An edge to her voice that makes her sound much older, much wiser. Peter has already learned to love her for that.

"Ten times as much at the very least," he says. "Maybe as much as fifty times." He reconsiders. "Could be a hundred."

"A hundred times as much?"

"As I said, it's hard to say." But he lays it all out for her: the way he moved from real estate and small business investments into larger construction concerns. Then railroads; he's got a small piece of the empire the Van Sweringens are building. But more, too. Cars. Steel. Shipping. The stock market. Some foreign investment, most of that in Europe, but some in India and Latin America. A bender across the financial world but so much of it is still in Cleveland. She has no idea how he's done that and still kept such a low profile in this town. How he's had time to see her, when William's been so busy.

"Where did all this come from?" Caroline says.

"One investment led to another."

"But what was the first one?" she says. "It couldn't have been my brother. It can't all be my brother."

"No, it wasn't," he says. Both frightened and delighted that she's smart enough to ask the question.

"What was it?" she says again.

"Illegal."

"How do you mean illegal?"

"I mean that I borrowed from one of our fair city's most illustrious crime operations."

"How much?"

"A lot."

He waits to see if she'll run away at that. She doesn't.

"I've been paying them back, if that's what you're asking," he says, "almost in full, though there are kickbacks involved all the time. Pretty high, in fact, but not compared to how much I have. And, now and again, there's the occasional dubious venture that can't be passed up." Peter smiles. "The ties that bind, still bind. But I don't think they always will. Someday I'll be clear of them. I'm just not sure when."

She doesn't say anything. Doesn't give him any sense of what she's thinking.

"You're not going to turn me in to the police, are you?" he says.

"No. I just don't understand how on earth you ever got involved with them."

Now Peter doesn't say anything. For a few seconds, she thinks maybe she's overstepped. He's going to open the car door for her, gesture for her to get in, drive her home. Then she'll never see him again. But he doesn't do any of that.

"I'm not from Connecticut," he says. "I have no family there. I didn't go to Cheshire, or to Yale. And my name isn't really Peter," he says. "Not strictly speaking."

She can see the transformation before he says a word. It looks like magic, like voodoo, her husband-to-be possessed by another man.

"I'm also Pete the Uke," he says. "A gangster, a bootlegger, a criminal."

Then it happens again.

"But, but," he says, now with an accent she's only heard from the people from the South Side, the newsboys, the ragpickers, the women who look in the windows of the stores downtown and never buy anything, "before I was any of them, I was Petro Garko. My father and mother came here from Ukraine, before I was born. They met on the South Side at a dance. My father died when I was a boy. My mother and brother are still alive. I almost never see them, but I never stop thinking about them." He becomes Peter again, in the blink of an eye. "For almost five years, I have been giving them enough money to live on. More than live on. Live well. They could move out of Tremont if they wanted to, but my mother doesn't want to."

Caroline's just staring at him. Her mouth is open, just a little bit.

"What are you?" she says.

"To be honest," he says, "that's one of the few things I don't think about that much. I'm just who I need to be to get what I want."

She doesn't know what to say to that.

"I'll understand," he says, "if this is too much for you. I won't blame you if you walk away. But I very much hope you'll stay."

It is too much. At first, she wants to run. But she looks at the man again, and sees under the surfaces—all the surfaces—to the person beneath. A man who can cage his thoughts in the name of his ambitions, who protects and cares for his family. And in the last few words he says, she catches a glimpse of the boy. Petro Garko, age seven, on the sidewalk in front of his house. It's sunset on a Saturday night, and he's watching his parents sashay down the block, on their way to a dance. They've left him in the care of a neighbor. He doesn't want them to go. He wants to go with them. He just wants them all to be together, even though he can't make that happen, because he's just a kid.

They're married on May 15, 1926. A hasty calling of an engagement. A ceremony in St. Alban Episcopal Church. Only the bride's side of the family is represented; the groom's family is nowhere to be found. *Shouldn't we at least have invited them?* Caroline's mother says. *But you're my family now,* Peter tells her. Says it in just such a way as to imply that he hasn't spoken to them in years, hopes she'll leave it at that. She does, at least to him.

"Aren't you at all worried?" she says to Caroline.

"What do you mean? You said you liked Peter."

"We do like Peter. And we know he can take care of you," her mother says. "But what kind of man doesn't keep in touch with his family? Doesn't even tell them he's getting married?"

"You don't know that he hasn't."

"Well, he hasn't invited them."

"He has his reasons," Caroline says.

"Do you know what they are?"

Caroline, right then, makes the biggest decision of her life. She already can feel the way Peter's deceptions pull at her, force her to choose, between him and her family, him and an honest life. That wall in front of the house in Bratenahl might be the most important thing about it, she realizes. It means most people will never see how they live, never be in a position to ask them any questions they don't want to answer. But they can't stay in the house all day, or keep everyone out. Being with Peter means dancing around a line for the rest of her life. She can see it all coming, the millions of tiny lies she'll tell, about where Peter is, where Peter's gone. Where the money comes from, why they have so very, very much of it. If she's not careful, she'll lose her whole family over it. That thought almost makes Caroline back out right then. Almost. She doesn't think of what could happen to her children.

"Yes," Caroline says. "They're between him and his family. And frankly, I'm a little insulted that you seem to think so little of me as to ask."

"I don't think so little of you," her mother says, in a quiet voice. Her mother's just worried, and Caroline knows it. Knows, too, that her mother can see how her daughter's holding all the cards. Her mother can't be angry. Just hurt.

"I'm sorry," Caroline says. "Perhaps I misunderstood you." She'll regret all of it later, but relishes the power now. And a month after the wedding, after they've made arrangements to deliver furniture to the giant house in Bratenahl, empty except for the bedroom, the kitchen, and two chaise lounges on the long porch overlooking the lake, they take the car west along the coast, into downtown Cleveland, where the steelwork for Terminal Tower is starting to go up. Drive over the Cuyahoga, where the Flats are clanking and roaring. Peter doesn't look. They drive through Ohio City, pass the West Side Market on Lorain; Caroline can't get it out of her head that it looks like a train station, clock tower and all. As if they're going far away. Then they've dipped into the valley and come back up again, and they're in Tremont, they're on the South Side.

Caroline's never been there—she's an East Side girl—and it hits her, hard. She always knew Cleveland was an industrial place, knew that's how people earned money around here. She just didn't appreciate the difference between making a living from it and living with it. On the South Side, it's all church spires and smokestacks. The people living in obvious poverty. The streets are lined with picket fences instead of sidewalks, and they're so narrow that two cars almost can't pass each other. The alleys are open gutters. Children appear from gates and run out in front of them without warning. People keep green hedges and flower gardens, ivy and foxcomb, but the paint on the houses is covered in cinders and soot, the pigment bleached out by sulfur fumes.

They have to drive slow to get down to the house where Stefan and Galina still live. Stefan's been to college, is working for the Ukrainian

National Association as an accountant. *You're not going to make any real money doing that,* Peter tells him. *Yeah, but I don't need to be ashamed of what I do make,* Stefan says back. Both of them tough enough to say what they have to say and not flinch, laugh about it a little bit afterward, though they both feel it later, like a burn they didn't put the ice on fast enough. The fight they had years ago that they both still remember. And Stefan can't hit him with everything. The Ukrainian identity Peter left behind. The people he could be helping—the money he could be sending back—if he only gave a shit about them. It's hard for Stefan not to think it, being part of the UNA. He's too aware of the war that's fought over Ukraine from 1917 to 1922, just when everyone over here says the fighting's over. That war ends with the Soviet Union and Poland dividing the place up; well over a million and a half Ukrainians die for their privilege. And at the beginning of 1922 *Svoboda,* the UNA's newspaper, runs a few pieces so Ukrainians in America won't forget it. *Everywhere there are Ukrainian tears; everywhere the spilling of Ukrainian blood; everywhere the wounding of the Ukrainian soul. Everywhere we were on our native land, but surely not our own. Svoboda* covers, too, the famine in Ukraine in 1922 and 1923. There are conflicting reports of bread shortages in the country and the export of bread from it. *At first it appears the two reports are contradictory,* the editor at *Svoboda* writes. *If one of the reports is true, then the other is a lie.* It's the setup for pointing the finger. The editor sees through the Soviet ruse even then, believes without hesitation that Moscow would sell bread abroad and let the Ukrainians starve. He doesn't know how right he is, or how it's going to get much, much worse ten years later.

But Stefan can't push Peter that far. He's gotten used to Peter's surprise visits, has learned to accept the money he gives them with a measured grace. They've absorbed, in its entirety, the complex of shame and pride, love and obligation, that keeps Peter coming back, even as Stefan's education—beyond high school, all the way through college, thanks to his brother—separates him from his friends, who are still working in the factory. *Hey, ask your brother if he can help me out, too,* one of them says. *He's not like that,* Stefan says. He tries not to wince when he sees the expressions on their faces, calling bullshit without having to say it. The money alienates all the Garkos, from their neighbors and themselves. And with Caroline beside Peter, Stefan and Galina are awkward all over again, awkward like they were in the first seconds when Peter arrived with the first envelope full of money, that first thousand. Stefan notices the ring on her finger when he opens the door; Galina sees it before they take five steps into the house.

"Who is this, Peter?" Galina says. She's learned never to use the name she gave him again.

"Ma, this is Caroline, my wife. Caroline, this is my mother and my brother Stefan."

Caroline doesn't know what she was expecting. Some kind of drama. Screaming, maybe, from joy or anger, she couldn't say. Some real discomfort, the beginning of some intense family politics. *Aren't all families political?* she thinks to herself. Those endless questions of who has the power, over what domains. The favors and slights that get banked in people's heads. The rising and falling values of the familial bonds, traded in a market like any other, she thinks. At least that's how her family operates. But Galina just looks Caroline over from head to toe and nods, and Caroline realizes that Peter's mother has sized her up, knows everything she needs to know, while Caroline doesn't understand the first thing about her. If there were politics in this family, Galina would be at its head, a dictator, severe but fair. But there isn't any time for politics. Just fighting, fighting and moving on.

"Caroline," Galina says. "Catholic?"

"No. Episcopalian." She can tell the word means almost nothing to Galina. She's aware of Episcopalians as a far-off tribe whose customs she doesn't pretend to know. The older woman nods three times.

"Kids?"

Caroline smiles. "We haven't been married that long."

"Ha!" Galina smiles too. "I mean kids and church. You will take them?"

"I intend to," Caroline says.

"Church is good for kids," Galina says.

"I think so, too."

"Then we understand each other?" It's like Caroline's signing a contract before she knows there's a pen in her hand. She stops. Looks down.

"Yes, we understand each other."

"Good," Galina says. Turns to Peter. "She's too good for you." Doesn't give anyone in the room a clue as to whether she's joking or not. But Stefan chuckles anyway, goes into the kitchen to get Peter and Caroline something to eat. A small bit of sausage he bought on Professor a couple days ago. A triangle of cheese he's been saving for himself. A bottle of homemade wine he got from a neighbor in exchange for helping him dig holes for fence posts in his yard. Bread. A dense bunch of small grapes. He brings them in on a platter. Galina has Peter and Caroline seated at the small table in the living room and is pulling up a chair to sit close.

"May I?" Caroline says, before she reaches for the platter.

Galina chuckles. "Oh, this is a nice one," she says, though it's unclear who she's talking to. Then to Caroline: "Of course you can. You must eat until you are no longer hungry."

"Why?" Caroline says.

Galina pats Peter's knee. "Long trip ahead with this one," she says.

Chapter 11

On February 27, 1933, Galina Garko develops a cough. She ignores it. But the next day, the cough is worse, much worse. A fever comes down on her that makes her head spin. Then she has trouble breathing, and it puts her in her bed. She won't get out of it alive, and she knows it when she lies down. So Stefan heads downtown to see his brother.

Tremont, the South Side, has changed a lot in the past ten years; the Great Depression's hit the place hard. The churches, the houses, aren't as kept up as they used to be. People just don't have the money. There are no restaurants, no gas stations, one movie theater on Jennings, which they say used to be the Gold Coast of Cleveland, though there's no evidence of that now. Two of Stefan's neighbors are drunk all the time, the husband and wife both. Their four kids sleep in the same bed. Their water keeps getting turned off, and the kids end up showering and getting clean clothes at school. Ten boys are hanging around in front of the Ukrainian National Home, playing baseball, craps, and cards, sometimes playing music on an accordion. They're looking for a way to earn a little money; any errand will do. In Lincoln Park, the flowers and lawns for band concerts have become seven acres of dusty baseball fields where boys and men play games during the day. At night, after the policeman on duty goes home, the games turn into fights, and God help the woman who shows up there then. A bunch of the windows are broken at the Lincoln Bath House and they can't keep the faucets and fixtures in the building because the boys keep stealing them to sell for scrap. An old Indian lady with a machine gun runs pool rooms out of the vacant houses at the end of Fruit Street. The ruckus there goes until three in the morning. One Saturday night a gang bursts in and makes off with a hundred dollars after throwing the furniture, along with a couple chickens, in the street. Two priests complain to a couple government inspectors about a dive on Professor and College. *They have a beer parlor, a dance hall, and rooms where it is possible to retire,* one of them says. *Every Saturday night there are big doings over there. Not so long ago a gang of roughnecks over there stripped a policeman of all his clothes and beat him.* Stefan avoids the stoplight on 14th and Fairfield because of the pretty good chance that a gang'll hold him up there. Same goes for the hill on Jefferson Avenue—Big Jeff—if he were heading that way. And every night, Stefan hears the procession of women and children walking home from the Central Market, keeping together for protection. He sees the boys pulling wagons filled with boxes and bits of wood, sees them playing horsehoes in the Flats with bent wire, until it gets too dark to be out. Because unless you're looking for trouble, serious trouble, being out at night is not a good idea.

Peter's a world away from that now, even though he's just on the other side of the Cuyahoga. He's got an office in Terminal Tower. Looking at the marble and bronze of the lobby, Stefan feels underdressed, disheveled. He wants to brush the snow off his shoulders, but he has to wait until he's gone up in the elevator and is standing outside the door to the suite. He leaves snow on the carpet in the hallway.

"Do you have an appointment?" his secretary says.

"I'm his brother."

"Please wait here," the secretary says. Rises and goes into the next room. She's trying to be discreet, but Stefan can hear her through the door. *I didn't know you had a brother, Mister Hightower.* She comes back out, leaves the door open.

"Please come in, Mister Hightower," she says to Stefan. He can't quite bring himself to correct her.

Peter's at his desk. Papers in neat piles. A sleek black telephone on his desk, the same curve on the handset that Stefan sees in the metalwork of the Terminal Tower; he doesn't know the phrase *Art Deco*, but he recognizes the style when he sees it. His brother looks up and smiles.

"To what do I owe the pleasure, Stefan?"

"Ma's sick. Really sick."

Peter nods. "You'll get the best doctor I can find."

The doctor's car stands out in Tremont. It fills the street, seems bigger than the house it's parked in front of. It's the first house call people have seen on that street in a while. The smart suit, the little black leather bag. Everyone knows he's not from the university, not from the city. Only the ones who don't know the Garko family wonder how Galina can afford him. Inside the house, the doctor notes Galina's symptoms, gets out his stethoscope, bends over her on the bed. Her breathing is fast and raspy by then, faster sometimes than the second hand on the clock. Her sentences come out in pieces; she can't get through more than three syllables at once. Through the stethoscope, the doctor can hear it in her lungs, crackly and dry, like the sound you hear when you rub your hair between your fingers behind your ears. He knows what it is.

"Pneumonia," he says. "Almost certainly."

"What can we do?" Stefan says.

"Well," the doctor says. Gives a small sigh. "You shouldn't let her out of bed. Make sure she gets plenty of rest. Does her cough let her sleep?"

"No."

"Well, do what you can."

"That's it?"

The doctor considers. Remembers who's paying him. "There is the possibility for serotherapy," he says. "Injections, you know. Like a vaccine."

"For pneumonia?"

"It's a new treatment. Controversial. They tried it out in army hospitals a few years ago. They've tried it in New York. Now they're starting a big study in Massachusetts. We don't know how well it works on a large scale, but the initial results have been promising." In a few years, after the study's finished, there'll be a big push for serotherapy, because it will seem to work, at least for some people; more people will live because of it. There'll be a government program in place to bring the treatment everywhere, to hospitals and homes, to give everyone a shot. A campaign from the public health service to try to convince private doctors to go along with them, complete with lurid posters. One with an army of Grim Reapers, flags and all, marching together: heart disease, cancer, pneumonia, nephritis. A skeleton captain with a sword leading the way. *Among the men of death, pneumonia ranks third.* Another poster has Hermes sprinting across it, the winged helmet on his head, caduceus in his hand. *Speed is the great factor in the diagnosis and treatment of pneumonia. Take no chances with this disease!* Then antibiotics will come and change everything. But that's a way off.

"We might be able to try serotherapy in the hospital," the doctor says, "but we can treat her better there in any case. In fact, we should take her right now."

"No you shouldn't," Galina says. She's been quiet through all of this, because talking is too hard, but nobody's making any decisions for her. "I don't want to go anywhere. Not even to the hospital. I'm staying here." She thinks of the farm she grew up on outside of Kiev; her memory of it is as strong as ever. The vibrant light, the endless fields crossed by lines of thin trees. The houses of thick walls and animals in the yard. She thinks, too, of the view across the Cuyahoga, the perch on the lip of the valley she's kept going to, because its meaning has only deepened for her as she's gotten older. Her oldest son works in the spires of office buildings on the other side. Her poor, dear Mykhaylo's still somewhere in the valley below. She's so much richer for it, for everything she's seen and done. Though there's weight to that wealth, too, and she's tired.

"I've lived long enough," she says. Sets her mouth and squints at them. Nods a few times. There's no more discussion about it. Everyone comes to see her, one after the other. The priest from St. Peter and Paul, friends and neighbors. Baskets of food and flowers. She won't kiss the baby Henry when Caroline and Peter come by; she doesn't want to make him sick. She just lays her shaky hand on the baby's head. *Be good,* she says. *I know you will be.*

After she dies, they bury her in Riverside Cemetery, in the plot Peter's bought. The ceremony is quiet. There's Peter, Stefan, and the stepfather, who isn't far behind his wife. Caroline holding baby Henry. The stepfather tells Caroline that one of Galina's great happinesses in her final days was that she'd lived long enough to see the child. It's the longest conversation they've ever had, and they lapse back into silence fast. The loudness comes a few hours later, at the reception back at the house, where the friends and neighbors bring food and drink and instruments, enough party to help the ones who are grieving unburden themselves however they want to, without judgment or consequence. But Peter isn't there.

Stefan sees his brother a few days later when he drives out to Bratenahl in his Chevrolet 6. The car's a bit of a splurge, though it makes a difference for his job. He's a bigger accountant for the UNA now, does a bit of recruiting and fund-raising, visiting his fellow Ukrainians to impress upon them what the UNA can do for them and what they can do for Ukraine. He finds that people have a little more faith in the UNA when they see that their representative makes enough to own a car, though not a fancy one. They want the organization to be healthy, not wealthy; there's such a thing as having too much. Stefan doesn't go to his brother's house much, thinks back to when the last time was: to visit the baby just after he's born. Before that is 1928, when he borrows a coworker's ride to get himself out there, all for the mission of telling Peter, face to face, that he can stop giving him money, that he's doing all right for himself. *That's great to hear,* Peter says, and seems to mean it. Stefan doesn't realize then that it means he'll almost never see his brother after that, because the money for Galina starts coming when Stefan's at work. He doesn't even know if Peter delivers it himself after that, and Galina never tells him. He's cut himself out of the deal.

Stefan arrives at the house in the midafternoon, a fall day, the trees in front of the house on fire from the foliage. Peter is there in the driveway when he pulls up.

"I heard you coming," Peter says, and invites him in. The house is all oiled oak and chestnut, covered with Turkish rugs. The sleek couch, the polished end tables. Long, empty walls waiting for paintings or photographs. They're still putting the house together, even though they've been in there for years, but what they've done so far has all the marks of people with real money. There's not a single object in any of the rooms that doesn't cost more than what Stefan would be able or willing to pay for it. It makes him nervous about touching anything, even the short, elegant glasses on a table next to a few bottles of what looks like some very good booze.

"Islay Scotch?" Peter says. "We can drink to it being legal again."

"Not that it ever stopped anyone when it wasn't," Stefan says.

Peter laughs. "Isn't that the truth." Telling Stefan, as if he didn't know already, just where all his money started from.

"How's business?" Stefan says.

"Business? Business is business," Peter says. "Just like it always is."

"They say it's bad now."

"It's always bad. Even when it was good, it was bad. And sometimes when it's bad, it's good."

"You talk like a real businessman now," Stefan says. "It almost sounds like philosophy, some of the things you people say, except it doesn't mean anything." He's surprised at how pointed it sounds coming out of his mouth. But Peter just laughs again, and Stefan isn't sure whether it's magnanimous or condescending.

"You've got us all figured out, don't you," Peter says. "That's the one thing the lower classes have on the upper classes, that they can see right through them. And meanwhile, the upper classes can't understand the lower classes at all. It's as if things are only clear when you look up, never when you look down."

"More philosophy," Stefan says.

"I'm only saying it's just as hard, or just as easy, to make a lot of money as it ever was."

"Once you have a lot of it," Stefan says. He's maybe the only person in Peter's life who'd say something like that, who'd start the class war right in his living room, and Peter likes him for it. Up to a point.

Peter nods. "I'll allow that. But now *you* sound like one of *us*."

"I've been paying attention," Stefan says. Takes a sip of the Laphroaig and remembers, all over again, that he doesn't like the stuff very much. He doesn't think he ever will. That mossy, peaty taste the aficionados rave over just reminds him of someone's basement.

"It's good, isn't it?" Peter says.

"Yes. Excellent."

"That's what the end of Prohibition really means: You can get really good Scotch again. Someday, I think, we'll be able to get the best in the world, all the time. And you know what? There's so much more money involved, then."

"And if you make enough of it, you can erase the line altogether."

"I don't follow you," Peter says.

"The difference between legal and illegal. Enough money, and it doesn't matter very much."

Peter looks at him for a while. "Are you turning into an anticapitalist?" he says.

He knows enough not to say *Communist;* it's that distinction between socialist and communist again, which neither of them will ever forget to make. The socialists are the ones who organized labor, on the South Side and everywhere else, who took a look at the mills and factories, the railroads and the furnaces, and decided that maybe the people who worked there deserved better. When their father was political at all, he was one; if the changes the socialists fought for had come sooner, maybe he would have lived longer. But the communists—well, it's 1933, and the Ukrainians under Stalin, socialists, capitalists, and everyone else, are all starving to death, starving by the millions, ten thousand a day, on the most fertile land in Europe, which they've been farming and feeding the continent with for centuries. It's all because of the Communists, because of Stalin, who's forced them off their land, taken away their bread and livestock, exported what harvest they had. He's made the people eat their seed grain, even though they know what that means, and in time he takes away the grain, too, and has the secret police shoot anyone who tries to take it back. The Ukrainians eat their dogs and cats. A few of them start eating each other, and then die all the same. There are corpses everywhere, in bedrooms, in kitchens, in the street. A band of traveling musicians sent by the government to cheer up the dying—it'd be funny if it wasn't so horrific—find entire villages empty. No one's left to play for. At last they find a house with people in it. Two girls are lying in bed, dead. A man's legs are sticking out of the stove. An old lady, clawing at the dirt floor and ranting, is the only one alive. In another village, a starving man digs his own grave and then lies in it. A father buries one of his children in the graveyard. His other child dies before he gets home. A girl dies in school, in class; she just closes her eyes and dies. Parents leave their children in train stations, send them to the cities, because they can't feed them anymore. Some of them die on the trains. A brother tells a sister: *Mother says that we should eat her if she dies.* The final thing she can give to her children.

In 1933 you don't know any of that from reading *The New York Times* because its Moscow correspondent, Walter Duranty—who's won the Pulitzer for his coverage of the Soviet Union the year before—has decided to ignore it all. The Western intellectual left loves communism right now. Malcolm Muggeridge from *The Manchester Guardian* visits Ukraine and calls it like he sees it. He loses his job and can't find another one. Gareth Jones, on his own dime and against Soviet law, goes to Ukraine for three weeks and reports, in the Hearst newspapers, on what he calls famine on a colossal scale. *Everyone is swollen from starvation,* people tell him. *We are waiting to die.* Duranty attacks that report. *A big scare story,* he writes. *There is no actual starvation. There is widespread mortality from diseases due to malnutrition.* It's just what the Soviet press censor told him to write, after a night of vodka and celebrations. But there are still reports if you know where to look. William Henry Chamberlin in *The Christian Science Monitor* reports on it. And so does

Svoboda, the UNA's paper, maybe more than any other publication in North America. They publish letters from people in Ukraine. *Here in the village there is not a chicken, nor a duck, nor a pig, nor a cow, only hungry people. They have cleaned us out, as if with a broom.* It's the headline story for months. *Ukraine on the brink of death from famine. Bolsheviks execute hungry people.* There's an editorial in December 1932 that once again sees right through what Stalin is doing. *Even the Bolshevik sympathizer from* The New York Times—they mean Duranty—*admits that this winter two-thirds of Russia's population will have nothing to eat. Today they are not blaming the government but the peasants. Is it possible to blame here the serf living in Soviet slavery? Who can possibly believe that?*

A lot of people do. But Peter and Stefan don't, and in that shared understanding of where their people came from, for just a moment, Stefan sees the South Side boy, the older brother he grew up with, lean and strong, who protected him not with his money, but with his hands. He smiles, then. But Peter doesn't return it.

"I didn't mean to turn this into politics," Stefan says.

"You didn't," Peter says. "We're brothers. We can talk about anything." He chuckles. "I just might not answer you."

Now Stefan's angry, because Peter can and will always talk to him like that, and Stefan can't do it back. They'll never hit each other again like they did when they were kids, because there's too much money now. It's all about money, it always will be about the money. It's all right that Peter has so much more than him. Stefan can live with that; he's comfortable, he has nothing to complain about. These days, he feels lucky. And he's seen enough of the business world to know that what you have to do to get that rich isn't worth it to him. But it's also that Peter gave him so much for so long. Stefan thinks, again, about how Peter's the reason, the only reason, that he could go to school all the way through, go to college, get a job better than the one his father had. It was a gift, the biggest Stefan's ever gotten, but because Peter's the kind of man he is, it's also a muzzle. Peter tells Stefan they can talk about anything, but they both know that's not true. If Stefan pushes back too hard, he'll just be acting ungrateful, disrespectful, to the man who changed his life. But Peter can push as hard as he wants, and does.

The truth, dear reader—and Stefan can feel it a little, in the edge on his brother's voice—is that Peter now hates his brother a little. He doesn't resent giving Stefan the money; he resents that what Stefan has is enough for him. He's not married, doesn't have much in the way of prospects for a wife. He can hear, in his mind, the way the women in Tremont talk about him. *He's a little on the feminine side.* Their brows furrowed, one hand lifted, the fingers wiggling. But he has the little house, the job with the UNA, a ton of friends in the neighborhood, who he and Peter grew up with and who are like family to Stefan now; Stefan's making them into the horde of cousins people always say they must have back in Ukraine, if they only knew for sure where their parents came from, though their parents never told them. Peter can see how all the decisions Stefan's made about his life are coming together now into something cohesive, something real. Where he lives, who he works for, who he knows. Stefan is Ukrainian; in the past few years, that word has gained a lot of power, and it makes Stefan powerful, too. Peter imagines Stefan strolling down Professor and running into twenty-five or thirty people he knows. It takes him a half an hour just to walk a few blocks, and it's a few blocks of constant conversation, asking for and doing favors, catching up on small talk. *I'm so glad your sister's feeling better. Please say hello for me. Listen, I was wondering if you could help out a friend of mine. He has four children and needs a job and he's a really dependable worker, I can vouch for that. Oh thank you, he'll be so grateful. Yes, yes, I think there's a chance a loan can be arranged. How much do you need? Let me talk to the office and we'll see what we can do.* He's even reclaiming the language, which Peter almost can't remember, so that he doesn't talk like a child, but the man he is. It all makes him wanted, needed—Peter's thoughts go all the way to the word *loved*—a part of the community that you can't take away without losing something. If Stefan were to die tomorrow, the funeral would be gigantic. The wake would last for two days. They'd fill St. Peter and Paul for the service, and afterward the party would go for hours. And if Peter were sitting there in the house, he'd hear nothing but great things about his brother. The jokes he told. His kindness, his willingness to help. His faithfulness. All the great things he did for the neighborhood, for the community, for Ukrainians. There'd be talk, maybe, of putting his name on a bench somewhere, or on a plaque in the church. Something so that fifty, a hundred years from now, people would see his name and know it, even if they didn't know what he did. They'd talk like that in the living room and the kitchen, on the front porch, in the street in front of the house. And Peter would be sitting there on one end of the old couch, wearing shoes that cost more than all the furniture in the room, one of the most powerful businessmen in Cleveland, and nobody would know or care who he was. That is, until they knew he was Stefan's brother, and then they wouldn't care about anything else; it's all they'd need to make him part of the family, too.

Against his will, Peter thinks of his father: *Pa would be so proud of Stefan, I know it. What would he think of me?* It forces him to dwell the things he's done and why he's done them—and not the little why, but the big why. For Peter, the question of why is almost always a question about strategy, about what can be gained, in money, power, influence. His brain, it seems, is very good at doing that kind of math. He makes decisions fast and doesn't look back, and it's served him well, well beyond what most people dream that they're capable of. But when he steps back from it, at the thing he's made, he doesn't like what he sees. It's a creature, a predator, made of lies and disguises, with murder at its heart, so terrible that he has to hide it from everyone who's not caught up in it themselves—most of all his family, even though he uses it to give them everything they have. His stomach flips when he thinks of it. He wonders what would happen if the thing ever got loose. Whether it would eat his family whole. He wonders how he could ever kill it without losing everything he has. And he thinks then about his own funeral, the precious few people who would go. How would they have anything to say about him afterward? No one's ever seen the beast, not even Caroline. No one knows what he is. And then the final awful thought: *Do I know?*

"I brought some things from Ma," Stefan says.

"I was wondering what's in the box," Peter says.

"It's just a few things. Some photographs of us as children. Some of her and Pa. A few other things from around the house, from growing up."

"Are you sure you shouldn't keep them?" Peter says.

"No, no," Stefan says. "She told me you should have them. Made me pack the box in front of her." *So you won't ever forget who your mother is, or where you came from,* he wants to say. But won't, ever; he knows that it's cutting too close, too far in. "Are Caroline and Henry here?"

"No. They're out with her family," Peter says. He can't help but push that last word a bit, hopes it hurts a little. But Stefan doesn't seem to notice it.

"Listen, Peter? I wanted to tell you something," Stefan says.

"Anything."

"I want to be a bigger part of Henry's life. Henry and any other children you have. I'm their uncle, after all, and I want to be an uncle to them. Do you understand?"

"Of course." Though the way Peter says it makes Stefan think his brother has no idea what he's talking about.

"Could I talk to Caroline about it? Maybe find a time when I can come visit Henry?"

"That sounds like a perfect plan," Peter says, and gives him a quick nod. With that, the last meaningful conversation Stefan will have with his brother is over. Stefan knows it even then, that when their mother died, the last bond between them was broken. He wonders if Peter knows—if he'll never know, or always knew. If he cares enough to worry about it. Stefan worries, though, and so a few months later, on a day when he's sure Peter's away, he comes to the house to call. Caroline answers the door with Henry, still small enough for her to carry him on her hip.

"Good morning, Stefan," she says. "How can I help you?" Pleasant and wary.

"I was wondering if I could talk to you," Stefan says.

"Of course," she says. The same tone of voice as her husband. *So that's where Petro got it*, Stefan thinks; God help him, he just can't think of his brother any other way, after all this time. Peter and Caroline have been swapping each other's phrases for a while now. Caroline just happens to mean it. They end up talking for three hours. It begins and ends with the baby, who's already standing and is working on walking. But it goes everywhere in between. Caroline learns more about her husband's family right then than Peter's ever told her. The death of the father, the nonexistent stepfather. And Galina, Galina, so much about her. *I should have gotten to know her better,* Caroline thinks. The regret threatens to overwhelm her; then she pushes it back, clears her head, because Stefan is telling her something else, about the time he and his brother went to Whiskey Island when they were kids. They were going to dive for bottles—or steal them from the men who lived in the shantytown there—to sell back to the bootleggers. The story takes Caroline all over the island, from the loading docks and the cranes to the ships coming across Lake Erie, to the houses made from scrap lumber and pieces of old billboards. Two chases, first from the men who lived there, then from the police who thought they were thieves, or working for the bootleggers—*now they're contracting out kids, the police must've thought.* Stefan says, and laughs. Caroline laughs too, incredulous all over again that her husband grew up that way.

On the carpet, Henry stands, takes a step, and falls; stands, takes two steps, and falls. Walking is still two months away.

"I'm so glad we talked," Caroline says.

"Me, too," Stefan says. So the wife and children start to see more of Peter's brother, at holidays, weekends, more in the summer. Stefan takes Henry for a few days when Sylvie's born, shows him the neighborhood where his dad grew up, without saying anything beyond what they see, hear, smell, taste, though it's hard not to impart the lesson that almost nobody in the world lives like the people of Bratenahl do. The uncle looks after all the kids whenever Caroline needs him. Years later, when she tells him she needs to escape, he understands, and then is the closest thing to a parent Jackie will ever know.

But Peter won't know any of that. When the trouble starts, he'll feel like he's all alone. By the time it's over, he really will be.

Chapter 12

It's the evening of June 24, 1947. More than twelve thousand people are packed into the Cleveland Arena on Euclid Avenue, filling all sixty rows of the place, cramming themselves into the floor seats, until the place can't fit another soul. At home, in bars, they're gathered around the radio. They're talking about it on the street. It's all for the fight between Sugar Ray Robinson and Jimmy Doyle, the first championship boxing match Cleveland's seen in a while. Robinson's held the world welterweight title for just a few months. He gets it in December 1946 after he goes fifteen rounds against Tommy Bell; he wins by unanimous decision. *He should have been champion a long time ago,* some people say then, because going into that December fight, he's got seventy-three wins, one draw, and only one loss, against Jake LaMotta—you know, Raging Bull—but they've fought five bouts already, and Robinson's beaten him in four of them. The draw is with José Basora; they go ten rounds in Philly in 1945, but when they have their rematch in 1950, Robinson knocks out Basora fifty seconds into the first round. The rumor going around is that it takes so long for Sugar Ray to get to be champion because he won't deal with the mafia, because of racism. But after a while, Robinson's just too good for all of that.

So, the packed arena. It's hot and getting hotter, and loud. Peter Henry Hightower's in the third row of the floor seats, on an aisle. He's there by himself. Caroline's home with the children; Jackie's only two, and is turning out to be anxious, emotional, while Muriel, who's five, just wants to talk all the time. Sylvie and Rufus—nine and seven—are the opposite: so quiet, calm, always heading off somewhere, vanishing together. Henry, fifteen, is a serious kid, tall and strong. In the spring he plays baseball for his school, and it's pretty clear he'll be the team captain by the time he graduates. He has a discipline, a focus about him, that makes him seem older than he is. Because Henry's athletic, Peter suggests just before he leaves that maybe he could take his oldest boy with him ringside, and Caroline just glares. She hates boxing, Peter knows that. But it's something else, too: She knows Peter will end up conducting business at that fight one way or the other. There'll be too many knowing handshakes, too many pats on the back. Way too many sentences with vague nouns in them. *Henry's not stupid,* Caroline's look says. *Do you really want him to know you're a criminal?*

Things change between Peter and Caroline. In the early years of their marriage, there's a part of her that can't get enough of the crime, the deals, the conniving. It teaches her how to manipulate her own family, the Andersons, even through her first falling-out with them. In 1936 her brother William finds out at last just how much better off Peter has become than he is, and there's a night when he's angry about it. But it's so easy to smooth over, just a matter of months. A generous gift over the holidays, a promise of a retainer in one of Peter's business ventures, an apology from her husband that sounds authentic, and soon they're laughing at Anderson family gatherings again, patting each other on the back, wishing her the best. Caroline notices that the days of William confiding anything to her have ended; a trust has been broken, and it'll never be restored. But she decides that what's left of the affection between them after that is enough for now. *After all,* she thinks to herself, *I love my brother; I don't need him.* She's twenty-nine then, old and smart enough to see how callous she's being, but still thinks the sincerity behind it matters, and that it'll let her fix the damage later.

The realization that she's wrong takes years to sink in, but hits her at last on a Saturday morning in March 1942. She's sitting at a table on the long sunporch over the lawn that rolls down to the lake, a cup of hot water in her hand; she's a tea drinker, but she's six months pregnant with Muriel, and something about tea makes her want to throw up. She looks out to the horizon, toward Canada. There's a light rain over the water. The newspaper's folded on the table next to her, but she hasn't read it. It's full of news from the war, though you could say there's still not enough, because we seem to get through the entire thing without knowing just how bad things get for the soldiers fighting it—anywhere, let alone east of Germany. Rufus and Sylvie are playing in the living room. Henry's upstairs. Her husband is still sleeping, from a very late night; she's not sure, but she thinks he didn't get back until dawn. *He's getting too old to be out like that,* she thinks. It's an idle phrase, one she's thought before, and often, even though she knows why he's out like that: It's when the other side of his business gets done. But this morning, it irritates her more than usual. It occurs to her that this criminal thing has been bothering her for a while. No. A long while. Maybe years. Now her brain is off and running, and it goes all the way back to their courtship. The first time she saw the house. *Someday I'll be clear of them,* he said to her then, and she knows he might have meant it as an aspiration—Peter, for all his directness, never speaks in absolutes—but the young Caroline heard it as a promise, a condition for marriage. And the older Caroline realizes that she's been waiting ever since for him to give it all up, to cut those ties. At Henry's birth. At his mother's death. At Sylvie's birth, the first girl. At Rufus's birth two years later. There's always been that hope, that one day he'll come home, wait until everyone else is asleep, take her in his arms and say it: *We're safe. We're free.* Because what made the crime thrilling when she was younger was the certainty—buried so deep she couldn't see it then, even though it affected her—that someday it would end. But now it's been sixteen years, and they have three children, soon to be four. And she keeps reading in the papers about the violence gangsters inflict on each other. It's not thrilling anymore. It just seems dangerous. And she thinks, then, of what she's lost: her brother's trust, and her parents' with it. Even Cecily's. *Was it worth it?* she thinks. *To live like this?*

That Saturday morning, Peter wakes up to find her just a little bit more distant. Over the next five years, there are fights, every eight months or so. *When are you going to get out? Why do you still do this?* Sometimes she's screaming at him. His calm is infuriating. *It's complicated,* he says. *We need to wait for the right time.* This line is the worst thing he can say to her in 1945, when she's pregnant with Jackie, and fighting even more. *It's been nineteen years,* she seethes, *and there has never been a right time.* He's reduced to his last defense then. *Keep your voice down,* he says. *Do you want the children to hear?* As if he's the one trying to protect them from her. From then on, that's the weapon they use against each other. The first one to accuse the other one of hurting the children wins, and they accuse each other of it often enough that, by 1947, each of them is starting to believe it about the other.

In the Cleveland Arena, the bell goes off for the first round. The crowd sucks in its collective breath when the people see how fast Sugar Ray Robinson is. They know he's the champion; some people are already saying that, pound for pound, he's the greatest boxer who ever lived. But it's another thing to see it. He keeps his distance a little, *like a man admiring the cut of another man's suit,* as his biographer will write about him later, and then moves in, throwing punches faster than Jimmy Doyle can keep them off him. Doyle's a real fighter, too. He's from Los Angeles and he's been pro since 1941, with the busted nose to show for it. He gets a reputation when one fight of his becomes a *fight,* the two boxers falling through the ropes of the ring and onto the floor, Doyle still going at it. *He wasn't afraid of nothing,* another boxer will say years later. He's single and lives at home with his mother, and he has this idea that he can make enough from boxing to set her up: buy her a house, some nice things. Enough that she can be comfortable. If he hits it big enough, he says, maybe he'll stop fighting, too. But right now, he's boxing. He gets through the first round, the second, the third, and Robinson's still coming. In the fourth round, a good hit from Sugar Ray shuts Doyle's left eye, and it stays shut.

The seat next to Peter is empty because he bought it for Henry, and he's got his hat on it while he sits, impassive. The boy in him wants to put two fingers in his mouth and whistle, loud, every time Sugar Ray lands a solid hit. But that boy hasn't had a chance to speak in a very long time.

"Do you mind if I sit down?"

Peter looks up. There's a man in a yellow suit standing in the row. Young, maybe twenty-six, Peter thinks. But trying to look older with that mustache. He points at Peter's hat.

"Do you mind?"

"No, of course not," Peter says, and takes his hat, puts it in his lap.

The man nods, sits. Watches Jimmy Doyle catch a blow to the side of the head that makes beads of sweat fly out of his hair.

"He's some fighter," the man says.

"Sugar Ray Robinson?" Peter says. "Yes, he is."

"I mean Jimmy Doyle."

Peter nods. "It's a good match."

"Excuse me for asking," the man in the yellow suit says, "but you're not Peter Henry Hightower, are you?"

Peter looks at him now, much longer, and the man has a sense of Hightower's brain memorizing him. The lines on his face. The tangled whiskers in his mustache.

"I'm sorry, do I know you?" Peter says.

The man gives him a broad smile. "Joe Rizzi," he says.

"Lou's son."

"That's right."

"I knew your father very well, Joe."

"You did? I didn't see you at the funeral, Mr. Hightower."

Peter blinks once, and Joe wonders if he can already see where all this is going.

"I didn't know he had died," Peter says.

"Yeah. Throat cancer. You must not have called much in the last couple years."

"No, I hadn't. I'm sorry I didn't."

Things are awkward for a couple minutes. The fourth round ends and the fighters go back to their corners, then come out swinging again.

"I'm very sorry to hear about your father, Joe."

"Well, thank you."

"I did think of him often."

"Well isn't that nice. He used to talk about you all the time."

"Did he, now?"

"He did. He mentioned this little routine you could do. A shtick, really. You know, talking like me."

Peter smiles. "Yes, I could."

"You don't mind if I hear a bit of it, do you?"

"Oh, no. I haven't done it in years."

"Come on. It's got to be in there somewhere."

"Oh, it is, it is," Peter says. "But I don't think I could summon it now."

"Why?" Joe says, and looks around. "Because of where we are?"

"Yes, that's part of it."

"But it's part of you, too, isn't it? Pete the Uke?"

Peter smiles again. "I haven't heard that name in years."

"That's funny, because I heard it *for* years. My father was real proud of you, you know. How big you got, and so fast. *That boy's got a head on his shoulders,* he used to say. He respected you so much." He licks his lips. "Even though—maybe because—he knew what you had to do to get there."

"He exaggerated," Peter says. "I was just lucky."

"I don't think *lucky* is the word Rinaldo Panetti would use. I know for sure it's not the word his wife and kids would use."

"Who's Rinaldo Panetti?" Peter says.

The tone of voice, the rhythm, is perfect, suggesting nothing but benign ignorance. *I'm sorry, I haven't met the man.* As if Pete the Uke didn't pull a razor across Rinaldo Panetti's throat and get three guys to dump him in the lake. Joe Rizzi's father told him that in confidence. It wasn't information he was supposed to use; it was only to know, to understand the man. If anything, it was a warning, and a warning Joe Rizzi's getting again right now, that Peter Henry Hightower is not a man to mess with. But Joe Rizzi's come a long way to get here. He's been asking around, going through his dad's old things to find a cooked book or two. He's linked it all up, the chain of crimes that starts in Tremont and ends in a giant shackle around Peter Henry Hightower's ankle. The money laundering, the tax evasion. The payoffs, the kickbacks. The financing of a dozen or so operations over the years that turned a couple guys into corpses. And at the very beginning, the murder itself, the story that's an open secret among the wiseguys of Cleveland, that Peter Henry Hightower is one of them. They respect him enough, know the system well enough, to never tell. But Joe Rizzi's not quite smart enough and a little too ambitious to pay attention to respect. So something that could have been done anytime, by anyone in Cleveland's criminal underground, Joe Rizzi is at last doing: He's going for blackmail.

"Oh, you know who Rinaldo Panetti is," Joe Rizzi says. And then twirls his left pointer finger as though it were a knife and drags it across his own throat. Smiling the whole time, staring Hightower down.

"Joe," Peter says. "Do you mind if I call you Joe, Joe?"

"No."

"We can't talk about this here, Joe."

"Sure we can. Nobody's paying any attention to us. We're alone here."

"Alone?" Now Peter laughs. "All right, then," he says. "Since we're alone, I'll say it plain. You have a choice to make right now. You can get up and walk away, and if I see you later, I'll be cordial, nice and friendly, because I held your father in that kind of esteem. Or, you can change that tone of voice of yours right now, and we might even become friends. But continue with what you're doing, and by God, I will ruin you. You will be like the walking dead."

For maybe a second, Joe Rizzi's afraid, but it doesn't show. "It's interesting to hear you talk like that," he says, "when you're the one in the quicksand. You got nothing on me, see, because everyone knows I'm a dirtbag. But you? You're squeaky clean. All those cocktail parties and business meetings you go to now, and no one suspects a thing. All those secrets tucked away safe in that big house of yours. But I can let them all out." He's feeling almost cocky now. "You ruining me? There's nothing to ruin. But I can ruin you with a couple phone calls, a couple letters. First to your business associates. Maybe your wife's family, too. Then to the police. Maybe they won't have enough to put you away, but it'll be enough to destroy that precious life you've built for yourself, won't it? Because here's the thing: You have all the power, all the money, all the influence. But I've got the truth. Nothing but the truth." Now he can't resist. "So help me, God."

The fifth round ends and they go into the sixth. Doyle's still taking punches; he's outstanding at it. Sugar Ray'll say later how amazed he is at the hits Doyle takes. Then Doyle gets Robinson back, at last, right over the eye. Sugar Ray staggers back and starts to bleed. They fight the rest of the round to a draw. Doyle's surviving. But in the seventh round, Robinson starts hitting him, hard, again and again.

"What do you want?" Peter says at last. "Money, I assume."

"You're smart," Joe says.

"How much?"

"Let's not put a number on it just yet. But you might want to think twice about getting ponies for your daughters."

"So you're planning on ruining me anyway?"

"I wouldn't put it that way," Joe says. "But, hey, if that happens?" He shrugs.

"I see." For a moment Peter's breezy. "So since it doesn't matter to you, then maybe I'll just ignore you and get on with my life." Then Joe feels it before Peter speaks, the ice in the air. "You fucking wop lowlife. You two-bit imbecile. I could break your neck with my little toe and you're too fucking stupid to even notice."

Peter's not watching the fight anymore. He's watching Joe Rizzi. And Joe Rizzi turns and looks back at him.

"Sure," he says, "but what about your children?"

Peter swallows. Joe sees it and is satisfied. He's already broken one rule today—the code of silence, a big one. Why not break a few more?

"Oh, yes. Because I know where you live, and you can't keep all your children in your sight all the time, can you? Can anyone? You have so many. It would be impossible to keep one of them from going missing. And if one of them does, Peter, there won't be a ransom. Oh, no. None of that fucking around for me. I'll make it look like one of the torso murders, like the Mad Butcher of Kingsbury Run did it. Yes I will."

It's been nine years since the last victims were discovered: On August 16, 1938, at the dump on the corner of Lake Shore Drive and East 9th Street, three men come across what look like human bones, and get the first policeman they can find. Turns out there's a human torso there, a woman's, wrapped in heavy brown paper, a striped summer coat, and a quilt. The thighs are right under it, bundled in the same paper and held together with a rubber band. There's another package five feet away; the head's in there, with silky light brown hair. The arms and lower legs are in a cardboard box made from two different boxes, one for biscuits, the other for seafood; it says so right on the side. Just a few hours later, a machinist there to see the police activity finds the bones of another murder victim, in a depression in the ground near an outflow pipe. The head, now just a skull, is in a can nearby. They're the eleventh and twelfth people slaughtered this way around Cleveland since 1934. They find the parts in the river. They find them in the lake. They find them on hillsides, in baskets on curbsides. The papers have gone mad every time. *This torso killer—what sort of madman is he? A cunning madman with the strength of an ox. He's as regular, as coldly efficient, and as relentless as an executioner when the mood to kill comes over him. Never has an intended victim escaped his relentless knife, never has a "friend" lived to tell the tale.* The police have been investigating for years, following one trail after another that all go cold. In 1938 Eliot Ness, then Cleveland's safety director, rounds up dozens of hobos who live in the Flats and Kingsbury Run and burns down the shantytown there. It parts a lot of people from their houses and their jobs, and it doesn't do anything for Ness or the case except stain his own reputation. In 1947, when Ness is running to be mayor of Cleveland, shaking hands and going to rallies, riding around town and waving from the back of a convertible with his wife in the backseat, it's a big deal, but people haven't forgotten how he couldn't catch the Mad Butcher, and when he loses the campaign, they say that's part of it, that the killer's still out there, that no one is safe.

"Take your daughter Sylvie," Joe Rizzi says. "Maybe they'll find her hand down in the Flats somewhere. Or a leg on the beach. Or they'll find the rest of her body just bobbing along at the mouth of the Cuyahoga. The head? Maybe they'd just find that in a trash can somewhere. And they'll just blame it on the Butcher. Nobody'll know it was me. But you'll know. And you won't be able to say a thing. Which, you know, means I get one for free. Free? What am I saying? You'll pay me for the privilege."

And that's it, the code's broken all the way, because a threat like that is going way too far. See, organized crime in Cleveland is bloody: They stab each other, shoot each other in the heads and stomachs, and over time, they escalate to car bombs. In 1976 there are thirty-seven explosions in Cuyahoga County, twenty-one of them in Cleveland. Shondor Birns and his Lincoln Continental are blown to pieces in 1975. In 1977 John Nardi's torn apart in his Oldsmobile by a shrapnel bomb of nuts and bolts set in the Pontiac parked next to him. Danny Greene's detonated in the parking lot of his dentist's office by a bomb in a Chevy Nova. It's a massacre. But you could also say that they keep it in the family. Nobody's killed who isn't involved. When someone gets it, everyone knows why. There's a reason, a logic to it; stay out of the racket and you're safe. When the new crime syndicates start in the 1990s, that'll all change, because those rackets won't be based on anything human, not family or friendship, history or culture. Follow the market, make money any way you can: Those will be the only rules, and the new criminals will follow them all the way. The police'll find people shot, drowned, drugged, dismembered. Their bodies hollowed out, all their organs removed. Everything used until it's used up. It'll be just like the Mad Butcher of Kingsbury Run, but they won't call it sick or psychotic then. They'll just call it business. So you can say Joe Rizzi's crazy, or an idiot, or a sociopath. But in 1947, he's also the future.

It's the eighth round of the fight, and the people are getting what they came to see. But what comes next happens so fast that Peter Hightower and Joe Rizzi—along with dozens of other people who were looking the other way for that second —miss it. That includes the reporter for the *Los Angeles Times,* there to cover the hometown hero. *The left hook that lifted Doyle off his feet, crossed his eyes and turned his face gray must have been as clean and perfect a knockout blow as was ever landed,* he writes later. *The writer can only say must have been, for, truthfully, he didn't see it. The round was drawing to an end and I had turned my head to pick up a piece of paper on which were scribbled some notes when that ripping left cut Jimmy down.* There's a picture that's taken just after the punch, from behind Jimmy Doyle. Jimmy hasn't hit the mat yet. He's halfway down, pivoting backward on his heels, his arms out in front of him, his trunks filling with air. He looks like he's underwater. You don't have to see his face to know it's bad, because you can see Sugar Ray's. Robinson's hands aren't up anymore—that's how fast that punch must have been—and his body's still ready to fight. But his expression tells you everything. His eyes are wide, his mouth is open, like he's going to say something. Like he knows what just happened.

Jimmy Doyle falls to the mat. Everyone who missed the punch is watching now. Doyle's manager hollers at him to get up. The referee starts the count, but he knows something's very wrong and beckons the manager into the ring with the other hand. Jimmy's sucking in air, loud and hard. Robinson's manager shouts for the ref to call a knockout, and he does, puts Robinson's glove in the air. But everyone's looking at Doyle. His cornermen lift him. It's like he's dead already. Now there are twelve guys, more, in the ring, circled around Doyle. Two of them are doctors. For fifteen minutes, Doyle is just there, in the middle. He doesn't move.

"Be seeing you, Petey Ukeleley," Joe Rizzi says.

At last, at last, the ambulance arrives, and they carry Doyle out on a stretcher. In the hospital they discover he's got a blood clot inside his skull. At three in the morning they cut into his head, look inside, and find out it's a lot worse than that. For twelve more hours, Jimmy Doyle's still fighting, even as the doctors and nurses run out of ways to help him and call in the chaplain. He's pronounced dead in the afternoon. When he dies, there's talk of trying Sugar Ray for involuntary manslaughter, which could put him away for years. The charges are dropped after a quick investigation determines that Jimmy Doyle came into the fight with brain injuries from an old fight. His number just happened to come up against Robinson.

It's the market for violence, and we're all involved: the mob, legitimate businesses, all of us. It's all for the money. People don't want to see a man die, but they do want to see a fight, and they pay to see it, and everyone who's involved in that racket takes their cut of the spoils. It'll mess Sugar Ray up a bit, because it's something, getting paid to beat someone to death with your own two hands. In the investigation, the coroner asks him if he knew Jimmy was in trouble during the fight. *Getting him in trouble is my business as a boxer and a champion,* Sugar Ray says. But as soon as the investigation is over, he announces that he'll hold a series of fights to raise money for Jimmy Doyle's family, and he does it. Two of those bouts end with Sugar Ray's opponents—Sammy Secreet and Flashy Sebastian—knocked out on the mat. They hold the last fund-raising match in Los Angeles, Jimmy Doyle's hometown. At the end of it all, Jimmy's mother has enough money to keep her solvent for life.

But that's not quite the end of it for Robinson. Years later he'll say that the night before the fight, he had a dream that he killed Doyle in the ring, just like it happened. *I got up that morning and I told the commission that I wasn't going to fight,* he'll say. *They said why and I told them what I had dreamed, you know. They told me it was just a dream. They called a Catholic priest and a minister, and they came and they talked to me. They told me to go ahead with the fight. And just like I dreamed, I hit him with a left hook and he died right there in the ring.* And almost as soon as those fights for Jimmy Doyle's mother are over, he starts giving money away, showing up at orphanages with presents for the kids. Hitting the market back, though he knows there's no way to knock it out.

Chapter 13

"What's wrong?"

It's October 1947, two months after the Sugar Ray Robinson fight, and Caroline's been asking this question a lot. Her husband isn't insomniac; he doesn't pace in the halls or lose his temper. Peter's too good at what he does for that. But there are a couple phone calls he says he needs to take at home. His voice drops a little more than usual. There's a shakiness in his appearance, a little less directness. And he spends more time with his children, watches out for them more. Sylvie, Rufus, Muriel, and Jackie don't ask why; they just love it, the attention, the games, the joking around. They laugh as if they've been saving it up all their lives. Caroline comes in from the kitchen one evening, just before dinner, to find the five of them in the parlor pretending to be orangutans, like the ones you see at Monkey Island at the Cleveland Zoo. Sylvie, Rufus, and Muriel are perched on the ridge of the back of the couch. Jackie's standing on the coffee table. Peter's in a crouch; he bangs his fist against the floorboards, and the children clap and hoot, while Peter thinks of his own father, bearlike, roaring. And on the other side of the room, there's Henry, old enough to know better, just standing there. He looks at his mother, and Caroline can see on his face what he's thinking: *What is going on around here?*

She assumes that it's just about business; maybe things are going south for them at last, because for Cleveland it's as if the Depression never quite ended, and she knows that, for all his financial cunning, her

217

husband's money never quite left the town. Their fortunes rise and fall together. She can see it all around the house, in the paint peeling in the corner of the ceiling, the dust in the rafters, the loose shingles on the roof. She can see it all over the city, in the shantytowns, the tenements, the lines for soup kitchens, little children holding their parents' hands. The people shuffling down the sidewalk, asking for something, anything. In the city, there are more people than jobs. There's not enough for everyone, and it's making things ugly. The people fleeing the city—let's just call it like we see it, okay?—the white people leaving don't want the black people following them. Caroline's heard about what's happening in Woodmere from Cecily. Black families are buying land and trying to build houses there. First, someone keeps trying to burn the places down before they're done. When that doesn't work, they use the law, ordinance after ordinance, fee after fee, to keep the families from building. The families are angry; they know what's going on. *This is my lot and my property,* a man named Eddie Strickland says to a reporter from the *Call and Post, and I'm going to build a home on it or die in the attempt.* He doesn't die. But he doesn't get his house, either. They arrest him for illegal use of lumber. *It's a bad move, hitting Negroes like that,* Cecily says. *One of these days they're going to hit us back. And you know what? We'll deserve it.*

Cecily's being dramatic, but Caroline doesn't disagree with her. She's forty years old now, starting to look back as much as forward, and the curve of her life and the city she lives in is clear to her. The teens and twenties were such a rush; it was so easy to imagine it would all just keep going, until it didn't. Now it's hard not to see how out of balance things are getting. So many people need so much, and they don't know how they'll ever get it. She and her family have so much, and they don't know how to keep it. And nobody, but nobody, has just enough; or if they do, they don't know how to recognize it. It's an American thing, she knows that, but sometimes when Caroline's alone with her husband, after the little ones are asleep and Henry's up in his room, she wants to turn to him and ask him all the questions he doesn't have answers to. *Did we have to go so far? Did we need to get so much? Was it necessary to hurt so many people along the way?* They have too much now, way too much, she thinks, and it's killing her. Because she can't let go of the idea that, once, maybe for just a second, they had it—enough, everything they needed and nothing they didn't. It must have been before the office in Terminal Tower, before the house, back when they were courting, because that's when they were happiest. The past few weeks, she's thought that maybe it was that night at the Allen Theatre, the streetlights blurred with fog, Lon Chaney on the screen in front of them, Phil Spitalny waving his arms in the pit. William and his girl— whatever happened to her?—right next to them. Her hand in Peter's. It was all promise and contentment that night, her family all around her and her man at her side. Did they feel like they did because they had all that they would ever need? And if Peter had known that, could he have stopped? She can't help but imagine it now. A conversation between Peter and William: *That's it. I've made my fortune.* William patting him on the back, shaking his hand. *Congratulations. Welcome to the family.* Then a dinner, or a cocktail, somewhere on the East Side with a man in a sharp suit. *I'm out, I'm done,* Peter says, and hands the man an envelope stuffed with cash. *Paid in full.* The man squints. *Why do you want out now, when you're doing so well?* Peter says it plain: *I'm getting married, having a family. I don't want them mixed up in this.* Then the man frowns and nods. How could anyone argue with it? Everything would have been different after that, Caroline thinks. No house in Bratenahl. No long hours away from it, either. He could have been whoever he wanted to be then, all the time. There would never be any need to tell her anything about who he was before he met her; though after he was out, he could tell her everything.

"What's wrong, Peter?"

She's standing in the front doorway. He's going out to the car. He stops, turns.

"It's nothing I can't fix," he says.

"You have to tell me what it is."

"No I don't. I've always said I never give you details, remember? It's safer that way, for you and the kids."

"Why are you bringing up the kids now?"

"So that if something goes wrong, you'll be able to stay with them. Someone has to raise them."

"You've never talked like this before, Peter."

He blinks. "No? I must have just thought it to myself, all this time." He walks back to her and puts his arms around her. Kisses her forehead. "Please don't worry," he says.

He's just a couple days from his third meeting with Joe Rizzi since the boxing match. The first time, in early July, Joe's waiting for him in the lobby of the Terminal Tower building, and Peter glares at him as he gets off the elevator. He walks out of the building pretending not to know him. Joe catches up to him, puts his hand on his shoulder. The tone of voice a little wounded.

"Hey, what are you—"

"Don't touch me," Peter says. "Don't even look me in the eye."

"What's the big deal?"

Peter walks another two blocks, turns into an alleyway, then lets Joe have it.

"Look at you," he says. "The way you look. The way you're dressed. The way you talk and smell."

"Yeah?"

"Now look at me. Do we look like we belong in the same world? People know who I am, Joe. If they see you with me, they might start asking the kinds of questions that will make what you have on me academic. If you're going to blackmail me, at least have the courtesy to do it right."

Joe doesn't have anything to say to that.

"All right," Peter says. "Follow me. At a distance."

Peter takes a right onto 9th Street, one hand holding a briefcase, the other with his hand in his pocket. A straw fedora on his head. Following behind him, Joe can only see the brim, the bob of the head.

They reach Erie Cemetery, the place where Lorenzo Carter and all the people who made this town are buried, and Peter walks around to the back wall, where there are fewer people. Stops and takes out a cigarette; he's almost a third of the way done by the time Joe's in earshot. Then, without putting it down, he opens his briefcase, just wide enough to pull out a thick envelope.

"Here," Peter says. "Your first payment."

Joe starts to open the envelope.

"What are you doing?" he says.

"Making sure it's all here."

"Right here?"

"Yes, Peter. Right here. You want to stand in front of me while I do it, that's fine with me."

"Next time, I decide where we meet and when," Peter says.

"Sure. We'll try it your way." Joe enjoys saying that; he likes that Peter isn't used to having anyone tell him what to do, and now Joe gets to do it.

"Thanks, boss," Peter says.

"Don't mouth off," Joe says.

Now it's obvious that Peter's angry, and Joe smiles. "Relax," he says. "I'll call you when I need you."

Joe Rizzi's price goes up after that. Peter first seethes at him over the phone, then gives in. They meet again at Edgewater Park in late August, early on a Sunday morning. This time the envelope comes out of a jacket pocket, thicker than before.

"What are you doing with all this money?" Peter says.

"Same thing you did with it," Joe says.

Then there's the third meeting, at Edgewater Park again, another Sunday morning. Peter gets there before Joe arrives. It's the first time he's sat still since he can remember. The day is clear and bright; he can tell it's going to be warm. The Five-Mile Crib gleams offshore in the morning light, looking like a ship coming in. It's the intake for the city's water system, and Peter, almost against his will, finds himself thinking of the people who died building it. The multiple gas explosions that killed fifty workers in all. The five men who died in a fire; the three who drowned trying to escape it. The one who died trying to rescue them. It's the memory of his father getting to him, again. He isn't sure what Mykhaylo Garko looked like anymore. But the idea of him, the way that he died and the stories of how he lived, still visit him. *What would he think of me?* Now Peter invents a man, tall and skinny, with an expressive face, like a comedian. Sometimes the man smiles. Sometimes he dances. Now and again he frowns. *This is not the boy I would have raised. This is not the boy Galina raised.* Today he's giving Peter a slow shake of the head, his lips drawn tight. *You knew this would happen in time, didn't you? You should have gotten out sooner, when you had the chance to make it clean.*

This whole idea of the self-made man, the guy who leaves all his past behind and rises into the financial firmament. He's hated it from day one because he's always seen how it's either shallow or a lie. Some of the people on top are so afraid of the world, and at the same time, get so upset over nothing. A botched dinner reservation. A slight mistake on a bill. A spot on their suit lapel. These things can ruin an entire day for them. He has never understood how that happens. Maybe it's because they stop hearing the word *no*; the money props open doors for them that people without it don't have a chance to unlock, and after a while, they're so used to seeing all the doors open that they have no idea what to do when one of them's closed, or broken. It looks like anger, but on the inside, it's bewilderment, confusion, resentment that their lives are still outside of their control, that the world, the truth, has punctured the fiction they made for themselves. So up go the walls around their houses, here come the private security guards. Out they go to a place far from the city, or up to some secluded office, where no one can see them. Or when they go out and see other people, they play the whole thing down; they're chummy with their hired help, a little too magnanimous with cabdrivers. They think they're still one of the boys. They've forgotten how transparent they are. Maybe people envy them, want some of what they have. But there's also contempt, that grown men could let their money turn them into babies.

It doesn't happen to all of them, though, Peter knows, and he hasn't let it happen to him. He hasn't been able to afford it, because of who he's become. The Tremont boy, the mobster, the baron, all at once. Everyone who goes from poor to rich and doesn't let it go to their head has to become at least two people, because it's a motherfucker, becoming the thing your parents used to mock. People like to see a man rise and fall and rise again; nobody wants to hear from a guy who rose and stayed there. Peter doesn't even want to hear it, because the Tremont boy and the mobster won't tolerate it. His father won't tolerate it. Sure, Peter was clever. He played his hand well. But there was luck in there, too, luck and timing, that he was born when he was, tried his stunt when he did. The world cooperated, he knows that, but he can't say it out loud, because it sounds too much like false modesty. The truth is that he can't say very much at all anymore. The words twist and turn in his brain before he says them, until *yes* means *you owe me*, and *no* means *you just haven't offered enough yet*, and *I love you* means *I will bleed you dry*. There's still such a thing as *yes* and *no* and *love* like he used to understand them, but he doesn't know where they are, hasn't known for years. And now his luck has run out. The world isn't cooperating anymore. The arrow that used to point up and out has bent back on itself, made a closed loop. Two of the three people that make up the man called Peter Henry Hightower are trapped inside, and they're fighting each other to the death. And there's Petro Garko, back on Whiskey Island with his brother Stefan, first so full of ambition—*we're going to make some real money off those bottles, boy*—and then terrified when those ambitions are thwarted, and the men on the island are coming to get them. *We have to get out. We have to get away.* They talked about it years later, once, Stefan and him. Stefan started laughing halfway through the retelling. *We were crazy, weren't we?* he said. *What the hell made us do that?* Peter couldn't laugh. He knew all too well what compelled them. Still does.

Pa was a sucker. He remembers himself saying that, way back in 1921.

If he'd had any ambition at all. Then they could have left Tremont, and Mykhaylo wouldn't have been in the way of that train. It all seemed so obvious to Peter then; he was so fucking full of himself. He thought of his ambition as an engine, purring and powerful, running on his desires, for what he thought were better places, better things. But now he understands that it's an animal, and it's taken him places, all right. But it's hungry, and it's been feasting on him for years. If he waits too much longer, there won't be anything of him left. *Then what was it all for?* he thinks, and it goes off like a bomb in his head. He realizes he's been avoiding that question for almost three decades, but here it is, now, running him down, and he doesn't have an answer.

And there on the shore of the lake, Peter Henry Hightower comes to his own big realization: He wants out, out of the whole thing. The graft, the rackets, the swindles, the deals. All those hustles. The crimes and the transactions. The illegal and the legal. He wants to be done with all of it. There's a way out, he thinks to himself. It took years to put together, to make it grow, but it shouldn't take more than a few months to leave it all behind. Building a tower, that takes time. But walking out of it only takes a minute. It's just a matter of selling things, selling things off, being willing to take some losses. They can still keep the house, still live like they do; he has more than enough for that. His business associates will be shocked, because he's given them no warning, no indication that he isn't as hungry as he was when he was twenty. But it won't take more than a few days for them to get used to the idea, and soon they'll be picking over what he's selling, offering to take his business interests off his hands for a reasonable price. Then it's just a matter of paying people off. *I'm out,* he'll say. *I'm out of this game.* They'd all understand. Everyone except the man he's about to meet. But he has to start somewhere.

Joe Rizzi pulls up in his car. It looks new. "Morning," he says.

Peter doesn't move.

"You got the money, right?"

"No," Peter says. He's lying; it's in his jacket pocket. But he's made his decision.

"Price just went up again, then," Joe says.

"Did it?"

"Sure did."

"That's a shame for you, Joe. Because I'm not planning on giving you any more."

"Your friends and neighbors will be very interested to hear about this."

"So you say. But I don't know my neighbors and they don't know me. And I'm not sure you even know who my friends are."

"You willing to bet on that?"

"I am. You seemed like you knew what you were doing when we met in the Arena. But now I'm not so sure. So I'm calling your bluff and I'm getting out."

"I don't think that's a good idea, Pete."

"I'm calling it, Joe. We're through here. I'm through with all of it." He turns his back on him, starts walking back to his car.

"You're going to regret this," Joe says.

Peter keeps walking. Doesn't look over his shoulder. "What I'm doing right now is the only thing I don't regret about this," he says.

That feeling lasts for about five weeks. Early December 1947 is still warm, warmer than anyone would have expected, even if it's still late fall. The first Tuesday of the month, Caroline is letting her kids out of the house in hats and jackets, no gloves. It's after school, and Muriel, Sylvie, and Rufus are playing under the trees in front of the house. Caroline can hear their voices from inside, yelping and laughing, settling an argument. There's Muriel's high voice, complaining over some small injustice. Rufus defends himself. Sylvie brokers a deal. More yelps and laughing. Then there's a long stretch of quiet that Caroline doesn't think too much about, not until Rufus knocks on the door, fast and loud. *Mom, Mom. We need you. We need you, Mom.* Caroline feels a chill ripple across her skin—it's panic, the panic that only a parent can feel, racing toward the ability to do violence—and before she knows what she's doing, she's running to the door, pulling the handle, throwing it wide.

There's a stiff breeze and she doesn't have a jacket on, but she doesn't feel it. Rufus is standing on the steps in front of her in his brown coat and green cap, hands at his sides. He looks scared. Sylvie's just a few yards away, down the driveway, her back turned. Caroline can't see her face, but she can see what her daughter's looking at. Muriel is standing up straight in the ivy under the bare trees in her bright blue coat. There's a man in a dark coat standing right behind her, smiling. He's come in past the wall, the wall that was supposed to keep everyone out. He's in the garden and he has her daughter, he has Muriel. He has black leather gloves on. His left hand is gripping Muriel's shoulder. His right hand is covering her throat.

"Who the hell are you?" Caroline says. The words are sharp with fear, but more with anger—more than Joe's ready for, and he loses his smile. *She'd kill me right now if her daughter wasn't in the way,* he thinks, and he's surprised at how frightened he is. But Peter hasn't left him with too many more moves, and he's not quite bright enough to know what else to do.

"Mrs. Hightower? I'm a friend of your father's."

"You're no friend of his. Muriel, say something, sweetie." She doesn't know if Joe's choking her. "Please say something."

"Mom, come and get me," Muriel says. She starts to cry.

"You're scaring her," Caroline says. "Let her go."

It's not a plea; it's a command. There's so much threat in her voice. It isn't how Joe imagined things would go. He pictured them all scared, all crying. But except for the girl in his arms, none of them are. The other two kids aren't saying a word; they're not moving. Just looking at him, hard. *What is this family?* he thinks.

"I'm not going to hurt her," he says. "Just tell Peter I came. Remind him about the deal we have. He'll know what I mean."

"Let her go," Caroline says.

"Remind him about the deal," Joe says. He loosens his hands on Muriel's shoulder, her throat. "Tell me you'll do it and I'll let her go."

"I'll do it," Caroline says.

Joe gives Muriel a push, and she falls into the ivy, scrambles up again, runs tripping and falling again into the driveway. Her bright coat's covered in dirt. Caroline lunges forward and picks Muriel up, crushes her daughter in her arms. Muriel is bawling now, into her shoulder.

"Don't ever come back here," Caroline says.

Joe is already backing away. "Just remind your husband about our deal, and everything will be fine."

They stay outside, all four of the Hightowers, to watch him turn and walk down the driveway. At the very end, before he disappears around the corner of the wall, he gives a little wave with his black glove. As soon as he's gone, Caroline grabs all her children, *come inside, come inside,* and that's when Rufus starts to cry. He's been holding it all in, being brave, but now that it's over, he needs to let something out. Inside the house, Jackie is screaming, wondering where everyone went. It takes Caroline a good half hour to calm the three children down, and realizes only then that Sylvie hasn't shed a tear.

Caroline calls Peter at work, but can't reach him. She leaves three messages with his secretary and then gives up. Henry gets home later, just before dinner, and Caroline doesn't say anything to him. But she can hear the other kids telling him all about it upstairs as soon as the table's been cleared. Henry's incredulous—*what happened? what?*—he keeps saying. Caroline can hear him from the kitchen. *He sounds more like his father than ever,* she thinks. It's the rhythm in his voice, the directness. The questions he's asking moving toward a plan, though he's too young still to put one together.

Peter Henry Hightower gets home even later than usual that night. He's expecting everyone to be asleep, is a little surprised to see Caroline waiting up for him. For a second, his thoughts are amorous, until he gets a better look at the expression on her face. She tells him everything, point-blank. The man standing in the ivy. The hand on their daughter's throat. How they cried at the end.

"What are you involved in, Peter?"

"It's business as usual."

"Nothing like this has ever happened before. Ever."

"That's because he's stepped outside the lines," Peter says. "Did you call the police?"

"No," Caroline says, and realizes all over again how crazy that is. She didn't even think about it. She's gotten so used to this life of hers, even though she's come to hate it.

"Good," Peter says. "I'll take care of it."

"What are you going to do?"

"No details," Peter says, and then uses the line he's been using for decades. "It's better that way."

"Better for who?" It's the first time she's ever asked, but Peter's ready.

"Everyone except the man who thought it'd be a good idea to threaten our children," he says.

Caroline's on edge for the next three weeks. She holds her kids tighter when she hugs them, watches them every minute they're at home, worries about them every minute they're at school. Her husband isn't home at all, won't talk when he shows up. He's exhausted. She makes Peter take her and the kids to spend Christmas with her own family in Cleveland Heights. It's cold by then, at last. A little snow in the air, frost on the windows. The Anderson house is decorated as much as a house can be, with branches of holly, strings of lights, a sprig of mistletoe in the kitchen doorway. Peter's there just long enough to not be considered rude. He and William exchange the pleasantries you see between people who've given up on each other, and then Peter's gone again. Caroline spends the evening with a glass of eggnog in her hand that she doesn't drink. She's lost in envy. For her children, who are overcome by the holiday and chasing each other around the house. For the rest of the Andersons, who've slipped into good cheer; today, they don't have a care in the world. She keeps the kids there as late as she can, then calls Peter to pick them up. When they get home, she looks over her shoulder down the driveway, hustles them inside, and not just because it's cold enough to freeze their breath in their noses. The next day, while Peter is out, she calls Stefan.

"Merry Christmas, Caroline," Stefan says.

"Merry Christmas. I'm sorry we didn't get to see you yesterday."

"That's all right. We still have plans for New Year's Eve, yes?"

"Yes. Though I'm not sure Peter will be able to join us."

"That's all right."

Everything's always all right with Stefan, Caroline thinks. *I married the wrong brother.* She envies the honesty of his life, his ties to his neighborhood, to his church; he still goes every Sunday and prays for his mother, or to her, because his Christianity is shot through with some of that serious Old World superstition, the one that took the order the merciful God offered and embedded it in a darker, more chaotic universe, where those big concepts of sin and redemption work only inside the village walls, and only at the sufferance of the forces in the ancient woods, who can intercede and disrupt whenever they feel like it. So that, for the people who believe in it, if forbearance doesn't work, there's always hostility; if justice fails, there's always vengeance, and without consequences, if you're clever enough.

"Listen, I have a favor to ask you. It's about the children."

"Name it."

"Do you think you could take them for a little while?"

"Of course."

"Henry can help you with the younger ones."

"I said of course, Caroline. I will be happy to take them."

"You're sure."

"Of course. But I have to ask if you're all right, Caroline."

"Yes. I think so."

"You and Peter? You're all right?"

"I think we will be."

Stefan doesn't ask whether the problem is between them, or with Peter. He used to, when she called and wanted to talk. He used to think that Caroline and Peter had all the usual problems of marriage, the friction you get when two people have to deal with each other for a long time, and that the person Peter had become, the life he had made for himself, was apart from that. He used to think that if only Peter could find a way out, they both would be happier, and their children with them. He hasn't seen that much of his brother, hasn't talked to him in a long time. But he's talked to Caroline a lot, he's heard the way she speaks, about him, his work, their kids. And he sees something Caroline doesn't: that the years have taken everything—Peter's past, his work, his marriage, his family, his crimes—and made it one living thing. But that thing is a monster. When they slaughter it, there will be blood everywhere. It's only a question of how much time they have left, and what the children will do then.

Chapter 14

I t's January 8, 1948. Peter comes home early in the afternoon, before the kids are back from school. He almost never does that, and it startles Caroline, who's on the second floor. *Who's there? Who is it?* she calls down. *It's me, Caroline,* Peter says. *Come down, I have something to tell you.* He's standing at the bottom of the stairs, watches her descend. She stops.

"Why are you looking at me like that?"

"I'm out, Caroline."

"Out of what?"

"The business. All of it. Everything. We still have the money, but's it's all just investments now. Passive. I'm out."

At first she shakes her head; it's too hard to believe. But then it makes sense, how quiet he's been, how far away. He's always been that way a little, not revealing anything until the work is done. It was like that when he proposed, showing her the house for the first time. It was like that when he broke his business connections with her brother, and when he told her his mother had died. But this is beyond that: It's the dismantling of his own life, and though the past few months have felt a lot longer, when she gets her head around the scope of what he must have done, it seems to her that he must have moved fast, with complete determination. The phone calls, the drinks, the dinners, the cigarettes. Making sure the businessmen never saw him with the criminals, that the criminals never got close to the businessmen, even though Peter's joked that he has trouble telling them apart now.

"And that man who came to the house?" she says.

"We'll never see him again."

She doesn't say anything after that. Just opens her arms, beckons him upstairs. Leads him into the bedroom. They hurry. They're feeling young, like they're misbehaving, getting away with something. Neither of them knows that they'll never sleep together again.

Because, dear reader, Peter is lying, to himself as much as her. Not about the business; ever since his meeting with Joe on the shore on the lake, he's been extracting himself from the financial kingdom he built. He's been naming successors, setting up managers, creating funds to pay for his transition out. *Shooing away some of the vultures,* he's thought to himself. His business associates are at first jolted by the suddenness of it. They say they need a couple days to think about it, but it always turns out they need less. Within a day, sometimes a couple hours, they're talking about what they'd like to be in charge of. *If that sounds good to you, of course,* they say. A little too deferential for Peter to buy it; he knows that as soon as he relinquishes power, takes his hands off the steering wheel, the real jockeying, the serious squabbling, will start. By then he'll be a silent partner. Showing up for quarterly meetings, if that. Taking a phone call now and again. He's been moving his investments around, too, setting up an array of stocks, bonds, real estate holdings that don't need him to look at them every day to see how they're doing. The money won't perform as well that way, he knows that; he just doesn't want to think about it that much anymore. Most of his money is in this city, his hometown, and maybe he knows it's not the smartest decision, that there are better places to put your assets. But he knows his town so well; knows, too, that so far it has risen and fallen with the fortunes of America. *If Cleveland goes down,* he thinks, *it's because America is going down, too. There'll be no place to hide.* He's not an idiot; he knows that can change. Though in another way, he's right, will always be right—even in the 1960s, when it's sunny in California and Cleveland is on fire. In 1995, the people of Cleveland are living in the future. They're still living in it now. Stand on the west side of the

Cuyahoga's valley and take a good look around, at the giant machinery, the rusting bridges, the white arcs of new buildings downtown hard against the sooty older ones. Look at the colors in the water below, the unmoving barges, the flocking seagulls. Take a good fucking look. Then turn around and listen to the way people talk. The friendly sarcasm in their voices, the skepticism. They're through pretending they're sure of anything. *Things'll get better,* you might try saying to them. *They always get better here.* By *here* you mean America, but they know better than to think that means anything. See if they don't laugh a little. Not bothering to ask you how you're so sure, because they know you don't know. They know that nobody knows. And in the way they laugh is a message for you: *Things are always getting better, always getting worse. Always something. Get used to it. You might be next.*

No, Peter's not lying about the business side. It's the crime he keeps from Caroline. He's not trying to be devious. He lies because he thinks it's just a matter of timing, and he doesn't think he's asking too much. He tells her what he wants to be true, what he hopes will be true in just a matter of months. He thinks, too, that she'll never find out the difference. Which means he underestimates Helene Rizzi. Joe's wife.

It's March 8, 1948. Caroline is standing under the overhanging roof of Clark's Colonial Restaurant on Euclid. A few flakes of snow in the air. Her daughter Jackie holding her hand. She's just had lunch with Cecily, a couple plates of scallops and vegetables, a little heated conversation. The outspokenness that Cecily was all about when she was younger has turned into her way of talking to people, by debating them, and Caroline's one of the few people she knows who'll argue back without making it personal. Her father gave up on her years ago; he's never quite accepted her opinions, has despaired that she'll never get married. One evening in May 1940 he stands up at the dining table and accuses her of being a lesbian. Her mother is shocked. Caroline, for the first time in a while, doesn't say anything. Lesbianism is just the beginning of what the last decade or so has been like for her, if they're going to talk about things the family considers immoral, and Cecily doesn't need their condemnation of the things she's done, the people she's done them with. So she likes talking to Caroline. There's never judgment, and Cecily's told her a few times over the years how grateful she is for that.

Which is why Caroline is surprised by what Cecily says now. Before the scallops have arrived, they're arguing about the Supreme Court decision that day—McCollum v. Board of Ed—which is all over the papers. The sisters start with the question of banning religious instruction in public schools, run through the separation of church and state fast—because they agree—and then, because of the spiritual persuasion of the case's plaintiff, they get into atheism. They haul out the usual arguments. Then, when Caroline mentions that she's herself an atheist, Cecily's eyebrows rise.

"Really?" she says.

"Yes," Caroline says.

"Aren't you concerned about your immortal soul?"

Cecily's teasing her a little; both of them are smart enough to know that if you're an atheist, you're not worried about whether you have a soul, never mind its immortality. But something else sneaks into the statement, a certain concern. *I'm worried about you,* Cecily is saying. *You don't seem okay. Do you need help?*

"No," Caroline says. "And you shouldn't be concerned, either."

The check comes and Caroline pays. In front of the restaurant, Cecily bends down and gives Jackie a long hug. Then her sister. *It's always so good to see you. Take care.* Then Cecily's off, leaving Caroline there with her daughter in the falling snow. Caroline's about to raise her arm to hail a cab when a woman approaches her wearing a black scarf on her head.

"Mrs. Hightower?"

"Yes."

"My name is Helene. Helene Rizzi."

"Pleased to meet you, Helene."

"I wish I could say the same, Mrs. Hightower, because you seem like a nice woman, and you have a beautiful daughter. But we need to talk. It's about your husband."

She's serious, and Caroline knows it.

"What do you have to tell me?"

"Not here," Helene says.

They find a coffee shop without too many people in it, a place where they can sit down. Helene insists on buying Jackie something sweet to eat. Then clasps her hands on the table in front of her, shaking her head. Working up some courage.

"How much do you know about what your husband does?" Helene says.

"It depends on who's asking," Caroline says.

"Do you recognize my last name? Rizzi?"

"As in, Lou Rizzi?"

"Yes," Helene says. "Good." Caroline can see Helene relax, and realizes why she was so nervous; there was a chance, of course, that Caroline knew nothing, that everything would have to be explained to her, and what Helene had to say would be lost in it all. It all would have been too much to get through at once.

"Do you know he had a son, Joe?" Helene says.

"No."

"Joe Rizzi was my husband."

The past tense, Caroline notes. The black scarf.

"I'm sorry for your loss."

"Not as sorry as you're going to be, after what I have to say. Mrs. Hightower, your husband killed mine. Well, he didn't do the killing had him killed is more like it—but it's the same to me."

Caroline's skin is buzzing, the hair on her arms standing up. She knows Helene is telling the truth. She has no reason to lie; and Peter has every reason.

"There's no body yet," Helene says, "and everyone's saying they just sent him away somewhere. But I've seen this before. I know what happened to him. He's down on the bottom of the lake, or he's been thrown into an incinerator, or he's in a drainpipe somewhere. And I'm not saying my husband didn't deserve it, Mrs. Hightower. God love him, but he wasn't too smart and thought he was."

"Why would Peter have him killed?" Caroline says. She can't get her voice above a whisper; her brain is on fire.

"My husband was the one who came to your house. He broke a few rules by doing that, Mrs. Hightower. It made him fair game. Fair enough, anyway."

"I see," Caroline says. She's almost not holding it together.

"He'd been blackmailing your husband for a few months already. Your husband called him on it. Then my husband went too far."

Caroline is having trouble seeing.

"Why are you telling me this?"

"Because I have something for you," Helene says. "I know that Joe overstepped. Your husband wasn't wrong to act as he did. But I want to make sure that it ends here, Mrs. Hightower. I have kids that need me, you understand? We both have children. I don't want anything else between us." She reaches into her purse and takes an envelope. It's pretty obvious what it's filled with. "This should be everything my husband took from your family. If it isn't, my phone number's on the back. Please call me. We can settle this between us. Mother to mother."

Caroline's crying now, and she can't stop. Helene takes Caroline's hand in hers, pats it. *There, there.* Then looks over at Jackie.

"I'm sorry your daughter was here for this," she says. "But that's how it gets passed along, doesn't it?"

It's never this easy—marriages more than two decades long don't just come apart in one shot—but if there's a moment when you could say Peter and Caroline's marriage is over, this is it. Because Caroline thinks it: *This is it.* Everything's recast in her mind. The power she thought she had, the partnership she thought she shared. All of it is revealed to her as a delusion. Her husband has been playing her, she thinks, letting her believe a fantasy, that the crimes he committed amounted to cooking some books and evading taxes. She reads the paper; she knows what the mafia does. But she imagined that her husband dodged all that, never got any blood on his own clothes, even as it flowed all around him. She understands all at once how stupid that was to think; and now the entire thing comes apart. The animal is slaughtered. She wonders what else he's lied about. How many other people he's killed. Whether any of their money is theirs, or if it's all borrowed, all leveraged, a complicated farce. How much of that speech he gave her in front of the house all those years ago was true. If she'd never met his family in Tremont, it would all be open to doubt, that he grew up in Cleveland, that he's a South Side boy. That his name is Peter Henry Hightower, or Pete the Uke, or Petro Garko. That he's anyone he's ever said he's been.

Years later, Caroline and Peter will both remember 1948 and 1949 as a long string of awful fights. At first there are a few rules. They wait until all their children are asleep or out of the house. If it's at night, they try to keep their voices down. But by the end of the second year, they've stopped caring. So in 1949, family life for the kids is a small boat in a rough storm. They never know when the next big wave'll pitch them over. The waves break at breakfast, in the afternoon, very late at night. They don't hear them coming. There's a tiny comment, a tone of voice. Sometimes just a glance from one parent, and the other says *what. What.* Then the shouting starts. The kids learn to read the pitches of their parents' screams so they know when they're as angry as they can get. Their father's highest note is a holler; his throat opens up and the words pop out, like small bombs going off. Their mother, they find out, can yell so loud that their eardrums cut out the higher frequencies of her voice, so it sounds like they're listening to her underwater. Their father likes to point his finger when he's angry. Their mother shakes all over. In time, the older kids have their own responses worked out. Henry, who's seventeen, goes to his room and shuts his door. Sylvie and Rufus, eleven and nine, head off together to the opposite side of the house, as far away from the fight as they can get. But Muriel's only seven and doesn't know what to do. She just stands there and cries; after ten minutes or so, Jackie, who's four, starts crying, too.

The last fight is near the end of 1949. The parents scream at each other until their children can't recognize their voices, and they all end up in Henry's room, scared. *Are Mom and Dad going to hurt each other?*

Muriel says. *Is Dad going to kill Mom?* She's heard it too many times now, that her father's a killer, and she believes he's capable of anything. Sylvie's wise beyond her years even then. *No, Mom and Dad are both going to be okay,* she says. Telling Muriel what she needs to hear. Rufus is angry. *Why can't they just stop fighting already?* he says. *Will you all just be quiet?* Henry says. *I want to hear what they're saying.* He opens the door without a sound and goes out into the hallway. *Stay here,* he whispers, and closes the door behind him. In the hallway, he hears everything. Who it was that had his sister in the front yard. What he was there for. It will never leave him. For the other kids, there's a lot of language they can't quite decipher through the door, because their parents are talking so fast. *You sold us out, Peter,* Caroline says. *Every time. You sold us out. Over and over again.* Then they hear her say this: *I hate you so much. So much more than I ever loved you.* The kids all look at each other. Muriel starts crying. If they were different children, the others might have hugged their sister then. But they're too much like their parents to do it.

By January 1950 the marriage has been shot in the head, torn limb from limb, dumped in the lake. But it's 1950, and people don't get divorced; not people like them, anyway. So they all go on living in the same house, or at least sleeping there, until the death of their marriage is enough of an open secret that Peter can take a small apartment downtown, close to his office, the kind of apartment the young Caroline always believed he lived in when they were courting. There are rumors of affairs, that Peter's taken up with a younger woman from somewhere on the West Side, that Caroline has a lover somewhere in Shaker Heights. These rumors are unfounded. The truth is that as much as they despise each other, they miss what they had. Maybe each of them could find something as good again, but despair keeps them from trying.

When Caroline's diagnosed with cancer in 1962, Peter pays for everything. The treatments that don't work, the painkillers that don't work well enough. She won't see him, but she will see Stefan, and they talk for hours, though she never tells him what occurred to her back in 1947. Only that she's always so glad to see him. *You should see Peter, too,* Stefan says. *Even if it's just for me. He's my brother.* In February 1963, she relents and tells Peter to come visit her while there's still enough left of her to visit. They hold hands for two hours and don't say a word. She dies toward the end of May and he pays for the funeral, suffers the nasty things her family says about him, and they don't know the half of what he's done, because Caroline never sold him out; all they know are the rumors. It's been a long time since Peter's been to church, but he's still Catholic enough to know that he didn't deserve someone as good as Caroline was, and deserves her family's loathing now. Deserves much worse than that. By then, Henry's been in New York for years. Rufus is just out of college and has no permanent address. Muriel's in college and restless. Jackie's halfway through her second stay in a hospital. Which leaves Peter, sixty-four years old and feeling older than that, alone in the big house with Sylvie. He has three years left to live, though the left-hemisphere stroke comes sooner than that.

And he can't hide anything from his daughter. Even before the stroke, she hears him on the phone, sees how he comes and goes. Starts asking questions. *Who are the Rizzis? Who are the Ukrainians?* And when Peter starts to explain, starts to give her the history, she just has more questions: *Why did you start with the Italians instead of the Ukrainians, anyway?* Peter's proud at how hungry she is for the details, how good she is at putting them together. The various little organized-crime concerns in town all have their own little rackets going, the protection and loan-sharking that's tied to neighborhood, to ethnicity, language, food, home. It's the logic of the family applied to an economy; values on everything are bargained for and agreed. *You love me? How much? You say you trust me? How much?* But when the money gets big, it breaks the family logic; the calculations need to be colder, the partners not as connected. That's where Peter lives, has lived for Sylvie's entire life. There's camaraderie, of course: Peter and just about every crime boss in town can have a drink together, and the congeniality smooths the edges of every transaction. But everyone makes sure it doesn't get too friendly, because one day, they know, they're going to have to screw each other over. It's all right if they think of that as part of the deal, a decades-long game of poker, millions of dollars whirling around their heads while they sit at the table, hiding their cards, looking at each other and smiling. At that level, it's when things get too close that they get ugly. The honor killings, the stabbings, the shootings, the drownings, the explosions. *That's why families should never be rich,* Peter says to Sylvie, in spite of himself, and then stops there, because to keep going would be to unravel his entire life, his life and Caroline's and the lives of all his children. He'll never admit the crimes he's committed against them. But by mid-1964, Sylvie's handling her father's books, knows where all the money is, what to record in one ledger and leave out of the other. The structure of her father's organization is right there in front of her, all the names of everyone involved, though she's never been to a single meeting. There's no need to do that; Peter's still as sharp and able-bodied as ever. Until, on October 24, he isn't.

When it starts, Peter's alone at the kitchen table. There's a throbbing behind his left eye, a hammering pain, like the eye's trying to pop itself out of its socket. He looks down at the cup of coffee he's holding and doesn't recognize his own hand. Doesn't see how his hand is separate from the cup, how his clothes are separate from his body, his feet not part of the floor. He's losing himself—Peter Henry Hightower, Pete the Uke, Petro Garko—and expanding, growing, rising, flowing into the house, into the lawn outside the window, the trees turning orange and red near the shore. Into the lake. He's in an infinite present, forgetting who he is and what he's done; he can't say whether he's there or not anymore. It's euphoria, to feel it all fall away, and in that second— maybe it's a second, maybe it's an hour, he's not sure—he's never been happier in his entire life.

Then he realizes he can't move his right arm. He tries to get up and walk, but his right leg is paralyzed too, and he crashes. His right wrist breaks when he hits the floor and he hollers. Tries to form words but they won't come out. His voice goes *raaahhh, raaahhh,* like an engine that won't start. Sylvie rushes in and scares him; he can't put together that she's there because she heard him fall. He looks at her and her mouth is moving, he can hear her voice, but he can't understand what she's saying. He panics and flails on the ground, smacks his left shin into the table seven times until Sylvie drags the table away from him, gets the chairs out of the way, too. Then the floor feels like an ocean, the walls a million miles away, and he's alone in a tiny boat, until the ambulance comes and takes him away. That's when all his energy leaves him and he gives up. He's out. *Did you hear that, Pa? At last, at last, I'm out.*

From then until the second stroke kills him in 1966, nobody's sure if he's there anymore. The right side of his body stays paralyzed. He stops talking and only murmurs in his sleep. It's never clear that he understands what's said to him. Sylvie and Stefan move his bed to the first floor of the house, get him a wheelchair. She parks him on the sunporch, where he seems to like it best, for most of the day. She bathes him, changes his clothes, helps him in the bathroom after she learns to read the signs. Tries to give him his favorite things to eat. He doesn't seem to know what to do, seems to like being told. *It's time for lunch now. Time for your bath. We need to get you dressed because your brother's coming over. We need to get you in a tie because Michael Rizzi's coming over.* Yes, Michael Rizzi, their contact with the Italian side of Peter Henry Hightower's criminal activities. Lou Rizzi's nephew, Joe Rizzi's cousin. They have their meetings in the living room, Michael on the loveseat, Sylvie on the couch, Peter in his chrome wheelchair. Coffee's in a French press on the table in front of them. Michael's there about once a month, explains what's going on. Peter's eyes are on him when he talks, but he never says anything. So Sylvie speaks for him. At first she's all deference. *I know my father had told me he wanted to do what you're describing, so I think it's okay if we do it now. If it's all right with you, Dad.* They both give him a couple obligatory seconds to respond, even though they know he won't. He stares at his daughter when she speaks and nods his head, maybe because he likes what he's hearing, maybe because his neck muscles are tired. It's impossible to say. After a few months of it, Sylvie starts to speak for her father with more confidence. *I know my father would want this. I don't think he'd think that's a good idea.* Peter's still in the room, still nodding. Michael starts smiling more, being more supportive. He's impressed with her; he can already see what she'll become. *When she takes over,* he thinks, *look out.* Decides that he wants to make sure he's on her side when she does; the love between them, the marriage to show that everything between their families is forgiven, will come later. In early 1965 she says it at last—*I think we should do it*—without mentioning her father at all. If she notices what she's done, she doesn't let on. Michael looks at Peter, still in his wheelchair, staring at his daughter and nodding. *Your father would be proud of you,* he says, and notices that Peter Henry Hightower's eyes don't shift toward him at all; they're still fixed on Sylvie. *He knows the score,* Michael Rizzi thinks. *We're talking about him like he's already dead.* He feels a twinge of guilt for the disrespect, but there's no way around it. There's business to get done.

Chapter 15

D o you see it now? Where the spine of the story begins and ends? It runs along the length of the rise and decline of the family, the city, the country, because the system, the animal, runs its course and then keeps running, longer than it should. Call it capitalism. Call it American. Call it what you want. There isn't an animal born yet that doesn't get sick someday, and it gets sick in Cleveland in 1966, because too many people have been left out, and decide they've had enough.

It's Monday, July 18, 1966. In the afternoon, a prostitute walks into the Seventy-Niners' Café, a bar on the corner of 79th Street and Hough Avenue. She's there looking for money; she needs to get some together for the children of another prostitute who just died. Owner Dave Feigenbaum tells her to leave. She balks. Soon they're swearing at each other. She storms out, and Feigenbaum says something under his breath about serving Negroes. It's about five o'clock in the afternoon. A little while later, a guy walks in and gets a pint of wine, asks for a pitcher of ice water and a glass to go with it. It's ninety degrees out. Feigenbaum says no; someone says he overhears him talking to his waitress, too. Don't serve *no niggers no water*. Maybe he's thinking back to the winter, when someone tried to burn up his car. Maybe he thinks the people in the neighborhood don't like him and has decided to be hateful and return the favor. Maybe he's a virulent racist. Or maybe it's just too hot and things are too tough in Cleveland, not enough is going well for anyone. Maybe it's everything all at once, the race, the poverty, the sense that it's all coming apart. But that's how it starts. The guy who doesn't get his water gets angry. He tells all his friends in the place what happened, and he's nice and loud about it. Then he's out of there. Minutes later there's a brown paper bag stuck to the door of the place with writing scrawled on it: *No water for Niggers.* Now there are a bunch of people gathered around it, and they're not happy. The Feigenbaum brothers call the police and then step outside themselves. They've got a pistol and a rifle. Then the police show up, and everything explodes.

Three grocery stores are on fire, a drugstore, a clothing store. Then the fires are everywhere. The police set up blockades, cut off twenty blocks from the rest of the city to try to contain it. The firemen go in and get bottles and rocks thrown at them. The fire hoses get slashed, along with police cruisers' tires; the cars' windows get broken in. The police set up a command station at East 73rd and Hough, and soon they're taking fire from snipers nesting in the apartments around them. The police captain there says later that it's like a western. A woman named Joyce Arnett dies in the crossfire that night, trying to get home to her baby daughters. Three other people are shot. Eight people go to the hospital with wounds from rocks and bottles. A policeman who served in World War II says it reminds him of London during the blitzkrieg. The next day the looters are selling what they stole as fast as they can. The mayor thinks about Watts and Chicago and calls in the National Guard in the afternoon. The shooting starts before they arrive. A stray bullet gets a man named Percy Giles right in the head, they say, while he's trying to help a friend board up his store. He dies in the hospital. The National Guard arrives and things settle down, but there's still plenty of looting the next day. The third night, Hough is quieter; there are three National Guardsmen at every intersection, soldiers accompanying the police. There's a fire just south of the place and the police shoot up a family in their car who are trying to get to safety. On the fourth day, there's an outbreak of over a hundred fires, half of them started by Molotov cocktails. It doesn't settle down until the end of the week, and by then, the damage has been done.

A year later, Hough Avenue's still destroyed buildings and streets full of garbage. The kids walking it don't have enough clothes or enough to eat. There are more murders, more firebombs. They say later that the only thing keeping the entire neighborhood from going up in flames in the summer of 1967 is Carl Stokes's run for mayor—Stokes, Cleveland's only black candidate for mayor who stands a chance of winning. *Cool it for Stokes,* they say. They do, and Stokes wins. But Stokes can't save Hough. Thirty years later, they're calling it an urban prairie because most of the houses and apartment buildings are gone. There are just the streets and the sidewalks, the telephone poles, a house or two left on an entire block next to an apartment building that's boarded up and falling over. The rest of the block is weeds turning into forest. From the air, you can see the dark outlines of the foundations where all the other buildings used to be, and it breaks people's hearts. They argue, then, about what happened in 1966, about whether the riots bled Hough out or whether they happened because Hough was already bleeding. Fifteen years later the city makes a move, and houses get built in Hough again. The empty blocks get filled in. But then it looks like a suburb, and people are angry about it. *The city's giving up on being a city,* some people say. *No,* say others. *The city sees the writing on the wall. All those people left, all those jobs left, and they're not coming back.*

They're having an argument about the future, and the public version of it is all sparks, thrown off from the friction between practicality and ideology. The nostalgia for the past, the push for progress, the American stubbornness in insisting that everything always gets better. But it's getting harder and harder not to see how the big wheel's turning. How they've been on a long arc going up, and now they're on the other side going down. Some of the people, in America and elsewhere, want to turn around; there must be a way back, they think, a way to climb up the rim as it's moving downward beneath them. Some of them are turning and facing it, trying to save what they can, to prepare their children for the harder world that's coming. And a few of them are checking out the approaching chaos, speculating on just how things will fall apart. How the laws will weaken, and how the market—the market for everything—will rise to fill the space. How the people around them will become more vulnerable, more desperate. And then they think about where they need to be to profit from it.

It's August 1966. The second stroke, the one that kills Peter Henry Hightower, gets him in his sleep. For Peter, it's like a switch is flipped, a plug gets pulled, and the dreams and memories left in his head are gone. Lights out. Sylvie comes into his bedroom in the morning to check on him because she doesn't hear him stir. She can tell from the doorway what's happened. The covers are off him and his right leg is bent, his foot tucked underneath his body. His left arm is out straight, hanging over the edge of the bed. Sylvie doesn't make a sound. Maybe for her siblings, the line between their father alive and their father dead is bright and clear, a crack in the sidewalk. But Sylvie's been living with no one but Peter for years now. She's seen how there's a gray country between life and death; her father's taken his sweet time walking across it, and Sylvie's been standing on the edge of it, watching him go. She's had a long time to prepare. She goes to him, arranges the body like he's still sleeping to give him some dignity. Puts his pillow beneath his head and tucks the blankets around him. Then makes the calls, to the hospital, to the police. To Stefan, who sighs and thanks her for the news, agrees to break it to Jackie. She calls the rest of her siblings, first Henry, then Rufus. Muriel last, and only after the authorities have arrived to take the body away; she knows that Muriel would have rushed over, lost it a little bit, made the necessary parts of dealing with a corpse harder. There's some ruthlessness in that decision, to deny Muriel the chance to see her father by herself before he's packed away. But there's compassion in it, too; she knows that their father's body isn't going to give Muriel whatever sense of completion she's looking for. *It'll never end,* Sylvie thinks. *Never be done.* And something moves in her, a sense of acceptance, of where she finds herself. Of what she has to do.

So she's quiet, quieter than usual, when Henry comes a few days before the funeral to sort out the paperwork for their father's estate. He gives Sylvie a good look when he finds out just how orderly it all is.

I know you're smart, Sylvie, he says, *but I still underestimated you.* Sylvie just smiles. *Let me know if you need anything else,* she says, and gets her first taste of the power her mother felt when she married Peter Henry Hightower. Sylvie knows something Henry doesn't, a big thing. To her, it's like Henry's going through everything in a grand house, and as thorough as he prides himself on being, he never finds the switch under the shelf of a bookcase in the library that would make the walls part, show him the wing of the house he didn't know was there. She doesn't say anything even during the fight in the dining room. *Raise your hand if you think equitable doesn't mean equal, but fair,* Rufus says. He thinks he's saving her from poverty. *What's wrong with you, Henry? Don't you ever see regular people anymore?* She's still mum even to Rufus hours later, when he explains to her in the garden what he's going to do. *I'd do anything to keep you in this house,* he says. *I don't need the money.* She feels a little guilty; it would be so easy to tell him what reins have been handed to her, the direction she's going in. But nothing is certain yet, her transition to power in the underworld isn't assured. So she just gives him a hug. *I owe you one,* she says. *I owe you everything. Someday I'll pay it back.* And after the family departs and the house is quiet again, she meets with Michael Rizzi. Tells her how much Rufus gave her and what she's planning to use it for. *I don't want to take my father's place,* she says. *I want to be bigger than he ever was.*

In time, she is. Big enough that she needs to tell Henry how she's still living in that giant house in Bratenahl, because he's sensitive enough to the money to know that the legitimate numbers don't quite add up, even as she doesn't need to tell any of her other siblings anything; she lets them think she's just being careful with what she has. Big enough that she can't launder the money she makes fast enough to spend it; she has piles of cash in the bedrooms, in the basement, under the stairs, but she can't hire anyone to fix the roof without drawing the authorities' attention to her. She has her hands in everything in town, in all that's left of Cleveland's criminal heyday—the Irish, the Italians, the Eastern Europeans, the Jews. She does the financial stuff, the loan-sharking, the money laundering. She's the bank for some of the drug trade, for gambling circuits, for real estate swindles, for human trafficking. They always tell her she doesn't need to know what she's investing in, where the money's coming from, but she always finds out, she always knows. They don't know how she does it; her own husband goes to his grave in 1986 not knowing how she's always four steps ahead, even of the FBI, which is aware only of the fact of her existence. When the criminals don't call her the White Lady, they call her the Goddess: She's the all-seeing eye, knows what everyone's up to. And in the early 1990s, when the Soviet Union implodes, her eye turns east, to the criminals rising up there, and she buys in. *What are you doing that for?* Kosookyy says to her, over coffee in the living room. *They're bad news over there.* And Sylvie gives him a little smile. *For protection,* she says, *I want to know who they are.* She sees how the criminals in Eastern Europe are just capitalists run amok. The governments and the borders between the countries are dissolving, there's no one in charge; there's only the logic of the market, putting prices on cars, factories, houses, towns. People. *What are you made of? How much are you worth?* It's all for sale, and the price is so low, for everything, everyone. No wonder it's so brutal. But then Sylvie looks out the window, thinks about what her city, her country, is becoming, and thinks she sees the future on the other side of the ocean. *The new gangsters are coming here,* she tells Kosookyy. *And when they arrive, either they'll eat us alive or we'll become them. Though I'm not sure I see the difference.* Even before her nephew Peter, Rufus's son, shows up at her door, she's figuring a way out, and she's learned from her father's mistakes. Right before she goes, she has to try to kill it all and set it on fire. Not just one man. All of it, all that she's built since her father's death and all her father built before she was born. She has to slaughter it and light it all up, make it burn quick and hot, until there's nothing left but ashes. That part is easy, though there'll be so much blood. The trick, the hard part, is in escaping the bullets, the knives, the flames. In making sure that the blood that flows doesn't belong to her or the people she loves; and that no more flows again.

Part 3
1995

Chapter 16

*O*ur family is destroyed, Muriel thinks, *and I'll never see my son again.*

It's August 1995. Muriel doesn't sleep at all after she drops Peter off at Sylvie's, and the way he and Sylvie are acting when she picks him up the next day scares her. *Muriel, honey. We're already ruined,* Sylvie says, and Muriel's too upset to ask her what she means. She and Peter don't say more than a couple words on the ride out to the airport, because Peter looks shell-shocked, and Muriel thinks she knows why. Or maybe it's better to say it this way: *thinks* she does. All of Peter Henry Hightower's children know their father was a criminal. They all know he had a man killed. But after he dies, for Muriel, it's as if there are rings around their family secrets, rings of knowledge and power, and she and Jackie are on the outermost edge, knowing the least. She's aware that Henry knows more, and Rufus must, and that Sylvie knows the most. In the past, before their falling-out, she might have worked up the courage to complain to Henry about it. *You're always keeping me in the dark.* Except that she thinks of it the other way around: At the center of the ring, it's pitch-dark, so dark that she can't see her older sister, who's standing inside the shadow, and she can only just make out the faces of her brothers. She has seesawed for years between hating them for leaving her out and being grateful to them for letting her live in the light, to meet Petey's father and then marry Terry, to live her life of relative normalcy on Edgewater Drive, without having to answer for the rest of her family, succumbing to it like Sylvie did, or running away like Rufus did, or struggling with it like Henry always will. She knows she doesn't have the stomach for any of what they did, and her gratitude swells in her whenever she thinks of Andrew and Julia, who she thinks are so safe. But now and again she's wanted to call up Henry or Sylvie and talk to them, really talk. *I know more than you think I do,* she wants to say. *I see more than you give me credit for.* She doesn't do it, though, because she's afraid. Not of what she might learn—she can handle it, she knows she can—but of what it might do to her family. It has all seemed so precarious to her, like since their father died, they've all been held together by spiderwebs, and a push from the smallest breeze would send them all floating far away from each other. She can't see how strong the connections still are, the tendons between them all, of commerce and history, loyalty and regret, and it's the great tragedy of her life. Because if she knew the family could take it, she would have pushed harder, and maybe her oldest son would have been saved.

But the people involved—her family and the criminals around them—can see what binds them all together. Most of them can't see very far. The cords disappear into the darkness, and they don't know where they go. But a few people can see everything. The sinews from Cleveland to Connecticut to Eastern Europe, stretching across the world and the years. And Sylvie, the White Lady, is about to take them in her hand all at once, pull them, and cut them. Cut them and then hope that the ones that matter, the bonds between her and her family, can heal themselves. She knows she can't fix everything. That it's not just the Wolf she's up against, the Ukrainian crime lord who wants her nephews dead. It's not just the police either, or the feds, or Feodor and Kosookyy, the new and old criminals who had a hand in making her what she is. She's dealing with the market for violence, with the almighty dollar and the things people will do for it, and she can't change that. But she thinks she can get everyone she loves out. Which is why, after she talks to Feodor, she calls the cops.

FBI agents George Guarino and Anne Easton are sitting in their car, in front of the big house in Bratenahl, under the shady trees. Guarino's scanning the house, amazed that there are no security cameras, no bodyguards he can see.

"She's been that good," he says. "Staying under the radar, making alliances, paying off who needs to be paid off. She's never been in any real danger, never put her head out. It's always just been about the money."

"Looks like," Easton says.

"Makes her more like the new criminals than she'd probably want to admit."

"She's not stupid, George," Easton says. "I think she knows."

They get out of their car and are walking toward the house when Sylvie opens the door. "Come on in," she says.

"You have a beautiful garden," Easton says.

"Why, thank you, Agent Easton."

"You can call me Anne if you'd like."

"I'd rather call you Agent Easton, if that's okay."

"And what should we call you?"

"Anything you like," Sylvie says.

The agents know who her father was; the legitimate side of the story is just enough to explain how the house came to be, how Sylvie came to be living in it. It's not that Sylvie's never come under any scrutiny. She's been audited three times over the years, accountants questioning just how she can hang on to the house without ever seeming to leave it. Each time she's managed to satisfy them with cooked numbers about investments, and so the bigger investigation never happens—the one that might connect tax authorities with the police and federal agents who have been looking for the White Lady for years. It rankles Guarino and Easton, sitting in Sylvie's parlor, that she's been here in Bratenahl for so long, an arrest as easy as a knock on the door. They're suspicious about having been called now. Wondering what the White Lady might be using them for.

Sylvie comes in with a tray, a French press, cups and saucers. "You seem like coffee drinkers," she says. So unhurried. As if they're just chatting.

"Before we start," Easton says, "I want to tell you how pleased we are that you've decided to talk to us, and also assure you of the protection you'll soon feel as part of the Witness Security Program. Not everyone in it is as important a figure as you are, Miss, um, Hightower—"

"Rizzi," Sylvie says. "I took my husband's name."

"Rizzi," Easton says, and writes it down. "I'm sorry."

"It's no problem," Sylvie says. "Please go on."

"Not everyone is as important as you are, Ms. Rizzi. But almost no one has kept as discreet a public profile as you, either. That, combined with the various levels of protection that the program offers, should ensure your safety."

"And where will that program place me?"

"Usually out of state." Easton regrets it as soon as she says it. It's a routine thing to say, but she's forgotten who she's talking to: someone who, to the best of her knowledge, has spent almost all of her life in Cleveland, much of it right in the house where she's sitting. The agent tries not to give herself away, but Sylvie notices it—just a slight wince—and decides, what the heck, to exploit it.

"I see," she says. Lets it hang without a tag for four long seconds. "Well, it will have to do."

It's a good way for Sylvie to throw them off, to buy herself some latitude in being cagey. She knows the agents know she's planning something, that she has some ulterior motive. But she still wants the agents to believe that the trade they're making is safety for information; she wants them to think that when she withholds knowledge from them, it's because they haven't convinced her that the protection they're selling her is worth it. She can't let them know what she's really up to, and it'll be hard to hide that she's keeping things from them when she knows almost everything. But she only needs to hold it together for a few days. After that, it won't matter what they know.

She doesn't want to end crime in Eastern Europe, or bring down an organization. She can't, because she knows better than the FBI agents do that the organization never ends, the money never ends. She just wants an escape, for her and the rest of her family. The crime syndicates to her are a thicket of thorns; everyone on them gets hurt, and if she cuts them down, they just grow back. But she can burn a hole through them, big and wide enough for her and everyone she loves to pass through. By the time the thicket's grown back, they'll be long gone. She just needs to lay down some tinder. The FBI agents sitting in front of her are the match that starts the flames.

"There are quite a few international crime syndicates now working in America," she says, "from New York to Florida to California. And here. How could there not be?"

Agent Guarino lets himself smile. He reminds himself that he's sitting across from maybe the hardest criminal he's ever seen. But another part of him kind of likes her.

"If you're willing to draw some arbitrary lines to separate them," Sylvie says, "I've invested in maybe seven of them. And I think some real damage can be done to all of them, but only if we do this in the proper order. I can give you the names, addresses, phone numbers, of operating criminals from Los Angeles to Mumbai. But you have to give me some time to straighten a few things out before I do that."

"Can I ask you a few questions first?" Agent Easton says.

"Of course."

"You'll forgive me if this comes across as a suspicious question, Mrs. Rizzi, but you've been involved in organized crime for thirty years, it seems, almost without leaving your house. Why are you coming to us now?"

Sylvie's done the math already, knows what to say.

"One of my nephews is in real trouble," she says.

"Peter Henry Hightower," Agent Guarino says.

"Yes, my sister Muriel's boy."

"We've had our eye on him for a little while."

"Do you know where he is?" Sylvie says.

"No. Not today we don't."

"That's what I'm afraid of," Sylvie says. "I want to do everything I can to make sure he's safe. For my sister's sake. She has no idea the kind of trouble her son is in."

"Does she know about you?" Agent Easton says.

"Nobody in my family knows about me," she says. And thinks: *Henry's more than good enough a liar to make that stick. And they'll never meet Rufus. He'll see to that.*

The agents are there for another two hours. There's so much to talk about, a lot of information to go over. But once they're outside the house, they don't say anything to each other until they're in the car, at the end of her driveway, turning onto Lake Shore Boulevard, and the high wall is out of sight.

"She's using us," Agent Easton says then.

"Yup," Agent Guarino says. "But how?"

"I don't know."

They reach the highway back to the city of Cleveland. They're both thinking the same thing. Agent Guarino says it first.

"We could just arrest her, couldn't we?"

"Bring in the White Lady," Agent Easton says.

"Right."

They're almost back to the city.

"But here's the thing about that," Agent Easton says. "I'm scared. It's like she's keeping a lid on something, something that'll explode on us if we just take her out."

"I think it's going to explode anyway," Agent Guarino says.

"How many people do we hurt if we intervene now?"

"How many more get hurt if we wait?"

In Negostina, on the border of Ukraine, Claudiu—Madalina's father—is closing up the house for the night. Madalina's mother, Georgina, is already asleep; Claudiu can hear her snoring in the next room. They live in an old house with thick plaster walls, low ceilings, small windows. The kind of house that knows how precious warmth in the winter is, coolness in the summer, even if it means it's always dark inside. They compensate by making the house as bright as possible inside: the walls are lime green, pale turquoise, bright salmon, throwing the light from the smallest lamp around. Then there are the pictures on the walls, of grandparents, of a scene from the Carpathians. A picture of a tropical place that Georgina cut from a magazine; the location changes every time a guest asks her where it is. *Fiji,* she says once. Then the next week: *the Bahamas.* She'll never go, though she's always going in her mind, and, Claudiu thinks, in her dreams. It's where Madalina must have gotten it from, Claudiu thinks, the restlessness, the need to move, to see so much of the world. Nights like these, after her mother has gone to bed, Claudiu always, always thinks of her. Where she is, what she must be doing. He's never seen her apartment in Kiev and never will. In his mind, it looks like a typical apartment in the housing blocks in Botosani, where a friend of his moved when he got a job as a pharmacist there. The thirty-year-old design just full of the old Communist mind-set: *All families will require and should be happy with space like this.* A square living room. A small kitchen with the tile on the walls reaching to the ceiling. A small rectangular sunporch, the glass fogged over. But Madalina, in Claudiu's mind, has made the space her own. She's hung bright fabric on the walls because they won't let her paint them, draped her modular furniture with woven cloth; she sleeps under a bright blanket of twenty different colors that the fluorescence from the streetlights outside can't bleach out. When her father imagines her at night, she's always sleeping, a sleep so deep that the only movement is from her chest, rising and falling under the sheets. It's the consolation he gives himself, that everything she did has worked out so well for her, that every night she rests better than she ever did in the town she was raised. So it's best that she left Negostina behind and will never come back. Even though he misses her so much.

The knock on the door startles him; he's pretty sure no one has ever come by this late, so he knows before he gets to the door that something's wrong.

"Who is it?"

"It's Alexandru. Open up, Claudiu."

Alexandru is standing there in a light coat over what must be pajamas; Claudiu's never seen him look like that outside, not near the open space in the center of Negostina near the bus stop, not heading into the store in Siret for crackers. He looks exhausted. There's a young man with him who looks like he's close to homeless, and maybe sick. There's dirt on his face, his hands, his clothes. A hole in his pants just below his left knee. This young man has come a long way. He's taken days to get here, hitched four rides from Kiev across the Ukrainian steppe to the Romanian border, in a blind panic, sure that he's being followed, until the ride's ended and he's found himself in a village he's never heard of, and he's collapsed from exhaustion in a hotel he can't read the name of. He's walked, run, and stumbled six miles out of his way to cross the border where no one's looking, because he's sure someone's waiting for him there. And he's knocked on three doors in the middle of the night in Negostina, trying to find out where Madalina's family is, but because no one can understand his Ukrainian, they've given him to Alexandru—who speaks a little English—instead.

"This boy says his name is Petey," Alexandru says, "and he knows your daughter. He's in a lot of trouble."

Petey. Yes, Petey. The boy he's never met, the one his daughter loved. There's no way, just no way, that he's here to give good news. Claudiu feels a hot prickling along his skin, like someone's doused him in oil and is about to set him on fire. Now it's in his head. A bomb has gone off in his brain and put a crack in his skull from his forehead to his crowd and down to his neck. *Madalina, my Madalina.* He knows the answer, the only answer that matters, before he asks the question: *Where is my daughter?* He says it twice, in Romanian and Ukrainian, and his jaw drops when Petey can't answer. The American starts shaking his head, asks Alexandru something in English, in a very small voice. Alexandru's been studying from books, movies, and tapes. He practices in his yard sometimes, speeches from Shakespeare and gangster movies. Lots of time spent rolling the words around in his mouth, though it must come out all wrong. He says the four words that Claudiu thinks must make up the question as if there's a question mark at the end of every one. It's obvious that Alexandru's not sure he's saying it right. But Petey seems to understand, because that's when he shakes his head even more. He looks at Claudiu and his face twists with sadness, sadness and guilt and terror. He says something in English over and over, until he's sobbing too much to speak. A rope of spit hangs from his open lips until he's covered his face with his hands, his fingers so tense that Claudiu thinks, just for a second, that it's as if he's trying to rip the skin off. So that nobody would recognize him, and he could be someone else.

"Alexandru," Claudiu says. "What did he say?"

Alexandru gives him a good long look. Holds out his hand.

"He says he's sorry."

Chapter 17

B y now, dear reader, I bet you want to know where Peter is. You
know, Rufus's son. Maybe you think of him as the good Peter,
your first friend way back at the beginning, at Sylvie's wedding
on the lawn of the house, and in Granada, when he was forced
to start running. That Peter is still running. If this were a different kind
of story, that Peter would do everything. He would travel the world
himself, uncover the criminal enterprise, tip off the authorities, and
help bring the whole thing into the light, family and syndicate and all.
Maybe he'd kill the Wolf himself, put a bullet in the man's head. Or
no, wait: Maybe there'd be some standoff with his cousin Petey, his evil
twin, in which the bare fact that they haven't seen each other in years
is ignored so that Petey can get down on his knees before the cousin
he's wronged and atone for his sins. Then maybe Petey would sacrifice
himself for the cause, go on a suicide mission that lays waste to his body
but redeems his immortal soul, as the organization can't be brought
down without it. That would leave the good Peter standing on top of
the wreckage he's made and wondering what on earth he's going to do
next, until Sylvie somehow appears to give him more money than he
could spend in his life. A fresh start. An earthly reward for the work he's
done serving a higher justice.

But all that would be telling a lie, a bigger lie than the ones that fiction
allows. It would be giving you false hope, that one person could do all
that. I'm not saying that no one person can ever right a tremendous
wrong. God knows it's been done, and maybe it's the only thing, in

the end, that keeps the rest of us going, or just alive. But the problem here—of what happens when the laws get weak, the market takes over, and people get hurt—isn't something one person can fix. Only decide how much to be involved, and how hard to push back. Or how much to steer clear, because nobody ever thanks the guy who stands in the way of other people making money. Peter doesn't steer clear, because it's his family under threat, the family he's always wished he was closer to, wished things were different with, and he loves them, even though he hardly knows them; even though he knows, now, so much they've done.

So Peter's running, by which I mean that he's flying, back to Africa, to warn his father. He flies back to New York from Cleveland, then has to wait six and a half hours for the connecting flight to Johannesburg. After that is another flight to Victoria Falls, Zimbabwe—this is before Zimbabwe takes its serious nosedive—which puts Peter within spitting distance of his father, who's put himself down in Livingstone, Zambia. A lot of thoughts cross his mind in the almost two days he spends on airplanes and in airports. By the time the plane's stopped for refueling in Cape Verde, he's taken his own life apart and put it back together in his head three times. Because what Sylvie told him—and she told him almost everything, more than she'll ever tell the FBI—is driving him a little crazy.

It all hinges on how much his father knew about it before he left the United States forever. Peter had always thought Rufus was driven by something more personal, a version of the mix of conflicting feelings some rich hippies feel, the shame at having so much, wrapped up in a childish selfishness, the glorification of being able to live with so little. It's impossible to imagine that it's not part of the equation. But it never occurred to Peter that maybe Rufus was also protecting himself, and after Peter was born, him, too. That Rufus's refusal to tell him much at all about his family, his complete ambivalence about Peter wanting to visit them, wasn't just him projecting some long-held grudge onto his son. If his father knows as much as Peter does now, then it took some strength—holding back for so long, not unloading the entire family story onto him the minute Peter said he just wanted to visit his cousins. At the end of this train of thought, Peter's respect for Rufus rises, until he's proud of the way the man raised him, of how Rufus taught him to get by in the world, to survive on so little and yet be able to do almost anything he wanted, even if he didn't know what that was. He wants to call his dad and tell him he's sorry. He wants to thank him over and over. But then he starts swinging the other way. If Rufus knew everything, why didn't he just tell his kid after a while? He could have just let it all go, let it go and stayed with Peter's mom. Peter's only seen one picture of her, a woman with dark hair and a long face. They lost it years ago, somewhere between Addis Ababa and Kampala, but he had memorized it by then anyway and still thinks about it all the time. In the picture, her arm is flung over Rufus's shoulder; she's thrown her head back and letting out what must be a huge, big-toothed laugh. Rufus is smiling so wide you can see it under his mustache. They could have stayed together, the three of them, stayed even in the town where Peter was born. Lived a simpler life, one that didn't involve cash in bottom drawers, cash under the bed, cash in kitchen cupboards. Just clothes, a few toys for him, pots and pans, plates and spoons. They might still be there, then, and this whole misunderstanding, the mistaken identity, that's drawn Peter into something he didn't ask for and wants no part of, would never have happened. Then Peter wants to call his father and scream at him. But both extremes assume that Rufus knows. *How much do you know about your sister, Dad?* Peter wants to say. *What do you know?* But then what if Rufus doesn't know anything? How much is Peter allowed to tell him? Because his family's toxic legacy is still alive, the animal is still out there and coming for him, and he's scared of it, of what it can do. Scared of what Rufus might do if he learns just how much Peter's been pulled in.

Peter doesn't know who his father is right now, and he just needs to talk to him and can't, because he's on an airplane and this is 1995; because there's no way he's going to talk to Rufus about any of it over an airport payphone. In a flicker of self-awareness in between the bouts of self-doubt, he thinks of how awful airports and airplanes are for people who are in a real hurry to get where they're going. All that waiting around at the gate, not moving at all. All those hours sitting on the plane, which feel like you're not moving, even if you are. It's dead time, dead space, and Peter's the kind of person who winds up counting every minute. He doesn't know that Sylvie's done the same thing; that she's using him as much as she's helping him. Stalling with the FBI until she's sure Peter's on the ground in Zimbabwe and crossing over into Zambia. Banking on what Peter would never assume: that Rufus is, in the end, much more his father's son than he would ever admit, and when the beast comes for him—because after what Sylvie does, it will—he'll know what to do.

Sylvie's liquidated almost everything now, her legitimate and illegitimate holdings. The legitimate transactions, she knows, the FBI can see, but she can explain it as getting ready for the witness protection program, to go into hiding. They'd be able to see the illegitimate ones after a while, but by then everything will be done. She's moving too fast. She knows so much about the Wolf's organization, thanks to years of dealing with him, getting him to let his guard down by putting so much money with him. She knows who's involved, who's been doing it for a while, who's new to the game. She knew when Petey joined as a fellow investor and asked Kosookyy to try to talk him out of it. She felt a little sick to her stomach when Kosookyy told her later that he hadn't. She remembers what Kosookyy told her then. *You could stop him, you know. All you have to do is tell him the truth.* She winces a little at how she responded. *It'll blow my cover. He has too big a mouth.* What Kosookyy must be thinking now. *Look what your silence cost you and everyone around you. And so many people you don't even know.*

And thanks to Feodor, who's been spying on the Wolf, just as the Wolf has been spying on him, she knows who Mercedes is and how to get to him. Mercedes—a government official who, for some reason, has decided to name himself after a car—works for the Moldovan ministry of the interior and also the Wolf. He's in his office, in a blocky

Communist-era building overlooking a small park with a bust of Stefan cel Mare, the hero and icon of Moldova who, some say, also cursed it. His beeper goes off, gives him a number he doesn't recognize, but that doesn't matter; he knows that whoever has his beeper number means business. Hours later, Mercedes is in a part of Chisinau where he never goes. He gives twenty dollars to the owner of a hardware store with a painted sign out front to let him use the phone. Makes his call. It's Feodor on the other end, though Mercedes doesn't know that.

"You've wasted a lot of time, waiting so long to call," Feodor says.

"I had to make sure it was safe. Who am I talking to?"

"An acquaintance of the Wolf," Feodor says.

"Do you have a name?"

"Is it important to you?"

It is. Mercedes is very suspicious; it's how he's gotten this far.

"I can wire you money to indicate my seriousness," Feodor says.

"That would be better," Mercedes says, and gives him the details for an account in his uncle's name, a man who died a few months ago of tuberculosis, though he knows the various authorities involved haven't put the picture together enough to shut the account down. He'll use it for maybe a month more, he thinks, and then close it out. But what he's wired turns out to be a lot of money, much more than Mercedes thought it would be. And the number isn't random; it's just under the limit where the bank starts to ask questions before allowing the transfer. That evening, Mercedes finds a tailor in a different part of town, gives her fifteen dollars, and calls the number again.

"You're going to need a lot more accounts," Feodor says.

"I figured," Mercedes says. "How many?"

Feodor tells him, and Mercedes, for a moment, balks. It's a huge transaction.

"Can you come up with the accounts?" Feodor says.

"Yes," Mercedes says. "But before I do, I have to ask what this is for."

"I have learned that there's a mole in your organization, sir," Feodor says, "and to scare him out, each member of your organization has a part to play. I thus need contact information for everyone down the line—"

"I don't have it."

"Of course you don't. But you have it for the next in line. And you can distribute the money."

"Yes."

"Perfect. Tell me how to contact the next in line."

"How many of them?"

"All of them."

Mercedes takes a deep breath. Then gives Feodor information on more bank accounts than he ever thought he would in one phone call. The money's wired to them the next day. Then there's a third phone call from a barbershop in yet another part of town, when Mercedes gives Feodor the beepers for the eighteen managers he oversees, tells Feodor to wait a couple hours before calling so he can tell them, in a general way, what's up. Feodor agrees and thanks him for his cooperation; if they find the mole, he says, there'll be something in it for him. They hang up almost at the same time. Mercedes walks out of the office and gets a haircut. Looks at himself in the mirror, himself and the other men getting their hair cut, the men waiting in a row of seats by the door. Outside, it's a beautiful day. If he were in a better mood, he would think of the light as bright, but today, it seems hard to him. Harsh. Glaring. Angry. The barber, who hasn't seen what happened between Mercedes and the owner, asks him a routine question—*do you live around here?*—and Mercedes struggles to answer before remembering that it's better to lie and say yes. The minutes in the vinyl chair seem much longer. His eyes are always on the front door reflected in the mirror. He's waiting for someone to open it and come for him. If it's the police, he thinks, they won't wait for the barber to finish. They'll drag him out of there with the cut half done. The pictures in the paper will be embarrassing, enough to earn him a nickname in the press. He doesn't want to think about what it might be. The police'll finish the job in jail by shaving his head, as if he had lice. But that's better than the criminals who might come for him instead. He realizes that, as many times as he's talked to his managers on the phone, he doesn't know what any of them look like. They're all high up enough in the organization that it's been in everyone's interests not to know. It means they can't identify each other to the authorities, can't acknowledge each other on the street if they happen to be tailed, which is great when it comes to protecting themselves. But now the problem is inside the organization. What if one of them is the mole? Or what if, somehow, the organization makes a mistake and thinks Mercedes is—despite, or no, no, because of his eagerness to cooperate? *I'm fucked either way on that one,* Mercedes thinks, and feels sick to his stomach, swallows back the bile rising in his throat. Either way, one of the people he oversees could come for him right now. He could walk into this barbershop, get right behind Mercedes, and blow his brains out of his face, all over the mirror in front of him. It wouldn't take more than five seconds, because Mercedes knows that the rumors are true: some of them are ex-KGB and know what they're doing when it comes to executing people. Nobody in this barbershop would save him; they wouldn't pretend to be able to identify the killer, because nobody's that stupid, or righteous. If there's a difference.

For the rest of the haircut, Mercedes is in a cold panic every time the door opens. He regrets everything he's ever done for the Wolf's organization, every little thing. *When this thing dies down,* he thinks, *I'm getting out.* He pays fast, leaves too big a tip, and walks home—it takes him over an hour—because he's too paranoid to get in his car. There's someone hiding in the back, he thinks, or there's a bomb under the driver's seat. He decides he'll come back for it later, and the bus is just out of the question. But halfway home, the terror leaves him. *They'll find out who it is very soon,* he thinks. *They'll know it's not me.* If this was the Wolf testing him, he thinks he might have passed, maybe excelled. He starts to feel almost euphoric, thinking of the good things coming his way. He wouldn't mind moving up in the organization one bit. Maybe in his official job as well. Maybe he'll take over from the Wolf one of these days. Meet the man at last, just in time for him to shake Mercedes's hand before he retires to a villa on the Black Sea. *Someday you'll be here too,* the Wolf will say to him. Mercedes can't wait, and his impatience makes him reckless. He calls all seventeen of his contacts from a phone in a hotel lobby in central Chisinau, maybe six minutes from his office. *You're about to get some very specific and very important orders. And yes, the compensation to carry them out.* The news shoots down all seventeen branches of the organization's operations, loses a bunch of the official finesse along the way. *You're about to get a weird order and a lot of money.*

The letters are all over Moldova the next day, delivered by Feodor's boys. They're in Chisinau and Balti, in Orhei and across the countryside. A manager named Ion gets an envelope slipped under the door of his apartment. It has a mark on it that indicates it's from the Wolf. He opens it fast, before his wife can see it. Inside is a wad of American dollars and a printed note. *We suspect that Evgeny Razin, your underling, has been informing on the organization to the authorities and that a police raid of the organization is imminent. If you have any indication that this is true, including an increased police presence around your activities, you are sanctioned to dispatch Mr. Razin as soon as possible. We trust that the compensation in this envelope is enough to convince you of the seriousness of the threat and to secure your vigilance. You will receive double this amount again if you are required to carry out this order and do so.* The wad is thick; the denomination on the top is pretty high. Not everyone believes the letter they get, of course. But enough do to set the whole organization on edge, stretching the connections between everyone inside the network. And they're all afraid enough, of the enforcers, the spies, their superiors, and the Wolf himself, that nobody says anything, at least for the first few hours. Sylvie knows that'll change. For all the money she's thrown at the scheme, the lie at the center of it is rotten; it's decaying fast, and the longer she waits to use it, the more it's going to smell. But she guesses that for the next two days, they'll all feel like they're in incredible danger, and the truth is that almost all of them are. About the only person who's safe is Mercedes, which means he almost pissed his pants in the seat of a barbershop for nothing. He's safe because Sylvie doesn't want to assassinate a public official, and because she's a good enough judge of character to understand that without the organization around him, he'll be harmless. It's the Wolf who isn't; getting him will be the most important of all, if she wants her and her family to be free. She's counting on creating enough chaos to get him, for once, to lose his cool. To forget one of the protocols that keep him out of harm's way. To make himself vulnerable. It's the one part of her plan that requires her to be, above all, lucky.

But for now, a lot still has to happen. Which is why, as soon as she's talked to Feodor and they've agreed on their plan, Sylvie calls Agent Easton and Agent Guarino again.

"What's the FBI's relationship with police in Moldova right now?"

"It depends," Agent Easton says. "On the city, on the province, on specific police chiefs. There's a lot of red tape and bureaucracy to deal with over there."

"What if I could hand you an entire organization?"

"That would be incredible."

"When could you start to act on the information?"

"As in, a raid of some kind? Not soon. But beginning to investigate? Sure. Why do you ask?"

"Because if the investigation were to start, say, tomorrow, I would need protection very soon after that."

"You got it."

She hands over the information. Names. Addresses. Phone numbers. Everything she has. The information moves fast, from the FBI to Interpol, to local police in Moldova. Some of those police officers have been paid off. Some of them just don't have the manpower or the firepower to do anything with what they're given. But some of them can do something. They start spying on the addresses they can reach, and they try to be inconspicuous about it. Agent Easton and Agent Guarino are delighted; for them, it's a huge breakthrough, and they go out for a quick dinner to celebrate before they go home to their families. It also feels like the beginning of a long process for them. There's entering Sylvie in the witness protection program deep. They're thinking somewhere in Nevada or Arizona. And there are the many, many leads to follow, the trips to take, the people to interview. *We're still being used somehow,* Agent Easton says, *and I wish I could see how. Yeah,* Agent Guarino says, *but there's only one real way to play the cards she's given us, right? Besides, isn't it something that we started moving this boulder forward, at last?* He holds up a wineglass. He doesn't know he's using the wrong metaphor: They've started a fire. They just can't see the smoke yet.

Livingstone, Zambia. Rufus is living in a low-slung house in town, behind a tall cinderblock wall that was painted white and yellow maybe ten years ago and has been chipped away at ever since, by the rain, the rocks that passing trucks kick up, the cars themselves. Three years ago, a drunk taxi driver backed right into the place, messed up his bumper and a piece of the wall, but got away without anyone seeing him; he hasn't been back down that street since. The house is a pretty simple affair: tile floors, white walls. Some square wooden furniture Rufus bought in town. A few carved hippos on the coffee table that he bought in the central square—he traded them for two American dollars and an empty plastic water bottle—just to give the place a little touch of home. He's almost the only white guy in town. There are the owners of the two backpackers' hostels and the couple of backpackers who were just passing through but got roped into working for them. There are the owners of a couple of the businesses on the main drag, a restaurant and a souvenir shop. There are also what Rufus thinks of as the exploitation scouts: All along the long, straight road from Livingstone to the Zimbabwean border, which passes right over the canyon the Zambezi tumbles into to make Victoria Falls, some white people with money have plans to build a series of very exclusive hotels. Rufus pretty much hates this idea, it and the giant land-clearing construction equipment it brought along with it. He doesn't know where these white people are from. Maybe they're Europeans, or South Africans, or both. But they stand out more than he does, and Rufus feels like he's a lit candle every time he walks down the street. The Livingstonians know he doesn't work for one of the businesses they can see. Not for the fancy hotel at the end of the main drag, where the traffic doesn't obey all the laws and has to dodge baboons besides. Not for any of the other small businesses, most of which are run by Indians. They get the impression that he's either a criminal or just sitting on a big pile of money, and they lean toward the pile because of the way he dresses, as ever, in linen clothes, and because of his ridiculous salt-and-pepper mustache. He's earned a nickname, Yankee Doodle Dandy, which is a term of endearment. Rufus has stuck around longer than any of the other Americans the people in town can remember, and he's done his best to ingratiate himself. He's not like some of the white people around Livingstone, who almost act as if they're under siege, driving from place to place in an air-conditioned truck with tinted windows, spending as little time as possible outside. Rufus is out during the day, walking around, buying overripe fruit and cassava, shooting the breeze with the friends he's made when he meets them in the shadow of the broken-down colonnade that the British built and nobody has the money to keep up. He's out at night in the club that pumps out highlife music on the stereo as loud as it can, playing cards over coldish bottles of Mosi, winning and losing money fair and square. Not long after moving to Livingstone, he's broken into and held at gunpoint while the home invaders liberate him from his cash. The people in Livingstone expect him to leave after that. Instead, he shows up at the club the next day, has a talk with the right people, gets himself the right talisman for his door. He's never broken into again. The people in town nod when they talk about it. *Yankee Doodle Dandy knows how to live here,* one of them says. *Mmm,* says another. *But why do you think he's here at all?*

When Rufus hears Peter's voice on the other side of the metal gate to the house, his heart fills, almost cracks under the pressure. He rushes to the gate and opens it, expecting that it won't be his boy, because he can't get his hopes up too much. But it's him, it's his son. He's covered in a thin layer of light dust, on his skin, in his hair, and he's been wearing the same clothes for two days. He looks so good. The father can still see the kid he knew in him, and he's so proud of the parts of him that he doesn't recognize at first, the man that Peter's becoming. Rufus can't even speak; he just opens his arms.

"I've been here for hours, looking for you," Peter says.

"Come in, come in," Rufus says. He wants to hug his son so much, but doesn't know how. "Are you hungry?" he says.

"No, I just ate."

"Why did you do that? You know I always have food."

That's not true, Peter wants to say, but decides it's a little hurtful, and keeps it to himself.

"Bad timing, I guess," Peter says.

They come into the house. Peter throws his backpack down.

"Sit down, sit down," Rufus says. "It's so good to see you. Tell me how you are. How long are you staying for?"

"Dad, we need to talk."

"Do you need work? It's fine if you do, I know a reporter in town if you still want to do that. Maybe he can throw some work your way. If not, I also know—"

"Dad. Dad. We need to talk about your family."

Now it's Rufus who sits down.

"Oh," he says. He runs his fingers through his hair and closes his eyes. When he opens them again, his face looks like he hasn't slept for a week. Then, in a tone of voice Peter's never heard in him: "What's happened now?"

And Peter begins to talk, telling his own story. For the first time in his life.

Chapter 18

Sylvie's on the steps of the house, looking into the garden. Two suitcases are next to her, a floral pattern on them that went out of style decades ago; they belonged to her mother. Behind her, in the threshold to the house, there's a man on his knees, attaching wires to the lock.

"Almost done here," he says. "Are you sure this is a good idea?"

"Yes, I'm sure," she says. She doesn't bother turning around to say it.

"What if your sister comes by?"

"She doesn't have a key," Sylvie says, "and besides, that door hasn't been locked in thirty years."

"What if someone else comes by?"

"Nobody comes by," she says.

The man looks at her and shakes his head. "All right," he says, "all right. This is the last one." There are wires all over the first floor of the house now. "I'm going to close this up. You have everything you need?"

Mmm hmm, he thinks he hears her say. She's just looking into the garden, going back through the years. There's the memory of Joe Rizzi standing there with his hand on Muriel's throat. But so many more better memories. Her wedding on the back lawn, the lights down to the water. Her whole family together, all of them who were alive. It was the last time that happened, though none of them knew it then. Her years of marriage, quiet, peaceful, to a good man. Then years of her own quiet contentment, pushing her fingers into the soil, planting flowers. And further back into her childhood, of she and Rufus, far enough away from the house that they thought no one could see them, telling each other secrets. She understands why Rufus took off, understands even more why he never came back. There's never been anything for him here, nothing he wants. But she's missed him every day since he left. It still surprises her that the feeling is so strong, after all that she's become since they saw each other.

The man finishes his work, puts his tools away. Gets up. Checks three times that he has everything he came with, his tools, his wallet, his car keys.

"You sure you have everything?" he says.

"Yes," Sylvie says.

"Want to take a look around?"

"I already did."

Amazing, he thinks. "All right," he says, though he doesn't sound convinced. He's careful closing the door, gives the lock time to settle into position.

"Ready?" he says.

Sylvie turns her head to look at him. Picks up a suitcase in each hand.

"Let's go," she says.

New Canaan, Connecticut. Henry's phone rings at two-thirty in the morning. The phone's on his nightstand, and he picks it up halfway through the first ring. He turns to look at Holly, again, to make sure she's still asleep. Then cups his hand over the receiver and whispers into it.

"Hello?"

"Henry, it's Muriel."

"Just a minute, okay?"

He gets out of bed, goes to his office, picks up the phone, and leaves it on his desk. Goes back to his bedroom and hangs up the phone in there. Walks back to his office. His phones are old, even for 1995; they still have cords on them, and he's willing to fight about it with anyone who decides to bring it up. *Aren't you tired of just standing in the kitchen to talk on the phone?* an acquaintance in New Canaan says. *On a cordless phone, you can talk anywhere in the house. No you can't,* Henry says. The unpredictable static on cordless phones irritates him, even as the businessman in him admires the cordless phone companies for convincing people to pay more for technology that doesn't work as well as what they already had. He's heard that cell phones are even worse—you can't hear on the phones very well, the person you're calling can't hear you very well either, and the phones drop calls without warning—but he knows they'll take off in just a couple years, whether they iron out the kinks or not.

"Muriel, it's late," Henry says. It's awkward. He hasn't known how to talk to her for years, and he wishes he did.

She does too. "I'm sorry to be calling you. I'm so sorry. But I can't sleep, Henry. I can't get Sylvie on the phone. It's been a couple days. First Petey and now Sylvie. Henry, what's going on?"

Henry forces himself to wake up, because he needs to make sure he doesn't misstep. "I don't know," he says. "But I'm sure they'll both turn up somewhere."

There's a long pause on the other end of the line. He can hear how his sister's breathing; she's nervous, excited, angry. Something. *I wasn't convincing enough,* he thinks.

"Is that all you have to say?" she says.

"What else can I say? I don't know any more than you do."

"Is that true, Henry? Is that really true?"

See, he and Sylvie have been lying to Muriel for years. She doesn't know that Sylvie's still involved, the way their father was involved; in 1985, when Muriel asks Henry how it is that Sylvie can still maintain the house, and Henry can't dodge the question anymore, he gives Muriel the answer he and Sylvie cooked up years before: Sylvie gave Henry the money left over from Rufus's share—after the house was covered—and asked him to be very aggressive in investing it, to try to make some big money. *So I did,* Henry tells Sylvie then, *and we had some excellent years. Sure, the late seventies were a little touch and go. But the past few years have been exceptional, very good years for Sylvie.* Then Henry says what he's almost sure will end the conversation. *You know, you could get in on it, too, if you wanted.* It appeals to the hippie left over in Muriel, the one who gave birth to Petey on the bus outside of the hospital, who still holds a profitable activity at arm's length like it's a piece of rotten chicken, because she can't get her mind off wondering who's getting exploited to give her what she has. And it works. *Oh, no,* Muriel says. *You know I'm not interested in that kind of thing.* She never asks again, and Sylvie and Henry never tell her anything. Every couple years they've talked about it, and while they can't deny that they enjoy keeping a secret from their sister a little bit, they've also agreed that it's for her protection. *Muriel's got too big a mouth to know what's going on,* they say. Like mother, like son.

But now, maybe because they're nearing the end, the end of the game, it looks to Henry like the whole thing's been flipped on its head. That the longer Muriel's in the dark, the more in danger she is, because the fire that Sylvie's starting is going to spread everywhere, and Muriel needs to know it's coming. If he keeps the lies going, he'll read about Muriel next in the *Cleveland Plain Dealer,* an awful, inexplicable murder. Maybe of the rest of her family, too, and whoever else happens to be around. He wishes he could talk to Sylvie right now, to get her agreement on what he's about to do, but he knows she's made herself unreachable. *Here's hoping I don't fuck up everything, Sylvie,* he thinks.

"Is it really true?" Muriel says again. He hasn't answered her yet.

"All right, Muriel," Henry says. "No. No, it's not true."

He can tell she's surprised before she starts talking.

"What do you mean?"

"Well," Henry says; and then he tells her everything, pretty much from the beginning. It takes about an hour and a half. Muriel says *oh my God* a lot, and *I don't believe you,* and *how could you have kept all this from me,* and, at first, *wait until I tell my husband,* until Henry says he'll stop talking right now if she breathes a word of it to anyone. There's some crying. But by the end she knows just what kind of trouble her son is in, what kind of person Henry and Rufus and Sylvie have always been. How much she and her family are in danger.

"What do you expect me to do with all this?" she says. She sounds almost like a teenager again, Henry thinks. Just before the boyfriend and the bus.

"I don't know, Muriel," Henry says. "Just be careful."

"How do I know when I'm safe?"

Her voice is so small that Henry spares her his real answer: *The truth is that you've never been safe.* He thinks about it a second longer.

"I'll call you when everything's okay. Okay?"

"Okay."

"Okay?"

"Yes."

"Good. And Muriel? I'm sorry we kept all this from you."

"I know you are," she says.

"Look, don't act hurt. We've always just been trying to protect you."

"I know you have."

She's too angry for Henry to get anywhere right now, and he knows that what he's saying sounds too much like self-justification to work anyway.

"All right," Henry says. "Take care of yourself, all right?"

"All right."

"And I really will call you, okay?"

"Okay."

"Good night."

"Good night."

He sleeps for another two hours. Holly gets up and can tell it's been a rough night for him. Makes him a cup of coffee. He sits for a while at the window in his kitchen, scanning the woods, the driveway, the road. The cars passing by. He's waiting for one of them to stop, and for three men to get out who aren't going to be scared off by anything. Who aren't going to leave until what they've been paid to do is done.

"Holly?" he says. "How do you feel about going into the city for a little bit? Like five nights or so?"

"That's a great idea," Holly says. "We haven't done that in so long. When should we do it?"

"Today," Henry says.

"What?"

"Why not?" he says. "Who's going to stop us?"

She smiles, walks over behind him, and puts her arms around him. Kisses the top of his head. *Sounds like fun,* she says. *A lot of fun.* He smiles back. Wonders when he'll have to tell her everything, too, and whether she'll still be around when he's done.

Chapter 19

Sylvie's fire starts—at last, at last—in three different places. The tinder's driest in the parts of the Wolf's organization where the money's the biggest and the regard for life the least. The organ harvesters, the ones who do the cutting, are a crew of borderline psychopaths; if they didn't start out that way, the job has done it to them. It's a hell of a thing, that the work is so brutal, so inhuman, and the pay is so high. When some of them walk around Chisinau now, they find out that they can't turn it off. The woman in the green dress standing on the corner, her arm in the air, waving at a friend across the street. The man smiling behind the counter at the pharmacy. The children balancing on the edges of the steps in the central park. For the organ harvesters that the work has changed forever, all those people have prices floating over their heads, dotted lines drawn on their bodies where the incisions would be. Some of them then play the entire scenario in their heads. The screaming, the hasty operation. The disposal of the body. They wonder how big that kid's heart is, how much it would weigh in their hands. The ones who enjoy the work wonder how the rape before the operation would be. They're told not to do it— *don't damage the merchandise,* their commander tells them—but some of them can't seem to resist. *I don't damage the parts they want,* they think to themselves. It's maybe their final, hideous self-justification, the last one put on a pile of flawed rationales and moral dodges that led them deeper and deeper into the work. *My family needs the money. There's no hope for these people anyway. Someone else might do the same to me. It's a rough world.* If any of them had the chance to survive it, to get out of the trade, some of them would end up in mental institutions. Some of them would commit suicide. Most of them would just drift away, become feral people. Then they'd get what's coming to them. They'd starve to death, or be hit by a car, or get shot trying to do something they shouldn't be doing. How could they ever return to society after breaking every trust, almost every taboo? Why would anyone want them?

So when Sylvie's message trickles through the Wolf's organization, the organ harvesters don't need to see the police. The suspicion—some of it kindled by corrupt policemen who get the message through official channels and tip off the criminals, just like Sylvie hoped—is enough. It spreads from the bottom up. On one branch of the organization, there are two kidnappers. One of them gets Sylvie's note about his colleague and contacts his boss, a doctor who can harvest organs, offering him a quarter of the ransom money, though he tells the doctor it's half. He then suggests that he and the doctor split the proceeds from the partner's parts. The doctor agrees and tells him where he and the other kidnapper should meet him. They cook up an excuse about needing to meet to work out some financial details, and the kidnapper's satisfied, goes and picks up his partner. But the doctor, having also gotten one of Sylvie's messages, has already ratted on the kidnapper and tells his boss to meet in the same place so they can harvest both the kidnappers' organs and sell them. *I don't like to do the actual killing,* the doctor says. *I'm not very good at it.* The doctor can almost hear his boss shrug over the phone. *Leave that to me.* So the kidnappers, the doctor, and the doctor's boss all meet in a cinderblock building that used to be an auto garage at the edge of a tiny town near Orhei. Everyone's smiling. They all think they're going to make some easy money.

It happens fast. The first kidnapper strangles the second one as soon as they walk in the door and the doctor gives the nod. The doctor and the kidnapper put the corpse on the table while the boss gets a set of coolers from the back of his car. The doctor's a quick worker; the organs are on ice fast. Then the boss walks over to the kidnapper who's still alive and, without any warning at all, shoots him in the side of the head. The boss is a real professional: The bullet goes in one ear and out the other, without touching those valuable eyes. Then the boss helps the doctor get the second body onto the table and goes to get another set of coolers from his car. The doctor's about halfway done when he gets back. The boss stands behind him, looks him up and down. *It's too bad I don't know how to do the operations,* the boss thinks. *Then I could make some real money off this whole thing.* As soon as the doctor has all the organs in the second cooler, the boss shoots him twice, before the doctor has time to turn around. Now the boss has a situation he knows what to do with. He hacks the bodies into small pieces so he can put them in garbage bags he can carry himself. It ends up being a lot of garbage bags and it takes the boss all night to get rid of them. But he does it. By then it's almost dawn and he doesn't smell very good. He goes home and changes his clothes. Calls his superior to tell him what happened. His superior congratulates him and says they should get together to celebrate. Of course, the superior then kills the boss. For the next two and a half days, this keeps going right up to the guy below Mercedes, who by then knows what's going on inside the organization and kills the man below him just because he doesn't need the aggravation. Then off he goes with a big wad of cash, to Vladivostok, he thinks, where the money can last a long time and no one will know who he is. But he won't be there for more than a month before someone else kills him, not for who he is—the killer has no idea who he is—but for the money he's got. On this branch of the Wolf's organization, the destruction is so complete that you might call Sylvie the right hand of God, even though Sylvie's no angel, at all, and she's doing what she's doing just to save her family. Maybe this is what they mean by mysterious ways.

But it's messier for the rest of the organization, and it takes a day or two for the results of Sylvie's plan to hit the papers. There are dead gangsters all over town. They've been killed every which way, found every which way. In an apartment block in Chisinau, someone is found in the doorway to a near-empty apartment. His skull has been smashed in, as though he were dropped on the tile floor on his head five or six times. A piece of his tongue is lying on the floor nearby, as though he bit it off one of the times he was dropped. The squatters in the apartment across the hall aren't saying anything. In Balti, another man, who had a wife and child, is found in a field with a gigantic hole in the side of his head. Someone's found burned alive in a car. Someone's stuffed in an outflow pipe. Someone else is sitting upright at his kitchen table. The problem is that he's tied to the chair and his throat is cut. The carving knife that did the work is on the table in front of him. There are no prints on the handle. The police have found twenty-six bodies already and are expecting a lot more. They see a rash of death inside the Wolf's organization, like the sweep of a scythe, the rampage of some giant predator, from Moldova to Ukraine to Romania. Even a few deaths that might seem random otherwise: a man killed in Paris, two in London. Five in Berlin. It's devastating—most of all, for the police, to their investigation. Almost all the information Sylvie gave them, in three days, has become the roll call at a morgue. The police have almost nothing to follow it up with, and someone at Interpol calls Agent Easton in Cleveland to tell them that they've been played. Agent Easton tries to call Sylvie, and when she doesn't answer, goes to the house and shouts at the door. But Sylvie's long gone.

In time, the Moldovans get tired of living in a country run by criminals, and not in the way that Americans mean when they say that politicians are crooks, but for real, run by criminals, who do whatever they want, among themselves and with thousands of innocent victims, while nobody tries to stop them. In time, they vote some of the Communists back into power—well, they're not calling themselves Communists anymore, but it's the same people, just a few years older—because if nothing else, the Communists were good at security. The police get stronger then, the army gets bigger. Fifteen years later, legitimate capitalism still looks a little shaky. In the center of Chisinau, the bright signs for new stores are put up on old buildings that need a lot more money than the store's making, as though capitalism is a thin layer over everything that you could peel off in maybe a week if you wanted to. But the crime isn't as rampant or as obvious. There are far fewer guys in crew cuts and leather jackets strutting around like they own the place, which they used to do. Spring comes in the week before Easter, and the benches of the parks in the center of Chisinau fill with people. Old men in jackets and caps. Old women with their hair covered in scarves. Young people, the boys in tight jeans, the girls in high skirts. They don't have jobs but they do have cell phones. They sit next to each other and everyone talks to people who aren't there. Or they pair off and share headphones, or just neck for hours. In the afternoons, when the schools are out, the playground is full of children, the parents hovering near. Still almost no one goes out at night, because so little is open, but people know things are better. They start to think of the mid-1990s as the bad old days, though they're too smart to consider themselves past all that now. This is Europe, and it's been a rough century; it can't afford to believe, like America still does, in the story where things always get better. Not with what they've seen. Not with what they know.

But we're still in 1995, and the Wolf is in Kiev, furious. He knows he's been screwed, and it doesn't take him very long to find out who did it. He has more information about Sylvie and Petey than the police do, and though he never made the connection between them before—there was no reason to—within a couple hours, he has. It's more than a coincidence, he thinks, that Petey should get in trouble with him, and then his aunt descend on him. *Mother hen stuff,* he thinks. He has no idea why Sylvie would go so far, can't grasp that Sylvie is trying to do much more than just bail out her nephew. It occurs to him that maybe the man he sent after Petey killed him already, and somehow the White Lady found out about it before he did. It's possible. The truth, though, is that he wouldn't understand what Sylvie's doing even if someone explained it to him. This need to get the whole family out, to end things that started almost a century ago. *Why would anyone want to do that?* he would say. *Can you do that?* In about two seconds, he chalks up what Sylvie's done to hysteria and sentimentality. It's not a satisfying explanation. He knows the White Lady is tougher than that. But it's enough that his brain can stop thinking about why and get down to the business of revenge.

One of the Wolf's boys—Pocketknife, remember him?—gets a call at one in the morning. He's in a casino near the center of Kiev, at the bar, sipping on a neat whiskey. Watching the room. He likes being around gambling, but doesn't like to put his own money down. The odds aren't good enough for him; he's too careful for that. Besides, he wants to be there with a loan ready when one of his friends goes broke over a game of blackjack and needs money. Not that he likes extorting money from his friends, he tells himself. He just likes them being in his debt, and it tells you something about what kind of life he leads, the kind of man he is, that the distinction matters.

His beeper goes off and he checks the number, knows who it is. Heads toward the bathroom where there's a payphone.

"Pocketknife," the Wolf says.

"It's me."

"You have heard about everything."

"Of course."

"Where do you stand?"

"Do you still have money?" Pocketknife says.

"Of course."

"That's where I stand," Pocketknife says.

"Good," the Wolf says, "because I have an expensive job for you. It's because you did so well with that woman Petey was fucking. You have a good crew."

"What's the job?"

"To go to America."

"I don't have to go," Pocketknife says. "I have people I can call."

"I want you to do it yourself," the Wolf says.

"That will be more," Pocketknife says. "There are engagements I will need to disentangle myself from, which will cost me." Pocketknife is lying, and he's pretty sure the Wolf knows it. But he also knows that the Wolf isn't in a strong position to argue now. Why shouldn't he use it to his advantage?

"That's fine," the Wolf says.

"Okay. The job."

"It's three people, plus any witnesses. I don't think any of them will put up too much of a fight."

"That's what you said about that woman and she bit off a part of my man's hand."

"You call that a fight?"

"There were medical expenses involved," Pocketknife says. "We understand each other, right?"

"Yes."

"Where are the people?"

"Two in Cleveland," the Wolf says. "One outside of New York. In a town called New Canaan. Full of rich fucks, I think." They both laugh, just for a second.

"How much time?" Pocketknife says.

"As soon as possible." Then the Wolf sighs. "A week at the most. Call me when you're done and not before. If I don't hear from you in a week, understand, I may send someone else after you."

You don't have anyone else, Pocketknife wants to say, though he knows it'd be counterproductive to completing this transaction. "I understand," he says.

They agree on a price. The Wolf starts low and Pocketknife bargains him up. They end the conversation as genteel as can be, as though they're royalty or diplomats. On the way back into the bar, one of Pocketknife's friends approaches him. *Hey, can you spot me a thousand? I'm low. Sure,* he says. *We'll talk terms later.* He reaches into his pocket and smiles. Business is good.

And in the early morning, Feodor's beeper goes off. It's a number he doesn't recognize. If it were a normal day, he would ignore it. But things are a little crazy right now.

"Feodor. It's the Wolf."

Feodor wants to ask how it is that the Wolf got his number, but he's way too smart for that. "I figured I'd hear from you soon," he says, as if they're old friends. As if they've ever spoken before. The truth is that Feodor didn't think the Wolf would sound like he does. Didn't expect his voice to be so high-pitched.

"You know what's happened," the Wolf says.

"I've heard, yes."

"It's that bitch the White Lady. She fucked me."

"How do you know it's her?"

"There's no one else it could be."

"Uh-huh," Feodor says, as noncommittal as he can sound.

"I'm hoping you're already thinking what I'm thinking," the Wolf says, "that someday she'll fuck you, too, hard, as hard as she can. And that it's best if we just cut her out."

"Cut her out," Feodor says.

"Yes. Perhaps we could take the opportunity to merge our operations."

"I see."

"Yes."

Feodor can't say he was expecting the last part. It isn't something he and Sylvie have discussed. It's not quite in the script. He wishes he had a minute, but he doesn't.

"I mean this with a great deal of respect," Feodor says, "but what's in it for me?" He lets the weight of the words sink in a little. They both know how vulnerable the Wolf is right now. There's almost nothing left of the organization under him, and he's teetering in the air. The Wolf names a very high price tag that surprises Feodor even more. He knew the Wolf was doing well, but he didn't know he was doing that well. *How is he making so much money?* Feodor thinks, and then stops. Yes. The harvesting. The harvesting and God knows what else that Feodor won't touch. Why did the White Lady ever get involved with that man?

But it's so much money, too. Enough that Feodor could get out himself, sooner than he planned. Stop and then buy a house on the Black Sea. Meet a nice young lady, have a family, and never think again about everything he's done for the past ten years. It sounds nice. Very nice.

"We should meet," Feodor says.

"Good. When?" the Wolf says.

"Soon."

"Tomorrow night."

"Okay."

They agree on a place outside of the city, where no one'll know who they are. Bodyguards are fine, as long as they wait outside and don't draw too much attention. After they hang up, Feodor just walks around his office, pacing. He runs his operation out of an apartment he's bought in one of Kiev's newest buildings, a tower with some serious geometry on the top of it, triangles of mirrored glass. From the window he can see the curve of the Dnieper as it flows through the city, the traffic moving on the highway beside it. The bridge to the Hidropark. The Friendship Arch on the edge of the cliff. The red, yellow, and blue of the Ferris wheel and the circus tents beneath it. A bit of the blue and gold dome of St. Andrew's Church. *I love this city,* Feodor thinks, *but it's making me old, too.* He's glad he has a day before the meeting. He needs some time to think.

Chapter 20

In Negostina, they've been up all night. Claudiu, Madalina's father; Georgina, her mother; Alexandru, the neighbor who speaks English; and Petey Hightower. For three of them, it's the worst night of their lives. Alexandru, who has to translate everything, who can't find a way out and has to be there for all of it, won't ever tell his wife or children a lot of what he saw, what he heard, beyond the barest facts. *Look, I just should never have been there,* he says. *I felt sick, I felt dirty. That's how much I didn't belong.*

It starts with the revelation that Madalina's gone. In his panic, Petey can't remember a word of Ukrainian, and he's never known Romanian. He says it in English, in the most evasive way he can think of—*they took her*—but Claudiu knows what he means. He tries to be quiet; even there, in the second that he realizes his entire life is coming apart, he's thinking of Georgina, asleep two rooms away, and he tries not to wake her. But then his grief takes over. First he chokes on it. Then he wails, *oh, oh, oh,* and Georgina comes out in a nightgown. *What's going on, Claudiu?* Looks at Peter. *Who is this?*

For Petey, it feels like a nightmare, because he can't understand what anyone is talking about. Claudiu says something to his wife. It's short, only a little longer than what Petey's told them so far, and Georgina's eyes widen, her mouth opens. She keeps saying the same word over and over, and then breaks down and shrieks, followed by a long, stuttering breath that sounds like she's drowning. They stand there in their kitchen, holding each other, and just talk and talk, crying and crying. They say a lot of things that make Alexandru realize that it's as if he and the American aren't there. The parents don't care. Their despair has made them too honest for things like politeness. There's only the annihilating truth. It goes on for maybe forty-five minutes, minutes that feel like hours, and then Georgina looks up, stares straight at Petey, startled, as if she's just noticed he's there, and asks him what happened.

Petey tries to get out of it at first. *I don't know,* he says, still thinking he can somehow avoid responsibility. He tells himself that in the strictest sense, he's not lying to these people. He doesn't know, not really, what's happened to the woman he says he loves. She could be anywhere. They could have done anything to her. He tells himself he's trying to protect them. But he's not good enough a liar to sell that to Madalina's parents. He gives Georgina a look he thinks will let her know that he wants to spare them. But Madalina's mother is way too sharp for that. All she sees on his face is the hope that he can spare himself. She sees a boy trying to be a man and not knowing how much he's failed. A stupid kid who's turned the world sideways in his head, has convinced himself that it's still right side up, and thinks he can convince everyone else, too. *You disgust me,* she thinks. And she's going to let him know it. She looks at Alexandru.

"What does he mean, he doesn't know?"

"I don't know," Alexandru says.

"No. Ask him what he means. I want to force him to talk."

Alexandru asks, and Petey repeats himself. She doesn't need the translation.

"Well, what was she doing when he last saw her?"

Alexandru asks Petey, and there's a long pause. Then he says one word.

"He says she was driving," Alexandru says.

"Where?"

"Um. He says nowhere."

"Why?"

"Because there was a car in front of her, and a car behind."

"Like a traffic jam."

"No, he says. No. Not like a traffic jam."

"Like what, then?" Georgina says. "Tell him also that I'm getting tired of guessing. Very, very tired."

She's angry now, and looks at her husband, who's getting angry, too. A tiny part of her almost feels sorry for this stupid American, this child who fucked her daughter and doesn't know anything about anything. They're going to rip him apart.

Petey's quiet again for another half minute and then starts talking. Alexandru asks him to say some things again, to slow down, to use different words. Georgina knows how bad it's going to be by the expressions on Alexandru's face. The surprise. The horror.

"What did he just say? Tell us what he's saying," Claudiu says. There's a growl in his voice. Something primal is coming out. Alexandru looks scared when he turns to Claudiu and Georgina. He slows down, tries to be as precise as possible. Tells them the whole thing. They came down from Madalina's apartment, got in her car. Were surrounded, blocked in. Then these men came for them.

"So he was in the car with her?" Claudiu says.

"Yes, I think so," Alexandru says. Checks with Petey and he nods.

"How is it that he got away and she didn't?"

Alexandru turns to Petey and asks him the question. For almost a minute they watch him while he just stares at the floor.

"Answer the question, you fucking piece-of-shit coward," Georgina says. "You have the balls to fuck my daughter, you should have the balls to tell us what else you did to her."

Alexandru stares at her.

"Tell him," she says. "All of it."

"I don't know if I can," he says. "My English—"

"Just do it."

Alexandru's words are slow and careful, and after he's done, Petey just looks at Georgina and starts crying. Talks more and more, blubbering and weeping, though he seems to be saying the same thing again and again.

"What's he saying?" Claudiu says.

Again Alexandru stalls. He's trying to find the words.

"Tell us," Claudiu says.

"He says he ran. He jumped out and ran before Madalina could stop the car. That some guys chased him but he got away. But he heard Madalina say something, just as he was running away. Just as that bunch of men came down around her. She said: *You sons of bitches. You fucking animals.*

A sound comes out of Claudiu that isn't language. It's a shriek, a roar. The sound of a man losing himself in his own rage. He seems to grow, until his head touches the ceiling. The air seems to darken around him. His hands come out and they're claws. For the next few seconds, Alexandru believes that if Claudiu and Petey were alone right now, Claudiu would kill the American with his bare hands, bury his fingers in Petey's body until he found the places where the muscles were weakest, then pull until they came apart. The arms, the legs, the chest. Somehow Claudiu would find a way into Petey's guts, too, maybe with his nails, maybe with his teeth. Then, at last, the boy's face and neck. If the police came after Claudiu was finished, they'd find the boy in pieces on the floor, know what color his intestines are. Know what the underside of his scalp looks like. Claudiu wants to do it all to Petey, so much, and Alexandru can't do anything to stop him.

But Georgina can. She just puts a hand on Claudiu's chest, tells him to go to their bedroom and come out when he's ready. He gets quiet and gives her a slow nod. Then leaves the room. Though they can still hear him howling.

Georgina turns to Petey. Gives him three taps on the cheek with her hand that aren't gentle.

"He has it in him to kill you right now, do you understand?" she says.

Alexandru translates and Petey nods.

"Good," Georgina says. "Keep fucking around and I'll let him. You're going to tell us everything. Everything you know, so that we don't spend the rest of our lives wondering more than we have to. Get it?"

Petey nods again.

"Good. Now wipe the snot off your nose and start talking."

And so he tells her everything, from start to finish. What he was doing before he came to Ukraine. What he got himself involved him. How he met Madalina. It takes a long time because poor Alexandru has to keep translating, asking for clarification. *I love her, I swear I love her,* he says, and Georgina almost softens, but then remembers how responsible he is for her not being a mother anymore. She wasn't ready for it to be over, was hoping it never would be. Thought it was her job to go first. Claudiu comes back in the kitchen about halfway through it and Georgina looks at him. *Are you okay?* she says. *No,* Claudiu says. *I never will be. Me neither,* she says. It's almost dawn when Petey's done. Then there's just the question of what to do with him.

"I hope you'll understand," Georgina says, "why we can't bear the sight of you."

"Yes, I do," Petey says. He's put himself back together enough to say it in Ukrainian. Alexandru agrees to take him and escorts him back to his house. Tells his family that Petey is Madalina's boyfriend and something's happened to her. *Please don't ask me any questions right now,* he says to his wife. *We'll talk when this is over, but not right now.* But like I said, he'll never tell her everything.

Petey's sleeping a few hours later when Claudiu gets another knock on his door. He hasn't slept at all and looks as if he's been in a fight. He's ready for it to be Alexandru, and he finds himself hoping that he's come to say that Petey's killed himself. Hanged himself by his belt from the rafters in Alexandru's barn. Claudiu hates himself for thinking it, but he can't help it. Can't stop thinking about it, either. The way the body moves on the end of the belt, swaying just a little from side to side. The knife they'll use to cut him down. He's still thinking about it, wondering if he'll feel any better, at all, when he opens the door.

It's not Alexandru. It's a tallish man in a leather jacket with a crew cut. Claudiu's never seen him before in his life, which means he's not from Negostina. He can't be from around here at all. The shoes are wrong, the pants are wrong. The stranger's hands are in his pockets, and he licks his lips. His name is Gleb, and the truth is that he hasn't slept, either. He's been chasing Petey since he abandoned Madalina, first through Kiev, then out of it, because he's guessed—and guessed right, as it turns out—that they were heading to Madalina's parents' place. That Petey has nowhere else to go. But it's been a long trip, down a long straight road that, in the middle of the night, makes him feel like he isn't moving at all. Then there's crossing the border, the irritating bribes he has to pay. *The Wolf will be paying me back for those,* he thinks. And now this town, which he hates as soon as he pulls into it. He looks at the lines of houses, the unpaved roads, and shakes his head. *The sooner I'm out of this place, the better.*

"You're Claudiu?" he says in Ukrainian.

"Yes," Claudiu says.

"I'm Misha," Gleb says, "and I'm with the police." He flashes a badge that Claudiu doesn't get a good look at. "I'm looking for an American. His name is Peter Henry Hightower. I believe he is an acquaintance of your daughter's. Have you seen him?"

There's no way this man is a policeman, Claudiu thinks, and the image of Petey hanging from the rafters comes back. Now there are more images. What will this man do to Petey if he finds him? Maybe just do it fast and shoot him, right through the head, from temple to temple. Or if Petey tries to run, the man'll shoot him twice in the back to bring him down, once in each knee to make sure he doesn't get back up, and then get him in the back of the head. Then again, maybe the fake policeman isn't the only one who's here for Petey, and they have every intention of taking him alive, a young, healthy man. Then it'll all be much slower. He's not a doctor, and he's only heard stories about what the organ harvesters take. But it's enough for him to picture it. Petey strapped to a table, with a man sitting on each of his limbs, as a fifth man cuts into him and pulls things out. In Claudiu's imagination, Petey's alive and awake for all of it, and because they do the eyes last, he sees everything.

"Claudiu?"

"I'm sorry," Claudiu says. "I'm a chronic insomniac and last night I didn't sleep at all."

"I'm sorry to hear that."

"I did see Peter, though," Claudiu says. "He was here yesterday. But I told him to leave and he did. In all honesty, sir, I hate him and have no idea what my daughter ever saw in him. I hope that he's in a great deal of trouble, and that he pays for whatever crimes he's committed. Pays and then some."

It's a convincing performance because Claudiu means every word. And Gleb believes him.

"Do you know where he might have headed?"

"I couldn't care less," Claudiu says.

Gleb stands there at Claudiu's front door, nodding.

"Do you want to come in for a moment?" Claudiu says.

A look passes across the gangster's face that Claudiu can't read. *Not if I have to spend one more minute in this place,* he's thinking.

"No, thank you," Gleb says. "Sorry to have troubled you."

And the man is off. Claudiu watches him from the window, heading back to his car. Alexandru's place is only three houses away, and for a minute or so, Claudiu is terrified that the stranger's going to knock on a few other doors. If he finds Petey at Alexandru's, what'll happen then? It's carnage again, for Petey, his neighbor, his neighbor's family. Claudiu can't think about it this time. Afterward, he's pretty sure the man would come back to the house and finish with Claudiu, just to cover his tracks. Claudiu and Georgina. She's sleeping, at last, in the next room. *I'm so sorry,* Claudiu imagines saying to her. *I didn't think fast enough.* But the fake policeman just gets in his car and drives away. Claudiu waits ten minutes to leave his house, then takes a quick walk around town, just to make sure the man's gone. Doesn't see his car. So he goes to his neighbor's house.

"He's sleeping," Alexandru says.

Now Claudiu hates Petey even more. "Wake him up," he says. He can't bring himself to use his name. He waits in the kitchen. Petey comes out wearing the same clothes he had on last night. He looks worse than he did before, and Claudiu's at least glad for that.

"Someone came looking for you this morning," he says. "Someone who isn't a police officer."

He waits to see Petey's reaction; he's satisfied when he can see that Petey's more scared than he's seen him yet. The American says something to Alexandru and Alexandru turns to him.

"He wants to know what happened. What you said."

"I said you're already gone," Claudiu says. "Which is far more than you deserve. You are a danger to everyone you meet now. A danger to yourself. If I were you, I would turn myself in."

Petey doesn't say anything, but Claudiu knows he's about to tip. Knows, too, how to make him do it.

"For my daughter," he says, "it is the absolute least you can do."

There's one last, long silence. Then Petey sighs and asks Alexandru a question. Alexandru nods.

"What did he say?" Claudiu says.

"He wants to know if I'll go with him to the station."

Claudiu takes two steps closer to Alexandru and hugs him, hard. He tries to say thank you, but doesn't get past the first syllable before he's crying again. No. Bawling. Barking. Choking. It's the next giant wave of grief crashing over him, and he breaks down all the way; he can't put himself back together again. Alexandru brings him back to his own house, one arm around his shoulder, the other holding Claudiu's hand, as if Madalina's father overnight has changed into a ninety-year-old man. It takes a long time to get to his door, and when Georgina meets them there, she's already crying, too. They hold each other there in the doorway, Claudiu and Georgina, and it's easy to see that they will think of their daughter and how they lost her every single day, for the rest of their lives. The smallest thing will remind them of her. The wildflowers by the side of the road, which she used to like to pick. Beef stew, which was her favorite. The steps of the bus station, which Claudiu will remember seeing her sitting on, waiting to go into Siret, when she was a teenager and already so ready to leave. Another young girl in town who's wearing a dress like Madalina used to wear. For her parents, Madalina will be everywhere, always with them. After a few years, they'll be able to tell themselves, most of the time, that the memories they have of her outweigh the loss. It's what they know their friends want to hear. But they'll both know the truth, and feel it so much that they won't have to talk about it. The grief will never, ever end.

"Look what you did to them," Alexandru says to Petey; and when he's sure the American has gotten enough that he won't forget, they head toward his car. By then, the mayhem in Chisinau has already started. The Wolf has discovered what strings Sylvie's pulling, and he and Feodor are on the verge of meeting. And two more hired guns are taking long trips, one to the United States, one to Zambia. The police on two continents are counting the bodies, trying to piece together the story, trying to suss out just what's going on. They haven't seen anything like it in a few years, and they worry that it's all going to blow up this time, that it's all just going to get worse and worse. That it's the beginning of something huge. The toppling of governments, a sharp descent into the kind of violent chaos that'll make the fall of the Soviet Union look like a changing of the guard. It's what the threat has been since 1991, because it seems like when they put in the new world order, they also started a few time bombs ticking. Every once in a while, one of them goes off; a couple have already, in the Balkans and in Chechnya, and all the other countries to the east of what used to be the Iron Curtain take a look around, at their neighbors and themselves. They wonder who's next, or if they'll all go down together. And they wonder, too, if something's being revealed to them, even if they're not sure what it is; whether this is capitalism gone wrong, or if it's working just like it's supposed to when you let it run free.

It takes Pocketknife a day to get to New York, another half day to get to Cleveland. A long string of airplanes, airports, food that tastes like paper, bathrooms that have been bombed with antiseptic. It all annoys Pocketknife, a lot. In Kiev, he's only a medium-sized crook; he lives in an apartment he doesn't own, and when his boss calls, he comes. But he has something in common with people who have impossible amounts of money: He's used to being able to do what he wants, to ignore the rules that apply to almost everyone else. The velvet rope gets unhooked for him. There's always a table at a restaurant, a drink that's on the house. His car is always parked right in front. He doesn't pay too much attention to traffic signs, stoplights, speed limits. Those things, he thinks, are for people who worry about the law, about the police. He doesn't worry about them. He's hurt so many people, put so many in the hospital, into casts and splints, onto crutches. He's put more than a few people in the ground. The police have never come for him, for any of it, and he knows they never will.

But when he leaves Kiev, leaves Ukraine, all his privilege vanishes, and he resents it. The lines he has to wait in, to get his tickets, to get on the plane, to get a cup of coffee, to get through customs. He sleeps most of the way across Western Europe and the Atlantic just to not have to think about it. But as soon as he lands in New York, he finds out his English isn't as good as he thought it was, and it makes going through customs humiliating. He's angry switching from the international to the domestic terminals in JFK, just tired out by it once he's on the way to Cleveland. As the plane soars over Pennsylvania, he wishes, just then, that he'd never met the Wolf, that he had no idea who he was. He lets his impatience take over for a half hour or so because he knows he needs to burn through it, it needs to be out of his system by the time the plane touches down. So he calls the stewardess for a cocktail, gets more upset than he should when he learns they don't have the kind of whiskey he likes on the plane. *I'm sorry, sir, I'm sorry*, the stewardess says; she's been trained to just apologize, though Pocketknife knows he's out of line. He almost wants to tell her that he's just blowing off steam, but if he did that, he knows it would ruin it. At the end of the flight, the attendant checks into a hotel near the airport and worries that she might lose her job if that man complains like he said he would. Pocketknife collects his bags and feels better.

There's a car waiting for him at the terminal, a black Cadillac with tinted windows. The driver, whom the Wolf called himself in an unusual breach of protocol, is fluent in Russian and English. There's a briefcase on the backseat, all dark leather; he opens it up and finds a beautiful German pistol with a silencer and a full round of ammunition, more than he needs. He picks it up and holds it in his hand to test the weight. He likes it. On the highway into Cleveland, gliding into the city at night, he feels a bit of the power he knows he has in Kiev coming back, appreciates the respect that's implied by the Wolf giving him the right tools for the job.

"Do you want something to eat before you go to work?" the driver says.

"No, no," Pocketknife says. "Afterward, yes. Come and have a drink with me. Do you know a place?"

"Of course."

"Excellent."

It feels like they're hovering over the city. Cleveland stretches out all around them, darker than he expected an American city to be. It's way darker than New York. Except for the skyline downtown, which is all lit up. There's the Key Tower, just four years old, gleaming like a knife, a sliver of glass, next to the grand old dame of the Terminal Tower. Then there are the blocky wedges of the BP Building, the Tower at Erieview. A mass of others, all clustered around a few city blocks, like when it comes to making buildings for commerce, Cleveland remembers that it's a city, that it's supposed to build up, not out, even though the suburbs have been crawling into the farmland around Cleveland for decades; thanks to the Van Sweringens, it's been growing out for as long as it's been growing up. There isn't a lot of traffic in Cleveland after dark, and they're through the downtown in a matter of minutes, hit the highway along the shore of the lake that takes them out to Bratenahl. Now the light from downtown is gone, and Pocketknife gets little glimpses of the things that give Cleveland its reputation. The way someone's leaning against the wall of a tiny Chinese takeout place with dim lights inside. A car parked halfway down a street with two of its windows broken. They're just little flashes of something, without any context. Then they're gone, and the car is cruising down Lake Shore Boulevard. Pocketknife looks at those walls on either side of him, can almost smell the money that's inside them, all the anger and the fear that comes with it, the anger those families feel that they don't have even more, the fear that someone's going to come along and take everything they have away from them. Pocketknife smiles, because he knows that, for one of those houses tonight, the fear is justified. He's there to take everything away.

The gate to the Hightower estate is open. The driver tells him that's normal. *They say she never locks the door,* he says. *That's how protected she feels.* For Pocketknife, this is hard to believe. He tells the driver to drop him off and circle the block once every five minutes, but after fifteen minutes, just to take off. *What do you mean?* the driver says. Pocketknife doesn't bother to answer. When he's out of the car, he realizes just how quiet the long, wide road is. His footsteps are a lot louder than he wants them to be. He's expecting that, as soon as he's standing in front of the place, some motion sensors are going to kick in and the lights are going to come on, the cameras record him, and then the whole thing'll be blown; he'll have to work even faster to earn his pay. But no lights come on. He stands there at the edge of the driveway for a few seconds, then starts walking down it, stops to give his eyes a chance to adjust to the darkness. The driveway's a dark gray band weaving around a ground of even darker gray, the looming shape of the house. Two windows are lit on the second floor, but the curtains are drawn. He can't see in. He wishes the driveway wasn't paved with gravel. At last he's at the front door. He pulls out his gun, tries the door. It's locked, but the lock on the door is so old that he smiles at it; he could've gotten into this place when he was a teenager, back when he didn't have the first clue. He pulls out a pick, fiddles with the mechanism to make as little noise as possible. It feels a little heavier than he expected, but it doesn't bother him. He turns the lock, turns the doorknob, then starts to open the door.

The explosion that follows is so big and so fast that he doesn't feel it. He just sees a hint of the flash, and then it takes him apart. But two minutes later, the driver sees the aftermath, the huge fire, the thick smoke rising into the sky, passing through the branches of the trees in the garden. The neighbors are coming out of their gates, walking down the boulevard to see it. The fire engines are coming down the road; the driver can hear the sirens, see the flashing lights. He drifts by the place to get a good look. The Hightower place is gone, and nobody's coming out. Then he speeds up, lets the fire trucks through. He's gone before the police arrive. He tries to reach the Wolf. But nobody picks up the phone.

That's because it all happens at once. As Pocketknife is being driven through Cleveland, Feodor meets with the Wolf. It's that time of night when it's either very early or very late, and almost everything in the center of Kiev is closed. The hardest partyers are going home; the earliest risers are just getting up. Cabdrivers are sleeping in their cabs, waiting to take someone to the airport, to the edge of town. The single coffee shop that's open has three people in it, a man in a leather jacket who just sits there smoking, looking angry, and a couple in the corner, smoking more than he is. They stop taking drags on their cigarettes just long enough to kiss each other, make out a little. There's a shout from a side street, a whistle; then almost no noise on the wide boulevards, except for the bass still thumping out of the casinos with tinted windows, the ones with the Mercedes-Benzes parked in a slanted row on the sidewalk in front.

The Wolf's own car is a silver Bentley, a little inspiration he had a couple years ago when he decided he wanted to set himself apart from everyone else. He's been pleased at the way the news has spread; everyone who works for him and a few of his rivals all know that it's his car, though almost none of them have ever seen the man in the backseat. Now and again he has his driver take it for a lap around the city without him, just so people can see it and think he's always out there, in two places at once, like the KGB used to be. Like he owns this town.

The Bentley is gliding down the highway the Soviets built that runs right along the shore of the Dneiper. They pass under the bridge to the Hidropark, fly by the hill where there's still enough of the old city for Kiev to remember what it was like before World War II, before Stalin ever showed up and Ukraine's dreams of being its own country were postponed for a hundred years. Then he's in front of an older Soviet apartment block that looks almost identical to the ten other blocks around it.

"This is the place?" the Wolf asks.

"That's what Feodor's man told me."

They've agreed on a neutral spot, a vacant unit in a building neither of them owns. The driver parks the Bentley, leads the Wolf into the building, up the stairs. Knocks on the door, makes a show of putting himself between his boss and whoever opens it.

"Right on time," the man who answers the door says. He's in a neat black suit with a crisp white shirt, his hands clasped in front of him. He steps aside. "Come in."

There's no furniture in the place, but Feodor had the presence of mind to bring a little nightstand and a table lamp, a bronze thing with a cloth shade and tassels. It makes it all seem intimate, like they're here to fuck. Feodor's smiling.

"It has taken us a very long time to meet," Feodor says, and holds out his hand. The Wolf shakes it.

"It would have been better to meet when circumstances were more calm," the Wolf says.

"And when was the last time they were calm?" Feodor says.

Everyone in the room—the Wolf and his driver, Feodor and his two men, in identical suits and shirts—gets a good laugh out of that. They're all old enough to have been in a lot of trouble for a long time, even before the Soviet Union fell. They've always been capitalists, always been criminals, and it's impossible for them to separate the two. They don't see why they should. The laws got in their way back when capitalism itself was a crime, and they still get in their way now; they're just easier to avoid.

"Let's talk about our mutual problem," the Wolf says.

"The White Lady," Feodor says.

"Yes. She has done a great deal of damage to my operation, and while it's nothing I can't rebuild, I am not happy about it."

"What's the extent of the damage?" Feodor says. The Wolf explains. He lowballs it, though not as much as Feodor thought he would. The lowball is natural, Feodor thinks; it's what everyone does when they're trying to sell something. Though the essence of what the Wolf says is true. He's not trying to hide his hurt, and that makes Feodor stop and think. He wonders if the Wolf is more or less sticking to the truth because he knows that Feodor knows already. Maybe the Wolf knows that Feodor's the White Lady's accomplice, that he shares some of the responsibility for what happened to the Wolf's organization, which scares Feodor, because it means that there's an excellent chance he won't make it out of this apartment alive. Though there's also the chance that the Wolf is being honest because he respects Feodor, doesn't think Feodor's an idiot. Maybe the Wolf figures that Feodor will find out how bad the damage is anyway if they merge their operations, so he has a lot less to lose by being up front about it now. Either way, it's forcing Feodor to reevaluate the man. He saw the Wolf as cunning, ruthless, lucky; turns out he's just savvy, and not afraid to take a risk. Not afraid to fall down and get back up again. Not afraid to get really dirty. *He frightens me,* Feodor thinks, *but he'd be a good partner. Someone to make a lot of money with.* He thinks again about how much the Wolf has offered him. About the Caspian Sea and Western Europe. The second life he could have, the family. It's right there in front of him, and all he has to do is reach out and take it.

"What do you think?" the Wolf says.

"I think it's a lot of damage," Feodor says.

"It is. And I think she'll do the same thing to you, and soon, if we don't get her first."

"And what makes you think she'll do it to me, too?"

"She's in business, Feodor," the Wolf says. "Just like us."

Feodor decides to push it. "Yes, but does it make sense to you, what she's done?" he says. "It's so expensive, beyond what she can ever hope to make back."

"But that's just it," the Wolf says. "She's done it because, almost without a doubt, she could recoup her costs if she takes over my territory."

"In how much time?"

"Five years. Maybe six."

"I see," Feodor says. *Five years?* he thinks. *That's all?* It's enough to make him doubt that Sylvie was telling him the truth when she said that she was destroying her empire to do what she was doing, that her reasons had nothing to do with business and everything to do with family. That she wanted out. *What if she's lying?* Feodor thinks. *What if she's just telling me a story? What if the Wolf is right that I'm next?* The Wolf's version makes a lot more sense to him. It follows the new order of things to the letter. To be willing to say anything, do anything—to leave a lot of people dead—if it makes you a buck. To not worry too much about those old questions of right and wrong, to pat them on their heads as if they're stupid little puppies, because morality only applies to other people. For you, the profits you reap are the only validation you need. The money is the proof that what you're doing is right. And Sylvie's been so good at playing the new game. Why would she destroy herself now?

But Feodor still has questions. "What would you say your territory is?" he says.

"You're worried about creating redundancies between my operations and yours," the Wolf says.

"That's right," Feodor says. He's lying. He's still trying to figure Sylvie out, to decide what to do.

"There is some overlap," the Wolf says, "in the area of money laundering, the control of police and political officials. But that can be worked out. Perhaps our merged organization would pay them as much as they ever got when we were separate, as a sign of good faith. We can find some savings by letting a few people go, by . . . what is the English word?"

"Downsizing," Feodor says, in English.

"Yes, downsizing. You speak English."

"Some." Another lie: Feodor's just about fluent. It gives him hope that the Wolf doesn't know that. Maybe he can escape after all. Unless, of course, the Wolf is just screwing with him, playing his part; and now Feodor's nervous all over again.

"That will come in handy for several other areas of my business, areas that I don't think you're involved in now," the Wolf says. "Things to do with people."

"The human trafficking," Feodor says. "The organ harvesting."

"Those are the authorities' words for them."

"What do you call them?"

"Profitable. Very, very profitable. By some measures, the most profitable aspect of my entire operation. And you can share in it, provided that we remove the White Lady first."

That's what Feodor realizes he was waiting to hear, because he knows, all at once, what he should do.

"How do you propose we take her out?" he says.

"I've already started," the Wolf says. "I've sent a man after her and her family. If the White Lady survives it, she'll at least get the message. But then we can use your contacts with her to finish the job, yes? I'm given to understand that she trusts you."

Feodor squints, frowns, trying to equivocate. "I believe she does," he says.

"It's perfect, then," the Wolf says. "All you have to do is let me know where she is, and I can send five more men to do the work."

"I will almost certainly be able to reach her," Feodor says. "In fact, I'm supposed to call her after meeting with you."

"Perfect," the Wolf says. He's smiling now, nodding. "Do we have a deal?"

"Yes, we do," Feodor says. He steps forward to shake the Wolf's hand again, gives the Wolf's driver a look that's just big enough for him to catch. The Wolf misses it. His smile gets bigger and he takes a step forward himself. Their hands meet and clasp; Feodor brings up his other hand to give the Wolf's a good pump, allows himself a little chuckle to mask the sound of the Wolf's driver, his most trusted man, pulling out a pistol and leveling it at the left side of the Wolf's head. He fires. The Wolf is still smiling as the right side of his skull pops open. Then he cringes, brings both hands up to his head, like he's trying to keep it all together, though he's already falling. It takes less than a second for his body to slap against the floor. The blood's pooling out already. It looks thick, like there's some meat in it.

"Thank you for your service," Feodor says to the driver. "I assume this means you already received your payment in full?"

"Yes," the driver says.

"Excellent," Feodor says. "It's been a pleasure doing business with you." The next move—the last one—is maybe the easiest, because all it takes is for Feodor to knock the driver's hand aside, for just a second, so he can come in close and slit the man's belly open, from hip to hip, with a sharp knife he's had in his hand the entire time. The driver drops the gun, the hands go to the wound, as if by instinct, and you should see the look on his face, reader, when his fingertips understand that they're touching his own guts. He falls, too, no more than two steps from his former boss, and starts bleeding everywhere, fast. Feodor looks himself over, from the cuffs of his shirt to the tips of his shoes. Looks his two men over, too. *Not a drop of blood on any of us,* Feodor thinks with some satisfaction. He hasn't killed anyone in a long time, and it's nice that he still has that professional touch. The only thing that's left is to close the loop on all that death. Feodor scrubs the handle of his knife with a handkerchief, puts it in the Wolf's hand. The whole story's going to line up, now: All the carnage in the Wolf's organization is internal, all the money coming from the same set of accounts, using the names of a bunch of people from the United States, Western Europe, and the former Soviet Union who have no connection to each other at all, except for the fact that they've all died in the past three weeks. Nothing will lead the authorities to Feodor. If they dig deep enough, they'll find Sylvie at the center of it, Feodor knows. But that's her problem.

He calls her a few hours later from the kitchen of a restaurant in a town about a half hour from Kiev.

"It's finished," Feodor says.

"That's wonderful news," Sylvie says.

"Yes. Wonderful. An amazing word to describe what you've just done."

"Now, now, Feodor. Don't get sentimental on me."

"Another amazing word to describe this, considering why you've done it."

He regrets it as he's saying it, because he thinks Sylvie's going to be angry. But instead, she just laughs. He's pretty sure that's worse.

"Where am I calling?"

"Somewhere safe."

"You're still in Cleveland."

"Why should I tell you where I am?"

"You're right," he says. "You shouldn't." There's a pause in the conversation, then, that neither of them knows how to fill.

"Well," she says, "thank you for everything you've done."

"Don't thank me," Feodor says.

"But I have to. It's the only proper thing to do."

"Fine. If you must thank me," he says, "you can do it by making sure that I never hear about you again, in any way, except as someone else's memory. You can make sure that you really do what you say you're going to do. To disappear, altogether, forever. Because if I learn where you are, or that you're still in the business, at all, I will make sure you're dead the next day. Do you understand?"

"Yes," Sylvie says.

"I cannot have you alive."

"I understand."

"No hard feelings, then?"

"Oh, Feodor," she says. "With this much money on the line, every feeling is hard."

Muriel's sleeping on the other side of the city next to her husband, in their colonial between the mansions on Edgewater Drive. Henry's in a hotel room on the Upper East Side, awake, listening to the traffic on the avenue below, watching the curtains move in the yellow light from the street, in the breeze coming through the window. Jackie's in the same room she's been in for a decade, flipping between dreaming and waking; she's not too sure anymore which is which. None of them know what's happened yet. They don't know that the house they grew up in is a blackened ruin, or that they'll never see their sister Sylvie again. Or that they're safe. And they are, dear reader, at last, for the first time in their lives.

But Rufus and Peter aren't. The Wolf's last man, who goes by the name of Holliday, because he loves the old jazz singer so much, is already in Zambia, with no idea that his boss is lying dead. In his mind, Pocketknife has laid waste to Sylvie and all her family, and now the Wolf and everyone else are just waiting for him to get back so they can celebrate. It's taken him no time at all to deduce where Rufus lives— where Peter must be—and he's just waiting for the sun to set, and for night to come.

In Rufus's house, it's getting darker. Peter watches his father walk to a cupboard he hasn't opened since Peter got there, curl his fingers around the handle, and then turn and look at his son. A tired expression passes over his face, one Peter's seen before. One that makes Peter realize just how many times Rufus has done this, enough that Peter knows what he's going to say next.

"It's about time you went to bed, Peter," Rufus says.

When Peter was a kid, it worked every time. It even worked when he was a teenager, though he hated it then; he always thought he was because his father was treating him like a baby. Now Peter knows the truth. So he takes a long breath and tells Rufus something part of him has been waiting years to say.

"No, Dad," he says. "I'm staying right here."

"No you're not," Rufus says. "Go to bed, son." There's no hurry in his voice, though it's weaker than it used to be.

"I'm not going," Peter says. As if the strength Rufus lost has entered him. As if something's being passed along from father to son at last, though neither of them know what it is, and neither of them know what to say now, because the game between them, the rules, the history, are over. So they say what they mean.

"You think this is the first time I've done this?" Rufus says.

"I'm sure it isn't," Peter says.

"What's that supposed to mean?"

Peter ignores the question. "When were the other times, Dad?"

"A couple times in Nigeria and South Africa. One time in Egypt."

"Did you get paid for it?"

"What the hell kind of a question is—"

"Did you?"

"No. Never. I only had to do it when something went wrong. Only when they were coming to hurt you."

"How am I supposed to believe you?"

"Look," Rufus says, "I've committed some real crimes, but not like your grandfather did. If any of them went to trial, I'd win."

"Maybe. But you made sure they never went to trial."

"Of course I did," Rufus says. "I had to. Who would have taken care of you then?"

"You call what you did taking care of me?"

He can tell it hurts when he says it, but Rufus recovers fast. "We don't have time for this, Peter, not now," he says. "There's a man coming to this house who's going to try to kill us. I can't have you anywhere near him, do you understand?" He wants Peter to interrupt him, but it doesn't happen, so he keeps going. "I know how to do this. But you have to get out of here. Do you hear me? Do you?"

Rufus looks just angry, but Peter knows better.

"I'm not leaving," Peter says.

That's when Rufus's hand, the one on the cupboard handle, starts shaking. His shoulders follow. Then three sobs come out of him, quiet things, like he's in a theater and trying not to cough. He puts his other hand over his face. He still doesn't want Peter to see. Then he seems to make a decision and looks up at his son, tears rolling free down his cheeks.

"Why are you doing this to me?" he says.

And it all comes out of Peter, in a flash flood, all the years of anger and resentment, and none of the kindness. "Doing this to me?" he says. "Doing this to me? That's how it's always been with you. The things your family did to you, the things your brother did to you, the things my mom did to you, the things the world did to you. As if you're not responsible for any of it. You've spent your whole life, and all of mine, Dad, all of it, just running and running, faster than your fucking little legs can carry you, and what has it gotten you? Look where you are! Look! You don't have a friend in this whole damn country, and the only people in the world who care about you are so far away they can't help you when you need it. You haven't seen them in so long you don't know what they look like anymore. You took your family and broke it over your knee, and broke it again and again, and you'd rather die right now than try to fix any fucking little bit of it, the disaster you made of everyone you loved—"

"Don't you lecture me about my family," Rufus says. "You don't know the first thing about my family."

It comes out as a roar, and it makes Peter's voice catch in his throat. But he spits back.

"I know everything about it, Dad," he says. "Everything. And it's my family too."

Rufus is about to roar again, but doesn't. He just shakes his head, closes his eyes. Looks more exhausted than Peter has ever seen him.

"Sylvie told you?" he says.

"Yes," Peter says. "She did."

Outside it's gotten dark. The streetlamps are coming on.

"I was just trying to save you from all of that," Rufus says. "Because what little is good in me, anything good I've ever done, is in you. We're all trapped, Peter. Me, Sylvie, Henry, Muriel, even Jackie. But you don't have to be."

"Maybe after this I don't," Peter says.

"I have a lot of trouble believing that," Rufus says.

"Open the cupboard," Peter says.

"No."

"Open it."

Inside are two pistols and a rifle, all loaded. Rufus looks at them for a long time. Then makes a decision. Gives his son the two pistols. *You've got ten rounds in each of them,* he says. *Wish I'd taught you how to shoot.* He takes the rifle for himself. The idea is that they'll stand a few feet from each other, facing wherever the hit man comes in—the front door, a window—and just empty their guns into the guy. They kill the lights and wait. They're like that for a couple hours, standing in the dark, shifting from foot to foot. Peter almost drops one of the guns once, imagines shooting Rufus by accident. A bullet right to the stomach, or the face, or the neck. Doing the assassin's work for him. If that happened, Peter thinks, he'd turn on the lights and tend to his dying father, then let the gunman finish the job when he arrived. He just wouldn't want to live with what he'd done. In that moment, his love for his father burns through all the anger, all the confusion, that's been driving him for years. He looks at the silhouette of his father, just across the room from him, and wants to tell him. *I love you, Dad. I love you so much.* But there's no time for that now, not even to whisper it. It could kill them both.

Close to midnight, they hear Holliday coming, through the front gate and into the walled yard. By the light of the streetlamps they see him through the windows, circling the house, figuring out what the best way in might be. He must decide that the windows aren't worth it, because he ends up back at the front door. Rufus and Peter hear him try the handle, give each other a nod, and then raise their guns.

Rufus fires as soon as the door opens, three times, *bang bang bang,* and the noise makes Peter jump. Half of the bullets in his first pistol go into the ceiling. He gets the gun under control half a second later, but it's way too late. Holliday's no idiot, and he opens the door in a crouch, so Rufus's shots are high, and now Holliday's low-slung shape lunges across the room, quiet and quick, like an animal hunting. Rufus gets off a fourth shot that also misses before Holliday collides with him, and then they're both on the floor. Peter can't see anything but he can hear it, the panting and grunting, the scrape of shoes. A chair screeches across the floor, an end table flips, crashes, and splinters. Then there's a metallic click and a long groan from his father, a shuffling, a slap.

"Dad," Peter says.

"Shoot, for God's sake," Rufus says.

"I can't see which one's you, Dad. I don't want to hurt you."

"He's going to kill me. Just shoot."

There's a growl, as if the assassin is turning to throw himself at Peter. Peter raises both pistols and empties them. It only takes a couple seconds but it seems to go on forever, the flashes from the barrels, the horrendous noise. When it's over, it's a lot quieter, except for the ringing in his ears. Rufus is saying something, but it takes Peter a couple times to hear it. *Turn on the lights.* He does.

And it's just like I've been telling you: There is blood everywhere. Peter didn't think so much could come from two people. It's all over the floor in a smeared puddle; in Peter's reeling brain, it's crawling up the furniture, flowing up the walls. The knife that Holliday used to gut Rufus is painted with it. And the two men on the floor are covered, soaked. Rufus is lying on his back, staring at the ceiling. He's lost an eye, and he's clutching his stomach; the blood is welling around his fingers. Peter hit him three times, twice in the left leg and once in the shoulder. Holliday is on his stomach, pushing himself across the floor. He can't use his legs; he has four bullet holes in his back.

"He's going for his gun," Rufus says. Sure enough, there's a pistol by the front door; Holliday must have dropped it when he came in, his only real mistake.

"I'm out of bullets," Peter says. His voice is pitched high. He's in shock, panicking.

"I'm not," Rufus says, and nods toward the rifle on the floor. "There are four rounds left. You know what to do."

"I can't," Peter says.

"Yes you can."

Holliday's almost to his gun.

"He'll kill you without thinking twice," Rufus says. "And then me."

Peter still can't move.

"Do it now," Rufus says. "You've got it in you, I know you do. I'm sorry. Not everything I put in you is good, Peter."

Holliday's fingers are a foot from his gun's handle. All at once, something goes dead in Peter. He drops the empty pistols, picks up the rifle. Takes five steps and plants his foot on Holliday's hand. Holliday looks up at him with rage. The hit man tries to make words but it just comes out as barking and yowling. Peter can see the blood-flecked spittle on the man's lips as he pushes the end of the rifle's barrel into Holliday's forehead and pulls the trigger, pulls and pulls. The last four bullets all pass through Holliday's head and empty it out. There are pieces of the man's brain sliding down his neck now, pieces of his skull on the floor, and the rifle's all out of bullets, but Peter keeps pulling the trigger until his father tells him to stop. *Good. Good. Enough. You're done.*

The room is tilting and spinning. It smells like meat and burning metal. There is blood all around Peter's feet now, gore on his legs. A speck of something on his face. Something else in his hair. He wants to throw up. He wants to burn the house down. He wants to tear apart the body beneath him with his teeth until there's no man there, just the pieces of him. The eyes. The liver. The kidneys. The heart. Tear it all apart and then scream at the night sky, because he can't let in the words, any words, nothing that would make him think about what he's done. But then there's Rufus's voice, speaking like it did when Peter was little and scared, and his dad was the only thing in the world that made him feel safe.

"Easy there, Peter," Rufus says. "Easy. That's my boy."

Epilogue

The authorities never quite piece the entire story together, even after everything Sylvie tells them. There are too many bureaucracies in the way. It's too hard for the agents in Cleveland to talk to the police in Ukraine, Romania, and Moldova; too hard for the police in those countries to talk to each other. And not enough people are left alive to tell them how everything they see is connected. The ones Sylvie's plan leaves breathing aren't talking enough. In Moldova the police have a pile of bodies they know belonged to the same organization, but the other names on their list—the ones who survived—are all missing. In Kiev, the Bentley's stolen before anyone can report it, and it takes the police a few days to find the Wolf and his driver. The detectives on the case still can't say what happened after they learn who the corpses are. It doesn't make any sense to them that the Wolf and his driver would kill each other, but they can't come up with any other explanation. And though the police think they know what happened to Madalina, they never find her.

In Cleveland, Agent Easton and Agent Guarino feel played, hard; they had one of the bigger criminals on their beat in their hands and let her go, and now all they have are the burnt-out bones of a mansion on the shore of Lake Erie, a missing person in the form of Curly Potapenko, a body they can't identify but know isn't Curly, and a long series of money transfers that go all over Eastern Europe; even after they see that it spreads across what used to be the Wolf's organization, they still don't know why. They interview everyone they can think of, starting with

⋮

Sylvie's family. *I had no idea Sylvie was involved in anything,* Muriel says, and means it. Henry knows a little more. *I always knew she'd gotten into something,* he tells them. *I never imagined it was so bad.* The agents move on to her small group of friends, people she grew up with and hasn't seen in years. They make the rounds of the few organized criminals they know are left. It all gets them nowhere. Then there's just one small nagging question after another. *How long do you think she'd planned it for?* Easton will ask Guarino in the car four months later, as they're driving to the West Side to investigate a case that has nothing to do with the White Lady. *How did she keep all of it from her family?* Guarino will ask Easton six months later in the elevator. They'll be talking about it for the rest of their careers, and they'll never close the case.

Their only consolation is the trial of Peter Henry Hightower—Petey—which the newspapers turn into a regional sensation as soon as he's extradited from Romania to the United States. It's his second trial, after all, and plenty of people remember him from the first one, because the teenage Petey looked every bit like what he was then, a criminal who was also beyond privileged. A lot of the news programs like to run the pictures side by side, of Petey on the stand in 1986 and 1995, to show just how little has changed, to let people at home be their own judge and jury. *They should have put him away when they had the chance,* goes the general opinion. It helps when the reporters learn what the cops know, that what Petey was involved in is connected to the fire on the lake and his aunt's disappearance. There's the persistent rumor that Sylvie had a lot more going on than she ever let on, but there aren't enough details out there to put together a real story, and it fuels a hundred conspiracy theories, some of them more complicated and sordid than the truth. The worst of them involves every crime you could think of, including incest, a hint that the aunt slept with her nephew, or that some of the Hightower grandkids have siblings for parents. There isn't even circumstantial evidence for any of that, of course, but the details they have are lurid enough, and inconclusive enough, that they seem to point to only the most heinous crimes. Which is true—the crimes are heinous—but not the way that Americans are used to thinking. They make it into a soap opera. This is real life.

And Petey's trial is much narrower than that. The good evidence the prosecution has against him amounts to drug dealing and money laundering, the things he confesses to. They can't connect him to the crimes that made the laundering necessary because Petey doesn't know what he was laundering money for, or what he was investing in. They can't attach him to the Wolf with anything besides the information Sylvie gave the FBI, and for the defense, it's too easy to make Sylvie an incredible source. Petey ends up sentenced to twelve years in a state facility, which he serves in full. His scandalized mother, who two months before wanted nothing more in life but to see him, won't talk to him for the first three of them, except to lecture him. She visits him in prison just to vent. *Do you know what you've done to this entire family?* she says. *Do you know what people are saying about us? It's awful, Petey, just awful.* Then, when he tries to defend himself, she tells him to zip it and walks off. But during the fourth year, all Muriel's anger burns off. She stops visiting Petey for a few months because she's not ready to apologize, but then she does. When he gets out of prison, they let him come home. He gets a job working in a gas station convenience store by the highway, on the edge of Tremont, near the cemetery where his grandfather is buried. The owner knows who he is and feels sorry for him, starts him off shelving inventory and after almost a year lets him near the cash register. He has that job for a few decades. Over the years, a handful of people get up the nerve to ask him what really happened, what he was involved in over in Ukraine. What happened to Curly. Whether his aunt died in the house fire or is still out there somewhere. He tells them that everything he knows was in his confession and came out in the trial, that he never knew what the criminals in Ukraine were doing with the money, that he doesn't know what happened to Curly or his aunt. He always tells the truth, and nobody ever believes him. And for the rest of his life, he can't go a week without seeing someone who reminds him of Madalina.

For Henry, hundreds of miles away and at arm's length, the trial and fallout are easy to bear. He's mentioned a couple times in an article—*most of Hightower's family are still in Cleveland, although he has an uncle who lives in Connecticut and another uncle who lives abroad*—which gets back to him at work. He's on the phone for business, and right at the end, the person he's talking to can't help himself. *Is that your nephew in that Cleveland trial?* Henry sighs. *Yes, it is.* This happens about five times before he develops his stock answer. *You'd never have seen it coming if you saw him when he was a kid. He was a little angel.* Lets the person he's talking to tack on the moral to the story, button the whole thing up with a cliché. *Funny how things work out. It's always the quiet ones. I guess you never know.* It's a good trick; it seems to give the other person what they need, and it lets Henry make a quick exit. *Uh-huh.* That's all he has to say, and it's over. But he means what he says, too. His mind always goes back to Sylvie's wedding in 1974, on the lawn of the house where they grew up, the strings of lights in the white tents shining off the bells of the horns in the band. How happy Sylvie looked in Michael Rizzi's arms. They knew something no one else did. The two Peters, one of them in his little suit, dancing with his aunts, the other one trying to climb the tent poles, racing down to the lake and back again. What he said to Rufus then: *You really need to stay in touch more.* If Henry stays long enough in his memories, it starts to hurt. *Just because you have a shitty home life, it doesn't mean you have to make our home life shitty too.* He's a pretty happy man, now. He still has Holly, and the older he gets, the more he'll wonder what he did to deserve her. But he didn't treat Alex's mother very well. They haven't spoken in so long, maybe never will again. He doesn't see Alex even close to as often as he wants to. And he doesn't know where Rufus and Sylvie are. The truth is that he would do anything to bring them all back together, his brother and sisters and all their children, to be the paterfamilias that his father was, without the crimes he committed. Maybe, he thinks, he could be the kind of man Peter Henry Hightower would have been if things had been different. He could do it, he thinks. He could buy the big house they'd need, and his mind is still sharp, more than up to the job of making sure he knows where everyone is, making sure they're all safe. Once everything was all together, he could keep it together. But he doesn't know how to get it there, doesn't know how to start, and years later, he resigns himself to knowing that he never will.

But you could say it happens anyway, even if Henry doesn't see it. Because why tell a story if you can't make a point? What was the point of all that violence otherwise? During Petey's trial, being in the center of the storm is more than Muriel can bear, because for a while she's famous. There are reporters camped outside her house. People recognize her when she goes downtown. On Euclid Avenue, two people standing on the other side of the street can't stop looking at her. One points and turns to the other; they nod and keep staring, as if she can't see them, as if she's an animal in a zoo. She hates all of it, and at first, she takes it out on her son. The fights between them remind her of her childhood, make her wonder if it's genetic, the willingness and the ability to cut deep, to say things that hurt, a lot. But then she realizes that all she really needs is an escape. If Sylvie were there, she would visit her. Instead, she visits Jackie. She doesn't care by then that the couple of reporters who follow her might think she's checking herself into a psychiatric hospital. She's just there to see her sister.

"Hi, Muriel," Jackie says. "You look different somehow." It's because Muriel's older. She hasn't seen Jackie in a few years, though Jackie doesn't seem to know that it's been that long. Muriel doesn't know whether that's because of Jackie's condition or because anyone would lose track of time in a place like that. She won't get to the bottom of it one way or the other, and doesn't try.

"Yes," Muriel says. "But you look as beautiful as always."

Jackie smiles, big and broad. "Where's Uncle Stefan?"

Stefan's been gone for seven years; he dies at eighty-five in 1988, of a heart attack, in the kitchen of that same house in Tremont, which he stays in long after most of the people he knows have moved out to Parma. But they all come back for his funeral, just like his brother thought they would. Muriel doesn't remember the service very well, but the memory of the party afterward is as sharp as ever. The drinking. The jokes. The stories. As close to Mykhaylo's funeral, a proper Tremont send-off, as any of them will ever go to. It feels more like a birthday party and she wonders why more funerals aren't like this, or like this anymore, because they should be. Jackie's there, too, laughing along with everyone else, though because nobody has the heart to make her go to the funeral, or to tell her what the gathering's for, she's never clear on just where Stefan went. Stefan leaves everything he has to her, and it's more than the rest of the family expected. *He must have gone out of his way to save this much,* Henry tells Muriel and Sylvie. *He hasn't taken a dime from this family in years.* Lets them share in the collective guilt that they didn't do as much for their own sister. Stefan's will has instructions to sell everything and then manage the funds to best pay Jackie's way, get her the care and therapies she needs. *Tell your uncle thank you,* Henry says, after he's made the arrangements. *Thank you, Uncle Stefan,* Jackie says. *See you soon!* It's 1995, and she still doesn't know he's gone for good.

"He couldn't make it today, sweetie," Muriel says.

"Well, tell him I say hello and miss him."

"Yes, of course."

They talk about nothing. They play cards, the same games they played when they were kids. Jackie claps her hands every time she wins. When Muriel has to go, Jackie tells her how good it is to see her, and Muriel realizes that nobody's said that to her in a long time. So she visits again the next month, and the next. When Petey's trial is over, she switches to visiting every two weeks, then every week, on Tuesday in the late afternoon, a pattern that lasts for decades, until one day Muriel can't leave the house anymore. Not long after that, Jackie goes deaf.

But we're still in August 1995, before Petey's trial starts. Henry wakes up in New York City next to Holly, calls Muriel, now that they're talking again, and finds out that Petey's turned himself in and is coming home. It feels like a sign, but he's not too sure, so he stays a few more days that turn into a few weeks. He's still there when there's another knock on Rufus's gate in Livingstone, Zambia. *I'm coming, I'm coming,* Rufus says, and wheels himself to the door. He knows who it is already. Sylvie doesn't say anything when she sees him. She keeps smiling, because it's so good to be with her brother again, but Rufus can tell she's holding back tears; she knows he hasn't been in a wheelchair long, and the bandages over his left eye are fresh. Rufus pushes himself forward and she bends down and hugs him, hard. He reaches up and hugs her back. They stay like that for a long time, because it's been years, way too many years, and they need to begin something that never ended.

"Is Peter here?" Sylvie says, into Rufus's shoulder.

"Yes. He's still here."

"Tell me you're going to be okay. Both of you."

"We'll be fine, Sylvie. Just fine."

He tells her the story later. The break-in, the fight. A few days in the hospital. But one of the Wolf's boys is now at the bottom of the Zambezi, and the gun that killed him is tucked away safe somewhere in the house.

"And Peter?"

That's when Rufus lies. He tells Sylvie he does all the killing, that a friend gets the body out to the river, never asks any questions. That Peter's been saved, and now the animals of their past, the whole sad history of the Hightower family and all the hurt it's done, are in a cage; maybe Henry, Rufus, Sylvie, Muriel, and Jackie are all in there with them, and maybe they'll be eaten alive, but at least they're together. And there are the kids, Alex and Peter, Andrew and Julia, on the outside, free. Sylvie blinks twice when Rufus feeds his fiction to her, and she's quiet for too long. *She's not buying it,* Rufus thinks. *She knows Peter's doomed, that he's in there with us now.* But she doesn't say anything.

She has a fake passport with her mother's name in it—it makes it easy for her to remember on the spot and call her own—and one of her suitcases is full of cash. That's it, all that's left of the Hightower fortune, but it's more than they need. Rufus counts the money, takes a big pile of it out, and then tells the landlord he'd like to buy the place he lives in. The landlord doesn't care where he got the cash. Then Rufus has Sylvie push him around town to introduce her to the people he knows, to make sure they know her. She doesn't go out much after that, though, and for a while, when his friends catch Rufus out—at the market, at the club—they ask him who the lady is. *Where did you find her?* they say. *She's an old friend,* he says. Uses her false name. His friends all assume the two of them are lovers. They make up a backstory about them being childhood sweethearts before something separated them, a crime, a falling-out. Then they both lived their lives separated by thousands of miles—ten thousand, maybe—though they never forgot about each other. In time the crime was forgotten, or pinned on someone else, or they turned out to be innocent. Whoever was keeping them apart died. And now here they are, picking up where they left off, thirty, forty years ago. Rufus and Sylvie hear the story they've made up after a while and don't do anything to make people think it's wrong. It's a good cover, and some parts of it are even true. Henry still sends Rufus money and Rufus still takes it. He never tells Henry that Sylvie is there with him, but he suspects Henry knows anyway. In the backyard of their house, Sylvie starts another garden, much smaller than what she had, and she doesn't tend it as much, because it's too easy to think about how temporary it is, though it turns out they have more years in Livingstone than they think.

For Peter, it's like starting over, again. He knows so much now; too much. Everything. There's no going back to Granada. He's pretty sure that the few things he owned aren't there anymore, and neither is his job. If anyone noticed that his place was broken into, then the police are involved, and he doesn't want to talk to the police. And then there's his name. He doesn't want to tell people what it is, doesn't want to sign anything. He looks at his passport and cringes. It's a name that'll trigger a million warnings. It'll dog him for the rest of his life; he'll always have to answer for it, for the things his cousin did, the things his family has done. He'll always have to let the animal loose, and he doesn't want to do that. At all.

It's October 1995. A dry night with no mosquitoes. The streetlamp outside, beyond the wall, is buzzing.

"Dad?" Peter says. "What was my grandfather's last name again? Before he changed it?"

"Garko," Rufus says.

"And no one in the family used it since?"

"No one but your great-uncle Stefan, of course."

"Right," Peter says. Gives Rufus a minute to guess where he's going with this, but Rufus just lets the silence happen.

"I'm thinking of changing my name to that," Peter says.

Rufus nods.

"I think you should," he says. Nods again and shrugs. "At last you'll have your grandfather's name."

They both smile, both too tired to laugh.

"That means you're thinking of leaving soon," Rufus says.

"Yeah. In a couple days."

"You coming back anytime soon?"

"Are you going to be here?" Peter says.

Rufus looks toward the kitchen, where Sylvie's humming to herself, putting cut flowers in water. He pats the arm of his chair.

"I don't think I'm going anywhere anymore," he says. Then looks at Peter. "Keep in touch this time, okay?"

Peter buys new clothes, new shoes. Gets a haircut. Takes a taxi to the Zambia-Zimbabwe border, walks over the old railway bridge that spans the gorge of Victoria Falls. He doesn't have anything but a little backpack with a few changes of clothes, an envelope of bills Sylvie gave him before he left. Next to him is a man carrying a bundle twice as big as he is on his back. *Where are you from?* the man asks. *Morocco,* Peter says. *But my family's American.* The man gives a little chuckle. *You have all the power right now, in America,* he says, then shoots Peter a look that tells him not to get used to it.

In Zimbabwe, Peter takes the train from Victoria Falls to Bulawayo, and from Bulawayo to Harare. He finds an apartment, calls his old contacts at the wire services, sweet-talks a local paper into giving him a first assignment as a journalist. Gets his first byline with his new name. They realize fast how good he is and start giving him more, enough that Peter can eat and hold down an apartment in a part of Harare where white people don't live, but he doesn't mind. He's there to cover Zimbabwe's slide into chaos, the land grabs, the violence, the hyperinflation. People taking shopping carts full of bills to the grocery store to buy a couple vegetables. Reuters makes him a correspondent. The worse Zimbabwe gets, the better he does, and it starts to get bad. When opposition politicians and journalists start getting beaten and killed, he has a long talk with his editor. *You should get out of there,* the editor says. *Will you keep giving me work if I leave?* Peter says. *Sure. The kind of places you seem to live? Sure.*

He's everywhere after that: Africa, South America, Southeast Asia, Indonesia. But it gets easier and easier to keep his promise to his father to stay in touch. They end up with a long string of emails, long enough that Peter gets a separate address just for mail from his dad. Peter tells Rufus about his best assignments when they're over. Rufus tells Peter about small political fights in Livingstone, about how crazy things seem to be getting in Zimbabwe. *It's so sad,* he says. *I'm glad you left when you did. Everyone is leaving now, everyone who can. We get new people every day.* He tells Peter jokes, too, stories from when he was a kid. Stories about his mother. *Once we took a walk in the mountains and got lost. We might have died out there if your mother hadn't convinced a goatherd we found that we really were lost, and not just off in the hills to do drugs.* All the things he didn't get around to telling him before. *Your mother was the sweetest, fieriest person I ever met. I wish I had known how to stay with her. For your sake.* The emails get more and more personal over the months, but Peter doesn't quite see through it. He thinks his dad is making up for lost time. Then one day he gets an email, written from Rufus's account, from Sylvie. *Peter: You should come see your father. He's very, very sick.*

By the time Peter gets there, Rufus is close to dying.

"I bet it's cancer," Rufus says.

"You don't know?" Peter says.

"What's the point of knowing?" Rufus says. "I was never going to do anything about it anyway."

He's half drunk; *for the pain,* Sylvie says, and it doesn't seem to be an excuse. But he's lucid, or at least as lucid for Rufus. He holds Peter's hand and looks as happy as Peter's ever seen him.

"It's so good to see you," Rufus says. "I'm so glad we've been talking again." Gives him a big smile. "You're the best thing I've ever done, Peter. The best thing that ever happened to me. The best parts of me. The best."

It's too much for Peter to deal with at once, and he doesn't know what to say; the obvious answer doesn't occur to him, but will later.

"You should go," Sylvie says. "I'm glad that you got to see him, but you should go."

"Don't you need help?" Peter says.

"No," Sylvie says. "I've done this kind of thing before."

"I want to stay."

"Maybe for a few more days," Sylvie says. "But after that, Peter, he won't know who you are. And then everything gets much, much worse. Do you understand?"

"Yes. That's why I want to stay."

"Peter—"

"I don't want to be protected anymore, Sylvie. I want to be here for it." He sharpens his voice a little. "Do you understand?"

That's when Sylvie chuckles a little, and Peter feels as though he's passed a test.

"Okay," she says. "Okay." Two months later, they bury him in Zambia's sandy soil. It's a short, small service at the Church of Christ with Peter, Sylvie, and a few of Rufus's friends from town, who after the service tell the kind of jokes Rufus would have liked. And when they get back to the house, Sylvie hands Rufus a thick envelope.

"No. No more money," Peter says.

"It's all Rufus's, Peter," Sylvie says. "It's what he would have wanted to give you."

"But what about you?"

"You think I don't have a plan?"

He takes the envelope, turns it over in his hands.

"I'll come and take care of you when you need it," he says. But she just shakes her head.

"No you won't. Because I'm not going to tell you when I need it. How can I? I'm supposed to be dead already."

He says his goodbyes then, but comes back eight months later to try to surprise her, to make sure she's all right. She's not there. Someone else lives in the house and doesn't know who lived there before him. He walks around town, finds some of Rufus's friends. They say they have no idea where she is, and he can't tell whether they're lying or not. She's gone. He'll never see her again.

He stays in touch with Henry and Muriel, visits them a few times when his work allows it. He goes to Henry's funeral, to Muriel's. He sees Alex and Petey, Andrew and Julia, at all of them. At Henry's, they talk about nothing. At Muriel's, Peter takes Alex and Petey aside and tells them almost the whole story; he puts Rufus's lies at the end, like his father would have wanted him to.

Six months later he's covering a story about oil companies in Venezuela when he meets Silvana. She's a few years out of college and working as a photographer; she also helps her mother run a fabric store in Caracas. They meet because she has a few photographs—and connections—that he wants, and she's looking to sell more pictures to international news agencies, but after a few weeks of working together it's clear that there's more going on than professional camaraderie. *I'm seeing someone right now,* she tells him, *so nothing can happen.* He chuckles to himself. *Of course.*

He leaves Caracas after he files his story. Three weeks later she emails him to tell him that she's broken up with her boyfriend. *He was not serious enough for me.* After that they text each other at least once a day. *I miss you all the time,* she says, *which is crazy because I am not a sentimental person at all.* Four months later Peter takes the first vacation he has had in years to fly to Caracas to see her. He texts her from the airport. *What will your mother think?* She texts him back. *I've already told her everything about you. Just don't be different with her than you are with me and everything will be fine.* He smiles.

After two more trips, they're engaged. *Just one thing,* she writes him. *I don't want children, ever.* And Peter sighs, thinks to himself, *good. Maybe now it can all die with me.*

They're married by the time Jackie dies, and he takes her to the funeral. When Silvana is out of earshot, Alex and Petey descend on him, and they ask one another the big question, since all three of them have been carrying it around for a years now: *Have you ever told anyone?* They ask because it seems less and less important to keep it secret. Their lives seem so far away from what happened in the summer of 1995. But then they're not so sure that's true, because they read the paper and watch the news. They see how things are going over in Eastern Europe, in Europe, in America—all over—and can't shake the feeling that they've seen something, some truth about the future, about what's coming, and they don't have to know what it is to know how dangerous it could be.

Have you ever told anyone?

It's not an idle question. Peter never changes his legal name, just his professional one, so now and again someone makes the connection, a colleague, a new friend, a boss. *Hey, you have the same name as that thug in Cleveland who was wrapped up in that crazy mob thing.* And Peter tells the tiniest bit of the truth. *This is going to sound crazy,* he says, *but that's my cousin.* The expression on the other person's face is always the same. *Yeah,* Peter says, *long story. We never kept in touch with that side of the family.* After that, whatever he says is a lie. Then Petey dies in a drunk driving accident, and Alex and Peter see each other at his funeral, for what both of them are pretty sure is the last time.

"You going to tell anyone now?" she says.

He thinks about it all over again, because he's a journalist and it's a big story, and he has everything he needs to tell it. Between what he knows and the police reports, he could put it together like the police never could. He could solve the case, a dozen cases, more than a dozen, all at once. If he wrote it all up, it could be a career-making book, a real masterpiece of investigative reporting and memoir, a story about capitalism, the rise of organized crime and the fall of a family, all at once. The kind of thing other journalists would read and shake their heads afterward with envy. *Story of a lifetime,* they might say. It's so tempting because it seems so obvious how well it could do. The money he could make. *And almost everyone in it,* he thinks, *is already dead. Who's it going to hurt?* But then he turns that last question over in his mind. He looks at Alex, at Silvana on the other side of the room, playing a hand game with an eight-year-old he doesn't recognize. Thinks about the room filled with blood, the feel of that rifle in his hand. All the dead, the murdered, the dismembered, the disappeared. All those people eaten alive by the animals that made one great sweep across three continents and a century that passed in the blink of an eye. The beasts are still out there, still getting closer, and they're crazy with hunger. There are people in their way, and he doesn't know who. He can't even see them. So he never says a word.

Acknowledgments

This book could never have happened without the involvement of a lot of people, some of whom are great friends, some of whom I spoke with for only a minute, and some of whom I've never met and only read. Mark Olitsky showed me around Cleveland, Ohio, his hometown. Christina Crowder showed me around Romania and told me so much about living there. Andrew Fedynsky and everyone else at the Ukrainian Museum-Archives in Cleveland could not have been more generous with their time in helping me find what I needed. Same goes for the good people at the Western Reserve Historical Society and the Cleveland Public Library. Claude Cahn, John DeMetrick, Alexander Fedoriouk, Katharine Karpenstein, Jim Miner, and Brian Murphy let me talk their ear off, and told me so much that I needed to know. The people at the New York City Federal Bureau of Investigation organized crime office gave me precious minutes of their valuable time in explaining to a confused writer how certain aspects of organized crime work. Paul Ziats's memoir of growing up in Tremont and Marc E. Lackritz's paper on the Hough riots are the only reasons I could even think about trying to re-create them. Likewise, Wil Haygood's painstaking research and riveting description of the fatal fight between Sugar Ray Robinson and Jimmy Doyle in *Sweet Thunder* is the only reason I could think about trying to re-create that, though I don't think I did it nearly as much justice as he did.

I owe a lot to Cameron McClure, my agent, who stuck with me through all of this. I also owe an enormous debt of gratitude to Amber

Qureshi at Seven Stories, for believing in the book so much and also giving it the rigorous edit that it needed. Finally, my real extended family, for the record, is nothing like the fictional family in these pages; in writing about a deeply dysfunctional family like the one in this book, all I had to do was imagine the opposite of how my own family would act, and react. I'll always be grateful to them for showing me just how strong the bond can be.

BOOKS AND ARTICLES

Aslund, Anders. 2009. *How Ukraine Became a Market Economy and Democracy.* Washington, DC: Peterson Institute for International Economics.

Badal, James Jessen. 2001. *In the Wake of the Butcher: Cleveland's Torso Murders.* Kent, OH: Kent State University Press.

Executive Office of the President, Office of National Drug Control Policy. 2001. *What America's Users Spend on Illegal Drugs.* Washington, DC: Office of National Drug Control Policy.

Fisman, Raymond, and Edward Miguel. 2008. *Economic Gangsters: Corruption, Violence, and the Poverty of Nations.* Princeton, NJ: Princeton University Press.

Glenny, Misha. 2008. *McMafia: A Journey Through the Global Criminal Underworld.* New York: Knopf.

Harwood, Herbert H., Jr. 2003. *Invisible Giants: The Empires of Cleveland's Van Sweringen Brothers.* Bloomington, IN: Indiana University Press.

Haygood, Wil. 2009. *Sweet Thunder: The Life and Times of Sugar Ray Robinson.* New York: Alfred A. Knopf.

Kara, Siddarth. 2008. *Sex Trafficking: Inside the Business of Modern Slavery.* New York: Columbia University Press.

Kapuscinski, Ryszard. 2002. *The Shadow of the Sun.* New York: Vintage.

Kennedy, Maureen, and Paul Leonard. 2001. "Dealing with Neighborhood Change: A Primer on Gentrification and Policy

Choices." Brookings Institution Center on Urban and Metropolitan Policy, Washington, DC.

Kiev University. 1964. *Ukrainian-English Inter-Lingual Relations: Ukrainian Language in the USA and Canada.* Kiev: Kiev University. (in Ukrainian)

Kuropas, Myron B. 1996. *Ukrainian-American Citadel: The First One Hundred Years of the Ukrainian National Association.* Boulder, CO: East European Monographs.

Kuzio, Taras, and Andrew Wilson. 1994. *Ukraine: Perestroika to Independence.* Toronto: Canadian Institute of Ukrainian Studies Press.

Lackritz, Marc E. 1968. "The Hough Riots of 1966." Senior thesis, Department of History, Princeton University, Princeton, NJ.

Mencken, H. L. 1941. *The American Language: An Inquiry into the Development of English in the United States.* New York: Alfred A. Knopf.

Miller, Carol Poh, and Robert Wheeler. 1997. *Cleveland: A Concise History, 1796–1996.* Bloomington, IN: Indiana University Press.

Porello, Rick. 1995. *The Rise and Fall of the Cleveland Mafia: Corn, Sugar and Blood.* Fort Lee, NJ: Barricade Books.

Scheper-Hughes, Nancy. 2000. "The Global Traffic in Human Organs." *Current Anthropology* 41, no. 2: 191–224. Available at http://escholarship.org/uc/item/0fm776vf (accessed April 20, 2010).

Quammen, David. 2003. *Monster of God: The Man-Eating Predator in the Jungles of History and the Mind.* New York: W. W. Norton.

Svendsen, Margaret T., and Charles E. Hendry. 1936. *Between Spires and Stacks.* Cleveland, OH: Welfare Federation of Cleveland.

Ukrainian National Association. 1936. *Jubilee Book of the Ukrainian National Association in Commemoration of the Fortieth Anniversary of Its Existence.* Jersey City, NJ: Svoboda Press.

Van Tassel, David D., ed. *The Encyclopedia of Cleveland History.* Available at http://ech.cwru.edu/.

Wiese, Andrew. 2004. *Places of Their Own: African-American Suburbanization in the Twentieth Century.* Chicago: University of Chicago.

Ziats, Paul. n.d. *Tremont: Cleveland's Southside.* Self-published memoir.

NEWSPAPER AND ONLINE ARTICLES

Browne, Anthony. "Drugs Push Scarred Land to the Brink." *The Observer* (UK). December 2, 2001. Available at http://www.guardian.co.uk/world/2001/dec/02/anthonybrowne.theobserver (accessed July 24, 2010).

Candea, Stefan. "Abandoning a Broken Model of Journalism." Nieman Reports, Spring 2011. Available at http://www.nieman.harvard.edu/reports/article/102575/Abandoning-a-Broken-Model-of-Journalism.aspx (accessed September 19, 2011).

Keller, Martina, and Markus Grill. "42.90 Euros Per Arm: Inside a Creepy Global Body Parts Business." *Spiegel Online International*, August 28, 2009. Available at http://www.spiegel.de/international/europe/0,1518,645375,00.html (accessed April 20, 2010).

Marino, Jacqueline. 1999. "Hidden History: Did the Old Arcade Once Harbor a Speakeasy?" *Cleveland Scene,* October 7, 1999. Available at http://m.clevescene.com (accessed December 13, 2010).

O'Connor, Clint. "Welcome to Cleveland 1976 A.D.: Bombing Capital of America." *The Plain Dealer,* March 6, 2011. Available at http://www.cleveland.com/moviebuff/index.ssf/2011/03/welcome_to_cleveland_1976_ad_b.html (accessed January 2, 2012).

Scheper-Hughes, Nancy. "The International Organ Trafficking Market." Interviewed by Neal Conan on *Talk of the Nation*, National Public Radio, July 30, 2009. Available at http://www.npr.org/templates/story/story.php?storyId=111379908 (accessed September 21, 2011).

The Ukrainian Weekly, various issues. Available at http://www.ukrweekly.com/ (accessed July 24, 2010).

Zetter, Kim. "Scientist Turns Microscope on Herself." *Wired.* February 28, 2008. Available at http://www.wired.com/epicenter/2008/02/scientist-turns/.

Novelist, musician, and editor BRIAN FRANCIS SLATTERY is the author of three previous novels. *Spaceman Blues* (2007) was nominated for the Lambda Award and was a finalist for the Connecticut Book Award. *Liberation* (2008) was named by Amazon's editors the best science-fiction book of 2008. *Lost Everything* (2012) won the 2012 Philip K. Dick Award. As an editor, he specializes in economic development and human rights, working for a variety of public-policy think tanks and traveling widely. He was previously a senior editor of the *Journal of International Affairs* and an editor and co-founder of the *New Haven Review*. His short fiction is published in *Glimmer Train, McSweeney's,* the Revelator, and elsewhere. He lives with his wife and young son in New Haven, Connecticut.